P9-CFT-247

Also by Robert Coover

ROBERT COOVER

PINOCCHIO IN VENICE

Linden Press / Simon & Schuster

NEW YORK LONDON TORONTO

SYDNEY TOKYO SINGAPORE

Linden Press
Simon & Schuster Building
Rockefeller Center
1230 Avenue of the Americas
New York, New York 10020

This book is a work of fiction. Names,
characters, places and incidents are either the
product of the author's imagination or are
used fictitiously. Any resemblance to actual
events or locales or persons, living or dead,
is entirely coincidental.

Copyright © 1991 by Robert Coover

All rights reserved
including the right of reproduction
in whole or in part in any form.

LINDEN PRESS/S&S and colophon are
registered trademarks of
Simon & Schuster.

DESIGNED BY
BARBARA M. BACHMAN
Manufactured in the United States of America

1 3 5 7 9 10 8 6 4 2

Library of Congress
Cataloging-in-Publication Data
Coover, Robert.
Pinocchio in Venice/Robert Coover.
p. cm.
I. Title.
PS3553.O633P5 1991
813'.54—dc20   90-45706
                                          CIP

ISBN 0-671-64471-8

Portions of this work have been previously
published in *Antaeus, Conjunctions, Western
Humanities Review*, and *Delta*.

for Pilar, compagna

and special thanks to William Boelhower, Alide Cagidemetrio, Jackson Cope, Giovanna Covi, Carlo Lorenzini, Giano Lovato, Allen Peacock, Fernando Tempesti, and Rosella Zorzi.

CONTENTS

A SNOWY NIGHT

A BITTER DAY

PALAZZO DEI BALOCCHI

CARNIVAL

MAMMA

A SNOWY

NIGHT

1.

ENTRANCE

O n a winter evening of the year 19—, after arduous travels across two continents and as many centuries, pursued by harsh weather and threatened with worse, an aging emeritus professor from an American university, burdened with illness, jet lag, great misgivings, and an excess of luggage, eases himself and his encumbrances down from his carriage onto a railway platform in what many hold to be the most magical city in the world, experiencing not so much that hot terror which initiates are said to suffer when their eyes first light on an image of eternal beauty, as rather that cold chill that strikes lonely travelers who find themselves in the wrong place at the wrong time. "Ah," he groans, staring down the long dreary platform, pallidly lit with fluorescent tubing and garish hotel advertisements and empty now but for a handful of returning skiers disappearing through the glass doors at the far end, if those are indeed glass doors and not merely the swirling fog (he is sharing in his decline the martyrdom of poor Santa Lucia for whom this barbarously functional *stazione* was named), "whatever was I thinking of!"

He has arrived, as do most Italians, through what foreigners, who prefer always to approach this most remarkable of landing places by sea, think of as the city's back door, but, though Italian-born himself, not by choice or custom but by the simple dictates of the deteriorating weather: the airport was fogged in, he has had to land at Milan, where snow was already beginning to fall, then take the train on from there —and in haste lest he be trapped, speeding eastward ahead of the gathering winter storm as though pursued by assassins in coal sacks. The professor, while struggling despairingly through the congestion of Milan with his impossible baggage, had consoled himself with the observation, expressed aloud unfortunately, an embarrassing habit worsening with age, that such a prolongation of the journey would at least provide him more time to adjust to this precipitous return to his native land after so many years abroad and to prepare his mind for entering what was not only, in itself, a universally acknowledged work of art, but also the setting for what he has hoped will be the culmination (just as it was once the springboard) of his own life seen in just those terms: a work of art.

For it was here one day almost a century ago, here on this island then known popularly as the "Island of the Busy Bees," that he, fallen in abject surrender to his own knees, hugged the knees of Virtue herself, and so, but for a forgettable lapse or two (that is to say, he *wishes* he might be able to forget them: his brief and abortive career in show business, for example, a misadventure which is still almost too painful to recall, even when, as in his latest writings, he has, through excruciating self-examination, transcended it, or sought to), set into motion a life purified of idleness and fantasy and other malignancies of the spirit, a life worthy, he hopes (and in his heart believes), of those knees he once hugged so passionately, wetting them then with tears of gratitude, his infamous nose running with the high fever of what could only be called redemptive grace.

It is this life, as much hers as his, that he is now attempting to celebrate or at least to illuminate in his newest and perhaps (for he has few illusions) final work, a vast autobiographical tapestry in which are woven all the rich, varied strands of his unique personal destiny under the single predominating theme of virtuous love and the lonely ennobling labor that gives it exemplary substance—*Existenz*, as a great philosopher has called it. Monographs abstracted from this work have already, to general and by now familiar acclaim, been published, but the book's conclusion, like rectitude itself in an earlier unhappier time, continues to elude him. And thus, following in the footsteps of his great exemplar and precursor Saint Petrarch, he has been drawn back to this city, somewhat impetuously if truth be told, yet explicably too, seized as he was by the sudden vivid conviction that only by returning here—to his, as it were, roots—would he find (within himself to be sure, place merely the catalyst) that synthesizing metaphor that might adequately encapsulate the unified whole his life has been, and so provide him his closing chapter. That, together perhaps with a certain restlessness of the spirit, provoked by the alarming symptoms of his onrushing illness: if not now (to wit), when?

It is this opus magnum of his, in all of its physical manifestations (on the hard disk of his portable computer, on two sets of backup diskettes, and on voluminous printout, printout so edited and re-edited—he is nothing if not a perfectionist—as to resemble a medieval manuscript), that is the principal cause of his present distress. He is able to shift it only a foot or so at a time, carrying a portion of it a few steps ahead, returning for the rest in successive trips, advancing down the windblown platform toward the station proper like a crab, and with the mood of one as well, fatigued and headachy and in something of a stupor still from his unrestful doze aboard the over-heated train (in reality, the prolongation of the journey accomplished very little). Where are the porters? Perhaps it is too late. He has no idea what time it is. It is dark, but it has been dark all day. Whichever day it's been: he's not even certain about that, so numbingly intermi-nable has this ill-considered journey become. He is accustomed on his travels to being met everywhere by younger faculty, catered to, treated with the deferential esteem due his age and scholarly distinc-tion (only on the New York–Paris leg of his trip did it occur to him, for example, that he has not reserved a hotel room, something he has almost forgotten how to do by himself), and now, though it has been his express desire to guard his solitude and anonymity on this partic-ular occasion, an occasion he thinks of as reverentially sentimental, a voyage into his secret heart of hearts, as they used to say back at the studio in Hollywood, he nevertheless feels somehow betrayed and quite wrongfully neglected, such that when a porter finally does ap-pear, just as he is wrestling his bags and boxes in through the station doors, the professor, tears smarting at the corners of his eyes, blurts out at him: "Where have you been? I don't need you now, you idiot! Go away!"

"As you wish, sir," replies the porter with an obsequious bow (he is wearing the long-beaked bespectacled Carnival mask of the Plague Doctor under his blue "PORTABAGAGLI" cap, a bit of gratuitous sym-bolism the professor, in the grip of his strange infirmity and with his bags jammed hopelessly in the intractable station doors, could well do without), and he turns and trudges lugubriously away, pushing his empty trolley ahead of him.

The professor stares out across the desolate station, recalling a monograph he wrote early in his career on "The Tyranny of Perspectivism" and realizing with a sinking heart that he cannot even reach, on his own, the exit doors on the other side, much less some distant but as yet unbooked hotel. "Wait!" he calls out, his voice thin with petulance and self-pity (of course, the hotel will have its own boat, this city is not without its conveniences, even for the solitary traveler). The porter turns and cocks his white snout quizzically from behind his humped back. "To the tourist office, please! Come on, fellow, let's not be all night about it!"

"Can't make the step longer than the leg," mutters the porter sulkily, limping back with agonizing and perhaps mocking deliberation. "So don't fly off the hinges, padrone, he who hurries most arrives last, as they say."

"They also say that life's short, but talk's long," snaps the professor irritably as he watches the porter heave his luggage clumsily onto the trolley. "Be careful now, that's a computer—"

"There is time enough for paying and dying," the porter insists, picking up the computer and dropping it. "Ahi! Bad luck! Now you see where all your hurrying has got us! But let it be, dottore, don't make a big story out of it—we must take things as they come, life is not a path through the orchard, as the old proverb goes! Come along now!"

The professor, too exasperated to reply, follows the porter as he shuffles lamely, bent nearly double with the weight of years and heaped-up luggage (the years seem to have settled chiefly in his hindquarters), through the empty station, now echoing hollowly with recorded pop music and the porter's squeaking trolley wheels, toward the yellow tourist bureau sign at the far end. Where he has every intention of reporting the insolent scoundrel. He dropped that computer on purpose! Certain indignities are not, in a civilized world, to be tolerated, even if committed by the infirm. He is not thinking of himself, of course, a poor wretch like any other man, speaking loosely, but rather of that irreplaceable work of art, literature, and social thought of which he has been merely the medium and transmitter, as it were, the porter its temporary custodian—a work of major significance as has already been widely acknowledged, even before its publication, and one deserving of at least a minimum of care and respect. Moreover, if an insurance claim should be necessary, a report will have to have been filed; he has no choice.

But the tourist office is closed—or closing: the woman at the door is just locking up!

"Stop!" the professor cries out, stumbling foward in alarm. "A room—!"

The tourist bureau clerk, startled, drops her key, which clatters to the floor like a coffee spoon. "A room—?" she gasps huskily, her long auburn curls fluttering in confusion. Then she drops to a squat and fumbles about frantically for the key with one black-gloved hand, blinded by the mask she wears, which seems to have been knocked askew by her sudden movements.

"Allow me, signorina," says the porter, kneeling and poking his long curled snout under her skirts, startling the professor perhaps even more than the squatting clerk, who, when the porter shouts out from beneath her, his voice muffled by the heavy canopy around his ears, "Aha! I have it!" merely echoes wheezily, "You *have* it?" and lurches clumsily to her feet, stepping on her hem as she does so (there is an audible rip and, as she snatches desperately at the lowering waistband with her left hand, the professor observes that the poor woman is apparently deprived of its companion) and perhaps on the porter as well, who emits a coarse muffled grunt, something about the unclean hinder parts of benighted blockheads, then emerges with his paper nose bent sideways.

There is an awkward moment then with the tourist bureau clerk looking pale and abashed (of course, this is the expression fixed upon her mask, but the professor supposes this to be a true instance of art reflecting the reality beneath the surface) and holding her skirt up with her one hand, thereby having none with which to receive the key that the porter, seemingly unable to straighten up after his long stoop, is painfully holding out to her, and it is a moment, fleetingly rigid as an old photograph (except that all three of them are trembling faintly as though in horror and acknowledgment of that very rigidity), in which the weary voyager suddenly feels, like a cold wind down his back, the terrible vulnerability of his present situation. Perhaps this is, in all its irony, the end, he thinks, perhaps I shall die here, here in this deplorably vulgar hall with its resonant banalities, its aura of meaningless departures. And this thought is not an idle one, not a self-pitying one, but a simple recognition of his failing powers, his overwhelming debilities, among which he must now include, there being no other explanation for the sheer madness of this impulsive journey, the onset of galloping senility. Oh, a fool! A fool! And soon, perhaps even, only steps short of achieving his goal (home, he is thinking, I only wished to come home!), a dead fool . . .

"Don't *tell* me, cara mia," exclaims the porter suddenly, rearing up and stuffing the key, if it is a key, fiercely down the tourist clerk's frock, "that the office is closed!"

"Ah, yes, that's it!" cries the startled clerk, her curls bouncing off her shoulders as the key plummets into her bosom. "The office is closed! *Closed!*"

"But surely," insists the porter, "is there nothing available in all of Venice? Not a room to spare? It's the middle of winter and—"

"It's wintertime, you see, and there's nothing available," responds the clerk gruffly, clutching her skirts still, but recovering somewhat her composure. She pauses. She clears her throat, turns her head one way, then the other. "In all of Venice. Not a room to—"

"Yes, yes, I see. Which is no doubt why you were just closing up, you stupid creature," sighs the porter, bobbing his head dolefully, as though the dreadful foreboding that has overtaken the professor might just have gripped him as well.

"Er, I was just closing up," the clerk concludes as though inking in the final period, and for the exhausted traveler it is as if the entire world were closing its doors around him. In his thickening gloom, he finds himself leaning toward his luggage, as though his life were there and he wished once more to embrace it before being separated from it forever. "Because . . ."

"Ah, well!" exclaims the porter, suddenly perking up and lifting the professor to his feet again. "Un po' di cuore, professore, the devil is not always as ugly as he is painted! Volere è potere, as they say, what you wish shall be yours, for as fortune would have it, I heard only today of one of the great palazzi of our city being converted into a splendid new hotel, especially appointed for gentlemen of culture like yourself."

"Yes! Appointed! Culture!" echoes the tourist bureau clerk, then hobbles back a step or two as though the porter might have kicked her.

"Well, it's not perfect, of course, the renovations are still in progress," the porter says soothingly in his gravelly old voice, peering

down at the ancient traveler over his bent nose, "but, given the circumstances, it seems to be a matter of eat the soup or out the window,
if you know what I mean, unless you're wanting wet stones tonight
for a pillow. And, as the proprietor is a friend of mine, I am certain I
can, eh, pull a few strings, if you'll pardon the expression. Tomorrow
something better may be found, but for tonight, professore: better an
egg . . ."

"Yes . . ." Yet the old scholar seems rooted to the spot. This is not
hesitation, not doubt—what choice does he have, after all?—but a
simple loss of that willed power the porter, in his obliging way, has
wished upon him. He feels hollowed out—unstrung, as he might
have said in a former time (he shudders to think of it), his limbs
loosened by fatigue and deep foreboding. He fears now that that
metaphor he has come all this distance to find is to be one not of
encapsulation but of erasure, not of summation but of irony and
absence. He has envisioned a circle, traveling its circumference as
though enacting an oracle, but he now finds himself falling helplessly
through the hole in its middle. I have failed her, he thinks. I have
failed her after all!

The porter takes his elbow. "All right, signore, don't stand there
with your hands in your belt! Let's put the road between our legs.
Or a bridge or two, as the case may be! A little need makes the old
woman trot, as they say!" They bid arrivederci to the tourist bureau
clerk, who for no apparent reason turns and, with great haste, walks
straight into a wall. Then, together, they step out, the professor and
the porter, into the bitter night. "Courage, dottore! It's just two steps
away! Soon you'll be sleeping like the Pope!"

2.

MASKED
COMPANIONS

T he Stazione Santa Lucia is like a gleaming syringe, connected
to the industrial mainland by its long trailing railway lines
and inserted into the rear end of Venice's Grand Canal, into
which it pumps steady infusions of fresh provender and daily draws
off the waste. As such (perhaps it is constipation, that hazard of long
journeys, that has provoked this metaphor, or just something in the
air, but its irreverence brings a thin twisted smile to his chapped lips),
it is that tender spot where the ubiquitous technotronic circuit of the
World Metropolis physically impinges upon the last outpost of the
self-enclosed Renaissance *Urbs*, as a face might impinge upon a nose,
a kind of itchy boundary between everywhere and somewhere, between simultaneity and history, process and stasis, geometry and
optics, extension and unity, velocity and object, between product and
art. One is ejected through its glass doors as through the famous
looking-glass into a vast empty but strangely vibrant space, little more
than a hollow echo of the magnificent Piazza at the other end of the
Canal, to be sure, severe still in its cool geometry transposed from the
other world and stripped of all fantastical ornament, but its edges,
lapped at by the city's peculiar magic, are already blurred and mysterious, its lights hazed by a kind of furtive narcissism, its very air
corrupted by the pungent odor of the nonfunctional. The corpulent
Scalzi with its dingy overworked façade is, inarguably, little more
than a morose impertinent shadow of its luminous counterpart at St.
Mark's, the latter held by some authorities to be "the central building
in the world" (and who is he, in search here of such an anchor, to

dispute that? no, no, he accepts everything, *everything*), and across the Grand Canal, instead of the placid grace and power of the Salute at the other end, there is here only misshapen little San Simeon Piccolo with its outsized portico and squeezed dome—but even these poor creatures are monuments to locus, *place-markers*, far removed from the current architectural glorification of airports, superhighways, and space flight, and thus a part of the immense integral Self that is this enchanted city, after all, the Scalzi's baroque façade a kind of Carnival mask, both revealing and deceptive, the popping green bubble on San Simeon the Dwarf rising through the fog with the erotic suggestion of a Venetian double entendre.

Below the long arching stone bridge upon which the eminent pilgrim now stands, having paused a moment at the crest to contemplate this crossing, as he thinks of it, into the dark congested but alluring labyrinths of his own soul, his own core, so to speak (and to catch his breath, rest his damaged knees, vent a bit of spleen, unfray his temper; that useless fat-bottomed cretin of a porter has been unable to pull the luggage up the bridge alone, the professor has been obliged to push from behind, and more than once on the way up he caught the wily old villain with only one hand on the trolley), there would ordinarily be, as he knows, even now in the winter, a bustling traffic of waterbuses, barges, gondolas, private skiffs and motor launches and sleek speedboat taxis, all of them swarming in and out of the busy docks and wharves with their delectable clusters of souvenir stands and news vendors and flower stalls like bees at the hive, loading and unloading goods and people, and circled about all the while by wheeling gulls and fluttering pigeons, a most exemplary spectacle; but now it is night and the Canal is hushed and empty, save for a single light bobbing indistinctly in the cold fog or perhaps at the far side of his failing vision and, in the echoey distance, the audible rumble of a lonely waterbus sidling up to a landing stage. Not that he would have it otherwise. Perhaps it is the art critic in him, but he likes the stillness of the scene before him, its aura of motionless eternity. It comforts him. And the silence, the fog, the gloom excite him. It is as though the city, momentarily hushed by awe, were genuflecting before not him, but the nobility and solemnity of his pilgrimage. Here I am, the city seems to be saying, in all my innocence and beauty. Within my depths lies that final knowledge you seek. Enter me.

"The world is made of stairs. Some people descend them and some climb them," remarks the porter ponderously, breaking the spell. "Unfortunately, sire, we must do both."

"Yes," sighs the professor, tearing himself away from his revery (he has just been overtaken by a vague sweet memory of another time, another arrival, back when real steamers plied these waters, ferrying passengers all the way from the distant mainland where the stage-coaches and donkey carts, caravans and carriages stopped, a delicious time fragrant with friendships pledged from the heart and ripe with the prospect of endless gaiety and supreme clarity, when for a moment everything *made sense*), aware that the harsh icy wind has crept well inside his camelhair coat and professorial tweeds as though undressing him, preparing him for—for what? He prefers not to think about that. "I *told* you we should have taken a gondola," he adds crossly.

"In this weather? It is easier to find the sun at midnight, dottore," replies the porter, turning his masked eyes to the skies, which are black and heavy but faintly aglitter with damp reflected light swirling about in the wind. Below the paper snout, a long tongue lolls, seemingly real. The professor leans closer, not trusting his old eyes. "But come along now," exclaims the porter with a hasty slurp, slouching away into the shadows. "Let us pick up the old sticks, as they say, professore, it's just two steps away. You take the front end this time, and I'll—"

"What—?! I'll do nothing of the kind!" storms the professor, outrage gripping him by the throat yet again. Really, this is too much! Moreover, that reference to old sticks has stung him to the quick. "I'm an old man, and desperately ill—I'm not *allowed* to lift anything! Do you hear? Are you a porter or are you not a porter? You've been hired for this job, and if you don't fulfill your obligations, I shall be forced to take the appropriate—!"

"Very well," the porter says with that mournful shrug of his, or rather has said somewhere in the middle of this lecture, pushing the trolley dutifully toward the edge of the steps meanwhile, his back bowed and nose bobbing forlornly, the professor realizing too late that his tirade, however justified, has perhaps been impolitic and interrupting it now to stumble weak-kneed toward the trolley in the vain hopes of arresting its further progress, only to see it slip out of the trembling hands of the porter and commence, just beyond his grasp, its catastrophic descent. As he clutches at the tipping trolley, his forward momentum propels him out over the lip of the stairs and into the empty space as though he meant to throw his own fate in with his cascading luggage, but the porter, with a sudden display of unwonted agility and strength, snatches him deftly by his collar and, pulling him back from the very brink, saves his life. "Mustn't throw the handle after the axe," the porter admonishes morosely, still holding the professor suspended above the top step and watching the bags tumbling as if in slow motion to the gleaming pavement far below. "If you can't save the cabbages, at least save the goat."

"I-I'm very grateful," the dangling professor whispers meekly, his heart in his throat where his regrettable rage once was, and receives, as though in reply, a stinging swat from the white cane of a blind bearded monk hurrying by. The monk, seemingly confused by this fresh information at the end of his cane, turns to swish wildly at the professor again, backs off the top step, misses the second, finds only the lip of the third, lands gingerly, cassock flying, on the fifth, his momentum propelling him to the seventh and eighth, where he strikes the one bag that has not tumbled to the bottom, and, his heels soaring gracefully now above his cowled head, completes his descent on all but his feet, yowling all the way down like a baby with colic or a cat in heat. At the bottom, where he seems to have landed on all fours, if he has four, the monk scrambles about in bewildered circles, searching for his cane, then, finding instead the professor's umbrella, rushes away without a backward glance, so to speak, disappearing down one of the dark foggy alleyways, his frantic tapping slowly trailing away into the night.

"*Mezza calzetta!*" the porter shouts after him. He sets the trembling professor down on his feet at last, twists his finger meaningfully at his blue hat. "That turnip-head lacks a Friday, his stupid little wheels are out of place!" He pauses, seeming to regret his outburst, tipping his head to one side, stooping lower, clasping his hands in his armpits. "Still, a holy man, a happy heart no doubt, and blind as a mole in the bargain, we mustn't hit him with the cross, even if he does lack a bit of salt in his pumpkin. Eh, dottore? No, it takes all kinds, as the saying goes, saints are more famous for feast days than brains, we can't all be blessed with square heads. Come along now," he adds, starting down, planting both feet heavily on each step, "we'd better gather up your wares before the ants carry it all away."

The professor follows the decrepit porter down the steps, keeping close to the stone balustrade, snatching up the bag the monk tripped over when the porter passes it by and dragging it along, too shaken by his recent brush with disaster to feel imposed upon or indignant, his knees weak as water still from the memory of nothing but empty space beneath them, his heart still knocking in his chest. It was not any false attachment to property that led him to that rash and potentially fatal impulse, he knows, but rather a profound unconstrainable feeling of duty toward *her*, a feeling nothing short of chivalric devotion, at least that was how it felt in the hot rush of the moment, foolish perhaps but genuine and selfless, as though her own survival were somehow bound up in the safety of the contents of his luggage and she herself were about to suffer the shocks and blows of that calamitous fall. And once again, he thinks, picking up his damp, battered bags at the foot of the bridge and loading them onto the trolley, I have failed her. I have brought her here and then, like a false servant, I have deceived and abused her. Metaphorically speaking, of course. "Don't make an illness of it, dottore," as the porter says now, strapping the luggage to the trolley, "everything makes broth, as they say." Yes, he is all too easily carried away by his own turns of phrase. Everything is well packed, after all, his luggage is solid and water-resistant, his computer is nested in polystyrene—all things considered, it was probably the easiest way to get everything down from up there. And even his reckless solicitude, his terrible moment of mortal peril, his pang of remorse afterwards: all this, in the end, will serve him as surely and faithfully as he serves her. "Just two steps away! Volere è potere!"

"E patire," the old traveler adds, where there's a will there's suffering, but only in jest, for in truth his spirits, since he stepped down off the bridge, have been slowly rising. The bitterness that had gripped him in the railway station and then followed him up the Scalzi bridge seems gradually to be melting away, as though his own hard geometry, brought along from America like a kind of shield, or at least a badge of identity, were now being lovingly dissolved in the coiling Venetian fog. As the ancient bent-backed porter takes up the

trolley once more and leads him down a narrow passageway overhung
with balconies and laundry and dim yellow lamps, he feels something
like ecstasy overtaking him, an unfettered, unreasonable joy, unlike
anything he has known since childhood. He is here! He is home! The
way is tortuous and complicated, and there are more bridges, they
must wrestle his baggage up steps again and down, but the effort, far
from annoying him or aggravating his fatigue, seems to give him
increasing pleasure, as though the deeper they plunge into the shadowy labyrinth, the more replenished are his reserves of energy and
strength.

On the crest of one small bridge, he lets out such a sigh of rapture
(what is it? the row of little boats snuggled against the wet narrow
fondamenta glowing in the dim misty light? that distant bridge, delicate and pale, rising through the wisps of fog? the rosy cast of the
light near that wall with all its overlapping shades of faded red and
the little metal fountain near its base, trickling water from a lion's
jaw? or just the little bridge itself whereon he stands as at a rostrum
or a pulpit, the dark canal water slipping past beneath him like hushed
subversive laughter? all! all! and more!) that the porter turns to him
in alarm and, staring quizzically at his nose, asks: "Are you all right,
professore?"

"Yes, yes! Is it much further?"

"Just two steps away," the old fool says again, as he's been saying
all along, and in truth, though he's cold and his feet are wet and his
poor knees are killing him, the old professor feels that this long walk
has really been no more than "two steps," the porter's figurative eva-
sion being truer than he can possibly know. Indeed, so entrancing has
this homecoming been, so sweet this trek (above him now, a shutter
creaks in the wind, and, glancing up into the fog, he sees a bearded
god gazing benignly down upon him from a door lintel, its stone face
whitewashed, or perhaps so decorated by roosting pigeons, and he
feels almost as though he were receiving some sort of benediction,
greeting, some fraternal signal of recognition), he almost wishes it
could go on forever.

When he again finds himself on the same bridge as before, however, gazing at the same boats, the same distant bridge and damp red
wall, sees again there the same torn poster flapping in the wind, the

same peculiar misspelled graffiti announcing "JUVE! VIVA I BALOCCI!" and—faded but still visible—"ABBASSO LARIN METICA!" some of the magic fades as well. "Haven't we been this way before?"

"You speak, dottore?"

"I say, we seem to be going in circles! We've been on this bridge before!" He wonders now if this is only the second time. One of his elbows suddenly pains him sharply and his feet, he realizes, have gone numb with cold. He can feel his old childhood terror of the dark creeping up on him behind his back. Is this a trap?

"Venice is not like other cities," the porter explains soberly, easing the trolley down off the bridge. "To reach some places you must cross a bridge twice." His voice seems to be disappearing into the night. "Come now, no need to blacken your liver over bagatelles, padrone, we're almost there."

"Two steps away, I suppose?" he shouts scathingly after the porter, then clambers down the bridge and hurries after him, afraid of being left behind. Which way did he go? He can hear the trolley wheels screaking, but the sound seems to be coming from three directions at once.

"*Ipso facto!*" comes the distant voice, hollow as an echo on water, and as he turns out of a narrow underpass to follow it (why does he feel like something is chasing him? is it that bearded mascaron with his cadaverous veil of bird droppings—?!), the professor sees the porter standing in front of a dimly lit mansion at the far end of a long stony footway fronting on a dark canal. The devil seems to have managed the last bridge on his own; the professor, even unburdened, can barely drag himself over it. "Move your pegs, professore! We've arrived like cheese on macaroni! The room is yours, but let's not be all night about it!"

The flush of annoyance aroused by this mockery is immediately tempered by his great relief at not having been abandoned after all. Had he really thought he might be? To his discredit, yes. This city, he knows, has other names. "The extent of the step, I'm afraid, is governed geometrically by the length and triangulation of the bodily members in question," he mutters gamely with what good humor his terrible exhaustion still grants him, and, limping creakily up the damp riva toward the dim flickering light, discovers that he has indeed been brought to an old palazzo, not a very beautiful one perhaps, faded

and battered and quite homely and plain, with an air not so much of
decay as of quiet discouragement, as if it had rather missed its career,
its watersteps greasy and green with mold, its doorway blackened as
though it might have been gutted by fire, the damp stony hall within
lit by nothing more than a pair of plumber's candles, but a real Venetian palazzino for all that, gloomy and stately with characteristic pi-
lasters and arches all over the front of it and stone balconies from end
to end. His bags have already been moved inside, where the porter—
clearly he has misjudged the old fellow (though he's afraid to guess
how much all this personal portage is going to cost him)—awaits him
now beside an individual dressed in the city's traditional white *bauta*
mask, black cloak, and three-cornered hat, the two of them matching
the dilapidated old palazzo in gloom and stateliness with their ghostly
beaked faces and stooped figures. He hadn't expected to see so many
masks this long before Carnival, but he has read about the recent
enthusiasm for this ancient custom, and, for all its vulgarity and
promiscuous connotations, he is secretly pleased, for it recalls for him
quite piercingly that long-ago time of his own beginnings, call them
that, allegedly innocent yet somehow wicked (what penance he has
done for that!), certainly happy, and now under such close scrutiny
in his current work-in-progress.

"If you'd care to sign in, please," says the porter, standing before
an old wooden table with the two candles on it, and the person in the
bauta, the hotel manager no doubt, thrusts an old stick pen with a
splayed point at him and repeats this in a rather horrible cavernous
voice, befitting the macabre austerity of his costume: "Would you
please care to sign in?"

"It's rather cold," the professor remarks, taking up the pen and
gazing about. The huge dark hall, which runs the length of the building, opening out onto what is apparently a garden at the rear, is
empty save for two boats parked on dollies and this wooden table.
There is an intense unmistakable odor of cats and a glutinous damp
darkness all about. "Are you sure—?"

"The rooms upstairs of course are all heated," the porter assures
him with an impatient sigh. "Come along now, professore, when
you're between the door and the wall, don't try to look for the hair in
the egg. You're showing the rope, I know, but a little supper, a glass
of wine, and you'll soon be in fine leg!"

"A fine leg!" repeats the hotel manager.

"I'm not hungry," grumbles the professor, taking up the pen, though he's not sure of this, being too tired even to think about it. "I just want to get to bed."

"Ah well, appetite comes with the eating, dottore, as the saying goes. And my friend, not knowing you were coming, has only just put the heat on in your room," he seems to flick a foot out and give the hotel proprietor a kick on the shins, for the *bauta* mask dips abruptly and there is a grunt from behind it. "It will take a little while for it to warm up."

"I just put the hee-hee-heat on in your room," mewls the hotel manager, hobbling around in a small circle. "It will take a while to, eh, to, eh . . ."

"Besides," adds the porter, leaning closer to whisper in his ear: "the repast is included in the price of the room." The traveler, however, is staring in some amazement at the hotel manager's missing hand, the stump of which has just bobbed out from under the cloak to thump the table (it now ducks back in again): so many handicapped citizens in this town! Maybe it's the damp weather, all those miserable bridges, the slippery steps . . . "The war, you see," explains the porter, evidently following his startled gaze. "The Resistance. A national hero! This fellow, I tell you, this fellow has the heart of a Caesar!" The hotel proprietor modestly turns his masked head away, sweeping a candle to the floor with his remaining hand. The porter rocks forward and whispers in the professor's ear with a breath dizzyingly foul: "*And the balls of Caesar's wife!*" He chortles wheezily, then, straightening up, adds: "But come along now, it's time to go bend the proverbial elbow, professore. The kitchen is not yet in operation here, but there is an arrangement with a little inn just two steps away, where you cannot tell the polenta from Saint John's halo and there is at least as much wine in the wine as water. We will direct you there, but they will be closing soon so we must burn the laps. Animo! Don't worry about your bags, they will be waiting in your room for you when you return."

"Well . . ." Something is bothering him about all this, but he cannot think what it might be. He almost cannot think at all. He stares at his luggage, spread out in a heap on the cold stone floor like a careless jotting, his umbrella lying at one end like the line at the bottom of a long sum. Ah . . . "How much for all this? What do I owe you?" He is prepared for the worst, though admittedly, with the securing of his room here, the worst, in truth, is no longer the worst. But the porter merely shrugs, and it is a gesture so deeply iconic it almost brings tears to the professor's eyes. It means nothing, of course. And everything. Only rarely, in one "Little Italy" or another across America, has he seen its like. Perhaps the Plague Doctor's mask with its painted half-smile has intensified it: for it is an act of ultimate submission as well as negotiation, an acceptance, in effect, of mortality itself. There is a profit to be made, but the profit belongs to the act itself, not to the mortal through whose hands it is temporarily passing. The professor also shrugs, a different kind of shrug, one that says: Yes, we understand each other, I am a poor man, my fashionable camelhair coat which has caught your cunning eye notwithstanding, but not so poor that you do not fancy yourself a handsome return at my expense before we both must die. Yes, it is going to be a very daring figure. The professor, anticipating, not without a certain appetite in spite of his desperate weariness, a long ceremonial haggling, counts out a modest sum, fair but admittedly mean, and hands it to the porter.

To his amazement, the porter hands part of it back. "The dottore is too generous," he says. "I take what comes, to be sure, when the horse is given, one must not sound the teeth, but, alas," he sighs regretfully, "there are regulations, and this is more than they allow. I cannot afford to risk, at my age, you will understand . . ." He ducks his head as though winking behind his mask. "But perhaps the professore will invite us all to a small drop of wine at dinner . . ."

"Then the room—?"

"It is nothing," the porter says with a dismissive gesture.

"Nothing," says the hotel manager.

Which means it's going to cost him an arm and a leg—or an eye out of his head, as they say here—but, under the circumstances, it's cheap at twice the price, especially given the miserable condition of these afflicted parts of his. Though he cannot remember when he last ate, he truthfully has no appetite, but he dreads the chill and loneliness of his room and something deep within him—part peasant, part adopted Yankee—rebels against the idea of turning down a free meal. Besides, the thought of a glass of wine greatly appeals to him just now, a little Prosecco maybe or a sparkling Marzemino, a kind of effervescent libation, as it were, to consecrate his heroic return and to invoke a blessing upon his solemn quest. There are wines here from the Euganean Hills and the Friuli, from the Tyrol and the Piave and the Alto Adige, all but unavailable elsewhere in the world, wines he hasn't tasted since childhood—Refoscos and Amarones, Blauburgunders, Franciacortas and young Teroldego Rotalianos with their almondy bitterness, lush Albanas, Pinot Grigios, pale Tokais from Lison, Traminers, and golden Picolits, sweet Ramandolos: their very invocation resounds like a benison in his ancient head. "Well, two steps, then," he says with a crooked smile. "What are we waiting for? While the dog scratches himself, the hare goes free. As the saying goes. *Andiamo pure!*"

3.

THE GAMBERO ROSSO

It has begun to snow. At first just a flake or two like a fleeting dispatch sent from the world he has left behind, vanishing as quickly as glimpsed. Then a steadier fall, gently swirling, touching down, lifting up, touching down again, until the little square, or campo, outside the steamy window of the Gambero Rosso is aglow with a dusting of the purest white. Like a crisp clean sheet of paper, he thinks, and he is struck at the same time by the poignancy of this metaphor from the old days. For paper is no longer a debased surrogate for the stone tablets of old upon which one hammered out imperishable truths, but rather a ceaseless flow, fluttering through the printer like time itself, a medium for truth's restless fluidity, as flesh is for the spirit, and endlessly recyclable. The old professor sits there at the little osteria window, alone now with his reveries and musings, sipping the last of the fine grappa the landlord has offered him (he has forgotten how lovely the people are here, *his* people after all, to the extent he could be said to have any: how pleased he is to be among them again!) and staring out on the softly settling snow, letting himself be gradually submerged in a sweet melancholic languor. His erstwhile companions, perhaps sensing the onset of this pensive mood, have graciously slipped away for the moment, the porter to guide the blind hotel proprietor back to prepare the professor's lodgings for the night and to move the luggage up before returning for him here. Yes, blind as well as maimed. Upon leaving the hotel to come here, the unfortunate creature walked straight out the door and down the watersteps into the canal. "Now look what you've done! You've got your feet all wet!" the porter had scolded, pulling him out, and the hotel manager had whined: "My feet are all wet!" Which for some reason had made the professor laugh, made them all laugh. Then they had come here together, the ancient traveler in the middle holding both of the hobbling locals up, feeling quite jolly and youthful in spite of himself.

They had met no one en route except for a poor deranged drunk, shouting to himself in an empty campo, lamenting the hammerings he had taken and excoriating a no doubt imaginary untrue lover as though she were present, a deplorable reminder that even here, in the noblest of settings, loathsome disorderly lives are possible, beauty being no proof against asininity. Virtue, he had written (the line is now in Bartlett's) in his pioneering transdisciplinary work, *The Transformation of the Beast*, a "lucid and powerful prose epic in the tradition of Augustine and Petrarch," as it was widely heralded, standing as a fortress against the false psychologism of the day (there was perhaps in this work a youthful fascination with beastliness rather than its transcendence, since successfully purged, but it remained to this day the most convincing composite image of the Genius-in-History), *is* sanity. Indeed it would have done the crazy man in the campo no harm, what with all his ravings about untamable beasts and savage natures untouched by kindness and unredeemable evil fates (or fairies, his slurred ramblings were ambiguous), to have read that book before falling victim to his own self-fulfilling prophecies: natures *do* remain just as they first appear if they are completely mad. However, the poor creature, storming up and down a bridge over and over as though in the forlorn hope, a hope repeatedly renewed even when repeatedly baffled, that it might one time translate him to greater heights—up into one of Tiepolo's sky-high parades perhaps, though nothing so fair was above him now—did succeed in startling the professor as they passed by with what amounted to a demented paraphrase of another of his famous sayings, this one from the book the world best knows him by, *The Wretch*, his first essay in unabashed autobiography, stark precursor to *Mamma*, his current work-in-progress. Originally little more than a film treatment, notes for a storyboard, as it were, *The Wretch* had evolved into a program guide to the completed motion picture, sold in the lobbies, and from there into a comprehensive best-selling assault upon all the heretical modern and eventually postmodern (he was a man ahead of his time) denials of what in a famous coinage he called "I-ness," a masterpiece whose single message (other than learning not to be naughty and helping one's parents when they are sick and poor) was that each man makes

himself and thus the world: *"Character counts!"* "Making makes the
made mad!" is what the poor devil cried in his delirium, his voice
eerily hollow as though coming from the other world. "Crackers!
Curses! Listen to me and go back home!" Then he rushed to a church
wall and beat his dark bony head against it, wailing forth his "Woe!
Woe! Woe!" *("Guai! Guai! Guai!"*—or maybe it was "Cry! Cry!
Cry!") and eliciting from the beak-nosed porter in his role as the
Plague Doctor the laconic remark: "That's what happens to people
who get all their ideas on one side of their head, dottore: it tips their
brains over."

He has been introduced here at the Gambero Rosso as *un gran
signore*, and in truth has been treated as such by the beaming host,
who seems to be chef, waiter, barkeep, and master of ceremonies all
in one, as liberal with his wine as with his chatter, accepting their
incongruous lot with that democratic grace and forbearance typical of
the people of these islands, so leery of popes and kings alike, even
joining them briefly for a plateful of stuffed pig's trotters and a Pinot
Bianco from Collio, much recommended and indeed nothing amiss.
On entering this simple inn with its yellow painted walls and tattered
football posters and plastic wine barrels, he had felt suddenly that he
had been here before, not in this particular osteria of course, nothing
so mawkishly improbable as that—rather, it recalled for him all those
village osterias of his childhood, too long forgotten, this one now their
quintessence. What was it? A certain rancidity in the frying oil perhaps, the scrape of the cheap chairs on the wooden floors, the frayed
napkins, a sharpness to the Parmesan on the tripe—whatever it was,
he was overtaken by a sudden sorrow, and a sudden joy, as though
life itself were reaching out for him in one last loving embrace, an
embrace in which he feels himself still happily, if wistfully, enfolded.

Unable to sham an appetite which has utterly abandoned him in
his weariness and excitement, the professor has nibbled at all the
dishes for old times' sake yet eaten little, suffering, as it were, a
mental indigestion of memories and anticipations churned up in the
language by which he means to capture it all, the individual words
springing up and flowering now in his head like golden coins on a
magic tree, all atinkle with their manifest profundity and poetry. *Zin!
zin! zin!* they go. I should be taking notes, he thinks. The blind hotel
proprietor, likewise, complaining of a "grave indisposition of the gut,

as it is called," said he could eat very little, settling in the end for a few modest portions of mullet al pomodoro, grilled cuttlefish, sea bass baked in salt, razor clams, and stuffed crabs, the house specialty, and finishing with sweetbreads and mushrooms, plus a simple risotto with sliced kidneys trifolato, smoked eels, and prawns with chicken gizzards and polenta, all of it consumed noisily from beneath the grim visor of his *bauta* mask, pressed upon his plate like a pale severed head, his one black-gloved hand left free thereby to clutch his glass, from which he seemed not so much to drink the wine as to snort it.

The porter, contrarily, protesting that the night's exertions had aroused in him a most woeful discomfort in the stomach that closely resembled appetite, declared that he intended to consume at one sitting all that the liberality of *il buon dottore* had bestowed upon him, down to the last *quattrino*, speaking in the old way, and in demonstration of this proclamation proceeded to devour monumental quantities of tortellini and cannelloni, penne all'arrabbiata, rich and tangy, spaghetti with salt pork and peppers, heaps of thick chewy gnocchi made from cornmeal, tender pasticcio layered with baked radicchio from Treviso, pickled spleen and cooked tendons (or nervetti, as they call them here, "little nerves," slick and translucent as hospital tubing), bowls of risi e bisi and sliced stuffed esophagus (the professor skipped this one), fennel rolled in cured beef, and breaded meatballs with eggplant alla parmigiana. His doctor unfortunately having put him on a strict regimen (and here the masked porter patted his overflowing hips plaintively), he was denied the pleasures of the fish course, but he was able, in all good conscience, to round off his evening's repast with a dish of calf's liver alla veneziana, wild hare in wine sauce with a homely garnishing of baby cocks, beef brains, pheasants, and veal marrow, a small suckling lamb smothered in kiwi fruit, sage, and toasted almonds, and a kind of fricassee of partridges, rabbits, frogs, lizards, and dried paradise grapes, said to be another famous specialty of the house and particularly recommended for persons on stringent diets. "Ah, that was its own death!" he exclaimed on crunching up the last of the little birds, his gravelly old voice greased now to a mellow rumble. "I'm full as an egg!"

Of course there was an abundance of wine to be had with all this food, for as the porter put it: "You can't build a wall without mortar, professore!" True, true, and, given the hearty generosity of the hotel manager in providing such a feast, even if he himself in his jet-lagged condition was able to enjoy so little of it, how could he refuse them all a few simple bottles, especially since in this respect at least he was able to join in the festivities. Indeed, it was the delicate whisper of a fizzy Cartizze from Valdobbiadene, the soft cheeky blush in a Pinot Grigio from the Veneto, the meaty brusqueness of a young Friulian Refosco, the tangy, faintly sour aroma of a spilled bottle of Venegazzu Riserva as it spread through the tablecloth stiffened with stains (not to mention the evaporation of his own reserve as the wines coursed through his age- and travel-stiffened limbs: good wine makes good blood, as they say here) that most pungently drew him back to the drama of his origins, leaving him now in this delicious metaphysical torpor, blessed as it were with purposeful idleness, at rest in the face of perfection—the very indolence in effect of Paradise itself, wherein self-knowledge is not pursued but intuitively received: seek not and (a belch arises from some deep inner well like a kind of affirmation of the pneuma, and he welcomes it, clothing it in his spirit as it climbs toward the world, hugging it to his heart as he might a child, caressing it at the back of his throat as though to hone its eloquence, releasing if finally with a kind of tender exultation:)—*WUURRRP!*—and ye shall find . . .

"How's that, signore? You have lost something?"

"Ah! No, I said, I feel fine! Another round, my friend—while we wait!"

Though he shouldn't, of course. Thinking out loud like that, always worse when he's had a couple, but the magic of this moment and this place has him utterly entranced, and he wants to prolong the moment, to reach, if he can, the very dizzying heart of that enchantment. This, *this*, is what I have come back for, he thinks, sipping the pale grappa with its stalky aroma, its harsh green flavor, faintly reminiscent of winter pears and vanilla, his father's favorite drink. The old man brewed it himself, aging it under the stairs in an old oak barrel black with antiquity, and every week Maestro Ciliegia, as they called him because of his notorious love for grappa and the cherrylike nose it conferred upon him (he can't remember his real name, it doesn't matter), would drop by with a little something for them, some fried pastry or a basket of figs or a few scraps of firewood, and his father would invite him in then for "a drop of *riserva*," as he called it, dignifying it in that way, Maestro Ciliegia protesting all the way to the barrel. Then they would pull the broken-down table up to the cot and the rickety old chair up to the table, and commence a game of *bazzica* with cards as soft as empty pockets, or sometimes a chess match with little pegs and splinters only they knew how to identify, Maestro Ciliegia reminding his father each week that if he would only bring the table over to his workshop he would put a new leg on it, his father replying each week that the last time he visited that place he got pregnant, he would rather live with a ruined table than a ruined reputation. There would be more trips to the grappa barrel and sooner or later a piece would seem to move by itself on the chessboard or a card would magically turn up twice in one round, the joking would turn to insults, the words to pokes and punches, and soon the room would be a shambles, both men scratched and bruised, their ears and noses bit, their buttons torn off and their wigs scattered, and then from somewhere under all the rubble, his father would say: "Another drop, Maestro Ciliegia?" "One more spot perhaps before I go."

The Gambero Rosso landlord, yawning, fills his glass once more. Is this a gift or has he just asked for it? In either event, he thanks him, returning his yawn and feeling somewhat abashed. What is happening to him? It is as if the force of his reason and of a discipline which he has practiced since youth has suddenly abandoned him. In his time, it is true, he was young and raw; and, misled by his greenness and his admittedly peculiar identity crisis, he blundered in public. He lumbered about, he stumbled, he exposed himself, he offended against caution and tact. He has written about all this in *The Wretch*. But he renounced vagabondage and rebellion and idle amusements, and so, through discipline, has acquired that dignity which, as all the world insists, is the innate good and craving of every moral being; it could even be said that his entire development has been a conscious undeviating progression away from the embarrassments of idleness and anarchy, not to mention a few indelicate pratfalls, and toward dignity. Indeed, he is one of the great living exemplars of this universal experience, this passage, as it were, from nature to civilization— from the raw to the cooked, as one young wag has put it—or, as he himself has described it in his current work-on-hard-disk in the chapter "The Voice in the Would-Pile," "from wood to will." And now, suddenly, that voice has returned to haunt him, as though to avenge its long confinement by reclaiming, as his own powers weaken, its mischievous autonomy. Nor is that the worst that has beset him. What is most alarming is that—pain, sorrow, and the door on top, as the porter might say: if it's not one thing, it's another—he is turning back to wood again. It is poking out now at his knees and elbows, he can see it, bleached and twisted and full of rot, maybe even a worm or two. He can also see the osteria landlord standing in front of him with his camelhair coat over his arm and a long piece of paper. He stares up at him quizzically, lowering his sleeves and pantlegs.

"You said something about paying, signore, and to show you the door."

"Ah." His grappa is gone, though he doesn't remember drinking it. His stomach is not turning to wood, it feels like a soft collapsing bag, burbling indelicately now from under his napkin. "Of course." He stands, bumping the table, but luckily there's nothing on it left to spill. He'd rather sit for a while longer, it's quite peaceful here really, but he's too humiliated to admit it. "That's exactly what I said." But he can hardly say even that. Said, he said "said," he heard that part himself, it's still ringing in his mind, but he is not sure about the rest. He is reminded, as he stands there weaving from side to side, of certain particularly odious faculty luncheons of the past. Yes, I could use a digestive walk, he thinks, hoping he is only thinking it. He reaches for the bill, but the landlord seems to be waving it about. He pauses, studying its movements, the patterns (he has always been particularly skillful at discerning patterns), then, with an abrupt lurch that sends his chair flying, snatches it: "Got you!" he laughs. But he can't read it. Must have the wrong glasses on. He asks the landlord to explain it to him. "Just the general principles," he says with a generous wave of his hand. It seems he is paying for all three suppers. The figure is astronomical. Of course all sums expressed in Italian lire are astronomical. You have to take off three or four zeros, he can't remember which. And his hotel bill will be credited, the landlord says. That's his understanding. The landlord removes the requisite banknotes from his wallet, which the professor seems to have given to him for this purpose. There is apparently just enough to cover the bill, which is a good thing because he left his credit cards and traveler's checks back at the hotel. His good friends had not wanted to pay the bill for fear of implying he was not at liberty to have all he wanted to eat and drink, the landlord explains, handing the empty wallet back. It might have been an insult to a gentleman like himself. "I would not have minded the insult," the professor says grandly. He has one arm in a sleeve of the coat but cannot find the other one. The other sleeve, that is. He knows where the arm is. "In fact, it would have given me —*bwrrpp!*—scusi!—considerable pleasure." He has found the sleeve, but now he has lost the arm. This is because the first arm is in the wrong sleeve, or anyway that is the landlord's interpretation of the dilemma, an interpretation that proves functional if perhaps overly simple, for no sooner is it enunciated than both arms and both sleeves appear in their proper places. Whereupon a certain magic ensues: the professor finds himself, seemingly without transition, out in the snowy campo, all alone, bundled up in his coat and muffler, the Gambero Rosso behind him locked and dark, and such an immaculate silence all about that he can actually hear the snow falling upon other snow.

4.

NIGHT OF
THE ASSASSINS

He is lost. Lost, frightened, bewildered. And freezing his bark off. Somehow he has left his German fedora with its little bluebird feather in the headband back at the osteria, and his head, bald as an egg and becoming, alas, even balder, went completely numb under its peaked bonnet of snow before he discovered it. He brushed away the snow and wrapped his frozen pate then in his Andean llama-wool scarf, tying it under his chin like an old woman's shawl, and that has left his flimsy chest exposed. Ah, what misery! His calfskin gloves are gone, he knows not where. His twice-imported Italian shoes—he has always joked back in America that he liked to keep both feet in the homeland—have proven useless in this weather, leaving his feet soaked and aching from the cold, the thin leather taking a no doubt terminal beating. He might as well be barefoot. Hadn't someone he once knew died of fatal chilblains of the feet? Forsaking his pride finally and throwing himself upon the charity of his fellow creatures, he has rung a doorbell in a deserted campo, crying out in his despair for help or a warm hat or at least the loan of a city map, only to have a window open up and a bucket of water, or what he hoped was water, be thrown on him as if he were a potted geranium. Others in the square shouted out obscenities from behind darkened windows like a hostile audience from behind the footlights, even threatening to bring the police, and he screamed back at them, calling them all a lot of bloody assassins and murderers, shrieking and squawking in an altogether undignified manner unfortunately, overtaken momentarily by a fit of blind fear and rage. Or perhaps not so momentarily, for his heart still feels caught in the grip of that icy fist as he goes staggering through the white night, up and down the steps of bridges he cannot even see, across barren squares and through frighteningly narrow defiles, pursued by a fierce wind that whips around him from all directions, his spectacles frosted over and his wet clothes crackling now with ice crystals, unable to remember very clearly anymore exactly what he's looking for, even if he could see it should he miraculously come upon it. Something about a blackened doorway. But under the blown snow, all the doors look blackened. He feels utterly abandoned in a world without mercy or even logic. How he wishes he had left the osteria together with his "dear friends," as they liked to flatter themselves, instead of lingering for that last glass of grappa!

Yet how delightful it had seemed at first! He had stood for a moment in the radiant little square in front of the Gambero Rosso, one of those enchanting and forsaken places which lie in the interior of Venice as though within a secret fold, accessible only to intimates, his own interior aglow still from the generous infusions, thinking how right he had been to come back here! Here to this "vast and sumptuous pile," as a famous militarist once called it, this "peopled labyrinth of walls," magical, dazzling, and exquisitely perplexing, this "paradise of exiles!" She who called herself the Serenissima. Only hours before, he had been sitting in his lonely office back at the university at the end of the Christmas break, struggling to come to grips with the realization that his epic tribute to his beloved shepherdess and cynosure, thought concluded, was not. The "final" chapter was not the final chapter, after all. Something was missing. It was, like the stark New England landscape outside his office window, too cold, too intellectual, too abstract. Too empty. In his intransigent pursuit of the truth he had somehow neglected—virtue, truth, and beauty being, in the end (which was where, in the book at least, and in life too no doubt, he was), one and the same—the senses. Whereupon he was suddenly struck by a most remarkable vision, sensuous yet pure, of this very place, which his mentor Petrarch, who had preceded him here as though to show the way, rightly called the "noblest of cities, sole refuge of humanity, peace, justice, and liberty, defended not so much by its waters as by the prudence and wisdom of its citizens," and which appeared to him in that moment in flesh

tones as delicious as those of Giorgione or Tiziano. He reached out
and, seemingly without transition, by the miracle of flight, here, his
hands still outstretched, he was! He felt so happy just then that tears
came to his eyes, tears now frozen on his face and pricking him like
vicious little thumbtacks, but then warm and titillating as they ran
down his cheeks and nose, and as purifying as the snow frosting the
delicious little campo, turning the stone cylindrical wellhead in the
middle into a kind of large pale lantern. *"Ah! Che bel paese!"* he cried
aloud. If his knees hadn't been hurting him so, he might have knelt
down and kissed it.

He had easily discovered the route back to the hotel and set off,
expecting at every turn to meet the bent back and broken beak of his
lugubrious guide, returning for him, and meanwhile enjoying his
digestive walk, as he thought of it, rejoicing in the luminous spectacle
of Venice in the snow and laying plans for the morrow when he might
encounter once again—in the flesh, as it were, the *unblighted* flesh—
his old friends Giambellino and Giorgione, Titian and Tintoretto,
Carpaccio, Lotto, Veronese, and all the rest. For it was with them it
all began. Once all the other beginnings were over, that is. Now he is
better known for intellectual works of a tougher order such as *Sacred
Sins* or *Art and the Spirit*, his devastating indictment of theatricality
and amateurism in the plastic arts, but it was through the great masters of the Venetian school that his scholarly career, then as an art
critic and historian, originally—as they say in the Other World—
"took off" (here only the pigeons would understand such an expression, and they would not mean the same thing by it), with his seminal
studies on illusionism, transfiguration, and the motif of the ass in
Venetian paintings of the life of Christ.

He was first drawn to the study of art, being self-taught in this as
in all subjects, by a painting on the wall of his father's little room
under the stairs. His father was a poor man, unable to afford even a
fireplace or a kettle, so he had painted one, or had had one painted,
on the wall, with a fire lit under the kettle that looked just like a real
fire, a cloud of steam coming out of it that looked just like real steam,
and a kettle lid so convincing he nearly splintered his fingers trying
to take it off before he discovered the illusion. Locked in often by his
loving but, it must be said, ill-tempered father, and with little more
to eat than pear cores and his own hat, he had ample time to study

this trompe l'oeil, learning something therefrom about the function of appetite in scholarship (he has often argued that more interesting than the things that are studied by mankind is the infinite catalogue of things that are not), the implications of the wall (surfaces are *not* passive!), and the power of raw color upon the imagination: he found, on bitter days, he could actually warm himself by that painted fire, and indeed, even now, it might comfort him and still the rising panic in his heart.

For he does not want to die. Not yet. Not with just one more chapter to go. But the choice may not be his. He is nearing exhaustion. He no longer knows if he is walking or crawling. He cannot feel his hands and feet. The snow is everywhere, in his face, down his back, inside him as well as out—snow and the deep night, for the world is weirdly white and pitch black at the same time, just as his mind has gone blank and his spirits horribly dark. Somehow he has made a wrong turn. Probably more than one. He climbed that last bridge, expecting to see the old palazzo and its charred doorway, all warmly lit up and waiting for him, but it was the wrong bridge. He retraced his steps, but soon they disappeared under the fresh snow. He tried to find his way back to the Gambero Rosso, but the fold had closed. So his search became more random, more frenzied. His knees began to give way. Passages beckoned that, like his father's trompe l'oeil, were not ones, and he smacked his face on them. Or they let him in, then dead-ended in mazelike traps occupied by prides of mad squalling cats. He hobbled painfully over slippery bridges that led only to locked and darkened doors. He cried out for help, got doused, reviled.

Now he wants to stop but he cannot, he is too afraid. It is as though he is running not toward something, but from it. If he bumps into something, he jumps back as though struck; if he stumbles toward the edge of a canal yawning out of the swirling white night below him, he feels pushed. All the old childhood traumas have returned and he recalls with renewed terror that night in the woods when he was set upon by murderers who chased him, caught him, knifed him, hung him, a night that has haunted him all his life and haunts him now, driving him through this befuddling network of alleyways and squares like the pursued heroines in gothic movies. Except that he lacks the heroines' youthful strength. When he was just a little sliver, as his father liked to call him, he used to be able to run all day like a hare before hunters, to zip up and down trees, scale cliffs, leap hedge-rows at a single bound—indeed, on that "Night of the Assassins," as it has come to be called, he delayed his capture by leaping a wide canal of filthy water the color of a cold cappuccino just like these, his would-be killers falling in—*patatunfete!*—when they tried to follow —but now, far from leaping one of these wretched ditches, he cannot even pull himself over their bridges. He can barely walk. He is feel-ing, oddly, seasick. His head is pounding. He is beginning to turn in smaller and smaller circles.

But wait! What was that—? Something behind him? He stops dead in his tracks, stooped over, his knees knocking, sour breath tearing from his ancient ill-made lungs, afraid to turn around and look. All about him there is a deep hush, almost as though the whole island were frozen up, holding its breath, he can hear nothing but his own desperate snorting and the tormented creaking of his knees—and then suddenly a terrible flutter as of a thousand assassins comes roaring up out of the night, swooping down over him and away, and he screams and nearly jumps out of his skin, what's left of it. As his scream dies away, he can hear them, or it, circling back, so, terror reviving him —this is *real!*—he takes off down a narrow calletta, praying only that the little alley doesn't end in watersteps. Whatever it is that's after him—just a bevy of desperate pigeons caught out in the snow, he tells himself, but he doesn't believe it, pigeons aren't that stupid, for this kind of stupidity it takes a Ph.D.—chases him right down it, he can hear it, or them, bearing down on him, bellowing mightily, or maybe cursing (it sometimes sounds like belching), wings slapping and scraping the crumbly old brick walls, sending loose chips raining down, rattling the drawn wooden shutters, jostling flowerpots out of window boxes—no wonder this place looks so beat-up!

He emerges, dangerously, into an open square, no place to hide, the huge wings paddling away overhead—but in the nick of time he spies a low underpass, and he ducks down it. He can hear his pursuer roar with alarm *("Vaffanculo!"* he seems to hear the beast cry) before slamming into the walls and bringing down chimney pots and roof tiles in its frantic climb. The sottoportico, shorter than he might have hoped, leads him to another clumsy bridge, the bridge to a riva edging a canal full of docked boats sheeted with white snow, the riva to more streets and side streets past metal-shuttered shops and snow-topped heaps of garbage bags, the streets to other bridges and courtyards and passageways and squares, while, just above and behind him, the pounding wings bear down relentlessly, his assailant losing him and finding him in all these mazy turnings, as though it might be a game it's playing, like a cat toying with a trapped mouse. The old professor is not exactly running, but he's not walking either, it would be hard to say *what* he's doing, but he's picking them up and putting them down, all four of his wasted limbs at once and not in any special order, his head ducked for fear of having it snatched away, his torso bouncing along erratically like unwieldy luggage.

But then he finds himself again in an open campo, probably one he has been in before, and though his mind is racing down the next alleyway, his body is on its knees. It just does not want to go any farther. He crawls dutifully ahead, carrying through in the old way, holding fast, hauling his resistant carcass through the snow like a dull plow, a thing heavier even than his abusive old father was the night he had to wrench the old brute, hallucinating wildly on grappa he had made from seaweed, fish eyes, and ship wreckage, and fermented in his erstwhile host's digestive juices, a grappa too good, he kept blubbering insistently, to leave behind, out of the giant fish's belly. Which is where he is again, swallowed up as one sucks up an oyster and waiting to be digested, only now his daddy's not here and there's no escape. He can hear his assassin flapping fiercely in the wind above him, circling round as though, at last, to pounce. Well, let it, whatever it is, come. He curls up against the wall. It is not the wall of the painted fire and steaming kettle, but it will have to do. He can go no further. His opus magnum will remain unfinished. Our worst fears, he thinks, are always justified. He is going to "sleep like the Pope" all right, but not the present one. Above him, what looks for all the world like a flying lion is thrashing about in the snowstorm, roaring lustily and batting the snow away from its eyes with its massive paws. But it may be his own dizziness, his poor sight, his indigestion which delivers to him this vision. "PAX TIBI—*wurrp!*—EXCREMENTUM MEUS!" the fiendish creature bawls: "*Hic!*—REQUIESCET CORPUS TUUM!" and, its great ghostly wings churning up the snowy air theatrically, it circles a bell tower once to commence its murderous descent.

But then something quite unexpected happens. The winged monster dips and swerves erratically as though confused or blinded by the snow and (are its eyes crossed?) heads straight for the bell tower—or else the bell tower, which has been floating treacherously in and out of the whirling snow, sways suddenly and leans into the storm; from the stricken traveler's position in the nauseous pit of the orchestra, so to speak, it is hard to tell. The lion lifts its paws and spreads its wings, but too late: there is a thunderous earth-shaking ear-splitting clangor, followed by a frantic scattering of astonished pigeons, fleeing groggily from they know not what, the light fall of stone teeth and feathers upon the little campo, and a series of mighty reverberations that sound and resound through the frosty night as though a giant cymbal has been struck, a throbbing metallic clamor that seems to set all the bells in Venice ringing.

Behind the repercussions rippling out into the night, the professor can hear, up in the campanile where the din was launched, a great moaning and puling and thick-tongued cursing in the Venetian dialect: *"You turd! Rotto in culo! Oh! Ah! I'm dying! You head of a prick! I piss in your mother's cunt! Oh, my head! My ears! Shut up, will you, sfiga di cazzo? By the leprous cock of Saint Mark, you asshole of God, I'll have you melted down and turned into souvenir gondolas! Where are my teeth—?! Oh, you whore! I come on you, you sack of shit, on you and all your dead!"* And then, head in its paws, tail adroop, the pale beast goes flapping off sorely into the night, growling its oaths and imprecations, disappearing into the blowing snow and the fading tintinnabulation of tolling bells.

Left alone, the abandoned wayfarer, huddled miserably against the wall, accepts this melancholy tolling as his own knell. To be poised against fatality, to meet adverse conditions gracefully is more than simple endurance, he knows, it is an act of aggression, a positive triumph, but he also knows such triumphs are now beyond him. He just wants to cry. There are always endings, but there are not always conclusions. If you're out of candles, as his father used to say with a tired shrug, enh, you'll go to bed in the dark. These simple truths come to him, along with all the memories. But what is it he remembers? His own life or the film of it, the legends? This life of his: it has been like a kind of dream—but who was the dreamer? He cannot think. His brain is frozen. He tries to remember his own famous dream, the one that made him what he is today, *that* might warm him up; but all that comes to him there under his helmet of iced scarf is what he saw that awesome day when she spread her knees as though to reveal to him his fate. Ah, dear lady, and where are you now? He looks up, hoping for another miracle, even another flying lion, company at least. But there's only a ghastly white all around him as in the house of the dead. Except for the wall itself: a flaking ochre red softly reminiscent of the Trecento masters like Paolo Veneziano. It encourages him that he can remember Paolo Veneziano. I'm not dead yet, he thinks, or perhaps says, his cheeks pressed against the wall, I can still remember Paolo . . . Paolo What's-his-name. What was I thinking about? Already gone. Over his head, he sees now, there is something written. It seems to say "JESU." He's a sucker for words, he'll read anything, afraid of missing something if he doesn't. Might be a message, a final message (all my life, he thinks, I've been waiting for a message). He clutches at the snow-rimmed bricks of the wall, dragging himself up. Not "JESU," but "JUVE." And, yes, he brushes away the snow, here's the "VIVA," written like two birds in flight, their wings crossed in happy omen, and next to it the other one: "ABBASSO LARIN METICA!"—"Down with Larin Metica!" *"Viva abbasso!"* he cries. He laughs. He knows where he is now. He's almost there!

He scrapes the crust of ice and snow off his glasses, glances round. Right! There's the bridge, there's the narrow underpass! The joints of his knees are locked up, frozen solid, he has to totter ahead stiff-legged, rocking from side to side, his eyes watering, his nose running: but, yes, through here and turn right—*and there it is!* The long fondamenta, now a ghostly white and daintily pricked out with cat tracks, the stately palazzo rising through the eddies of swirling snow, the blackened doorway! He scrambles over the last bridge, more or less on all fours, *volere è potere*, his mind thawing now with glowing anticipations of pillows and eiderdowns and his own flannel nightshirt, his liniments and antacids (his stomach, he realizes, is in a ferocious turmoil), his computer, his books, his *Mamma* (he *will* find that climactic metaphor, maybe in fact he has *already* found it!), his earplugs and blindfold and sleeping pills and his hot water bottle. The thought of a hot water bottle alone propels him down the last stretch from the bridge to the door.

But it is all dark, the door is locked, they have given up on him!

"I'm here! I'm here!" he cries into the howling wind. He bangs on the door. He is so weak he can almost not hear it himself. There should be a doorbell somewhere, but he cannot find it. He rattles the rusted wrought-iron grills at the windows, shaking the snow off them, shouting through the broken glass. "My friends! Open up!" He can hear cats prowling around, yowling, chasing one another. Overhead, the windows are all shuttered or broken. *"Wake up! I'm here!"* He wants to throw something at the windows, but all he can find is a plastic cat dish. *"Help! Help!"* he screams. They cannot leave him out here! He has already paid! There is one pane left whole in the window just above his head: he flings his watch through it. There is a soft splintering tinkle and the cats stop yowling for a moment, then start up again. He is beginning to cry. He thinks he might be going crazy. He is still screaming, but there are no words now, he sounds like one of the cats. He is getting sick. His screams have become groans. His insides seem to be exploding and collapsing at the same time. He must squat somewhere, and quick. He could use the canal but he is afraid of falling in. There is a walled garden, he tries the gate, it is locked. No time for alternatives. He presses into the shallow sill of the gate, under a wild rough tangle of overhanging thornbrush and dead vines, fumbles feverishly with his trousers, ripping them down as far as his knees. But his coat is in the way. Struggling with it (he is already too late, much too late), he falls facefirst into the snow. He rises to his knees and elbows, can rise no further. Behind his ears, there are terrible eruptions. He feels like he is dying. Like the time when he was sick and lame and tethered, heart broken, to a stinking stable. Only now *no* one would want him, he is not even worth flaying. "I'm sorry!" he weeps, pulling his coattails over his head. "I'm so sorry . . ."

And so it is that *il gran signore*, the distinguished emeritus professor from abroad, the world-renowned art historian and critic, social anthropologist, moral philosopher, and theological gadfly, the returning pilgrim, lionized author of *The Wretch, Blue Repose, Politics of the Soul, The Transformation of the Beast, Astringent Truth*, and other classics of Western letters, native son, *galantuomo*, and universally beloved exemplar of industry, veracity, and civility, not a child of his times, but *the* child of his times, is discovered on this, the night of his glorious homecoming, head buried and ancient fulminating arse high, when the police come cruising up in three sleek sky-blue motor launches, spotlights glaring, and arrest him ("What are you *doing* there on the *ground?!*" they cry) for indecent exposure, disturbing the peace, suspected terrorist activities, polluting the environment, and attempting to enter a public building without official written permission. "*Avanti*, you rascal! And step lively! Or so much the worse for you!"

5.

ALIDORO'S RESCUE

Oh, he knows about the vagaries and terrors of the law. For years now he has lived a life of the utmost propriety, decent and law-abiding, crossing the street only when the light was green, avoiding swindlers and idlers and evil companions, speaking the truth with unflagging courage, and contributing annually to the policemen's ball. But it has not always been so. Once he got his own father sent to prison with a mere tantrum, then received a bit of his own back when, as the victim of an infamous fraud, he'd appealed to a judge for justice and got hauled off to jail instead ("This poor devil has been robbed of four gold pieces," the senile old ape told the police guards; "seize him therefore and put him immediately in prison!"), there to spend four of the worst months of his life, months of harsh deprivation, loneliness, and brutal abuse. In those lamentable days, all his worst crimes went unpunished, he's the first to admit that, yet when he tried to give help, for example, to his dear friend Eugenio, cruelly struck down by their own classmates, he was again dragged away as the main suspect in the case, and by police no more threatening than these. Oh, be sure of it, he knows full well the danger he's in! The abuse he suffered in prison was meted out by fellow prisoners and guards alike, he got it from both bells, as they say, they hated him on all sides of the law. His very existence seemed an affront to them, who and what he was, as though he demeaned them somehow merely by being in their midst, it was a kind of racism. In their merciless loathing, they used him as a nutcracker and knocked splinters off him for toothpicks and stuffed lighted matches up his rectum, hoping to get rid of him once and for all and toast their bread and sausages over him at the same time. And if anything, this lot tonight is even more violent, more heavily armed. Yet he can't stop himself. He has his father's pride and temper. And now, alas, his father's age, and then some. Long ago, when they'd tried to arrest him for Eugenio's injuries, he was able to run away, belly to the ground, so fast he stirred a dust storm; now he couldn't beat that old snail who took a week to serve him breakfast, there's no running left in him. Just helpless fury and terror and bitter indignation, his mind is literally reeling with it.

But how they've toyed with him, provoked him, how they've mocked and taunted him! "A stinking joss stick," they've called him, and "a twisted little twig," "shit with ears," and "a purulent polecat with a beanful of crickets." He's screamed back at them, threatening them with lawsuits and high-level investigations and public denunciations and even popular uprisings: *"When the world hears what you've done—!!"* Which has not been easy, of course, with his pants around his knees and full of the ghastly ruins of his night at the Gambero Rosso. "Foo! What a *puzzone!*" the officers exclaimed when they first grabbed him. "Someone get a lid on that pot!" "But that's my *hotel!*" he shrieked then. "I've already *paid!* My *bags* are in there! My *manuscript—! My precious Mamma—!*" "The disgusting old thing wants his mamma!" they laughed, pulling his pants up as they wrestled him toward their patrol boats, but failing to wipe him, leaving him feeling hot and sticky and chilled to the bone, so to speak, all at once. He was still blustering, so they picked him up by the scruff to watch him kick. They dropped him to watch him sprawl. They threw snow in his face to listen to him splutter. They tossed him from one to another in the glaring spotlights, shouting out vulgar jokes and proverbs about excreta and old age. They've threatened him with a hiding. They've threatened to take him out to the prison at Santa Marta and throw him in with their current catch of Red Brigade terrorists: "They'll know how to cook him!" They've rolled him in the snow. *"You fools!"* he blusters, spitting snow. "Don't worry, old man! It's always a consolation to fry in company!" they laugh and dangle him on high.

One of them reaches into his pocket to pluck out his billfold with two fingers and says: "Empty. Some American, looks like. The little prigger must've snatched it." And, seething, stamping his feet in space, he storms right back at him: "That's *my* wallet, you imbecile! I'm an American professor, an *emeritus* professor, do you hear me? Everybody knows me! This is an outrage! An atrocity! An—*oh!* Ah!" He's choking now, gasping, he wonders if he's having a heart attack.

They set him down, standing around laughing with hands on hips, kicking his feet out from under him whenever he tries to stand. "It's a—I'm—I've been—! *Stop!* You can't—! *I know the Pope!*" He is shrieking, bawling, his nose is inflamed (he doesn't know the Pope), he's completely out of control. He can't help it. His masterpiece! All he's worked for all his life—"Please—!" It's like when his father was beating him and he was crying for it to stop. Hugging the old man's knees as the strop came down. "You must open up! For pity's sake! You must let me—!"

"Here, here, you scummy old tart, stop that!" The young gendarme whose knees he's grabbed swats him across the noggin with his leather gloves and boots him away, while the others make sport about this, saying not to be hasty, it's the best offer any of them has had all night. The professor howls and fumes and crawls about in the tumbling snow and bright lights, demanding, pleading, explaining, chastising, but it's as though the language has lost its referents and is only good for the noise it makes. "My computer! My life! *My entire career—!*" "Ha ha! Don't give us that to drink, you miserable little blister!" they jeer. "You *pezzo di puzzo!* You piece of garbage! You shrunken scrotum! You stinking smoke salesman! You gangrenous turd!" They seem to be having a great time. "Look at that beak! Last time I saw one like that it was being used as a billiard stick!" "And bald as a cueball on top of it, the little freak's a whole game in himself!" "*Idiots!*" he screams. "*Scoundrels!*" "But not a very amusing game . . ." "*Delinquenti!*" "To tell the truth, the little asswipe is starting to get up my nose." "*Assassini!*" "Basta! Enough and period! Someone go wake Lido up! Let him have a gnaw on this old tramp! If there's less of him, there might be less noise!"

"Get up here, Lido! We got a live one for you!"

"Or almost live!"

One of the police launches sloshes about in the water as a huge ugly mastiff rises from it, growling throatily, so evil and monstrous in his appearance that even the hysterical scholar is momentarily silenced by awe. It's like some kind of hideous apparition, like a creature long dead rising grotesquely from the Venetian lagoon, pale and deadly, and the very sight of the dreadful thing makes the old professor's knees rattle. If he hadn't already emptied his bowels, he would probably be doing so now. "You're in bad waters now," an officer mutters sinisterly in his ear. "Lido hates presumptuous shitters like you."

"Some he eats straightaway," murmurs another as the beast slouches ashore, "some he promises."

"Eh, Lido, what do you think? One bite or two?"

"The little testa di cazzo even claims to be a professor! That should whet your appetite!"

"He certainly stinks like one! Dress him for the party, Lido!"

"Give him a little holy reason!"

He can feel the mastiff's hot breath on him. But the growling has stopped. The brute is sniffing him curiously, gazing blearily at him through muddy old eyes, drool spooling from his drooping lips. The professor can see that the old fellow is nearly toothless.

"What's this, Lido? We catch you a filthy off-season tourist and you're not even going to chew off a leg or two?"

"He says his name is Pinenut, Lido! Professor Pinenut! Ha ha! There's a tidbit for you!"

"Pinocchio—? Does my nose tell me true, is it really you?"

"Alidoro—?!"

"Ah, Pinocchio! My old friend!" cries the dog, his voice phlegmy with age and deep emotion. He throws his paws around him, laps him on the face and behind the ears, his stub of a tail wagging. Alidoro's coat is mildewy and flyblown, almost suffocatingly rank, but the professor hugs it to him like the sweetest balm, burying his face in it and weeping like a baby. "What has happened, my friend? What has brought you to this miserable state?"

"If you only knew!" the aged traveler wails. "This infernal—*sob*—night! I'll never—! The misfortunes that have—*boo hoo!*—rained down on—!"

"The little stronzo was waking up the whole neighborhood, Lido, making a bloody nuisance of himself with his drunken racket—then he tried to break into this old abandoned mansion here. We caught him with his—"

"Keep your mouth out of this, goose-brain! You're breaking my pockets!" Alidoro roars. "Can't you see I'm speaking with this gentleman?" He tugs the professor's coat collar up around his ears, licks his frozen pate with a warm tongue, then wipes it gently with a big soft paw, covers it with a few tufts of hair, torn from his own breast. "So, my friend . . ."

"It was terrible, Alidoro!" he sobs. "Just imagine! The airport was fogged in and I had to take the train from Milan and it was over-heated, I don't even know what time it was! I had no hotel reservation and the tourist office was closing and the woman dropped the spoon. I mean the key. But the porter had a friend so he brought me here, it was just two steps away, and they were dressed up for Carnival. Only the room wasn't heated, so we had supper in the Gambero Rosso, it was included in the price, but I got lost. The snow—I couldn't see! My old eyes—I nearly died! Someone threw water on me and I got chased by a lion who flew into a belltower! Then I saw the viva abbasso and I came here but it was dark. I was getting sick. I threw my watch—! All my bags—*choke!*—my computer! My flop-pies! Oh, Alidoro! My life's work—!" He's not sure if any of this is comprehensible. He doesn't understand it himself, he's crying like a cut vine, it's all just streaming out of him, words, tears, terrors, the lot, as Alidoro hugs him close. *"In there—! Everything's in there—!"*

"Gentlemen," says the dog, "this is a dear friend of mine. We once saved each other's lives. We are like bread and cheese, friends by the skin, do you understand? He is the most truthful person I have ever known. I'm sure he is all he says he is. You should believe everything he says."

"He says he knows the Pope."

"Well, almost everything." Alidoro raises his heavy snout and sniffs, then leaves the professor and goes to nose about the blackened doorway of the old palazzo. "Now, I think we should open up, gentle-men. There's something decidedly foxy on the air."

"La Volpe—?!"

"Very nasty, whatever it is. Hop to it now!"

One of the policemen fumbles with a big ring of keys. "It gives me a hell of a fright to go in here at night," shudders another, and a third laughs nervously: "Afraid of ghosts?" "A ghost—you know, that woman who died here in the fire." "Fire?" "That's just a legend," says the policeman with the keys, as he pushes the door open. "Beam one of those spotlights in here!" "Whew, when was the last time this pesthole was opened up?" "They say she was waiting for the return of a beloved brother or son who had abandoned her and that maybe in sorrow she set the fire herself. The place hasn't been used since."

"Except by cats. It stinks worse than the old man in here!"

"The woman," gasps the old professor, startled by the tale, his voice reduced now after all the hysterics to a hoarse whisper, "did she have . . . did she have blue hair?"

"Blue hair!" they laugh. "Whoever heard of such a thing!"

"Well, like you can see, Lido. The old ruin's as bald as your pal's conk."

"There's still a kind of smoky smell in this place. Like she's still burning or something. Let's get out of here—!"

"Wait a minute! What's this over here? Someone shine a light!"

"It's a watch! Do you recognize this, old man?"

"Yes, it's mine." This is not going to turn out well. The truth is beginning to sink in. And the story of the woman dying by fire has left him feeling frightened and confused. He knows about fire. He once burned his own feet off. He thought he was going to have to walk through life on his knees. Fire is his greatest fear.

"Did they steal your watch?" rumbles Alidoro, peering up from the shadows where he's been sniffing around.

"No. I threw it through a window. To wake them up."

"To wake who up?"

"His friend the Pope, no doubt. Lido, your mate's got his head in a sack of shit! He's a raving lunatic!"

"Let's take him to the Questura and lock him up. This place makes my blood freeze!"

"Really, Lido, come on, this is a complete waste of time. There's nothing else here except catshit and an old umbrella."

"Yes, that's mine, too. The umbrella, I mean."

"Aha! Did you throw that through the window, too, you daft old geezer?"

"No . . ." But there is something confusing about this, too. When he burned his feet off, they felt as if they belonged to somebody else. Which is how his head is beginning to feel now . . . "There was a blind monk—"

"A blind monk—! Madonna! What next—?!"

"He's gone from God's grace, this one, Lido! He's completely pazzo!"

"Maybe," sighs Alidoro, nosing at a piece of candle wax. "But they were here, just the same."

"You mean—?"

"I mean, gentlemen," rumbles Alidoro, stepping into the light from the doorway and rising to his full height, "that this distinguished visitor—and, indeed, more than a visitor, this native son returned here to his beloved homeland—has been the innocent and very nearly tragic victim of two of our city's most notorious felons. They have lured him here to this lonely site under false pretenses, no doubt playing upon his natural sympathies for the maimed and the infirm, for my friend is famous for his good heart, and here have robbed him of all his earthly goods. He's been sent for a walk, as they say in the trade, taken for a ride, put in the sack, he's been shorn, fiddled, landed, and gaffed. He's been worked like farm butter, boys, he's been had on toast. He's taken a crab and left his feathers in it, lost both lye and soap, do you follow? He was the pigeon, the pup, the one in the middle—am I right, my friend?"

"Yes! That's true, when we went to the Gambero Rosso, they made me walk between—"

"Then, having separated him from his possessions, they abandoned him to the elements—and on a night such as this! Gentlemen! The charge is not murder, not yet, but it might as well be! No hand was raised against him, true, but it was quite enough to lock all the doors. No hand, gentlemen, except your own!"

"Come *on*, mate, we were only doing our duty . . ."

"You're no shinbone of a saint yourself, Lido!"

"I know, I know, no one's paws itch for an occasional turn of tourist-bashing more than mine, you know that, boys, I'm not pulling your ear, I'm not hitting you with a paternale, I wouldn't think of it! All I'm saying is, you've done a duck here, this gentleman is not who or what he might seem, and you owe him an apology and a little courteous attention. I know him as a comrade, lads, I know his life, death, and miracles, as the expression goes, and believe me, he's good pasta, this one, a grand fellow and brave. When you're in over your head and it's drink or drown, when the fat hits the fire and the shit the fan, this is the man, speaking loosely, you want by your side! When Nature made him, as that old hound Ariosto Furioso once said, she broke the mold!"

"Yeah? Well, she might have waited at least until she was finished!"

"I'm not talking now just to give breath to my mouth, my friends! A serious crime has been committed here tonight! It's not just the theft of his luggage, you know me, I don't give a cabbage's fart for private property—*it's the theft of his dignity! His honor!* You can't restore that to him, you sadistic *coglioni,* but at the very least you should be trying to bring a little justice to bear! You should be trying to find the thieves and *get those bags back!*"

"All right, all right, we'll look for them, Lido—but do us the *favor,* enough of this *cacca*—!"

"And may I remind you, gentlemen, that you have been trying to clap those two rogues in a *gattabuia* since the last century? You and your fathers have always complained that they were too wily, you could never get the goods on them. Well, my boys, here's your chance, here's your case! In flagrante, ironclad, with ribbons and bows! If you grasp it by the hair, you'll be national heroes! In fact, come to think of it, it's probably worth a little reward to me and my—"

"But *no,* Lido! *Falla finita!* As far as we're concerned it's better to lose the little shit-machine than to find him, so if he's a chum of yours, do as you please with him, it doesn't do us hot or cold. But don't try to pass the plate, you old mutt, it won't go down! You're not getting the *centesimo* of a whore out of us!"

"Well, all right," says Alidoro with what might be a trace of a grin. "Give us a ride then." He puts a paw around the professor and leads him toward one of the launches. "Come along now, compagno, you've suffered enough. It's time to draw in the oars."

6.

THE PHILOSOPHICAL WATCHDOG

The benumbed wayfarer lies, swaddled in newspapers, blankets, and old rags like a wizened parody of the Christ child from a rigid Trecento nativity, on a bed of wood chips and sawdust under the umbrella of a corrugated tin roof, his back against an overturned gondola, his bundled feet pointed toward an old rusty barrel in which a fire is being stoked by the boatyard's watchdog, Melampetta. "Come Monday, they'll give me a rogue's thumping for letting thieves steal the firewood," she growls, "but così va il mondo, as the philosopher said, if it wasn't the poet—destiny's not to be tampered with unless the Party takes a hand in it, and the Party's hand nowadays is in its pants. So, nothing to do but face whatever comes with a good heart and stout buttocks, and if the evil beggars get carried away, the devil take them, I'll piss on their sandwiches." "That's letting them off easy," Alidoro rumbles from out on the lip of the old dock, where he is rummaging through a snowy heap of broken tiles and glass, bricks, rusted pipes, old paint tins and plastic bags, chain links, bottles, gas cans, and stiff old socks for any burnable bits of wood, rag, and paper. "You should piss in their wine, Mela, hit the tyrannical swillpots where it most hurts." "The wine they drink, cazzo mio, piss improves it, they'd be beating me for the profit in it," she replies. " 'When the masters drink pee and call it claret, the wretched of the earth must grin and bear it; but when the masters drink claret and call it pee, then hang the bastards from the nearest tree!' I think it was either Pliny or the blessed Apuleius who said that, or else it was Saint John of the Apocalypse."

"She's a quarrelsome old bitch, who fancies herself something of an argufier and a heavy thinker, she's got a mouth like a brass band, as they say, and a cunt like a mailbag, but she's a good compagna for all that, and I believe she will not shut us out on a night like this," Alidoro had explained on the way over, a way that was, in the end, too long for the collapsing traveler. Almost too tired and ill to know what he was doing, he had signed a general denunciation of the thieves, the police offering to fill in all the names, surnames, descriptions, alleged villainies, and formal criminal and civil charges back at the Questura, then he and Alidoro had hitched a ride in one of the patrol boats, Alidoro stealing a blanket as they got under way and stuffing it under the professor's coat, pretending to be buttoning him up. En route (and, yes, the railway station *was* just two steps away from the fraudulent hotel, that charlatan *had* taken him in circles: the police, annoyingly amused, promised to add this to his list of complaints), the old mastiff was the forbearant butt of a lot of more or less friendly banter about all his presumed mistresses, one or more of whom they were apparently about to visit, so the professor was alarmed to learn, when they were dropped off at the San Barnaba traghetto stop and the police had roared away, that the poor brute was broke and homeless ("I'm on the straw, old friend," he apologized with a woeful gaze, snow drifting down around his ears, "you've caught me between head and neck, to put it plain, I'm flat, I'm dry, I've neither bone nor bed. The last woman who, more in pity than in passion, took me in was on the prod and caught the plague from one of the fiendish instruments, sad to say, so I've been bedding down on my wits, what's left of them, ever since . . ."), and that their best hope was an old gondola repair yard at the backside of the island where he knew the watchdog.

So Alidoro wrapped the professor up in the blanket they had stolen off the patrol boat ("How did you recognize me?" he asked, and the old mastiff, cope-and-cowling him, replied: "You're the only one I've ever known, my friend, who gave off the smell of holm-oak." "So you've noticed then . . ." "Noticed—?") and they set off to come here, Alidoro plodding heavily ahead through the snow, the professor, hungover and weak-kneed, staggering along behind, afraid only of dying alone. What had been a partial misgiving back in America, a faint doubt as to the advisability of his expedition, had now become a bitter conviction that his own nature was somehow fatally betraying him. That dignity which has taken him nearly a century to cultivate and sustain had vanished in an instant, as though his very pursuit of a meaningful life were itself depriving him of it. He once stated quite plainly in some remote place (in his published lectures, perhaps, on "The Curse of Irony"?) that nearly everything great which comes into being does so in spite of something—in spite of sorrow or suffering, poverty, destitution, physical weakness, depravity, metamorphosis, the plague, being born a puppet—but he has never really considered the lingering power of that *spite* . . .

"What's that noise?" Alidoro had paused to ask. They were in a dark narrow street. The old dog sniffed the air, squinted blearily about him. "Sounds like an old rusty sign, swinging in the wind . . ." The ancient professor emeritus slumped, creaking, against a shop window. "It's-it's my knees," he gasped. "Something awful is happening, Alidoro! I'm-I'm turning back to wood again!" He felt tears pricking his eyes again and trickling down his nose. He'd never told anyone before, not even a doctor. "And this weather—*sob!*—the joints are seizing up. I'm so ashamed . . ." The shop, if his eyes did not deceive him, sold wooden puzzles. Such a gratuitous irony, which might have once offended him, now, in his deplorable humiliation, made his heart ache. "I don't think I can . . . go any farther." "Poor old fellow," Alidoro said then with a deep rumbling sigh, and he hoisted him up and carried him the rest of the way here on his broad bony back.

The old mastiff reenters their shelter now, rump first, dragging in a weathered beach chair, its torn canvas seat wrapped around a load of firewood. He has rigged up a green plastic tarpaulin on the windward side of the projecting tin roof to keep out the blowing snow, built short walls out of overturned gondolas on the two lee sides, the fourth wall provided by the rustic repair shed, then feathered their nest with sawdust, newspapers, and wood chips. "Here's a few more arguments for your fire, you old Jesuitical tart," he pants now, hauling the firewood up to the barrel, and the watchdog barks back: "Those aren't arguments, buttbrain, those are the a priori and assumptive *conditions*—axiomatic, absolute, and apodictical—of the argument, which hasn't even heated up enough yet to make your piss sizzle, so before you open your yap to answer back, just keep in mind

I've only started on the *As*, there's at least twenty-seven or twenty-eight more letters to go, if I remember rightly, and the soup's not on yet." Alidoro winks drily down at the professor and shakes the snow off his coat. "With all that hard thinking you do, Mela, I'm surprised your rectum doesn't fall out."

This was how they'd got in here, the two of them scrapping like strays, it was a kind of code between them, as though recognition depended on insult and invective, affection upon rhetorical display. On the way, rocking between Alidoro's shoulder blades in his stolen wool blanket like a withered seedpod, the old scholar had drifted off momentarily, dreaming of the little Tuscan village by the sea where he was born, with its one main street running from home to school and crossed by another leading to . . . to . . . ? He couldn't remember, but what he found when he turned down it was a little cottage as white as snow, or perhaps white *with* snow, except for its blackened doorway, where he was met by some junior faculty, blocking his entrance, to whom, when they suggested that with all due respect they desired to hang the distinguished visitor from the nearest oak tree, he was obliged to explain that he could not accept their offer at this time because he was still teaching at one of the East Coast I.V.'s, so named, he pointed out, because of their innovative method of education by intravenous feeding. They seemed to admire this insight, if that's what it was, an insight, and not an encyclopedia entry he'd been paid to provide, nodding their heads solemnly in unison, and they went on to ask him (though by now he might have *been* hanging, for the north wind seemed to be blowing and whistling, and he was swinging back and forth like a bell clapper on a wedding day), if, in his renowned wisdom, he might be able to elucidate a mysterious inscription on the back of a famous work of art attributed to one Paolo Venereo, or Venerato (a portrait of a cross-eyed yellow-haired Pope whose fat round face was dripping like candlewax), which read: "ABBASSO LARIN METICA." He understood the inscription instantly, and in fact was startled by the lucidity of his perception, but when he was jolted awake suddenly by Alidoro shouting out something about a black fart ("Melampeto!" he had bellowed—only later did the professor understand that this was a rude play on the watchdog's name), he found he could no longer remember what the perception was. Nor, for a moment, could he even remember *where* he was, he thought he might be on a ship at sea, bundled up in a deck chair or lashed to the mast, certainly he was feeling seasick—

"Melam*puttana!* Open the door, you ungrateful diabolectical sesquipedalian windbag, and let me *in!*"

"Aha! Is that you, Alidildo, you shameless eudemonist ass-licking retard? Everything I've got *you* to thank for I have to *scratch!* Let you in? Don't make the chickens laugh! You can go suck the Pope's infallible hind tit, as attested to by Zoroaster and the sibylline Teresa of Avila, for all I care! Addio, Alido! My regards to your worms and chancres!"

"Hold on, drooping-drains, don't put on airs, on you they smell like the farts of the dead! Remember who you're talking to! Your asster will be a whole lot sorer if you don't drag your vile syphilline cunt-flaps over here and open this gate up! Do you hear me, twaddle-twat? We're freezing our nuts off out here!"

"Oh, I *do* remember who I'm talking to, Alidolce, my sweet little bum-gut. I'm afraid your theoretical nuts were harvested years ago, if you feel something down there, it's probably just boils on the ass, for which cold compresses are highly recommended, *vide* Aesculapius' *Principles of Mycology,* and as for threats of violence, remember who *you're* talking to, you preposterous old humbug! I could split your hollow toothless skull quicker than Saint Thomas could split a hair from the Virgin's hemorrhoidal behind in four, in or out of the catechism! No, you can sing all you want, squat-for-brains, you're just pounding water in your mortar, as Leucippus of blessed memory once said to William of Ockham over an epagogic pot of aglioli, there's no room at the inn nor in this shithole either, and that's conclusive, absolute, categorical, and a fortiori finito in spades! So go spread your filthy pox among your misses of the opiates, fuckface! Arrivederci! Ciao!"

"I think she's weakening," Alidoro muttered then over his shoulder, and the professor, alarmed at all this vicious howling and barking, gasped: "Is this the right way to go about it—?" The storm had worsened, he could hardly see for the swirling snow—it was as though he were being pushed out of the world at full blow.

"Patience, old friend, it's part of the dance. For her all these citations, enthymemes, postulates, and premises are like a warm nose on her clit, the wormy old gabbler won't spread without them."

"Who've you got out there with you, you fatuous lump of clotted dookie? Are you on a sleigh ride with another of your cuntless junkies?"

"An aged compatriot, Melampieta, who is, I'm afraid, more there than here. I have carried him all this way on my back, not knowing what else to do, I tell you, mona mia, with my heart in my fore-paws, if you have no pity for me tonight, so be it and amen, a fartiari o'fuckem and spayed, I've weathered worse—but please take in my poor friend Pinocchio. If you don't, I won't know where to hit my—"

"Pinocchio—?!" There was a clattering and slapping of locks and bolts and the scraping of the gates against the flagstones. "Davvero? In flesh and bones—? But he must be—!"

"As you can see . . ."

"Ah, the poor little cock! I can hardly believe it! Why didn't you say so in the first place, you tedious fleabitten hothead, instead of standing out there and showing off for all the neighbors? Get in here and stop yapping like the damned fool mentioned by Saint Peter in his Epistle to the Cartesians, the one who claimed his farts were prayers and so got theophanically dumped on by what in effect he'd prayed for! Pinocchio, esteemed friend and comrade, you are wel-come, for as Julianus the Chaldean once wrote in an oracle, Whoso shitteth not on the dead earneth access forevermore to the privies of the living, or sterling sentiments to that effect, and if this walking mange-farm had only announced you promptly, you would not have had to suffer such prolonged exposure to the seventy-some provision-ally acknowledged elements, as well as all those not known but sus-pected, such as sewer gas and monads. In our family, if one can call such a bastardly plague of debauched egg-suckers a family, it has not been forgotten how you honored our great-grandsire Melampo with your eloquent silence when the poor beast, too dead to speak for himself, stood accused—and by a ruling class of lickerish unprinci-pled graspers born and spit—of the theft of his own meager suste-nance. To wit, the odd chicken or two he'd been hired to guard. Some said that great-granddad was bent, others that he was an old prole ahead of his time, and a martyr to causes as yet unformulated, but your mute testimony shut all their pustulous faces and left the old sonofabitch to lie in peace at the bottom of whatever stinking well they dumped him in. You earned thereby our eternal gratitude, though you'll probably get somewhat less than that, memory being the garbagey stewpot of doodoo that it is, and certainly your presence, which, if I may say so in passing, seems a mite fragrant, honors my poor hovel. So come along now, good sir—and easy, Alidodo, you blundering beffardo! You must transport the gentleman with the same cunning tenderness with which God's chosen ass is said to have borne the gravid Virgin so as not to tear her gossamery maidenhead, the frangibility of which was likened by Thomas the Rhymer unto that of crisp silk, and whose rupture would have detheologized the Western World, catastrophically orphaning us all. Come, come! I'll put a fire on!"

And thus it was that the exhausted pilgrim found shelter at last, swathed in the woolen blanket, the first thing he has stolen since those fateful grapes that landed him in the late Melampo's terrible brass-studded collar all those decades ago, and nested in sawdust and woodchips, his natural element—being, that is, the son of a carpenter. Melampetta immediately set to mothering him, digging a warm hole for him, feeling his pulse and touching his forehead with her dry nose, tucking rags and papers around him, stirring up a smoldering fire in a rusty oil drum, ignoring his protests and brewing him up some kind of pottage, scolding Alidoro for not taking proper care of him and directing the old dog in the construction of their little shelter against the winter storm, quoting various authors on the subjects of architecture, calefaction, climatology as related to nuclear accidents and flea sprays, and the general unpredictability of fate. "One never knows," she sighs, gazing down on him in wonder, "what might happen in this curious world," which is something his father might have said, though she attributes it to Alexander the Great at the time of his circumcision.

"The Great Dane, no doubt," growls Alidoro drily, smashing up the beach chair to add to the pile of firewood. "What good does it do to put up all these walls? It's windier inside here than out!"

"Sarcasm and parody," sighs Melampetta, "the final recourse of the mental defective. You can see, sir, what I've had to suffer all my life in this sunken and benighted haunt of farts and lechers. How I envy you your life in the real world!"

In spite of all he's had to eat and drink, the soup—which Melampetta, as she tips it down him, compares to the curative "hand of a saint, such as that of Saint Bernard of Clairvaux, the Thaumaturge of the West, for example, or six-fingered Simon Magus, or Hermes Trismegistus who once lanced a boil with a mere spoonful of puree of mashed peas"—does indeed taste good, soothing lips, tongue, throat, and belly in its healing passage. The fire is crackling away in the old barrel now, turning it a glowing translucent red in spots and casting a soporific dance of light against the corrugated roof overhead. He is warm and sleepy and his bed of sawdust and wood chips is cozy and sentimentally familiar, for in such did he sleep as an urchin in a corner of his father's workshop. Alidoro, with a gaping yawn, has settled down beside him, jaws on paws. Everywhere there is a deep and heavy silence like a down quilt being laid over him. But . . .

"I-I can't sleep. I'm sorry—it's my . . . my clothes . . ."

"Are they too tight, comrade? I thought you'd be warmer . . ."

"No, they . . ."

"He shat in them," Alidoro explains.

"Ah, well, why didn't you say so? All the time I thought this was your contribution to the unsavory atmosphere, old gutter-guts, ambulant orchard of dungballs and dingleberries that you are. Don't you know, as demonstrated by our spiritual but restless father Marx in the full blush of his prickly *Grundrisse*, that he who lies down in his own shit wakes up a sight for psoriasis? So what are you waiting for? We've had to listen to your drivel all night, let's put it to some practical use. For, as Jesus once preached to Mary Magdalene whilst she was anointing his bum, thereby freeing herself from at least seven nasty boogers: 'Blessed are the arse-wipers, Maggie, for they shall behold the Eye of God!' So let's make with the holy water, drizzle-chops, out with the tongue and into the pasta, as they say, for one must taste sorrow to appreciate happiness, and, once the bib's on, one might as well lick the plate clean!"

"All my life," the old professor whispers abashedly as Alidoro rises with a weary grunt and commences to peel the blanket away, "I have searched for meaning and dignity, striving to be true to . . . to her vision of me." He shudders, though not from the cold. He is anticipating their horror at what they are about to find. "But I have been so . . . so lonely . . ."

"Her—?" mutters the old mastiff, tugging his shoes off him.

He hesitates. He feels emptied out, shrunken, and more vulnerable and exposed than at any time since that half-remembered day when he first took rude shape under his father's knife and chisel. It is as though his insides and outsides were changing places, leaving his heart quite literally on his sleeve, and much worse besides, yet another bitter pill. "The . . . the Blue-Haired Fairy," he gasps, flushed with shame.

"Tell us about it," murmurs Melampetta soothingly, unbuttoning his clothes. "Make a clean breast of it, if you'll pardon the expression, empty the sack, let it all hang out, flat-footed, hair down, and no bones. Let it fly, sir. Trot it out. Spit the toad, as Saint Tryphone of Bythinia once said to the demon-possessed daughter of Emperor Gordianus, thereby bringing on the most awesome eructation and setting the bells to ringing." She licks him gently behind the ear. "Tell us about your life, old gentleman. Tell us about the Blue-Haired Fairy . . ."

7.

A STRANGE BIRTH

"**M**en, if lucky," he is quoting himself now, dredging up from what's left (not much) of his enfeebled memory this seminal line from his current work-in-progress, or once in progress, now perhaps arrested and lost forever, for he could never, not even with a final massive exertion of his notorious will, reconstruct the whole of it, not even with the magical assistance of that enigmatic creature upon whose intervention his own quotidian progress, also perhaps about to be arrested forever, has depended throughout his long career, a career and a dependency he has just, in his gathering (and altogether agreeable) stupor, been elucidating, or trying to, and which, by means of this allusive proposition which lies at the heart of the *Mamma* papers (if he can remember it), he is now attempting to sum up, "are graced in their lifetime by one intense insight that changes everything. Mine was the discovery that the Blue-Haired Fairy was pretending not to be dead, but to be alive, that in fact it was not she who had given me a place in the world, you see, but *I* who had called *her* into being. Grasping this seeming paradox altered my life forever . . ."

"Seeming—?" growls Alidoro indignantly, lapping his thighs, while Melampetta licks at his right nipple. "If Mela and me aren't the real thing, old comrade, then you've beshit yourself with zabaglione!"

"Oh, I do love paradoxes," Melampetta murmurs between strokes of her long wet tongue. It feels like oiled ebony paper, gently applied. She moves into the thoracic cavity now, pushing provocatively at his knobby sternum, then works her way slowly down the hollow between his ribs past his diaphragm toward what others, having one of the things, would call their navel. "It's like being in heat in a hailstorm, a kind of—*slurp! slop!*—ungratifiable arousal, as though the point of it all were not larking or litters but—*thlupp!*—mere longing itself. I believe it was Saint Catherine of the Festering Stigmata who wrote in one of her—*sklorrp!*—letters with respect to her peculiar inconvenience of having to menstruate out of a rip in her left—*thwerp! shloop!*—side that paradox was like a half-laid egg, speaking theologically of course, as the pious lady was always wont to—*ffrup! flawp!*—do, even when the curse was on her and—*sluck!*—bespattering her farthingales." She pauses to lick at her own coat a moment as though to wipe her tongue there, before returning to his abdomen, now tingling with the chill of her evaporating saliva. Alidoro, having nosed his thighs apart, is pressing toward his knees, panting heavily. "But this is a strange birth indeed," adds Melampetta. "A son pregnant with his own mother!"

"It's not easy to explain," the bared wayfarer sighs, gazing up at the corrugated tin roof, where still the flames' light dances as though to tease away the distance between reality and illusion, not to mention that between (he yawns) sleeping and waking.

"Nor to believe," harrumphs Alidoro. "Though I once had a cousin who fucked his own grandmother and so fathered his mother's half-sister who in turn—"

"*Ow—!*"

"Sorry, slip of the tongue," apologizes the old mastiff. "I think I touched wood."

"Yes, ah . . . it's tenderest just at those places where it's . . . it's pulling away . . ."

There are these moments of sudden pain when the edges are lapped (Melampetta has earlier sent an excruciating shock up from his elbow when she peeled his tailored shirt away), but they are only momentary deflections from the immense peace that has been settling upon the ancient scholar since he put it in the piazza, as they say here, and surrendered his body and its terrible truths, until now his solitary burden, concealed from all the world, to the intimate attentions of his two friends. "Come now," Melampetta had urged him when embarrassment momentarily stiffened his limbs and made him shiver, "there's no shyness in shit, as the saying goes, a saying straight from the *Textus Receptus*, otherwise known loosely as the *Beshitta*, it speaks volumes where farts do but slyly pretend, and now we must answer frankly with tongues of our own, keeping in mind that God so loved a clean behind that, having given his only begotten faeces, as they say in French, he invented the downy angels for bumfodder as humble examples for us all. So come along now, dear friend, you'll soon feel like a newborn babe. Off with those old rags, it's time for the divine services, for complines and eucharists, for libations, oblations, and ablutions, oralsons and lickanies, for leccaturas from the book of life—"

"They aren't rags!" he protested in his foolish confusion, clinging to his jacket hem as it was pulled away. "That's a seven-hundred-dollar suit from Savile Row!"

"Mmm," grumbled Alidoro, tugging his trousers down. "Smells like it, too."

"He said 'savio,' you suppurating imbecile, not 'sulfureo'!" Melampetta scolded. "Now give me those things, I'll put them to soak."

As she trotted out into the snow and down the beachlike slope to the water, the old professor, stripped to his shorts and socks, the wisps of cold wind leaking into their shelter making the frayed nerves at the edge of his skin tingle, literally pricking him on the living edge, closed his eyes and whispered miserably: "I feel like such a wretched ass, old friend. Sick, as my body is, I am far more sick at heart. You should have let them take me away."

"Better a live donkey, partigiano, mio partigiano, than a dead doctor," replied the mastiff, peeling his socks off with his ruined gums. "What my tinpot employers lack in subtlety, they compensate for in diligence."

"What does it matter?" he erupted crankily. "Listen to me. For nearly a century, I have lived an exemplary life. There have been trials, temptations, torments, but I have won through. I have earned the respect of the entire world. I am living proof of the power of redemption through education, endeavor's paragon, candor's big name. Do you understand? I have received not one Nobel, but two. I am a household word. I am the ornament of metaphors, the pith of aphorisms, what's liked in similes—in some languages, Alidoro, a very verb! My father would be proud of me, the Blue-Haired Fairy would! And now . . ." He shuddered as his shorts were pulled down. "Now I have lost everything. Even my pride."

"Ah, look at the poor old fellow, it's enough to make the stones weep," sighed Melampetta, having quietly returned, bringing with her the ashy odor of fresh snow. "He's thin as a nail, he's lost all his hair except whatever that is that's sprouting there on his feet, and he looks like he's wearing the tatters of old wallpaper where his hide should be. Even his nose has gone limp. What a scene he makes! Enough to make the jaded scuff in the galleries lose their suppers! And he's still no bigger than a piece of cheese, just a lick and a smell, you could stuff him in a matchbox if it weren't for the nose."

"In small casks, Melata, good wine."

"Yes, Alidote, if, alas, the cask is tight. But why is he sniveling like that?"

"He's embarrassed."

"Now, now, my pet, no need for that. It's not modesty that answers the call of nature, remember. And we dogs are great ass-lickers, as our comrades are all too quick to point out, we have a special aptitude for it. Not for nothing are we known as man's beast friend, his licking lackey. So, as Origen once said, whilst castrating himself in devotional zeal in the company of Saint John the Theophagist, 'When in a kennel, my peckish old bellybag, one must do as the curs do—the country you go to, as our epistles say, the custom you find—so, take eat, Zan Juan, these are my original ballocks, do this in mnemonics of me, good fork that you are, and buon appetito!' "

"Speaking of such matters, old friend," muttered Alidoro then, poking around in his thighs, "what happened to your own affair? There's nothing down here but a peehole."

"I don't know, it fell out one day. I didn't notice. It may have got sent out with the laundry."

"El desparà xe sempre castrà," murmured Melampetta, licking at it speculatively as though sampling an antipasto: "The destitute lose their balls to boot. But not to worry, for as La Volpe said after she sold her tail for a fly swatter: 'Who gives a fig, there's that much less acreage for the planting of whelks and buboes, may I soon be shut of the rest of it, speaking figuratively of course.' "

"You're touching a painful key, Mela, when you bring her up. It was those two old codgers who did him out tonight."

"What—?! Again?! But wasn't it you, dear Pinocchio, who bit the old Cat's paw off? You must have recognized them!"

"Well, they looked familiar. But then, with my eyes, who doesn't?" For a moment, he felt the abuse of it again, the indignity, and the bile rose in his throat. He felt stupid, outraged, humiliated, frightened, crazed, and embittered all over again and all at the same time. What would they say back at the university if they could see him now, lying here in a shabby boatyard, stripped of all his earthly goods, letting two old mongrels lick his devastated peehole? It infuriated him and shamed him, but what could he do about it, he was powerless. And, besides, it was beginning to feel good. "Anyway, that was in the last century."

"True. One forgets the power of such a life to seem coetaneous and omnifical, speaking in the grand manner, like Dionysius the Pseudo-Areopagite, for example, who once said, or was said to have said, while declaiming upon the angels in much the same highbrow panto-logical style, bless his gray-green heart, that the reason the little atem-poral beasts were sexless was because if they ever started fucking each other eternity itself might find itself in the family way, a superfeta-tion, as he called it in the classical tongue—at which he, whoever he was, was clearly no slouch—a superfetation that could well make twins of the Apocalypse, leaving God biting his own tail, so to speak, if he had one, and if he didn't, well, we're back where we started, like the universe itself in its tedious mechanical turnings, less acreage for buboes and all that." All this, though largely incomprehensible, was quite soothing, especially accompanied as it was by the soft warm strokes of the two tongues, gently bathing his body, poking into this crevice and that, unknotting the tight strings of muscle, swabbing away the foul incrustations, husking him, as it were, *desquamating* him (ah, the *words*, the *words!*), and he felt himself slowly slipping toward what that same Dionysius, so masked, called, if he remembered cor-rectly, "the darkness of unknowing." Whence all truth. "But tell us," Melampetta was whispering in his ear, the one she was licking with a tongue almost eellike now in its subtle acquatics, "tell us about the Blue-Haired Fairy."

And so he did, starting from the beginning ("It all began," he began), when, one terrifying night, running from murderers, he came upon a snow white house set in the deep dark woods and, knocking frantically with feet, fists, and head, aroused a little girl with sea-blue hair and a waxen white face who would have been quite beautiful had she not been completely dead. She couldn't open her eyes, much less the door, so the two assassins caught him and, after shattering a couple of knives on his hardwood torso, hung him from an oak tree, where, after crying for his daddy, he died. "I still have nightmares about it," he told them, succumbing gradually to the rhythm of their lapping tongues. "I was up there for hours, blowing about like a bell-less clapper, till at last my neck broke and my joints locked up and my nose went stiff. And all the while that dead girl was watching me with her eyes closed, don't ask me how I know this, but it's true." Eventually, eyes wide open and grinning like old Maestro Ciliegia on a toot, she staged an elaborate rescue with a bunch of circus animals and some crazy doctors (he has a vivid memory of waking briefly inside an airy coach padded with canary feathers and lined with whipped cream and custard, and thinking, in his unredeemed puppetish way, that Heaven was a sticky place that made him queasy, and he hoped they'd let him out soon), but why, he wondered, even as he described it for his friends, praising the Fairy for her ingenuity and her amazing remedies ("She brought me back to life again!"), did she wait so long?

Well, of course, she was just a little girl. This was the happy time. She was as capricious as he. They played doctors together, jokes on one another, house. They took rides on her birds and animals. She let him poke his nose in her long blue hair. He showed her how he could kick his own head, front, back, or sideways. She laughed at the wooden knock it made and showed him how she could turn her head all the way around seven times in the same direction without getting a crick in her neck; he managed only three before feeling all twisted up inside, but deliciously dizzy when he unwound. It was the most fun he ever had in his life, not even Toyland or Hollywood came close. She wanted him to stay and be her little brother, she even said she'd fetch his father, which somehow pleased him and displeased him at the same time. But it was too good to last. His trials, as it turned out, had just begun. He was dragged off to Fools' Trap by the Fox and the Cat to bury his money in the Field of Miracles, and then years went by, or what were probably years. He was still a puppet then and didn't know much about time. Except that it had something to do with beginnings and endings, this he found out when, after innumerable misadventures, he finally made his way back to where her cottage had been and found nothing but a tombstone with an inscription saying that the little girl with the azure hair had "died of sorrow on being abandoned by her little brother Pinocchio." "It nearly broke my heart. I tried to tear my wooden hair out. That was before I had real hair, of course. Now that's gone, too. I was so proud of it. Hair made me feel so human. But it all fell out. First, from my head, then from my chest and armpits, and . . . and on down . . ." Only on his feet is something still growing, and that probably isn't hair. Nor are they really, at root, his own feet.

The Fairy *wasn't* dead, of course. She who had taught him never to lie had lied, and not for the first or last time. Yet he accepted that. All part of his personal via crucis as he lightheartedly called it, though never in print. And, in a sense, she had died, for he never saw her as a little girl again. When next they met, here on the Island of the Busy Bees, she was suddenly old enough to be his mother, while he was still just a puny puppet. He didn't understand this. She pretended it was some kind of magic. Maybe it was, but he hated to get left behind. When he recognized her, he knelt and hugged her knees, and she gave him a glimpse of a possible future, more than one: he had to choose. Though his motives might have been mixed (there was something heady about having his nose there between her big tender knees), he chose boyhood, which meant he had to pass his examinations at school. But his classmates, hating him for the square peg he was, lured him to the beach and tried, as they put it, to knock his block off. Someone threw his own arithmetic book at him: it missed and struck down poor Eugenio, and the police came and arrested him for the crime. "That was when I met you, Alidoro. You chased me when I ran away."

"Yeah, we really tore up the landscape! When I was a pup, they trained me by making me chase a stick. I must've got carried away by your smell and lost my compass, nearly lost my life when you took to the water. I forgot I didn't know how to swim. Never did get the hang of it . . ."

"Wait a minute," said Melampetta, licking the hairless hollow of his armpit, "let me get this straight—"

"Careful! My ribs—!"

"Yes, I see. Some exhibit, you are, old fellow! You're like one of those mythical inside-out creatures mentioned by Abraham ben Samuel Abulafia in his postural studies of metempsychotics. They could use you as a foldout in an anatomy book. But, listen, do you mean to say that this fairy with the weird locks who liked to keep a magical menagerie and play spooky games with little boys—"

"Puppets . . ."

"Yes, well, like turning houses into tombstones and playing dead and conjuring up pallbearers and corpses and other such ectoplastic doodlings—do you mean to say that she gave all this up to pack school lunches and do the laundry, pick up toys and give baths—?"

"Actually, she oiled me down . . ."

"She abandoned fairyhood to be a *mamma*—?!"

"Well, *my* mamma. It seemed to be something she had to do. Though later of course she changed into a goat."

"A goat . . ."

"Yes. With blue fleece. That's how I knew it was her."

"Madonna! And udders hanging down the size of a theosophist's behind, no doubt?"

"She stood on a white rock in the middle of the sea trying to stop me from getting sucked up into the maw of the monster fish. Or maybe leading me into it, I couldn't be sure. It was the last time I saw her. Alive, that is . . ."

"She died? Again?!"

"Well, she just became . . . something else." How could he explain this? That, in effect, she became the house he lived in, the social order he embraced, even, in a sense, the universe itself at its most ineffable, its most profound . . . "But before that, I found out she was dying in hospital, too poor to buy a crust of bread. I sent her all my money. Everything I had. And with that she came to me at last . . . sort of . . . It was in a dream . . ." He was feeling very dreamy right now. Alidoro was tonguing vigorously the insides of his thighs as though to urge them back to youth again, while Melampetta was sliding up and down between hip and armpit with long soothing strokes, carefully circling the sore spots, making him feel almost like a ship at sea, awash in an airy foam. "It was . . . beautiful . . ."

"I don't know," sighed Melampetta. "All this melancholical hello and goodbye, all this gruesome hide-and-seek over an open grave, tombstones popping up like mushrooms—it sounds to me like either she was trying to cork up your ass with a motherlode of guilt, my dear Pinocchio, or else she had a terrific scam going."

"I know. That's how it seemed to me at times. And I haven't told you everything, either." He offered the old watchdog a replying sigh, and mostly in gratitude, for her tongue seemed to have spread out and was lapping him all over now like a warm wet towel. "Whenever I was a bad boy, for example, she seemed to go limp and cold and fall down with her eyes rolled back. It was really scary!"

"Oci bisi, paradisi . . . ," snorted Alidoro from between his thighs. "Remember that one, Mela? 'Gray eyes, paradise . . .' "

" 'Black eyes, hot romance . . .' "

" 'Blue eyes make you fall in love . . .' "

" 'White eyes make you shit your pants!' I know, I know—but how many times will it work? Once? Twice? This babau, this bugaboo, must have pulled her routine as often as she brushed her fangs. If I may say so, it seems to have taken you forever to eat the leaf, my friend!"

"I was a slow learner, Melampetta, as the world knows. But I'd suffered a lot of births and rebirths myself, I was used to the idea. I was a very lively piece of wood, you know, before the man I called my father—my *primum mobile*, as you might describe him—turned me into a puppet. Then the assassins hung me and the Fairy brought me back to life again. After that I became a dancing donkey and, when the fish ate all my donkey flesh away, I was reborn a puppet from the corpse, though naturally I'd hoped for something better."

"A dancing donkey! Do tell—!"

"Later, my father and I were delivered together from the belly of the monster fish, if that's what it was. Finally I died as a puppet and was reborn a boy. And now . . . well, you can see, it might not be over yet . . ."

"The 'miracle,' as a tourist here once defined it in a fine piece of Christian idiotology, 'of reborn ingenuousness,' a wonderful thing in principle no doubt, but you're like some kind of wind-up demonstration model. Round and round you go! Still I'm surprised you didn't get fed up finally with all this crazy vampire's pernicious horse-plop and just plant hut and puppets, if you'll pardon the expression, and walk out! Why didn't you send her to get fried?"

"Oh, I *did* grow to resent it, to resent her, Melampetta, I *did* walk out. I was a good boy, after all, obedient, hard-working, studious, truthful—but *then* what? I'd done everything I was supposed to do,

I'd become a famous scholar and exemplary citizen, the whole world loved me, I felt I deserved to have a little fun. But whenever I let myself go a little, I'd see her tomb again: 'Here lies who died because . . .' I couldn't get rid of it, it was worse than athlete's foot, and it ruined everything. Why did I want a boy's body in the first place, I began to wonder, if I couldn't use it? So I tried to run away again. This time to Hollywood—"

"Ah, Hollywood!" rumbled Melampetta, moving eagerly toward his nipple, which she circled playfully with her tongue. "Here comes the good part!"

"Not so good as all that," he replied, flushing with shame. "I suffered a kind of relapse out there, I even became a bit . . . reckless . . ." His heart gave a little regretful leap under his breast which Melampetta was swabbing, and his nose began to itch in admonishment. "I became something of an ass again, another sort of . . . well . . . Until one day . . ." And he told them then about his revelation, his sudden quite stunning perception that the Blue-Haired Fairy was not alive and pretending sometimes to be dead, but was truly dead, only pretending sometimes, when he helped her, to be alive. "It was not she who had given me a place in the world, you see, but *I* who had called *her* into being!" This explained the way she first appeared to him, her sinking spells, her desperate messages: goodness, she was trying to tell him, could die in the world. It was not an absolute, not a given, but something that got re-created from day to day, from moment to moment, by living and dying men. Either they kept it alive or it disappeared. Maybe even forever. "It gave me a mission. Her power was really *my* power, I had but to exercise it. 'I-ness,' I called it in a famous essay: the magical force of good character. My virtue, I felt, my decency, my civility, my faithfulness, might save the world!"

"Oh my . . . !" Both tongues were sloshing around in his groin now. "Aren't *we* the little Redeemer!"

"Or if I couldn't manage that," he has added, somewhat abashedly, "there were always the tombstones waiting to be done . . ."

"Whew, I haven't had such a workout since my last litter, bless their long-forgotten little hearts!" Melampetta exclaims now, panting heavily. "I think I have some idea now how John the Baptist felt, coming up for air amid the repentant multitudes after loosening all

their laces, as he liked to put it: 'You have to swallow the toad,' said
he, speaking about knowledge, of course, that bitter pill, 'to shit
pearls'! Or as Jesus himself, that notorious pearl-pooper, once declared, shouting out over the screams of the rich man he was trying
to thread through the eye of a needle, this not being one of his better
numbers: 'Hey, compagni, you can't suck an egg without making a
hole!' So don't hide your recklessness and edifying relapses under a
bushel, my venerable friend, don't skip over the beastly bits—the
seen, as they say in Hollywood, separates us from what we long to
see! Let's hear about the donkey days!"

"Ah, the donkey days . . . ! It's been so long, I can barely . . ."

"That's right, barely and baldly, it's the naked truth we want, the
unvarnished reality! Veritas in puris naturalibus—!"

"Scusa, Melampiccante, old suck, but I think this side's about
done . . ."

"What? Oh yes, Alindotto, you're right, it's time to turn the spit
and baste the other one—be careful, though, the little duck's as brittle
as croccante and flaking like puff pastry!" They straighten his legs
and tuck his arms in, then gently ease him over: "That's it—like
folding an omelette!" Melampetta urges, her sudden rash of culinary
metaphors no doubt betraying the effort to work up an appetite for
the awesome feast she is about to face. He shudders to think of the
spectacle he must now, in his procumbent attitude, present to his
friends' eyes—and other senses ("He's shivering, Lido, go put some
more wood on the fire!")—but at the same time, while being rolled,
he's caught a glimpse of the snow falling thickly through the night
sky outside their humble shelter, and it is as though the magical glow
it seems to cast upon everything has fallen upon him as well, for he
feels suddenly an intense flush of warmth penetrating his entire body:
this is what it is like (the fire is crackling, the two dogs are nuzzling
his thighs apart) to be among true friends! He had nearly forgotten.
Junior faculty may be attentive, but rarely like this. "Aha, I think
we've reached the font, Alidrofobo, you faithful old blister," Melampetta mutters (there is a cold nose poking at his rectum, perhaps more
than one), "that which Aristotle the Wise termed in his treatise on
The Classification of Dejecta the effervescent cause. We are at the source,
the wellspring, the root, the core—or what the divine Duns Scrotum,
confronted with the preserved contents of the Virgin's placenta,

called in his nausea 'the very stone of the scandal,' the *ultima realitas entis*. We are, insomma, if I am not mistaken, at the drippings. So, will you taste the soup please?"

"My pleasure," grunts the old mastiff with gruff simplicity, "it just does for me."

"Mmm. Al dente. Though maybe we've let him lie in the sawdust too long."

"Careful. Shoulder blades look a bit dodgy . . ."

"Yes, I see." She laps around one, stroking his neck and the back of his bald pate with her broad stroke ("The hairs of your head are indeed numbered, comrade," she murmurs in his ear, "and the number is zero!"), and slides her velvety tongue down his crenellated spine, pushing at the knots, stiffens her tongue to prod at the small of his back, then slips on down the crack to the gap between his thighs like a skier on a downhill run, curls up around one thigh, and, as though congratulating herself or getting her wind back, laps generously at his near cheek. As she does so, he has a dim fleeting recollection of being combed and curried, back when he was still a performing donkey and being readied for a show, an experience so comforting it nearly reconciled him to his unnatural life, a life indeed more like a dream than waking life, and so all but lost now to his living memory . . . "You know, I can understand humans wanting to tart themselves up a bit," Melampetta pants. "I mean, I wouldn't mind a little lace shawl or some beads myself, if ever some whoreson should offer me such baubles—naked we're only cute for a day and after that we need all the help we can get. But why people leave all their other orifices gaping, then cover their assholes up in this cumbersome tailoring is beyond me."

"Huh. Some philosopher you are, Melone mia. It's a great attraction to flies, that's why. Maybe you need to lose your tail like the rest of us here, there seems to be something too abstract about your fundamental principles."

"The Blue-Haired Fairy told me," the professor mumbles softly into the blanket under his chin (what he remembers is the day he *gained* a tail, that day of the transformation: he was laughing, he and his dear friend Lampwick, they were so happy and having so much fun, and then suddenly there was a seizure in his chest and for a moment he couldn't breathe, and then the laughter became . . .

something else . . .), "that little boys who do not wipe themselves properly not only grow leeks and cabbages back there and so become the village laughingstocks, they also lure rats into their beds at night and get bit in the behind with the plague." He sighs as a great soft tongue lathers a hip as though kneading pasta. Though the middle time is mostly gone, he can also remember the day he got changed back again, the day his new owner tried to drown him so as to make a drumhead of his hide, and instead the fish ate away his donkey flesh. It tickled more than hurt. It was liberating. Exciting even. Sensuous. It seemed to free him of a great weight. It was like the time the Blue-Haired Fairy sent a thousand woodpeckers to peck at his nose. It was like spring after a long dim winter. It was like . . . now . . . "She used to take me to the cemetery and show me the tombstones of all the little dirty-bottomed boys . . ." He yawns. As their tongues swab and massage his ancient hinderparts, he can feel the sleep that has been avoiding him since he left America steal over him like the caress of the Fairy's blue tresses. "Sometimes . . ."

"Yes . . . ?"

"Sometimes my life seems more like it's been . . . *ah! . . . !*" It reaches deep into his inner core, suffusing him with a powerful satisfaction, and a great leavening of his spirit, as if he were being freed from some wretched imprisonment. Well, life itself, he thinks, I'm probably dying. They know this. They're preparing me. It's wonderful. It is like a magical transportation, like the intimate and golden repose of a Bellini, like a Hollywood ending. Never has he known such peace since the day he first became a boy . . . "It's been almost like a . . . like a movie . . ."

8.

THE MOVIE
OF HIS LIFE

"It looks like you've indeed got that little something extra," is how Melampetta describes it in fond remembrance of the old fan magazines (they have just been discussing the big bang theory of the Hollywood star system with its dire implications, as Melampetta put it, of entropic twinkle), but what she is referring to is the clump of matted hair her excavating tongue has uncovered between his anus and the ridged seam of his backbone. "It's all coiled up here like the runout trailer from an old reel of film. Has it been there all the time?"

"When my father made me, all the hair was painted on," he explains, though he wonders if this is indeed an explanation, or more like a proposition—what his old friend Alidoro might call (and perhaps did, having just spat irritably and, muttering that "the old sporcaccione's barf is worse than his blight," wandered off on his own, leaving the ancient traveler and the faithful watchdog alone here on this sandy shore that slopes down to the sea, or else to a swimming pool) a "suppurating pustulate." What he has really wanted to say in reply to her question is, "Well, yes . . . but no . . . ," but he has been unable (the very effort seems to have pushed the boat shed some distance up the slope away from them into a circle of unmanned booms and cameras) to find the words for it.

But it's as though she understands anyway (she has meanwhile spooled the hair out from under the end of his spine so that it fans out over his cheeks and thighs all the way to the back of his knees), for she says: "Ah yes, I see, your skin is, after all, as one might have supposed, nothing more than a cheap veneer," and proceeds to lather his whole body at once, ferreting out vast hidden thickets of clotted hair: on his head, in his ears and armpits, down his back and legs, on his belly, chest, and chin, between his fingers, thighs, and toes. No wonder he's been feeling so inhibited! Out it comes! "This explains your infatuation with paradox," she howls.

"It's not an infatuation!" he screams, as though in pain, but really just to be heard, for she sits alone by his blanket now, far down the sunny slope below him, her head cocked archetypally, still as a plaster casting. Or perhaps that is a plaster casting. He in his elegant new pelt, which unfortunately is already attracting flies and ticks, is back up under the corrugated roof of the boat shed, where, as he was about to explain to Melampetta, they are making a movie of his life. "A new treatment," he says aloud, and seems to hear Alidoro laugh at that, or else the porter, that villain, though he, or she, is not to be seen, nor is anyone. The shed, for the purpose, has been fitted out like a sort of manger with heaps of straw, painted cutout animals, an imitation fire flickering in an old brazier. ("That's where I burned my feet off," he explains to Melampetta, or would have were she still beside him), white cotton on the roof, and Christmas presents secreted about like Easter eggs, but, though light streams spiritually through the broken rafters in imitation of, or homage to, the great Tintoretto, or perhaps dear old Veronese, the general appearance is one of artifice and desolation, the manger, suffused with barnyard odors and missing two of its four walls, uninhabited within except for a cheaply made wooden stick-figure lying in the straw and, without, surrounded by silhouetted camera gear looking about as reassuring as grave markers. It is as though those responsible have stopped in here only long enough to drop the little creature and hasten on, leaving behind nothing more personal than a yellow wig and a broken water jug.

"My mother died in the fire," the little wooden figure reminds him as they step out through the jaws of the smoldering doorway into the blazing but frigid sun, and, remembering, tears come to his eyes again, though whether of sorrow or exasperation, he can't be sure. He is, as it were, if he understands the storyline correctly, carrying himself on his back, having been awarded the role of the ass in recognition of his abundant hairiness and his recent achievements in the school metaphysics and polka examinations. Or at least this is, though its source forgotten, his understanding, an understanding beclouded somewhat by his uncertainty as to where they are supposed to be going and by the numbing pressure inside his head, a pressure he recognizes from previous experience as the donkey's stupid brain weighing heavily upon his own, a weight he had, in the intervening near-century, all but forgotten. "It doesn't matter where we are going," the little creature on his back tells him as if answering a question he might actually have asked, "what's important is to stay inside the frame."

"Hee haw," he replies, meaning: Is that all there is, then, this monotonous dynamics of inclusion and extrusion, of presence and absence (of pretense and abscess, he is thinking, or perhaps the little wooden man, mocking him, is saying this), this timid seizure of shadows, this insensible shying from the edge, and what the wooden man responds is:

"The public, oh holy ass, is never wrong."

Ah well, the *public*, he brays in reply, struggling against donkey-brain takeover (sometimes, he remembers now, this happened to him in his real donkey days, a kind of sudden slippage, or displacement, as if from one room into another, a synaptic leap not easily reversible, each brain aware of the other only as the mattress and the pea could be said to be aware of each other in that story of the fastidious princess, an alarming though not altogether unpleasant metastasis provoked, often as not, by the erecting of that outsized dangle between his legs, which is back, he is amused to note, slapping his thighs animatedly as he plods along under his chattering burden, the topic from the saddle now being the Renaissance use of the ass motif as a prototypical theophanic icon: the reluctant gait a trigger of passionate spiritual response, the upright ears emblems of devotion and orthodoxy, and the haunches, radiant as halos, more emotionally reverberant than angels' wings—one of the portentous themes of his own brazen youth, he is quick to recognize), the *public*—the *public* is always *dying* on you!

"Ah, where would we be," sighs the man on his back, who has been growing heavier and heavier with the weight of his discourse, "without the script?" And, as though to pursue the inquiry, he flings it away from him, the sheets scattering and tumbling in the air like sinners at the Last Judgment. Though they have made little enough actual progress (the boat shed, he feels certain, is still nearby), they have maintained the illusion of it by passing—or being passed by—revolving stages with painted backdrops representing the scenes of his childhood: the Tuscan village where his carpenter father lived, his fairy mother's cottage in the woods, the city of paupers known as Fools' Trap where all who came there lost their hair and plumage and other valued parts, the infamous Toyland, though here labeled "Pleasure Island" and looking a bit dated, even the little hill and coastal towns he toured as a marionette and dancing donkey, all gleaming and decorous as the backgrounds in a Bellini altarpiece. Now, however, they have arrived, by way of a gated and treeless city on an arid plain, desolate as a Western ghost town (a film set, of course: watching cameras no doubt lurk, unseen, behind the ruined walls), at a massive marble rock, white as candle wax and rearing ominously into the intense azure sky above them like one of Paolo Veneziano's primitive crags. Has he been here before? Alas, unlike the scenes on the revolving backdrops, this one has not been tagged. Gone, it's all gone. Or going. He can't remember yesterday. He shouldn't have thrown away the script. "What's the point," he cries bitterly, "of all these strenuous accumulations, if we only, in the—"

"Don't," groans the withering beast between his legs, limping now as it labors up the impossible rise, "give away . . . the ending . . . !"

At the summit, he is met (the fatally lamed donkey has crumbled away, turning to dust beneath him like a doused witch, he has had to scrabble up the last sheer face, hand over hand, alone) by a bearded ape in the scarlet robes of an opera buffa judge who, excoriating him for arriving so late ("But my poor knees—!" he protests, unheard over the strings of the studio orchestra), condemns him in an aria not unlike a love song ("The Picture That Could Change Your Life" is its title) to be rolled in flour and crucified.

He turns to address the gathered multitudes ("Blessed are they who turn the other omelette!" he cries), but snarling gendarmes swarm over him, strip him of his imported finery, lather him up with flour paste, and dress him for the party in his tattered old suit of flowered wallpaper, with a silver sash bedizened with bright ribbons bound round his waist and white camellias tied to his ears. Children are invited up from the audience to hammer the nails in, some of whom he recognizes as old schoolchums, who take pleasure in reviling him in the old style, calling him a stick-in-the-mud, pencil-peter, and a woodenhead, pulling his nose, covering his paper suit with graffiti ("HOORAY FOR TOYS!" they scrawl, "DOWN WITH ARITHMETIC!"), and tying strings to his hands and feet to make him dance, as though he were still a puppet and without the dignity of flesh and history. This is what it means, he realizes in his suffering, to be, of anything, incarnate. The children are clumsy and impatient, driving nails in randomly, some crooked, others only halfway, sometimes missing the nails altogether and hammering his flesh, and complaining all the while about the hardness of his bones and the wood, solid holly, of the cross beneath, which keep bending the nails and making their little hands sting.

Finally, a charge against him bearing the inscription "THE STAR OF THE DANCE" is nailed over his head and, to the accompaniment of fifes and drums, the cross is levered erect into the posthole prepared for it, the very hole, he sees, that he once dug in the Field of Miracles to plant the gold coins as seed for his magical money tree, he now rising as his own fruit, as it were, all of this taking place in exquisitely painful slow motion (there are so many nails in him, he hardly sags at all) as though they were overcranking the scene for erotic effect. *"Rispettabile pubblico, cavalieri e dame!"* bellows a voice from below: *"Your attention, please!"* He feels dizzyingly high, almost face to face with the sun itself, yellow as a patty of polenta there in the brilliant blue sky blanketing him. "Oh babbo mio—!" he whimpers as though cued. "Direct from the burning mountains and savage highways of wildest America, we bring you now in living color, speaking loosely, our feature attraction, in a performance more thrilling than the deeds of man, more beautiful than the love of woman, more terrifying than the dreams of children—" the children hoot and holler delightedly at this and heave their hammers at him, "—the final stirring episode in the Passion of Pinocchio! You will see before your eyes the farewell dance of the world's most notorious bad boy, this improbable son of an impotent carpenter and a virgin fairy, baptized by a chamber pot and circumcised by woodpeckers, part flesh, part spirit, and a legend in his own lifetime! Right this way!"

"Looks like this time you have, to make a phrase, barked up the wrong tree, dottore," remarks, amid all the burlesque whistling and cheering, a sour voice at his side: it is La Volpe, still in her porter's costume—he has been hung in the middle, he discovers, between her and her blind Gattino, now cackling on his other side with senile laughter. "You got the short stick, as one might say, you're out on a limb—you are, in a word, up the pole!"

"Up the pole!" wheezes the Cat, covering his mouth with the stub of his right foreleg: he hangs by one paw only, an empty black glove nailed up on the other side. "In a . . . in a . . . ?"

"Word."

"*Word!* Hee hee hee!"

"You two seem cheerful enough," gasps the butt of their badinage in his transfixed pain, beginning to worry that the movie of his life might suddenly have turned into a documentary.

"Enh," shrugs the Fox, as best, in her own pinned state, she can shrug, "you get used to everything in this world, professore, familiarity breeds consent, as the saying goes, though I do miss being able, what with all my blebs and buboes, to scratch my tormented old arse. If perhaps you have a hand free—"

"Don't even listen to those bandits, Pinocchio!" warns a voice at his back. He twists around to seek out the source, but there is no one back there, just empty space, blue, vast, and inscrutable. "If you lend those scoundrels a hand, they'll steal it!"

"Cross words," grumbles La Volpe sardonically, resolving the puzzle.

"*Words!*" repeats Il Gatto, sniggering hysterically into his empty cuff.

"Avoid evil companions, my boy, or you'll be sorry!"

"How could I be sorrier than I already am?" he groans, his wounds stretching as, losing strength, he slumps lower.

"You could be," replies the cross with a tremulous sigh, "like me."

"Ah well. As to that, there was a time when—"

"I know, I know, they send us dossiers, resumes, we get the publicity handouts. You're a famous case, a model for us all, you've—if you'll pardon the expression—crossed over. This is a big honor for me, I know that, I've got the star of the dance, top billing, I shouldn't complain. But do you remember what it was like before? Do you remember how it *felt* to be a piece of talking wood?"

So long ago. A time of darkness. He was innocent then. And

innocence, as his long life has taught him, is a form of naughtiness. Yet . . . "I had . . . no pain . . . no fear . . . I was free . . ."

"Free to get used for a chair leg or a clapboard! Free to soak, rot, and burn! Free to get chopped, hacked, whittled, split, and pulped! Hey, look at me! A tree made out of a tree! A joke! They gave me arms, I can't use them. Am I mad? Hell, I'm cross as two sticks, that's what the children say, but I don't know what 'mad' is, I don't know 'cross.' 'Pain,' you say, 'fear': it all sounds like magic to me—or it would, if I knew what magic was. I even envy that old Fox over there with her itches and scratches—I say, 'her,' but what do I know, right? I don't know '*knowing*'! While you, you've had a life! You've had *everything!*"

"You *don't* know. Men's lives are short and stupid."

"Stupid? You tell me stupid? What's two and two, you ask. I don't know. I don't know what's *two!* But *you* know, you're smart, you've got brains, whatever they are. You've got—I don't know, I can only imagine—which is difficult, I don't even have an imagination—but what? You've got charm, right? Dignity. Serenity. You've got—correct me if I'm wrong—hauteur, glamour, class, talent—how'm I doing?—dash and daring. And tenderness. Smoothness. Authority. Have I got the picture?"

"Well, I guess so—but how did you—?"

"I read it on a movie poster."

"You did?"

"You caught me. I'm lying. I can't read. I'm dumb as a stump, I'm thick as a plank, I'll never make my mark, or any other. Oh, I wasn't born yesterday, but that's just it. I wasn't born at all. Not like you, Mr. Star of the Dance! And I can't take steps to do anything about it, I can't keep my nose to the grindstone or listen to reason or kick the problem around, so what chance have I got? I'd be down in the mouth about it if I had a mouth. I can't even put my foot in it. I can't show my hand or beat around the bush or face the music. I don't even know where it is, the music, I mean, or the bush either, I'm too stupid. If I had a heart, I'd be wearing it on my sleeve, if I had a sleeve. So what have I got? A routine. A lumber number. A dumb show, a curtain dropper, an act with nails, halfway between a hanky twister and a creepie. But I'm a pro, a reliable standby, an understud, a support who never lets you down, I'm an old hand who hasn't even got one. People like to wear me on their chests. I'm vaguely sexy. I have a good silhouette. I stick out, as you might say. And I stick *it* out. I'm solid, I'm always there. And we're not talking lifetimes here, are we, we're not talking mere centuries—*you* remember!" But maybe he doesn't. The old boy seems to be hanging lower, his head drooping as if sniffing his armpits. "But you know what?" he whispers down his nape. "I like the blood! I soak it up! I can't get enough of it! I think: this must be what 'tasting's' like. Am I right? This must be 'appetite.' I like the writhing and the sweat: it oils me up. And I like *the crowds!*"

"Why are you telling me all this?" gasps the dying figure pinned to his crossbeam. The wretch seems to have gotten thicker and hairier, as though death were filling him up and leaking out in coarse filaments at all the pores. Below, he can feel a tail curling around his upright where the feet are nailed. There is a bad smell. "We were such good friends! We had such wonderful adventures! I showed you how I could pee longer than anybody. We used to make bets with the other boys. You showed me how your nose could grow . . ."

"What—?! Lampwick? Is it you—?!" The miserable creature lifts its long ears feebly, then drops them again. "Oh no!" He tries to throw his arms around his long-lost friend, but he cannot move them. "Lampwick!"

"And now . . . you're leaving me . . . hee haw! . . . to die alone . . ."

"I'm not leaving you, Lampwick! I'm here! I'll stay human! I promise!" But even as he protests, he can feel the place where they've nailed the charge twitch and stretch. A darkness is spreading everywhere like the darkness of unknowing. The sun seems to be falling from the sky. "Don't die, Lampwick! Don't die—!"

"Goodbye, Pinocchio . . . !"

"*No—!*" He struggles against the rigidity of his wooden arms to embrace the dying donkey, no matter what the consequences. All his heart is in it. He *has* a heart. He has *always* had a heart. And now he is straining it to the breaking point. He can feel the creaking and bending, the terrible splintering within. "Lampwick—?" And then the sky seems to tear like a curtain, there is a great roar (it is in his own throat), and he awakes to find himself grappling through his twisted blanket with Alidoro, his nose buried in the old mastiff's filthy coat, and bawling like a lost lamb.

"There, there," soothes Alidoro, breathing sleepily down his neck. He peels away the tangled blanket, then wraps him up again.

"It was Lampwick! He was dying! I could have saved him, but—!"

"It was a nightmare," says Alidoro gently, easing him back into the wood chips next to Melampetta, who watches him drowsily with one half-cocked eye. "It's all right, old friend. Nothing you can do now . . ."

"No, I mean," he mumbles tearfully, curling up inside the blanket, his shoulders aching still from his recent struggle, "I could have saved him when he . . . when he died the first time . . ." Gripped by this painful truth, unassuaged by all the intervening decades, the old professor snuggles down between his two companions, closes his eyes once more and, with the kind of diligence he once applied to scholarship and basket weaving, chooses to dream that, while his colleagues sit behind him on the stage, gravely exhibiting their noses, he is giving a ceremonial address to the American Academy of Arts and Letters on the uses, proper and improper, of somatic metaphor, a dream which is, he recognizes, even as he embraces it, a dream of, a surrender to, oblivion . . .

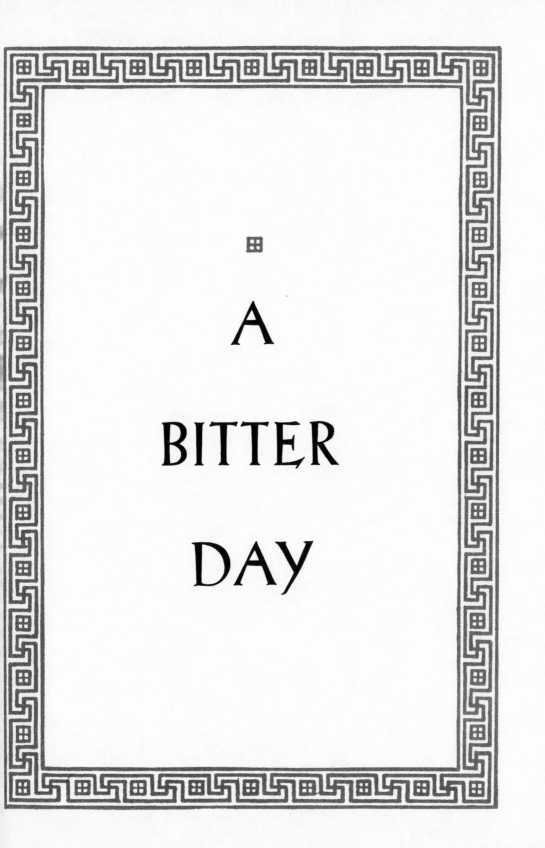

A

BITTER

DAY

9.

THE DEVIL'S FLOUR

"Impossible really," he says, describing for Melampetta the film studio's futile attempts to cast the part of the Blue-Haired Fairy, "like a painter trying to paint the color of air, or a composer reaching for the sound of grace—"

"Yes, or a theologian trying to imagine the taste of manna, which has been likened severally unto angel breath, Orphic eggs, the froth on a virgin's milk, pressed mistletoe, dream jelly, lingam dew, fairy pee, the alchemical Powder of Projection, and the excreta of greenflies on tamarisk leaves. I know what you mean. It's like going after the ineffable with a butterfly net, or trying to catch time in a teaspoon. Or, as the immortal Immaculate Kunt once said, in an attempt to describe by way of the practical reason the odor of sanctity: 'Toe-cheese is only the half of it.' "

"That's right, there are approximations, metaphors, allusions—but nothing close to the real thing." The aged professor emeritus, sipping his coffee and staring out quite blissfully on the little boatyard, blanketed this morning in newly fallen—and falling—snow, muses in this oblique manner upon reality and illusion, pursuing his own themes, as it were, even as the watchdog's salacious appetite for gossip seeks to deflect him from them. The front of the boat yard slopes down from the sheds to the canal like a beach, now completely white except for a few dog tracks and a yellow patch or two, and, though it's no bigger than a Boston back garden, its covelike nature takes him back to California and his once-upon-a-time passage through Filmland, where the two concepts in question—reality, illusion—were truly inseparable: even he could no longer tell them apart, and so he nearly lost his way again. "Finally they gave the role to a blond ingenue who looked like a highschool cheerleader from Iowa dressed up for the junior prom. She wore lipstick and blue eyeshade and plucked her eyebrows. Her complexion was nice, though I happen to know she had pimples back where her swimsuit covered them. And she refused to dye her hair blue, so they put her in a kind of slinky blue night-gown and shortened her name to the Blue Fairy. Instead of living in the forest in the house of the dead, she presumably came from some distant star as an answer to my father's wish—my father, who might have wished for the cheerleader, had he known about such beings, but never for a fairy or even, for that matter, a talking puppet. He always called me his 'little accident.' "

"Ah, povero Pinocchiolino . . ."

"She even wore one of those painted barrettes from the five-and-ten that were popular at that time, and gauzy wings like a mosquito or a blowfly. But they did me a favor, for it was this outrageous distortion of the truth, this callous misrepresentation of the very being to whom I had dedicated my entire life, that finally shook me out of my . . . my iniquitous indolence . . ." It is the indolence, of course, the iniquity, the outrage, that Melampetta has wanted to hear about. That's how it always is, he thinks, sipping his coffee while Melampetta trots to the edge of their little shelter to bark at a lone passerby on the bridge. A lifetime of scholarly diligence, of heroic integrity and self-discipline and an intransigent commitment to the loftiest of ideals, and what people always ask him about is the fun he had when he was naughty . . .

"So this Pimply Blue-Bottomed Fairy, I take it," rumbles the watchdog, stepping back in under the corrugated tin roof and shaking her coat, "was set up as a kind of synthetic milk-fed avatar of the Blessed Virgin, as she's called between theopathic farts at the Pope's table, who granted a pithless old carpenter his wish, in effect, to whelp without having to go through labor pains—?"

"You could say so, Melampetta. According to the script, she first brought the wood to life, then, after all the entertaining sin-and-redemption rituals, she changed the wood to flesh, more as a part of Geppetto's dream than my own, since the movie suggested I was more or less dead by then, or at the very least hopelessly waterlogged. When I pointed out to the director that I'd been a talking puppet for ages before I'd ever met the Blue-Haired Fairy, he said that was interesting but he couldn't use it . . ."

He is pleased to be talking about the Fairy, even if this is not exactly the approach he might have chosen, for his mind this raw and blustery Venetian morning is very much upon her. Having thought he'd lost her forever, he has her back again. In a manner of speaking. For he has awakened not only to hot coffee and a roaring fire (friends from the post office have dropped off a few bags of backlogged mail, Melampetta explained cheerfully, feeding the rusty oil drum appropriately through a tattered hole in the side), but also to the heartening news that his luggage has been found, Alidoro having already left for the police station to reclaim it. Soon he will have a fresh change of clothes, his own toothbrush and deodorant and mouthwash, money with which to procure a real hotel room with a real bath, his medicines and hair restoration elixir and linseed oil, his passport and credit cards, his scented handkerchiefs, his certificates and awards, his foot snuggies, and above all, in its manifold forms, his invaluable *Mamma* papers, the loss of which last night had seemed to him worse than the loss of life itself. The morning, as they say here, truly has gold in its mouth!

Indeed, he was rather surprised to find himself awakening to a new day at all, having supposed last night to be his last, whether as a victim and outcast, as he had feared at first, or, later, as an old companion being prepared lovingly, if humiliatingly, for burial. He had slept so hard he was certain that his sleep had been dreamless, but Melampetta assured him he had wept and laughed aloud more than once during the night, and on one occasion had opened his mouth very wide and from somewhere deep in his stomach had announced very clearly: *"We are all dead!"* He wasn't even sure, when he came to, if it was the next morning or several days later, or even some other time and place altogether, his arrival in Venice having seemed more nightmarishly unreal to him just at that moment than anything that might have happened in dreams. He reared up and would have cried out, but, bound tightly in the stolen police blanket, and with a fire blazing away somewhere nearby, he was afraid that he might be a prisoner again like the time he was caught and nearly fried by the Green Fisherman, a fear reinforced by the floury dusting of white snow all about.

"Aha! Sleeping Beauty blooms at last!" Melampetta barked out delightedly on seeing him start up in such alarm. "What a rising you make! Like the white goose's son, as the expression goes, beak and

all! You've really been sawing wood, compagno, if you don't mind
my saying so, you've been sleeping like a little log! Like a top! You
were hitting the knots! Caulked off! You were like the Seven Sleepers
of Ephesus all rolled into one and stretched out serially! It's nearly
noon! You've missed all the news!"

"I never closed my eyes," the old traveler grumbled then, falling
back again. He saw he'd been sleeping in sawdust and wood chips,
which reminded him, under the influence of Melampetta's terrible
puns, of his own mortality. Like a human sleeping in hair and bones.
"What day is it? What year?"

"It's the day they found your luggage," she replied. Which sat him
up again of course, this time with a shout, his weathered face split
with a smile. "It's down at the Questura, and so is Alidoro. He'll be
back soon. Now, meanwhile, dear friend, let's establish a few first
principles, as the Holy Peripatetics used to call those morning rations
of beer and porridge that preceded all their Olympian endeavors."
And, tail wagging generously, she brought him over warm bread,
coffee, and a thick chunk of unsliced prosciutto that still bore a dog's
toothmarks. It was delicious. He was suddenly ravenous. "Lido went
out and picked that up for you before he went for the bags, though
don't ask where or how, for as they say in the Lord's Prayer, 'Give
us each our daily bread, or else by the verminous ballocks of all the
cardinals in hell, we'll take it.' Poor old fellow, his tail-stub's really
drooping this morning. You were pretty restless, you know, thrashing about, yowling in your sleep, wheezing and snorting—the mangy
old eyesore was up all night with you, he's had no sleep at all."

"I'm sorry . . ."

"At one point you got free of your blanket somehow and stood up,
naked as a worm in the winter storm, and rendered a fair approxima-
tion of the Sermon on the Mount, blessing the weepers and wine-
growers, throwing pearls to the dogs, thank you very much, doing
unto thieves and profligates as they would do unto you, honking your
nose, turning your cheeks, unfolding your throat, and swearing
against oaths and blind men, salting the lilies of the field from your
peehole, prophesying against the foundations of the city which you
said were of rusty unleavened sand, giving advice on how to stay out
of the hands of the carabinieri, Romans, and other footstools of iniquity, plucking logs out of eyes and thistles out of figs and proverbs

out of the air like Simon Magus himself conjuring up heresies. And all of it at full split, you were really telling it big! A logomaniac of the first water! Where did you learn to speechify like that?"

"I don't know. I can't recall when I wasn't speaking. I was speaking before I was born . . ."

"It took both Alidoro and me to wrestle you back into your blanket again, you were really making fire and flames, you were climbing on all the furies, outside yourself, a devil in each hair, as one could say if you had any. You kept screaming something about rusty nails, hairy asses, and the forbidden fruits of firewood—what did you mean by all that?"

"I don't remember . . ."

"And your mamma, as you called her, was in it, too."

"She always is . . ." Last night, by the light of the fire, he'd thought the old watchdog quite beautiful. Now, by the harsher light of day, he could see she was a rather stubby and jowly old crossbreed with droopy ears and thick matted hair, mostly white—off-white— with a black Rin-Tin-Tin patch over one eye that made her face look hollowed out on that side. Nevertheless, he felt comfortable around her, he felt she was someone he could open his heart to, so, though he might have preferred to talk about his life as an art critic, philosopher, and theologian, and to discuss with her such topics as his concept of "I-ness," his definition of the soul, and his views on reality and illusion, beauty (the only form of the spiritual we can receive through the senses, as he has often declared), nasology, and the veracity principle, he did not really object now when she led him back, by way of things he had supposedly said in his sleep last night ("You kept crying for her floppies, it was some kind of mad infatuation, you said, and there was something about a missing hard dick . . ."), to his final crisis with the Blue-Haired Fairy and his sudden flight, a central theme after all of his work-now-once-more-in-progress, to Hollywood. Indeed, he would probably, if he had his computer here already, and if there were an electrical outlet he could trust, be taking notes . . .

"They asked me out there to be an advisor to a film they were making about me, based on one of my early books. I knew better of course, even then the place was notorious for its venal disregard for the truth, but they caught me at a weak moment, and I decided to go. I thought that maybe if I got away from this place, I could get away, finally, from her. From her and all her tombstones. At least long enough to think things out. Get a new perspective. And it did seem different over there somehow . . ." All those starlets, the auditions, they all wanted to take him home and play with him. There were beach parties and drunken nights by orchid-strewn swimming pools and wild drives to Mexico. They taught him how to mix American cocktails and drink champagne by the slipperful, though it tended to run straight through him, even as a human. They asked him to unzip their evening gowns. He lit their cigarettes for them. They cradled him in their arms and let him suck their pillowy breasts. They used him as a kind of bathtub toy. He was in all the gossip columns. Indeed, only his ignorance of his own anatomy saved him from fatal mistakes out there. He kept trying, at their urging, to put his *penis* in them, and it wouldn't go. It was more like a limp faucet. "It even *looked* like a faucet, my putative father's putative sense of puttanaio humor no doubt." The girls all thought it was cute. Only later did it suddenly occur to him . . . "But then the fights at the studio began . . ." The scriptwriters and storyboard people changed everything of course. The producers insisted on it. There were reasons: the need for metaphoric coherence and condensation, the temporal and technical limitations of the medium, the metaphysical riddle of the frame itself, the alleged infantilism of the American public, studio contracts with actors and artists, a growing dissatisfaction with Fascist Italy and with theology in general, the tight shooting schedule. "But the main points were there, I felt, even if the Americans did confuse beer and billiards with sin, redemption with technological ingenuity. And if they'd turned my heavy-handed ill-tempered father into a cuddly old feeble-minded saint, well, as I once said about your great-grandsire, Melampetta, the dead are the dead, and the best thing is to leave them in peace. And meanwhile I was the toast of the town, my face, as Jiminy said, on everybody's tongue, I was having too much fun really to argue about anything, doing interviews, judging bathing-beauty contests, turning up at premieres in the arms of the stars, trying to make my faucet work. So I took the money they threw at me, told them the truth whether they wanted to hear it or not, because what else could I do, and otherwise stayed away from the lot. Until it came to the Blue-Haired Fairy. There, finally, was the sticking-point."

"So she found you after all."

"She'd never lost me . . ." Even if he'd nearly lost himself. She was everywhere now, he'd realized, vast and immediate as the ocean outside his Malibu window or the blue sky overhead. The house he'd returned to after rescuing his father from the belly of the monster fish —*her* house, though the Talking Cricket claimed he'd got it from the blue-haired goat—had expanded to become the entire universe. He'd been a fool to think he could get away . . .

"Yet last night you said," she says, bringing over his washed underclothes and suit, and helping him out of his cocoon of blanket, "that without you she wouldn't even exist."

"It's our own creations that most possess us," he replies, pleased to be able to quote himself again, and thus, as it were, to clothe in some fashion his naked decrepitude.

"Yes, true, like blind Father Didymus in the demonic grip of the Holy Trinity, or poor old Pope Innocent the Eighth, who, populating Hell for the faithful, found himself nightly in the fiends' amorous clutches, a consequence, I take it, you have not suffered . . . ?"

"Not . . . not in that sense, no, I have never, so far as I know," he says, choosing his words carefully (his underwear is fresh and crisp, but his suit seems to have shrunk and is pocked, as though in imitation of his diseased flesh, with burn holes), "seen her again. Not since the night I . . . I became a boy . . ." He scrubs his itchy nose, holds his suit up to the dull light of the snowy day. "But what—?"

"Sorry about that. Must have been cheap material, dear friend— old sheep's hair of some kind, I suspect. I put it to dry on the barrel last night and it couldn't take the heat. I don't have much else to—"

"It's all right," he says, feeling very generous this glittery morning. "I've gotten by with less. There was a time when I had nothing better than wallpaper or a beanbag to wear, and stale bread on my head. And anyway I still have the overcoat."

"Yes, well, most of it . . . But wait!" She raises her snout to the air and sniffs expectantly, then barks: *"Here comes Alidoro!"*

"Ah, noble friend!" the grateful professor cries, stumbling forward, tears in his eyes, to embrace the great mastiff as he comes lumbering into the boatyard. "You have saved my life—again! And my life's work! How can I ever thank you? How can the *world* thank you?!" Lido does not immediately return his embrace. His old eyes droop rheumily. What—? A chill runs through the old scholar. He staggers back. "Is something—? Were the bags *not* found? Were they someone else's—?!"

"Nò, they're there. They're yours, all right—"

"Well, then, it's time for celebrations! Dinner tonight! At my hotel! With champagne! Cream puffs and panettoni! Tiramisu! Grappa from the last century! We'll have a week of Saturdays! Christmas and Carnival, all at once! For you, Melampetta, those shawls and baubles you've been wanting! For you, Alidoro, my most precious friend, *the world!*"

"The bags are yours," growls the old mastiff when he's able, "but they're empty."

"Empty—?"

"Ah," whispers Melampetta softly, tossing some more letters into the fire, "it rains on the arse of the unlucky, even when they are sitting on it . . ."

"Nothing in them but one sheet of paper."

"One sheet—?" he squeaks, beginning to choke up. "From all my work, just one sheet? But which—?" Lido hands it to him. There are three proverbs scrawled on it. Stolen money never bears fruit. The devil's flour is all bran. He who steals his neighbor's cloak ends his life without a shirt. He recognizes them. The last time he'd seen La Volpe and her stupid companion before last night was nearly a century ago. They were ragged then, maimed and destitute, begging out of need, not knavery, though it was only what they deserved, and so, his own conversion by then complete, he'd sent them both to hell: "*Addio, mascherine!*" he'd laughed, throwing proverbs at them like stones. And these: these were the proverbs. "Scoundrels!" he hisses. He is trembling from head to foot. "Villains! *Thieving treacherous fiends! Murderers! ASSASSINS!*" He finds himself beating wildly on Alidoro's chest. He clutches his head, which seems about to burst. They can't *do* this! Not to him! Don't they know who—? But what—? What's this—?! *There's nothing on the right side of his head!* "My ear! *What's happened to my ear—?!*"

Melampetta, head ducked, tail curled between her legs, glances sideways at Alidoro as though she might have just eaten a chicken. "Last night," she says meekly, "when we were trying to get you back into your blanket, it . . . it came off."

"What—?! My ear—?!"

"Don't worry, we saved it!"

"You knocked my ear off, you stupid animals—?! You slobbered all over me, you burned my clothes up, you made me sleep in all this filth, and then, on top of it all, you knocked my *ear* off—?!"

"Actually, it sort of fell off by itself . . ."

"Listen, my friend, you can stay here another night," suggests Alidoro. "The owners won't be back till the snow's gone, and Mela won't mind. Until we can—"

"Here—?! In this pestilent flyblown dunghill of a kennel? This loathsome flea farm, this squalid, stinking—?"

"You and Mela can talk. You know, about serious things. Meanwhile I'll go back and see if—"

"Talk?" he screams, his rage exploding. "With this dumb mutt, this illiterate foul-mouthed retard? Listen to her preposterous idiocies another whole night? Are you *crazy*, you stupid mongrel, I'd rather *die!*"

Alidoro, who has slumped to his haunches, now lowers his jaws and gazes mournfully up at him from between his paws. "For charity, vecchio—!" he rumbles softly under his breath. Melampetta stares at him a moment as though trying to see through the holes in his suit. There is a brief dreadful silence. Then she lifts her snout, closes her eyes, and commences to howl pathetically.

Oh no. What has he done? What has he said?

"My . . . my friends! Oh, my friends, *forgive me!*"

He rushes over, tearfully, to embrace them. Alidoro buries his nose deeper, Melampetta howls all the louder. All over Venice he seems to hear dogs howling. "Oh please! I'm just upset! Can't you see? It's been so hard! I'm an old man! I'm at the very edge, I've nothing left!" He is weeping, sobbing, all his pain concentrated now in Melampetta's terrible howl. "Oh what a wretched fool I've been!" His knees collapse, but Alidoro reaches for him now to steady him with a gentle forepaw. "You're the dearest friends I have in the whole world! Last night was, truly, one of the most beautiful nights of my whole life! Not even the day I got my Ph.D. was as wonderful! It's true! Please,

Melampetta! Don't howl like that! I'm so sorry! *I love you so!*" She releases one more anguished siren, then allows herself to be drawn into his arms. They are all hugging and licking one another now and whimpering and crying. "Oh dear sweet eloquent Melampetta! You're the greatest philosopher I've ever known!" he exclaims, then adds, to stop his nose from twitching: "In all of Venice!" They all laugh at that, and then they cry some more, and hug and kiss and promise always to be true and to help each other and not to say unkind things, and while they're all rubbed up together like that, his other ear comes off.

10.

THE THREE KINGDOMS

I t is all the old traveler can do, his traveling all but done, to put one benumbed foot in front of the other. It is not just the snow, blowing through the holes in his clothing and down his neck and ankles, it is not just the freezing cold snapping cruelly at his tender nose, or the pain in his elbows and locked-up wooden knees, the arduousness of the trek itself through the treacherously frosted city. It is also despair. Bleak, final, disabling. He no longer has anything left to live for. His conclusive and definitive work, his *capolavoro*, is gone forever, his life is ended. Why then must the suffering go on? "I have lived long enough," San Petrarca said. Perhaps while wandering these very streets. "If the Stage Director wants to break it off, very well." "We can but keep trying, my friend," Alidoro had insisted gruffly in a temper something between heroism and simple doggedness. "Death must find us alive." And so, without conviction, they have set out, the heartsick professor and the faithful old mastiff, bound for the Questura with the aim of providing the police with a list of the empty luggage's missing contents and perhaps a little monetary encouragement on the side ("Not for nothing is that band of shameless beggars known also as the *questua*—the Sunday collection plate!" Melampetta had growled good-humoredly, forcing upon him the few rumpled notes she and Lido had somehow scraped together, stuffing them into his pockets along with his ears), but the journey is as futile, he knows, as the larger one which brought him here. *Back* here, he should say, back here to Acchiappacitrulli, the infamous snare of simpletons, Fools' Trap, city of the shorn, where he himself once played, now plays again, the booby.

"I always thought of this as the Island of the Busy Bees," he had sighed somewhat grievously while they were bundling him up in his scraps and tatters of overcoat, which has the odor this morning of burnt camel dung, and Lido had replied drily: "Well, that's right, and what they're busy at, compagno, is skinning the tourists."

So he has returned, he has discovered, not only to the scene of his triumph, but to the scene of his ignominy as well, the place where all those years ago, in Acchiappacitrulli's Field of Miracles, he buried his gold coins, dreaming of orchards of tinkling money trees. He should have guessed. This infamous city of despotism and duplicity, of avarice and hypocrisy and subterfuge, this "stinking bordello," this wasps' nest of "insatiable cupidity" and "thirst for domination," as Venice's outraged neighbors once declared, this police state with the air of a robber's den, always out after its "quarter and a half-quarter" and "conspiring the ruin of everyone," this fake city built on fake pilings with its fake fronts and fake trompes l'oeil, this capital of licentiousness and murder and omnivorous greed: who else but these lagoon rats would *want* the tail feathers of a poor gullible pheasant or the hair of a dumb dog? One thing, surely, can be said of all who have come to this island: whether they left wiser, wearier, happier, sadder, enchanted or enlightened, exasperated or exalted, impregnated with beauty or disease or rabid hedonism, they all left poorer. Just as the Blue-Haired Fairy ever, in her profound maternal wisdom, warned him.

Yet it was for *her* sake he has returned and, though deceived, he can pride himself that on this occasion his intentions at least were nobler: the search, not without considerable personal sacrifice, for the consummation, as it were, of a virtuous life—and yet, and yet, he cautions himself, stumbling along, wasn't that dream of an ultimate life-defining metaphor as mad as the dream of money trees? What was he hoping for this time, another Peace Prize? Beatification? Another review that lauded his wisdom and stylistic mastery, whilst scarcely concealing an annoyed amazement that he was still alive? Another invitation to receive an honorary degree and put his nose on view? As he trudges miserably, step by leaden step, through this city of masks, its very masks masked this morning by the snow blown against its crumbling walls like the white marble faces masking Palladio's pink churches, a dazzlingly sinister mask, today's, as expressionless and macabre as the Venetian *bauta* worn last night by the hotel proprietor, the *alleged* hotel proprietor (fakes within fakes, deceptions upon deceptions!), he feels the mockery cast upon his own shabby self-deceptions, the impostures and evasions, grand pretensions, the many masks he's worn—and not least that of flesh itself, now falling from him like dried-up actor's putty. Ah, he was right to come here, after all, old piece of rot-riven firewood that he is, to share his shame with the defrocked sheep and peacocks, the wingless butterflies and combless cocks of Fools' Trap.

As the despondent prodigal shuffles along, "carrying through," as he would say, but just barely, dragging one ill-shod foot laboriously through the snow, then, after a deliberating pause, the other, his patient companion trots back and forth, sniffing this canal railing, lifting his leg on that boutique wall or Carnival poster, nosing around in garbage bags and emptied crates, lapping at cast-off food wrappers and paper cups, as though to pretend that this is the unhurried way he always goes to work. The streets are empty but for a few angry red-faced women under their dark umbrellas, carried like missile shields, a midmorning drunk or two, flurries of wheeling black-faced gulls, the occasional lost tourist. The heavy metal shutters are down on most of the shops, intensifying the city's blank stare (it is this blank stare he has been feeling, this cold shoulder, this icy scorn— there are no *reflections* today, even the ditchlike canals full of dirty slate-colored water, scummed with snow, are opaque), but from those that are open—a baker, a newsstand, a pasta maker, a toyshop and a cantina, a pizzeria—Alidoro receives and returns greetings, picking up scraps of this and that to nibble on which the professor in his desolation refuses.

Once they've passed out of earshot, Lido fills him in on the politics, in-laws, crimes, calamities, debts, spouses and lovers, foibles, fantasies, and farces of each of the shopkeepers, keeping up a steady rumble of conversation as though to stop the old professor's brain from freezing up. "Started life as a gigolo for the local contessas, that one, helped manage one of their Friends of Venice flood rescue funds, rising as you might say while the Old Queen sank, and then, when his little bird died, he retired into politics for awhile and, after the usual scandals and piracies, ended up in fashion leather, security systems, and the manufacture of decorative window boxes. Careful now, old friend, not too close to the edge there . . ." Lido talks as well about his career as a police dog, life in Italy between the wars, how the Fascists tore his tail off for some secret he never knew or couldn't recall ("You know me, I can't remember from the nose end of my muzzle to the other . . ."), his irremediable attachment to this island in spite of his loathing of tourists and his lifelong fear of water ("I always meant to leave, but you can't straighten an old dog's legs, my friend, I'll have to draw the hide in this infested overdecorated chamber pot, I'll fodder their boggy eelbeds in the end . . ."), his hatred of the modern world with its electronically hyped-up homeless transients, all of them nowhere and anywhere at the same time, even when they think they're at home, the humiliations of toothlessness and blindness (the professor, absorbed in his own debilities, hasn't noticed; he notices now: the old fellow navigates largely by nose alone), and life with his "mistresses," as he calls them, women he meets getting arrested, who take him home with them when he gets them off, and who are grateful and treat him well until they get taken back in again.

"They seem to get some comfort out of an old dog. I do what I can for them. Not much, of course, but the cask gives what wine it has, as they say, and at worst I've got this old stub of a tail to get me by when I'm not up to better. Unfortunately, a lot of the old dears have taken a bad fold of late, gone onto the needle, and are dying off now with the plague."

"There's a plague in Venice—?!"

"There's a plague everywhere."

In between stories, Alidoro, circling round and round in the bristling cold, asks the venerable scholar about his own career, about his books and his honors and his nose, about his prison days and life as a farm worker and getting swallowed by the monster fish ("You know what my father said when I went running up to give him a hug," he flares up, angry about something, though he can't say just what, "he said, 'Oh no, not you again, you little fagot! Even in this putrid fishgut I can't get away!' "), about his reasons for coming back to Venice (he doesn't give them—whatever they were, they were tragically stupid), about his problems with wood-boring weevils and fungal decay, and about America, about the bosses and the range wars, the recent elections ("How is it a country can stand tall, hunker down, sit tight, fly high, show its muscle, tighten its belt, talk through its hat, and fall on its ass, all at the same time?" the old mastiff wants to know), and the gangsters and centerfolds and dog catchers of Chicago.

Even though the professor is aware that his friend is provoking this dialogue as well-meant therapy against the despair which is threatening to halt him in his tracks, he cannot curb his sense of outrage and betrayal that he should be visited by such bitter despair in the first place—or the last place, as it were (and perhaps he even *wants* the despair, who knows, perhaps it is this that is making him crabby: he's earned it, has he not?), such that when Alidoro asks him: "How did you get so interested in painted pictures anyhow, compagno? I would have thought, wide-awake as you were—", he cuts him off snappishly with: "Because they don't move. And they don't ask tiresome questions." He groans faintly, regretting the outburst, though Alidoro seems unperturbed by it, maybe even pleased, in that it has carried him another three steps or so. They are trudging past silent black-faced gondolas with silver beaks, now laden with snow as though trying to disguise themselves as squatting gulls. Actors everywhere. Who can you trust? "I'm not a greedy man, Alidoro. I learned early on from my father's pear peels, the pigeon's tares, the circus hay, to be happy with little in this life. I have given up much for that little. And the little I wanted, here at the end, was to finish one last chapter of one last book before I died. But now . . ."

"Ah well, maybe that's a blessing," grumps the old dog. "Too many words in the world already. Like taking water to the sea."

"Enough words maybe," acknowledges the old scholar with a sigh, "but we still haven't put them together right. That, Alidoro, is our sacred mission."

"Bah!" barks Alidoro. "I shit on sacred missions!" And he squats right where he is in front of a barbershop to make his point.

"That's easy for *you* to say," replies the professor wryly, gazing blurrily upon the squatting dog. "If I try to make that kind of argument, your friends will want to throw me in jail again."

"To some son, to some—*unff!*—stepson," Lido grunts cheerfully, then lifts his rear, kicks a foot, and walks away. "Ciao, Mario!"

"Ciao, Lido!" shouts the barber, rushing out to spread sawdust on the turd.

"In Venice, Pinocchio my friend, in case you hadn't noticed, there is *always* a double standard. It goes with the scenery."

The professor is momentarily transfixed, however, by the mastiff's sawdust-sprinkled turd, sitting upon the glittering white pavement with all the authority of a papal announcement. Or a gilded prophecy. "Mine," he says dismally, his depression creeping over him again, "are coming out that way. There's . . ."

"Eh?" The dog turns back to nose his turd quizzically.

"That stuff . . . there's something wrong inside . . ."

"Mm, the sawdust, you mean . . . flour of your own bag, was it? Last night I was wondering . . ."

"The *devil's* flour . . . ," he sighs, trying to make light of it, but feeling tears prick the corners of his eyes. And standing there staring down upon Alidoro's turd, he feels the pang of his loss penetrate him once again to the very core, releasing afresh all those bitter memories of the more distant past, those times that heartless pair had cheated him, and lied to him, and set fire to the tree he was hiding in, then tried to murder him with knives and ropes. "After that," the abused traveler says, or perhaps adds, not sure whether he's been talking out loud or not, "the villains made me bury my money in the Field of Miracles. They took, then as now, everything I had!"

"Ah, *that* infamous patch, *that* pesthole—I'm afraid that's another story, my fr—!" Alidoro begins, but he is suddenly interrupted by a strange spindly fellow who comes leaping out of nowhere, black coat-tails flying, and lands with both feet—*SPLAP!*—on Lido's snow-frosted turd: *"Got you!"* he cries, laughing horribly. "Stamping out *wisdom!*" he shrieks at the postered wall, shaking his fist vehemently at it. Then he whirls abruptly on Pinocchio, startling him with his manic ferocity, and, staring straight through him, screams: *"Heads up! Heads up! Here she comes!"*

"What—?!" gasps the old professor, ducking, as the wild-eyed creature flings himself flat out in the turd-stained snow, crying *"WAAHH-H-hhh!"* Then he springs to his feet again and bellows into the swirling snow: *"Go to the devil, you ungrateful cold-assed nanny! You cuntless whore! You endless nightmare! Oh, what madness!"* He throws himself at the wall, kicks it, rips off an impasto of overlaid posters and heaves it at the sky, crying out his "Woe! Woe! Woe!", his *"Guai! Guai! Guai!"* (or maybe it's *"Mai! Mai! Mai!*—Never! Never! Never!"), and then, declaiming solemnly with a quavering voice, "I shall not leave until I tell you a great truth," the lunatic goes bounding off into the falling snow, the black tatters of his suit fluttering behind him like unpinned ribbons, and, at the far end of the little calletta, disappears into the storm suddenly like a candle snuffed in the wind.

"Poor old fellow," rumbles Alidoro, his rheumy eyes following his nose.

"I-I think I saw him last night," gasps the professor, still doubled over from having ducked, his knees creaking with their trembling. "He was beating his head on a church wall."

"Could have been. But Venice is full of them, my friend, you see them everywhere, bawling and squalling and abusing the masonry. Must be the water. Every campo has one. We call them our Venetian grillini, our little talking crickets, because they're always entertaining us, especially on balmy summer evenings. Days like this, I'm afraid, they don't last long." He sighs and seems to shudder. "Nor will we if we don't soon make bundle and—eh? What's the matter? Did you lose something?"

"No, I-I can't straighten up! I ducked and—"

"Ah! Here, lean on me, old man," says Alidoro, crawling under him. "Now, just relax . . ." The dog rises slowly, straightening him up. More or less. He is still leaning dangerously like a Venetian campanile, his nose dipping at belt level. "That's better! Don't give up, compagno! Get your soul between your teeth and bite down hard, we have to show a good face to a bad game!"

"It's-it's getting worse, Alidoro! Everything is seizing up!"

"Yes, hmm, but it won't do to stop moving, not in this weather. Hang on to my coat now and follow along as best you can, and I'll tell you about the real gold in the Field of Miracles."

"Real—?"

"If you'd left your money there, you'd be another Solomon today."

"Like those wretched beggars the Fox and the Cat, you mean," he gasps drily, stumbling along beside his friend, clutching his thick coat with frozen fingers, stiff as sticks.

"Those two," rumbles the mastiff, "must be the world's most unfortunate swindlers. Shortsighted is what they are, and shortchanged is what they got. Better an egg today than a chicken tomorrow was the way La Volpe always figured it, especially when the chicken might be plucked before it was born, so the minute they got an offer, fools that they were, they sold the field off."

"Hmm. It's true, she did tell me that a rich man had bought the field, that was why we had to hurry."

"Yes, a quick turnover, that was always her game, so when the Little Man made her an offer—"

This does straighten him up, with a noise like a squeaky rocker: "What—?! Who—?!"

"The Little Man—L'Omino, you know, that little fat guy who ran the donkey factory here, where—"

"Toyland? *Here—? But—?!*"

"That's right. In fact, we just passed the old dockyards where they corralled the little asses before shipping them out—but who am I to be telling you, eh? Anyway, as it turned out, the old Fox outfoxed herself on that one. The Little Man had found out somehow that there was good water running deep below it, so he bought the field and then resold it to petrochemical and electrometallurgical industries and steel plants and oil refineries and made himself a billion. It's called Porto Marghera now, you can see it from the Giudecca Canal. It's what you see in that direction instead of sky. Talk about your miracles! Sucking up all the sweet water sank this sinkhole another half meter into the sea and dried up all the wells."

"But wait! Do you mean to say—?"

"Oh, I'm not finished, my friend! For when the Little Man died, the Sons of the Little Man—Omino e figli, S.R.L., as they call themselves, the scheming little bastards—filled in the lagoon for more industry and airports and gouged out channels for tankers and that changed the very tides, eroding all the foundations. If you stand still and watch, you can actually see pieces of the city split off and fall into the canals. Some days now the sun turns red and yellow and even green, and all the walls are being eaten as if by invisible maggots. And I'm sure the Sons of the Little Man have more miracles in store for us yet . . ."

"But wait, Alidoro! Please!" he gasps, tottering under the dizzying impact of this new information. He lets go of his friend's coat. "Do you mean to say that this—this is Playland, too? *This is the Land of Toys—?!*"

The old mastiff pauses, peers down at him quizzically. "You didn't recognize it? Hm. You've been away a long time, vecchio mio." So! They were *all* here, then: the Three Kingdoms, as he has called them in his writings. Not "points on a moral compass" (his sanctimonious phrase) but overlays, a montage, variations on a theme . . . "Of course, the original operation is pretty much shut down—not much use for donkeys these days. And toys are a dime a dozen, the canals are clogged with them—ecologically, there's nothing worse in this town than another Christmas. Locally, the Sons of L'Omino are into tourist skins now—or Venetian sheepskins, as they're called—along with pederasty, restoration rackets, retirement scams, World Fairs, and the reinvention of Carnival. That's how the Little Man got started, you know: nothing more than a seedy Carnival sideshow down on the Riva degli Schiavoni in the old days. The landing place is still called the Street of the Donkey Cart, it's just behind the Piazza." Yes, this was Fools' Trap with its Campo dei Miracoli, this was the Island of the Busy Bees, and this was also Toyland—Pleasure Island, as they called it in the movie, and not so wrong at that. He had thought when he first visited those places he was seeing the world. But he was simply turning around in circles. On a moving stage. It was the world that was seeing him . . . "There are a few other landmarks—the Canal of the Virgins, the Fondamenta of the Converts, the House of the Incurables, where they put the transformations that didn't quite come off, the Streets of the Hoof and the Chains and so on, a couple of theaters, some old graffiti here and there—but the Sons of the Little Man, imitating the old doges and their gangs, are mostly international merchant bankers now, their deceptions and rapacities hidden away in corporate computers."

And yet, he thinks, the numbness in his feet having spread to his chest, is it really such a surprise? To what extent all these years, he must ask himself, has he truly believed in the physical separation of the Three Kingdoms because he *wanted* to? It was convenient, after all. His "psychogenetic geography," as he called it, to general acclaim —and he has *liked* the acclaim, *liked* being the famous professor and revered emeritus, whose exemplary pilgrimage moved the world. Would he have given all that up for so small a thing as the truth? He staggers, his knees sagging under the weight of his plummeting spirit. He squints up at the next bridge they must mount with a certain horror. He seems to see three bridges, piled on one another like a cartful of plague victims. Ah. No. Can't . . .

"You remember Eugenio, that ragazzo you laid out with your math book the day they sent me chasing after you—?"

"It-it wasn't me—!" he whispers faintly.

"He's running the show now. You should've killed him."

He stops. He can go no further. It's as though these revelations have peeled more of his skin away, exposing him yet more ruthlessly to the petrifying cold. He can hear the wood cracking and splintering in his limbs with each step. "Alidoro, my dear friend, I-I . . ." In his pockets, his hands are frozen like claws around ears now as hard as golden coins. And for some time now, he has been feeling something like loose marbles at his waistband. He shudders, and they rattle about down there. The dog gazes over at him from the foot of the bridge with his rheumy eyes. "Alidoro," he says, his chattering teeth clacking like wooden spoons, "I think I just froze my nipples off."

11.

ART AND THE SPIRIT

The monster fish that swallowed Jonah, sucking him up as a raw egg is sucked, was a pious creature devoted to virtue and orthodoxy, a kind of blubbery angel, conjured up by a God who liked to flesh out his metaphors. He—or she, the anatomy is uncertain, "belly" perhaps a euphemism—kept the runaway prophet dutifully in his or her belly or whatever for three days and three nights, long enough for Jonah to get a poem written and promise to do as he was told, and then, with a kind of abject courtesy, vomited him up, if that is not also a euphemism, on dry land. This is what Bordone's dark stormy picture, sitting like a mummy-brown bruise on the stone wall near the front entrance, is trying to show: Jonah disgorged like the metaphor's tenor emerging gratefully from its vehicle. He has often tried to see his own experience in the same light. In his now-lost *Mamma* chapter, "The Undigested Truth," for example, he has compared his brawling, boozing, recalcitrant father with the wicked Ninevites whom Jonah was reluctant to exhort, and from whom the prophet felt even more estranged once he'd saved them, has asked whether it was really truancy that landed Jonah in the fish's entrails, or whether God, like the Blue-Haired Fairy in her goat suit, might not somehow have lured the prophet into his crisis for reasons of pedagogy, and has indicated thereby how both his and Jonah's maritime adventures, often interpreted symbolically in Christian terms of baptism and rebirth, or else Judaic ones of exile and return (in Hollywood, quite literally: the raw and the cooked), might be understood more accurately—and more profoundly perhaps—as violent forms of occupational therapy. They were also living demonstrations of vocation's fount in the viscera: only he and Jonah—and perhaps poor Saint Sebastian up there, standing like a twisted tree with an arrow through his—could fully understand what a gut feeling really is.

Unfortunately, his own fish was not so decorous and accommodating as Jonah's. Attila was a decrepit, foul-smelling, asthmatic old tub of lard who slept heavily, snorting and eructating all night with his mouth open, airing his adenoids. Crawling out through his gorge was not so much dangerous as it was merely nauseating. His old man, he discovered, had been in and out many times. Old Geppetto had adjusted to the life and come to like it, brewing up his own lethal grappa in the fish's digestive juices, devising recipes for the tons of stuff the monster sucked up, one of his favorites being a cold porridge made out of mashed cuttlefish, live sea slugs, and walrus dung, and dressing up grandly in the uniforms of drowned sea captains. As far as he was concerned, he'd never had it so good. As a hobby, he'd taken up pornographic and religious scrimshaw, with which he decorated his chambers, ampler than any he'd ever known before. The place stank, but so had every other place he'd lived in. He'd fashioned playing cards out of bleached sea wrack, dice and pipes out of conches, smoked cured kelp. He'd developed, as though in imitation of his monstrous host, an Oriental pleasure in the swallowing of whitebait and polliwogs live to feel them tickle his throat as they died going down—that's what the old buzzard was doing when he discovered him in there and ran to give him a hug, getting in return a faceful of spat-up live fish and a smack on his tender nose. Mostly, though, his father just sat around hallucinating on his evil brew. It was this grappa that steeled his heart, as it stole his mind, and made him refuse to budge. He thought he'd never get the besotted wretch out of there. When he tried to plead with him, his father turned nasty, walloping him with an oar handle if he came too close and threatening to set him alight and smoke his herrings with him.

"This shit is magic, finocchio mio! It's the only magic I've ever known!"

"But what about me, babbino mio? Your little talking—"

"You, you little spunk, you sap, you sucker, you nutless wonder! You twist of tinder fungus! You're a thorn in my side! a splinter in my eye! a sprit up my ass! You stick in my craw! One step closer, knothole, and I'll make toothpicks out of you!"

Finally he had to pretend to go along with him, throw a party, tell stories, get him blind drunk and carry him out through the snoring fish on his back, the old stew by now completely demented and raving at the top of his voice about the snakes in Saint Peter's green beard and the treachery of stars and fink pigeons and about being impaled on the devil's nose, which he envisioned apparently as appearing miraculously on the Virgin's shiny cerulean and enigmatically uncleft behind, the poor brute having tried desperately at the last minute, when he realized what was happening, to drink up his entire production before having to abandon it forever. When he woke up in the Fairy's cottage three days later, he thought he'd died and it was the Second Coming. In fact, he never quite got this idea out of his crazed old head after, and insisted on being called San 'Petto ever after.

Maybe he should have just left the old ingrate in there. But already, unredeemed woodenhead though he still was, he had started reading his many trials as edifying metaphors, the didactic strategies of his blue-haired preceptress, and in their light he knew he had to bring his babbo out with him. Their light, with significance, has lit *all* his actions, without it his life would have been as dark and cold as this poor martyred church of a twice-martyred saint wherein, huddled in his tattered coat, shawled by his scarf, his ears in his pockets and his nipples at his belt, the old scholar sits, waiting for his friend Alidoro's return, frozen to the core and unsure even of his next minute—yet he can no longer say for certain whether the source of that imperiously guiding light was, all these years, without him or within. Did God, to put it another way, truly have plans for the Ninevites—they were spared, after all, nothing happened at all as Jonah said it would—or did Jonah, despairing of his own mortal condition, find himself invoking both God's plans and his own trials in reply, not to a luminous command from tempestuous skies, but to some inner storm of his own, his own career-engendering transformational wet dream, so to speak? A mystery frightening to ponder . . .

Paolo Veronese, whose church this is, having claimed it in the end with his very bones (his funerary bust gazes sternly down from the wall behind his painted organ upon its sickly visitor, shivering in his pitiable rags, and admonishes him with its straight classic nose, its unpocked flesh, its handsomely draped breast, its noble and contented demeanor, looking much like the benign host of some great and sumptuous feast, from which the visitor, though he may ogle, is forever excluded), toys with this problem of the light's source in his central altar painting, in which Saint Sebastian's pierced groin is vividly lit up, but his tormented face is cast in shadow by the thick cloud at the Virgin's feet. She hovers just above him with the infant Jesus as though in someone else's vision, stealing the scene, as it were, bathed in a golden Technicolor light not quite real and attended by angels fussing about like dressers, while the saint, his view obstructed (and looking a bit fearful that, what with all his other problems, something awesome might be about to fall on him), turns black with death and doubt.

Though it speaks in some ways to the abused traveler's embittered mood, this is not the classical Venetian Sebastiano. Veronese, as usual, has taken liberties. Traditionally the martyr is shown standing contented as a wooden post, bathed in golden light himself, and stuffed with arrows as though he might be sprouting them like twigs, an image that, while often ridiculed, once touched the professor deeply, especially as painted by his beloved Giovanni Bellini. The image—"a piercing of eternity's veil," as he called it—led him into his early Venetian monographs on traumatic transfiguration and on toys as instruments, simultaneously, of death and wisdom, and eventually lay at the heart of his controversial theoretical work, *Art and the Spirit*, the central theme of which was the absorption (the punctured flesh) of Becoming, fate, action, multiformity, naughtiness, discord, theatricality, bad temper, extrinsicality, evil companions, carpentry, negation, ignominy, and ultimately Art itself (the wooden arrows) by Being, will, repose, unity, obedience, peace, the eternal image, aplomb, intrinsicality, saints, teaching, affirmation, beatification, and all in the end by the transcendent Spirit (the languid gaze).

That languid gaze, he felt, had something to do with the mysterious shimmering *light* of Venice, a light that, paradoxically, seemed permanently to fix before the eye the very flux that excluded all fixity, patterns and archetypes emerging from the watery atmosphere like Platonic ideas materializing in the fog of Becoming, and so spellbinding the gazer in a process that more or less mirrored that of the moviegoer lost conversely to seeming life in the flickering sequence of lifeless film frames, movement there emerging from fixity, the viewer's rapt gaze seduced, not by eternal Ideas, but by illusory angels cast up by the enchantment of "persistence of vision," as they called it. And as he called it, too, when speaking of the Venetian masters, borrowing from the then-disreputable cinema industry, another revolutionary and controversial—"mischievous," as his adversaries bitterly remarked—critical act. The illusory, that is to say, *was*, for the great Venetian painters, *what was real*. *Change* was *changeless*, Becoming *was* Being. For them, "persistence" of vision was active, not passive: they *saw through*. Theirs was the art of the intense but reposeful acceptance of the turbulent wonderful.

This ground-breaking work, dismissed at the time as the "malicious prank of an irredeemable parricide," was to be sure an audacious frontal assault (though never, in obedience to the Blue-Haired Fairy's precepts, disrespectful to his elders) upon the established dogma of the day, a dogma that reduced Venetian painting to mindless decoration, mere theater sets for cultic spectacle, as it were, "unperplexed by naturalism, religious mysticism, philosophical theories" and "exempt from the stress of thought and sentiment," as the paterfamilias of aestheticians put it, but, disturbing as his youthful iconoclasm was, it turned out to be less controversial than the book's many alleged parallels with his own life story. In those long-ago days of faith still in progress and pragmatism, personality was seen as a hindrance to "pure science," and "spirit" of course was a dirty word, "I" anathema. He was accused of feeding, with works of art, "the great maw of a monstrous ego." His theories were ridiculed as "thin laminations, scarcely concealing a deep-rooted psychosis." "The confused work of a split personality," another said. "Dr. Pinenut cannot see the forest for the tree."

He could not entirely deny these charges. He was himself a product, after all, of his father's rude art and a transfigured spirit; the title had not come to him by accident. The quest for the abiding forms within life's ceaseless mutations was *his* quest, had been since he burnt his feet off; he too, rejecting all theatricality, sought repose in the capricious turbulence—freedom, as it were, from *story*. Even his decision to study the Venetians had to do with his own origins. If the beginnings of Venetian painting, as that same father figure of the priesthood who had dismissed Venetian art as "a space of color on the wall" argued, "link themselves to the last, stiff, half-barbaric splendors of Byzantine decoration," how could he help, pagan lump of talking wood that he once was, but be drawn to these magicians of the transitional? No, his reply to all these accusations in his germinal "Go with the Grain" manifesto was: "*All* great scholarship is a transcendent form of autobiography!" "It-ness," he declared (this was the first time he was to use the concept later to be made world-famous in *The Wretch*), "*contains* I-ness!" The victory was his. Even physics would never be the same again.

Oh, she would have been proud of him, she who had launched his great quest with her little Parable of the Two Houses, here on this very island, all those many years ago. He'd been cast up by a storm and was begging at the edge of town when she found him. She offered him a supper of bread, cauliflower, and liquor-filled sweets in exchange for carrying a jug of water home for her. He'd last seen her as a little girl, and moreover presumed her dead, so he didn't recognize this woman, old enough to be his mother, until she took her shawl off and he saw her blue hair. Whereupon he threw himself at her feet and, sobbing uncontrollably, hugged her knees. "Oh, why can't we go home again, Fairy?" he wept. "Why can't we go back to the little white house in the woods?" Her knees spread a bit in his impassioned embrace, and the fragrant warmth between them drew him in under her skirts. He wasn't sure he should be in here, but in his simple puppetish way he thought perhaps she didn't notice. He felt terribly sleepy, and yet terribly awake, his eyes open but filled with tears.

"Let me tell you a story, my little illiterate woodenknob," she said above his tented head, "about the pretty little white house and the nasty little brown house—do you see them there?" He rubbed his eyes and running nose against her stocking tops and peered blearily down her long white thighs. Yes, there was the dense blue forest, there the valley, and there (he drew closer) the little house, just hidden away, more pink than white really, and gleaming like alabaster. But the other—? "A little lower . . ." She pushed on his head, sinking him deeper between the thighs, until he saw it: dark and primitive, more like a cave than a house, a dank and airless place ringed about by indigo weeds, dreary as a tomb. She pushed his nose in it. "That is the house of laziness and disobedience and vagrancy," she said. "Little boys who don't go to school and so can only follow their noses come here, thinking it's the circus, and disappear forever." He was suffocating and thought he might be disappearing, too. She let him out but, even as he gasped for breath, stuffed his nose into the little white house: "And here is the house for good little boys who study and work hard and do as they are told. Here, life is rosy and sweet, and they can play in the garden and come and go as they please. Isn't that much better?"

"Yes, Mamma!" he said, and it *was* better, but he was still having trouble breathing. He tried to back out but he was clamped in her thighs.

"Don't be idle!" she scolded, and she gave him a spank on his wooden bottom that drove him in deeper. "Look around! Idleness is a dreadful disease, of which one should be cured immediately in childhood; if not, one never gets over it."

What he saw when he looked around was a glistening little snail peeking out under the eaves. "What are you doing there, with your nose in the door?" she asked, laughing. Or someone did, he wasn't sure, he was confused, and thought he might be about to faint.

"I odly wadt to stop beigg a puppet and becubb a little boy," he wept. "Wod't you help be, little sdail?"

"And will you ever tell a lie again?"

"*Ndo!*" he cried desperately and, alarmingly, his nose began to grow again as it had done the last time he'd been in the little white house when the Fairy was still just a girl. That time she'd unloosed on him a thousand prickly woodpeckers to peck it all away, a pecking he still sometimes felt out beyond his face like a nervous tingle as Il Gattino once told him he still felt his missing paw.

"Oh!" the Fairy gasped, giggling and wriggling about so, she seemed this time to be trying to break his nose off at the root. "A lie about lying, that's the worst kind, you naughty boy!" And then she began to spank him for real. No more playful smacks, she really let him have it.

When she finally let him out, he was too weak to argue: he promised that he would mend his ways and study till his eyes fell out and always be good and tell the truth and be the consolation of his aged father. "How nice," the fairy sighed vaguely. He was lying flat out on the floor with his little wet red nose in the air and the Fairy was sprawled spraddle-legged in the chair above him. He looked up at her dear sweet face, hoping she might be smiling down upon him, and then he saw it, the image that would haunt him for the rest of his life: the languid gaze.

Ah, Fairy! He can see it now! Not literally of course, not in here —no such languor on the face of Veronese's pinned Sebastian, nor in his other altar paintings of the twice-martyred saint either. The gaze is gone, most of the arrows as well, being used apparently to cross all the double-S initials of the saint which, looking like pairs of skewered serpents, decorate the church like a kind of company logo. Veronese's Sebastian is a man of action, a warrior, a politician of sorts who plays to the galleries, striking operatic poses (why didn't *he* get muscles like that, the old professor wants to know, sunk in his misery; why, when he put on flesh, did he still have to look like a spindly unstrung puppet, no bigger than a pennyworth of cheese, a veritable insult to the rules of human proportion—where was the heroic frame, the hairy chest, *where*—someone has a lot to answer for!—*were the powerful thighs?*), a kind of professional athlete who is used to pain, who has trained for it in effect and now receives the arrow like a gold medal. Still, for all the theatrics, the hedonism and decorative frivolity (this artist once likened his vocation to that of "poets and jesters"), there is something restful about Veronese, it is as though the languid gaze might have passed from painted to painter, invading the entire canvas, and the colors, flowing from that languor, are as soft and lush as old tapestry and vaguely warm him, much as the painting on his father's wall used to do.

He is, after all, even should this prove to be his final hour, exactly where his heart, in such extremity, would have placed him: back in one of those fine Italian Renaissance churches which he once proclaimed to be the acme and paragon of Western art, its glory and (because its moment was forever past, Western art now nothing more than, like scrimshaw, a decorated fossil) also its tragedy. His throat is raw and tickling him as if he were swallowing some of his father's live whitebait, his eyes keep watering up, his chest is rattling, and everything below that is still numb, but his eyes can still discern beauty, his fingers have come unlocked from his thawed ears, and his nose has begun to relax and hang from his face in the usual way. If anything, it is now a bit hot, at least at the tip. In his pockets, along with his ears and the rumpled money Melampetta and Alidoro gave him, he has found some bread and a wet sack of fresh mozzarella that Lido must have tucked there when they said goodbye, and he nibbles gratefully at these offerings now.

It was Lido who led him out of the snow and into this old church, like himself a crumbling ruin succumbing to the Venetian climate, faded and damp and veiled with mildew and tarnish, telling him to wait here until he returned. "I should at least be able to get your watch back, touch iron," the old mastiff growled gently after the professor had given him a shortlist of essentials from the bags' missing contents. "One of those thieving cunts must have snatched it last night." When he tried to give Lido his money back, however, the dog shook his shaggy old head and said: "Keep it, compagno. It's not much, but it might buy a warm hat or a hot meal. Besides, I don't have any pockets . . ." Which made him start to cry again—"I love you, Alidoro! You're the only real friend I have!" he sobbed into the mastiff's rancid coat, apologizing once again for all the stupid things he'd said this morning in the boat yard, but the venerable dog just lapped his nape tenderly and said: "Eh, vecchio, I've already forgotten, I told you I have a rotten memory. Now don't go away . . ."

Which was a joke. He can't even walk. When Alidoro left, he turned stiffly and, out of an old habit, started to genuflect. Or maybe something just gave way. Whatever, he went all the way down, knocking the marble floor crisply—ka-POK!—with his crippled knees. When he tried to straighten up, there was a cracking, splitting sound in his haunches that he felt all the way to the back of his neck. He had to crawl on all fours to a bench and pull himself up on it, still doubled over like a groveling penitent, an inconsolable mourner (oh, he *was* repentant, he *was* desolate beyond repair, his *Mamma* gone, twice—thrice—over, his life gone with it: *Oh non mi fate più piangere!* he wept, hoping that the echoes he heard, bouncing up off the checkered marble floor, were only in his imagination), unable to see anything for awhile through his tears but his shoes down between his knees. Boredom alone, in the end, drove the old art scholar's head up. The rest, unfortunately, has not chosen to follow. Though he's not yet as stiff as the Bishop of Cyprus stretched out up there on his marble tomb, he still can't unbend his knees or elbows, his back has locked itself into a fair imitation of a Venetian footbridge, and his backside on the hard wooden bench has now gone to sleep along with the rest of his nether parts. Overhead on the organ doors, Jesus is healing lepers and cripples at some spa or other. Relatively, they all look in pretty good shape.

Look on the bright side, he admonishes himself, beginning to wheeze. No more deadlines. No more bibliographical evidence to amass. No more *words*. Up on the Nuns' Choir, there are representations of saints holding what he takes to be the instruments of their martyrdom. Some of them are holding books. He can appreciate this. A kind of plague, reading them maybe even worse than writing them, and no end to it. The terrible martyrdom of the ever-rolling stone. Saint Pinocchio. He and his father, a new heavenly host. And now, think of it, for the first time in his long life, he does not have a book to write. That martyrdom at least is over. He is free at last. Which is probably just what they told poor Sebastian when they stripped his armor off him. "Free, my tortured *chiappie!*" he seems to be yelling, as they stuff him, up there beside the altar, into his second death. Trouble is, as martyrdoms go, the first was better than the second. This one hurts more and the compensations are more obscure. And this time: this time, no one's watching.

"Oh my *Ga-ahd!*" exclaims a loud nasal American voice, blowing in behind him. The professor makes a movement which to his own inner eye is that of shrinking down in his seat, though it may be invisible to others, as the intruder, stamping her feet and shaking herself audibly, comes blustering down the aisle. "Lookit *this!* Brrr! What a creepshow, man! Everybody's *dead* in here!"

12.

IN THE HOUSE
OF THE DEAD

"Gee-whillikers, prof, I feel really *flattered* to—*pffft! POP!*—
be able to talk with you all *alone* like this about art and life
and beauty and all that *great* stuff, I'm so excited, it's like
first day in class!" his former student gushes, squeezing his hands
inside her sweater. It does not feel like flesh in there so much as a
powdery cloud, like the materialization of his own flushed confusion.
"You never know," his father used to rumble drunkenly, wiping the
drool from his grizzled chops and tipping his yellow wig forward over
his eyebrows, "in this world, boyo, anything can happen." It was
about all the wisdom the old lout had: *In questo mondo i casi sono tanti*,
so save your pear peels, they might come in handy. It had prepared
the venerable professor for many of life's surprises, but it had not
prepared him for this. Perhaps only Hollywood could have prepared
him for this. "Everybody in class was crazy about you, you know.
'The beak's unique,' we used to say around campus. 'The Nose
Knows!' "

"I-I-I—!" he gasps. He feels, in such transport, like a fish out of
water, his gills flapping wildly. His chest is shaken by violent spasms,
which he is trying desperately to suppress. But his hands feel so
wonderful he wants to cry.

"We called you 'The Happy Honker,' you coulda had any girl you
wanted—and probably at least half the guys as well. And what a
dresser! A real zoot snoot, as we used to say, no disrespect intended
—and speaking of which, your snoot, I mean, snuggle it down here,
too, teach. Goodness sakes, but it's a mess! Is that an *acorn* growing

out the side of it? You poor dear man!" She puts an arm around him and hugs him to her bosom, which is alive and tremulous and fragrant as a Tuscan summer. Or an Iowa cornfield. Cape Cod in August. He doesn't even know where he is for a dizzying moment. He grabs hold so as not to fall, then nearly faints again to think of what he's clutching. "What you need, professor, is to let me take you back to my room and give you a good hot bath!"

"Oh, I can't—!" he squeaks, but his voice is smothered in fluffy blue angora. He tries to lift his head up, but she pushes it back down again. "I'm waiting for a frie—*mwmpff!*" She lays one hand soothingly against his nose, settling it into the warm hollow between her breasts, stroking it gently. It's as though it were made for it, like a violin case for its own particular instrument. Even resistance feels good . . .

What he'd felt when she first came storming in, disturbing his revery (his head had slumped again to his chest, for all she knew he might have been praying, had she no shame?), was more like outrage and repugnance and bitter vexation: To have traveled so far, to have suffered so much, and now, at the very end—! She'd swaggered brazenly through the place like she owned it, blowing bubbles with her noisomely scented chewing gum, hooting and snorting and loudly decrying the very sobriety that gave the church its celebrated beauty ("Stone corpses and little babies holding skulls—and lookit that skinny dude with the facefuzz—*ffpupp! squit! SMACK!*—hanging there like bagged game! Whoo, by his color I'd say he's not only dead meat, he's gone *off!*"), a sturdy middle-American blonde in a red plastic windbreaker, blue jeans, and white cowboy boots. Luckily, she seemed not to see him, and he sank lower in the pew. "And lookit the cute little butt on John-boy the Baptist there, and—hey, whoa, am I right? Has the Holy Virgin got her thumb up her kid's wazoo? Prodding his little poop-shoot?! His itty-bitsy *bumbo?!* Yippee! What a diablerie! Or are these supposed to be the—*ffpLUP!*—good guys? *Murder!*"

She brushed the snow out of her blond hair with hands ringed and braceleted in cheap costume jewelry, and, her windbreaker rustling, leaned over the altar railing. Her tight jeans seemed almost to squeak as they filled up, the worn seams spreading, her honey-colored hair clinging in snow-dampened rings about her neck and temples. "Ouch!

Bi-*zzang!* Right in his appendectomy scar! Musta missed his little dickydoo by a *whisper!* Well, what did it matter, what good's that old gap-stopper gonna—*splurpp! snap!*—do him now anyway, right? I mean, *that* sucker's *had* it! And, yikes, what're they trying to do to *that* guy, give him an *enema?* Weird!" She peeked into the side altars, stared up at the organ, gave the Veronese bust a high five, read the tomb inscription in the floor below it while blowing a huge rosy bubble. "I don't know," she sighed, sucking up the gum before it popped and turning around, "but it sure looks like a lotta heavy S and M to me, whips and bondage and dead bodies and all that, with some child porn thrown in for the kinkos—whadda *you* think, professor?"

He was thinking—had been—that she was an unspeakably rude and vulgar young loudmouth, but he was so startled by her addressing him directly like that, all he could do was raise his chin an inch and break into a wheezing cough. Under her windbreaker, he saw, she was wearing a gaudy blue angora sweater, still sparkling frothily with snow. She smiled, pushed out another enormous pink bubble. This one did pop, sticking to her nose and chin. She plucked it away with her fingers, looking cross-eyed at it, poked it back in, smiled again, chewing vigorously with her mouth open. She had even white teeth, the sort invented by American orthodontists, wide lips painted cherry red. "You *are* Professor Pinenut, aren't you? I recognized you by the . . . by your . . ."

"Ah! Yes . . . ," he coughed, shrinking abjectly into his miserable rags. He squinted up at her past his ducked and shame-enflamed nose. "But . . . Miss—?"

"Call me Bluebell," she said gaily, coming over, "the Underlying Principal of my graduating class, as they said in the yearbook, that's me, dumb as they come and gobsa fun!" As she moved, she seemed almost to bounce. Or maybe it was his blurred vision. Perhaps I have a fever, he thought, his eyes wobbling. "I was a student way back when in your famous Art Principles 101—Pinenut's Arse Pimples, as we called it—oh, I don't expect you to remember me, prof, those huge freshman cores, you know, a thousand and one faces, and no one in the whole auditorium giving diddly-eff-you-pee about anything except maybe sneaking in some shut-eye or passing a joint, you were a saint to put up with us." She planted her soft behind on the back of the pew in front, her spangled and fringed white boot propped on the bench beside him. "We were awful. You called us the living dead."

"I did—?"

"Oh, we deserved it! I sure did, I was rotten student, I admit it, I sat through all your lectures—the ones I came to, I mean—doing my nails. But, hey, at least I was doing something *artistic*, right? You used to call on me sometimes when I was fluttering my hands about and blowing my nails dry, and my answers were so stupid, you used to say you admired the absolute purity of my mind which clearly no idea had as yet penetrated. Boy, the nicknames I got called after that!"

"Oh yes . . ." But he didn't remember. He tried to recall the fluttering hands. Right then they were crossed on her breast, as though to emphasize her sincerity, as she leaned toward him, making her jeans squeak again. The nails were painted luminescent orange. To go with the blue sweater.

"But some things I never forgot, prof. You really helped me, you know, you changed my *life!*" She reached into her mouth, pulled out a long glistening ribbon of gum like a frog's tongue, rolled it up, and, turning back to the altarpieces, stuffed it back in her cheeks again. "I can see now, for example, how all these—*schloopp!*—paintings are really like moving pictures. *Nothing* stands still, so art, to be truthful, has got to move, too, right? It's why you said you—*yoomm! sploop! SPAP!*—always loved the movies. And theater—"

"No, I never . . ."

"I mean, 'images of eternity,' 'shadows of the divine perfection,' all that's just—*fffplOP!*—bullpoop, isn't it, Professor Pinenut? Like you always said!"

"I-I don't think you were, eh, listening very carefully . . ."

"And I can see now what you meant about churches being nothing more than fancy repertory theaters—I mean, just look around!—it's a place where you just *expect* something *wild* to happen—!"

"I said nothing of the kind—!" he rasped faintly, coughing and snorting. He felt infuriated by these stupid travesties of his deepest convictions, but at some remove, far behind his sinuses, which had filled up painfully, making his head bob heavily on his feeble neck.

"All the bejeweled props and snazzy sets, the stage doors and costumes and all the music and magical stuff—I mean, what actor wouldn't go apeshit for the priest's gig, it's a real headliner, isn't it,

it's got everything but dancing girls! And what with the whole amazing tonk dolled up in all colors of the rainbow, these glitzy dollar
signs all over the joint, kissing putti in the front row, and those big
chromos up there like crazy movie posters—what's a masterpiece but
just a high-class ad, a billboard for the bigots, like you always said,
right, prof?"

"Oh, please—!" he squawked, racked by a rattling cough.

"Jeepers, professor! Are you okay?" She slid in beside him then,
took his hand. "Hey, you're looking like a whoopee cushion that's lost
its whoopee! What's happened to all your fancy threads?!"

"I-I have suffered a—*wheeze!*—great misfortune . . . Now, please,
Miss, go—"

"And you're so *cold!* Here, tuck your hands in here and get them
warm!"

"What are you *doing—?!*" he yelped. "I—*rurff! hawff!*—I don't—!
Kaff! I never—!" But she had grabbed them both, stuffed them inside
her sweater, it was already done. One of his hands was still clutched
around an ear. He hopes she didn't notice. If it were still on his head,
it would be burning with shame. In fact it feels a bit warm under his
fingers right now. If that's his ear. Not much flesh left on his fingertips, can't be sure of anything any more. Not much in his head either,
his faculties hardening, his memory turning to dust: who *was* this
student? All the dense airless lecture halls of his endlessly protracted
career have blurred into one, his innumerable pupils into a vast shapeless, faceless mass. Waiting outside his office door. Waiting to have
their little strings pulled. Day after day. That was life, what he knew
of it. Closed now, that door. Forever. He nestles his nose deeper into
the soft fleece, wondering, vaguely, if he might have missed something . . . Well, and even if he did, what did it matter? *I casi sono
tanti . . .*

"You know that Mary up there hanging out over the skewered
saint, the one on the cloud holding up her little puppet," she says
suddenly, so startling him that he sets everything jiggling around
beneath his nose. "Hey! Be nice now, professor," she murmurs ad-
monishingly through the scarf tied round his pate, and gives him a
playful little smack on his behind. Which, to his joy, he feels. "Well,
you used to show us a lot of pictures like that in class. And what I
noticed is that the Virgin is always sad." She hugs him closer. He is

still, in his mind, protesting, but his body has completely surrendered. And the therapy is working: there is feeling now, quite wondrously, even to the tips of his toes. "I know what that's supposed to mean, that she has that faraway look because she foresees her little boy's tragic future, and that spoils the fun, but I think that's just dumb guys talking. What *I* see in that look is a disappointed mother." Even the tickle in his throat and the wheezing convulsions of his chest have faded away. He feels so grateful he wants to kiss something. "It's like, I don't know, it's like having a perfect son is not enough . . ." She sighs, and her breasts lift and fall around his nose like animated powder puffs. "Is that what you think?"

"Yes," he lies. He is too happy to argue. The gratitude wells up behind his eyes like the onset of a delicious sneeze. Before his eye, the open one, the tender blue hummock swells invitingly. *Che bella!* He lifts a finger under the sweater to touch the pointy part. "Exactly . . . !"

"Is—is something the matter, professor?" she asks in alarm.

"What—?!" he cries in panic, jerking his finger back and rearing his head up. It takes him a moment to remember where he is. "The matter—?!"

"Your *nose!* It seems to be—!"

"Ah, it's—it's a cold!" he mutters confusedly, his eyes watering. He turns his head away in embarrassment, pulls his hands back, hides his nose in his sleeve. "I'm sorry! Nasty thing, don't want you to catch it . . ."

She seems to be giggling behind him, but he can't be certain, and he's too ashamed to look. He ducks his head. What was he thinking —exposing himself—in his condition—and if she saw the rest—! He is wheezing again, his chest racked anew by a fit of coughing. "You sure you don't want to come home with me?" she asks, rising from the pew, her jaws snapping at the gum once more. "I could put an extra blanket on—"

"No! A friend! I have to wait!" he gasps between the painful spasms, keeping his offending part tucked between his knees.

"Well, can't blame a girl for—*flupp! POP!*—trying. It was terrif seeing you again, prof. You're really something *else!*" And—"Peace!" —she is gone.

"Wait—!" he whispers and, twisting round, catches just a glimpse of her tightly denimed posteriors disappearing provocatively out the door. "B-Bluebell—? *Miss—?!*" Too late. He has lost her, lost her forever! Of course, he cautions himself, turning back, shriveling once more into his terrible debilities, it's no catastrophe, insolent uncouth creature that she is, frivolous and disrespectful, no, good riddance, his final hours can be better spent without suffering yet another gum-popping American barbarian, her cockiness exceeded only by her ignorance, though she is not completely stupid, it must be said, brash, garrulous, but also fresh and winsome in her boorish way, blasphemous to be sure, impudent, a shamelessly wanton creature no doubt, but warm-hearted (he knows, he has been there), generous, compassionate, and willing to learn, yes, he could teach her, he has already changed her life, has he not, she said so, the soil is prepared, as it were, it's never too late—and think of it! a hot bath! What does he want to do, go back to that stinking boat yard? He finds he has already staggered to his feet. In the painting behind the altar, if his beclouded eyes do not deceive him, the Virgin Mary has opened her bodice to give baby Jesus and all the cherubs and angels crowding round a suck and is peering down now past her hiked skirts at Saint Sebastian, struggling in agony against his bonds beneath her but his eyes to heaven. And then (is something dripping on his face—?! what is she *doing—?!*) the holy martyr's nose begins to grow! Straight up! Oh my God! Even before the arrow in the saint's groin starts to twang obscenely, the old professor is out of his pew and scrambling stiff-kneed up the aisle. "*Miss—!*" he croaks. "*WAIT FOR ME—!*"

"What—?! Is the old sinner going to chase after that poor bambina, that little chick in the tow with milk at her mouth still?" comes an indignant voice, quavering eerily, from behind the organ. "Is he de-filing my tomb and sanctuary with thoughts of *pederasty?* Has the wretch no dignity? *Has he no shame?*"

"Beware of men who make public profession of virtue but behave like perfect *scoundrels!*" thunders a hollow voice above him on the left: the Bishop of Cyprus, he sees with horror, is sitting straight up, rigid and stony-eyed, blood dripping from the corners of his mouth as though he might have bit the host with his teeth. "It just goes to prove that a naughty person retains his evil character even if his outward appearance is altered!" And—*crash!*—he falls back onto his stone bier again.

"Let me give you some advice!" trumpets a voice from above, and others pick up the theme: "I want to give you some advice!" "Give you *advice!*" "Advice!" "*Advice!*" The entire church, as he struggles up the aisle (nothing's working right, it was his old babbo who taught him how to walk, he could use another lesson now), echoes and resounds with clamorous counsel: "Do not go for things bald-headed, woodenpate! Old codgers who, in an excess of passion, rush into affairs without precaution, rush blindly into their own destruction!" "Regrets are useless, booby, once the damage is done!"

"Stop it! *Stop it!*" he squawks, wheezing and snorting. He would clap his hands over his ears if he still had any ears and if he didn't need both hands for forward progress. The rose and white marble squares of the checkered floor seem to be on springs, rising and falling erratically, making him climb over some and out of others. Some drop away completely to reveal heaps of bones and moldering bishop's hats far below, forcing him to circle around, grasping pews and benches which are also on the move, sliding apart and then together again with great clashing noises like monstrous gates. "Woe to those blockheads whose minds are so beclouded by monkey business that they do not perceive the dangers that beset them!" cry the lugubrious voices, which seem to be coming from another world. Terrible odors, like hung game going off, rise up from the yawning chasms opening up in the floor. "Woe to those wicked ragamuffins who run away from their homeland! They will never do any good in this world!" "Woe to those who do not wait for their friends!" "They will repent bitterly!" "They will lose the bone of their neck!" "*They will pay through the NOSE!*" From the ceiling above, where Esther and her uncle Mordecai are subverting the reign of Xerxes, forestalling one massacre and launching another, come wild whinnies and a glittery blitz, as he fights his way over the undulating floor and through the crashing gates, of brightly gilded horse turds. *Splat! SPLAT!* they fall, bursting around him like thrown pies. "Eh, big shot! Pezzo grosso!" "Mister Nobel Laureate!" "Where do you think you are going?" Books are thrown at him from the Nuns' Choir, skulls rattle underfoot like bowling balls, arrows fly, the hanging brass lamps swing, clinking and clanking like muffled bells, the organ doors flap, the martyred saint screams in his reduplicated pain, masonry rains down, the whole church seems to be splitting and cracking and threatening him with destruction! "Eh, furfante! Vagabondo! Ragazzac-cio!" Splut! Crash! *Ka-pok!* "Come back! Come back, you little ninny!"

As he drags himself past the font of holy water near the door, the tumult now fading behind him, the carved Christ's halo falls off and, ringing like a coin, rolls around on the stone floor in front of him. "I say, pick that up for me, would you, Pinenut old man? That's a good chap! I can't seem to move my arms." As, still on his hands and knees, he snatches at it, the hung Christ dips a bit lower and, chin at his navel, adds in a whisper: "You know, from one woodenhead to another, old boy, let me give you a little useful advice—"

"*No!*" he screams, staggering to his feet. "*Why is everybody always trying to give me advice?!*" And he flings the halo into the suddenly stilled and dusty church: it sails like a Frisbee straight to the front where, in the deep hush, it blasts away a jar of pink and yellow carnations, startling an old bespectacled nun dusting the altar. She squeaks like a mouse caught in a trap and drops her feather duster, crossing herself in terror. As he turns to flee, the talking Christ is counseling him to "calm down, let things take their own course, dear fellow, let the water run along its own slope, as we say," whereupon, as though cued, the font tips over, threatening to inundate the church —he splashes through the flood and out the door, a fresh chorus of "Let me give you some advice!" ringing in his aching head like canned laughter.

13.

THE TALKING CRICKET

He's caged. As he ought to be. As Jiminy once said: You buttered your bread, now sleep in it. People passing by glance at him, stuffed there, shivering and sniveling, in the metal rubbish basket, and cast upon him weary expressions of pity mixed with undisguised loathing and contempt. They dump garbage on him, hang lost mittens on his nose. No more than he deserves. No more! Rushing baldheaded into this bizarre adventure, blind to dangers, deaf to advice, he has, just as all those madhouse voices prophesied, lost his neck bone in this one and all else besides. A lifetime of virtue, of self-conquest and in-spite-of's, an heroic career of the most rigid discipline and soberest endeavor, with all its books, honors, degrees, and endowed chairs, is no protection against the wild whims of senectitude, extremity's giddy last-minute bravado. Ah, Bluebell, Bluebell, you silly wise-cracking dumb-blonde murderess! he thinks, *hruff*ing and *hawff*ing and sucking up cold strangulated breaths that may well be his last. What have you done to me *now?*

All around him, even as his own devastated trash-bagged limbs petrify, he can hear through his wheezing a fluttering, pattering, pounding, and swishing, as the city, shaking itself, crawls out from under its strange white blanket to reinstate its restless habits of scurry and exchange. The storm is letting up. Shutters are grinding open. There are choruses of "Ciao!" "Ciao!" and bursts of laughter, the trampling of booted feet. Nearby, in the middle of this broad open campo, the wooden news kiosk has opened up, spreading its wings like a traveling puppet show, delivery boys are rolling heavy blue and green metal carts past the red benches, and the tarpaulins over the greengrocer stalls are being flung back, pitching clouds of snow into the glittery air. At the far end, a musical group of some sort seems to be setting up at the foot of a truncated bell tower with snow-frosted shrubs growing out the top, the only evidence remaining of whatever church once gave its name to this square. He hears the loose clang of cymbals being unpacked and a squeal like that of an overblown fife when a loudspeaker is plugged in. Crowds are gathering, mostly students with bookbags, housewives pushing strollers. The windows of cafés are steaming up, taunting him with the offer of hot coffee and grappa which he cannot, from his wire crib, alas, even though he has the cash for it, accept. As though to taunt him, on a door within reach of his failing sight, someone has spray-painted: "Only liberty is necessary; everything else is only important." Snow is being swept from shop entrances, sawdust spread. Not far away, as he knows, men in bright-colored slickers are scraping clean the bridges, shoveling the snow and ice into the canals to be flushed to the sea. Earlier, two of them, laughing, lifted him over one of the bridges when he'd been brought to a standstill halfway up, his knees refusing to bend enough to get his toe up past the next step.

"Ha Ha! Che brutta figura! Poor little cock's lost all his feathers!" exclaimed one.

"He's so light," laughed the other, "it's more like the feathers have lost their cock!"

That was his last bridge. Before that, how many, he doesn't know. He was in a kind of delirium. Fever probably. What's left of his flesh must be literally burning itself away. It was cold when he staggered out of the bedlam of that august temple gone suddenly berserk, colder than he'd remembered, and snow was being whipped about still in the sharp wind, obscuring the high bridge in front of the church, only meters away, his first obstacle, but he was on fire with terror, desire, and the hot flush of his infirmity, and the bitterness of the weather seemed only to invigorate him. Up the bridge he went and down, escaping and pursuing at the same time, hobbling to be sure, cracking and splintering and creaking with the cold, hacking and snorting, half blind, but on the move, his withered limbs at times outflung, tossed convulsively awry, to the casual onlooker appearing no doubt a bit whimsical and unstrung, but still clattering resolutely on down the narrow calle on the other side, feeling indeed like something of an athlete, a centenarian version of that spunky youngster who could leap ditches and hedgerows at a single bound, now with each lurching step making about as much progress laterally as forward perhaps, and having to improvise rather desperately at corners and bridges, but feeling that same exhilaration of the blood, that delicious conflict of pain and pleasure that characterizes a race well run, and keeping in mind all the while his noble goal—he will *teach* her! she will become his last great project! his pupil, his protégé, perhaps even his secretary, biographer, curator, and literary executrix!—as well as the more compelling images of a hot bath, a warm bed, clean sheets, and a pillowy blue hollow wherein to tuck his frostbitten nose.

Which was what, having no other guide, he had had to trust on that mad chase, following wherever it might lead, sniffing the crisp air for traces of her powdery warmth, her slept-in jeans, the tang of bubble gum and nail polish—and, at the crest of a short arching bridge, he was rewarded suddenly by a glimpse of azure blue, a distant flicker of startling color within the white blur, vanishing as quickly as seen, but which could only have been her sweater (had she taken off her windbreaker? was it a signal? a tease? was she walking backwards? he couldn't stop to think about this), and thereafter he seemed to see it more often, on a bridge, at the edge of a riva or the end of a little calle, fleeting and elusive as his famous last chapter, there and not there, yet drawing him on, though he couldn't be sure he saw it, saw *anything* for that matter, his vision, never the best, now hazed by icy tears and sweat and the crazy pounding of his heart in his temples and sinuses. So absorbed was he with the object of his pursuit that, as had often happened in the middle of books he was writing, he failed to notice the weariness, the physical and emotional exhaustion, that was rapidly overtaking him, overtaking him once and for all, his mind racing far ahead, abandoning his body, leaving it to drag along behind as best it could until it stopped. Which, inevitably, it did. Halfway up a bridge. He, who was very much afraid of the ridiculous, was then, with fearful ridicule, lifted laughingly to the other side. And stood for a time just where he was deposited, intent only on not adding to his indignity by falling over. It was not easy. Had anyone so much as sneezed nearby, it would have toppled him. And, straining thus to stay upright, he inadvertently pushed out a tiny gust of flatulence which escaped him like the shrill little peep of a wooden whistle.

"Ho! *Thou* wert a beautiful thought, and softly bodied forth!" declaimed a voice that seemed to come from the brick wall above him.

"Who is it that speaks so eloquently?"

"Not who is it, but *what?* It looks like a holdover from the last plague!"

"Or else something the boss might have had for lunch! Porca Madonna! If I had a stomach, I'd be throwing up!"

He was standing, he saw through his frozen tears, in front of a maskmaker's workshop, its entrance and windows lined with the painted faces of mythical creatures, wild animals, goblins and fairies, jesters, plague victims, suns and moons, *bauta*s and *moreta*s, death's heads, goddesses, chinless rustics, and bearded nobles. "Whatever it is, it's got more holes in it than a piece of cheese!" declared one of them, the pale pink-cheeked sun perhaps, a somber white-bearded Bacchus replying majestically: "Maybe it's a flute." "You mean, dearie," cooed an angel with cherry-red lips, "you don't know whether you should eat it or blow it—?" The ancient scholar, feeling now the full weight of his folly, wished desperately to escape these japes, but could not, his father's infamous joke—"What brought you here, Geppetto my friend?" "My legs!"—no longer a joke. "If I had a body like that," scoffed a freckled face with a red hood and golden braids, "I'd sell it for a pegboard!" "If you had a body, cara mia," whispered a ghostly voice from behind an expressionless white mask with large hollow eyes, "you'd sell it for anything!" From behind the window, he could see, he was being watched by a glowering figure with a wild black beard like a scribble of India ink, making hasty sketches on a pad. "But what's that lump between his shoulders with the pump handle on it?" the empty snout of a camel posted in the doorway wanted to know, and: "Look from what pulpit comes the sermon!" jeered a grinning noseless skull.

Then suddenly they all fell silent. Even the distant scraping of shovels stopped and the wind died down. Nothing could be heard but the water in the canals, far away, timidly lapping wood and stone. *"Who was it,"* thundered a deep ogrish voice from overhead, the very sound of which set the masks rattling on the wall with terror, *"laid this turd at my doorway?"* It was the maskmaker with his apron of black beard, smeared with paint and plaster, his roaring mouth big enough to bake buns in, and eyes so reddened by grappa they seemed to be lit from behind by a fire deep in his skull. *"Who has made this inhuman mess?"*

"It's—it's not my fault!" the old professor wheezed, indignant even in his indignity, bold even in his abject dismay.

"What? *What*—?! It *speaks?*" bellowed the black-bearded giant, leaning closer and baring his horrible smoke-stained teeth. "Talking turds have been *outlawed* in Venice! Is this the work of a rival seeking to discredit me? Is this—what you say—*dirty tricks?*"

"Believe me, my—"

"*Enough! Basta così!*" roared the maskmaker, snatching him up by the scruff. "*There's only one place for rubbish like you!*" And holding him aloft with one mighty fist, from which the unhappy pilgrim dangled limp as a skinned eel, the bearded giant strode into the nearby campo and, much to the amusement of the passersby—"Ciao, Mangiano! What's this? One of your rejects?" "Madonna! What an obscenity!" —thrust him, up to his armpits, into this plastic-lined wastebin.

Where, with the filling up of the campo, he has become the popular target of insults and horseplay. Mothers show him off to bundled toddlers to make them laugh; little boys, when they're not chasing bedraggled and dying pigeons, pelt him with snowballs; teenagers with ghetto blasters hugged to their ears flip their cigarette butts at him. He is crowned with fruit peels, pink sports pages, and rancid boxes from fast-food joints, christened with the dregs from supermarket wine cartons. "*Più in alto che se va,*" the musicians are singing raucously and tunelessly at the other end of the square while testing out their equipment, "*più el cul se mostra!*" The higher one climbs, the more he exposes his behind: a sentiment so apposite to the old emeritus professor's present humiliation, he might suspect them of malice had they not been entertaining the passing crowds with all manner of rude scatological lyrics since they began setting up. To add mockery to the damage, pigeons use him as a perch and public restroom, which causes one of the musicians drifting by, a swarthy snubnosed character looking more like a thief than an entertainer, to remark loudly and histrionically that "Every beautiful rose—" he lingers over this image to draw the guffaws, his plastic features twisted into a set painful smile, his hands flowering about the old bespackled professor's head, "—eventually becomes an assmop!" And the others in the campo gleefully pick up the refrain: "*Un strassacul! Un strassacul!*" The caged visitor, ever an emotional, even irascible defender of his own dignity when driven to it, would object, or would at least chase the pigeons off, but he is utterly and catastrophically undone, overcome by exhaustion and racked with pain and fever and a blinding cold in the head, suffering now, he knows, that final apathy of limb that marks, against his choosing, the end of the cold staggering race which he's, willy-nilly, losing . . . or however that old doggerel goes . . .

"It's the oldest truth under the sun: life is a race that can't be won . . ."

Something like that. And moreover, the abuse is warranted, is it not?—a fit judgment upon his perfidious heart, his capricious and ultimately fatal betrayal of Her and thence of himself, a betrayal that no doubt began back in America with his decision (if it was a decision—? it's all like a dream he can no longer recall) to return to this sinking Queen, this treacherous sea Cybele "as changeable as a nervous woman," this "most unreal of cities, half legend, half snare for strangers," this home of the counterfeit and the fickle heart, this infamous Acchiappacitrulli. The zany jester is mincing about, miming the crippled antics of an old fool, wheezing and snorting and tossing out his jibes on the comical debilities of the aged ("When one grows old," he croaks, wobbling about knock-kneed with his rear stuck out, his back bowed, and his toes turned in, "he loses his renown! His legs go flabby and his stockings fall down!"), his mocking parodies in the Venetian dialect about "this heartless city of nervous strangers and old queens" and "untimely fetal decisions" ("Ay, ay!" the fool cries with a quavering voice, pulling his shabby felt hat down over his ears, "I can't think, I've got this damnable bone in my head!"), but he does not even approach the true depths of disgrace into which the old wayfarer knows he has fallen. Up at the foot of the cutoff bell tower, the other musicians, augmented now by electronic keyboard and guitar, harmonica, and a set of traps (over their heads, on the scaffolding of cloth and boards, there's a sign painted every color of the rainbow, but the colors run together and he can't read it —no doubt yet another obscenity), are singing, to the same tune as before, if such hoarse shouting can be called a tune, can be called singing: "*El tempo, el culo e i siori, / I fa quel che i vol lori!*"—Time, one's arse, and the moneyed few, / All do just what they want to do!—and they might as well be singing about "*el tempo, el culo e i professori.*" When some within the jeering crowd pretend to come to his aid— "Now, now, remember that in this world, we must be kind to all such unfortunate creatures, that we ourselves may be treated kindly in our time of need—this poor old grillino, he really can't help it, you know!"—their patronizing remarks enrage him more than the abuse. No, no! he wants to tell them. I *can* help it, you idiots! But I'm a villain to the core! Believe me! A brute! An ass!

"Ha ha! Che parlare da bestia! Give him a hand, everybody! In fact, give him two, he needs them!"

But it's true! It's true! A fraud! A turncoat without even a coat to turn! I'm a vile unprincipled scoundrel through and through!

"He may have a small mind, ladies and gentlemen, but he knows it from corner to corner!"

Yet how can it have happened? A century of prudence and sobriety and effortful mastery blown away in a day, less than a day, vanished into the flux as though it never existed, leaving him not only the ludicrous dupe of charlatans, robbed of his every possession, arrested and humiliated by the authorities, stripped of his clothing as of his pride, indeed of his very humanity, enfeebled with illness and deprived even of his ears and nipples—"*Lai, lai,*" the grimacing clown is crooning sourly to the rhythm of a child's taunt, "*co se xe veci se xe buzarai! Ay, ay! Hugger-mugger! To be old is to be buggered!*"—but now, having abandoned his only true friend in the world in mad pursuit of a vaporous fantasy, a true *ignis fatuus*, a most foolish fire, he is hopelessly paralyzed as well, frozen, lost, confused by fever and hunger, left to die in a trash bag, taunted by cretins and crushed by his own shame, and all because of a vulgar American coed with a soft blue sweater . . .

"Oho!" cries the jester, leaping into the air and clicking his heels. "So *that's* the rock you've split your decrepit buns on, old man! Ha ha! Rispettabile pubblico! *Here* is where the donkey has fallen!"

He seems, alas, to have been talking out loud again. He doesn't know for how long, but fears the worst. It's almost as though he's forgotten how *not* to. Crowds of people, scarfed and booted, have gathered around, laughing and applauding and stamping their feet in the snow, whooping the prancing buffoon through his mocking routines—now, hobbling and cackling wildly, he is chasing all the young girls in the audience, making them squeal and clutch tight their coats and skirts. The venerable scholar has become, he sees through bitter tears, seeing little else, the very fool of fools. Butts' butt. But what, being four-fifths buried in refuse already and the rest soon to follow, does it matter? Oh, bambina mia, you little blue-jeaned and cowboy-booted barbarian, you twangy gum-popping red-white-and-blue siren! *You have been my death!*

"Well, at least your life has not been in vain for nothing!" the comedian exclaims with insolent bravado, as though egged on by the raucous crowd. He seems brash as a child yet ancient at the same time, his features beardless yet furrowed with grimaces and depravity, marred by warts and pockmarks and an enflamed carbuncular growth on his forehead, and with two deep wrinkles standing arrogantly, harshly, almost savagely between his bushy brows, like something out of a repressed nightmare. "Hee ha! Isn't it wonderful!" he brays, launching a little bowlegged dance around the wastebin, the professor shrinking into his trash bag and solacing himself with the thought, which in his feverish misery he only half believes, that at least—surely—nothing worse can happen to him now. *"Tutti quanti semo mati / Per quel buso che semo nati!"* the clown warbles out in a squeaky falsetto, rolling his eyes roguishly as he hops about. *"It's crazy how we're all inflamed / By that little hole from which we came!"*

But why is he surprised? For didn't the Blue-Haired Fairy warn him? "Puppets never grow up," she said, wagging her finger at him all those years ago. "They are born puppets, live puppets, die puppets!"

"Yes, well, dummy, that's show business! But do you mean to say—?!"

What a terrible oracle! He'd thought she was presenting him with an alternative, a moral choice; *she'd merely been pronouncing sentence upon him!*

"Hey now, here's a song and it isn't long: 'He who doesn't die in the cradle, / Will suffer for it sooner or later!' Hah! Who says there are no poets in Venice? Yes, at the end of the day, we're all just clay, give or take a sliver or two—we all bough down to the curse of events, you can't stave it off, speaking figuratively! So nothing to do, cavalieri e dame, but show a little spunk, as we say in the charade trade, brace up and stick it out as best you can, and let the chips fall where they may! But now tell me, old man," the entertainer murmurs, peering closer, the frown between his sunken eyes deepening, "what did you mean when you said—ye gods! Am I dreaming or . . . ?" And—*ka-POK!*—he butts him suddenly in the head.

O babbo mio! I am dying! There is loud laughter and shouting all around him, but the old traveler can hear it only intermittently through the reverberant clangor in his hammered head. What is this insane monster *doing—?!* "Oh please!" he wheezes, but this time no one hears him. "Help—!"

"It *might* be . . . ," muses the clown, leaning back, and then— *WHAACK!*—bangs heads again, hammering him brutally with the very knob of his carbuncle.

"*Ahi! o povero me!*" yelps the professor, whimpering in the old style, his head reeling, his eyes losing their focus. "*Ih! . . . ih! . . . ih! . . .*" And the jester cries: "*It COULD be . . . !*"

And then, even before the next blow comes, the distant memory returns and the old scholar recognizes his adversary—not an adversary at all of course but once his most beloved friend—a memory repressed to be sure, but not of a nightmare: rather of what was perhaps—before the glory of being human, that is, and all that shameful past was put behind him—the happiest night of his life! *Pa-KLOCKK!*

"*It IS! It IS! Pinocchio! It's PINOCCHIO!*"

"*Arlecchino!*" he gasps, his eyes still spinning around in his ringing head. Did he used to do this for *fun?* "My-my *friend!* Ow! Oh! It's *you!*"

"*Pulcinella! Pantalone!*" Arlecchino shouts across the campo, leaping up and down like a mechanical frog. "*It's Pinocchio! Colombina! Our dear brother Pinocchio is here! Flaminia! Brighella! Capitano!*"

"What—?!" cry the musicians of the rock band, dropping their instruments with an amplified clatter and bounding down off the stage. "*Pinocchio—?! Can it be—?!*"

And he is suddenly engulfed in a great commotion as they swoop down upon him, everyone kissing him and hugging him and giving him friendly head-butts and pinches and all talking at once—"*It is! It is really he!*" "*It's our brother Pinocchio!*" "*Evviva Pinocchio!*" "*Lift him out of his hamper there!*" "*Who has done this to him?*" "*Oh dear Pinocchio! Come to the arms of your wooden brothers!*" "*Give us a kiss, love!*" "*Easy! The damp seems to have got to him!*" "*Why have you been tormenting him so,*

Arlecchino? Our own brother!" "He saved your life!" "I didn't recognize him, he's been smeared with all this funny makeup!" "That's human flesh, you imbecile!" "Pinocchio, how did it happen?" "Why did you leave us?" "It's been so long!" "Careful, Brighella, don't drop him!"—and, trailing a litter of paper bags, old vaporetto tickets, and unspooled cassette tapes, he is lifted out of the trash basket, hoisted upon their shoulders, and paraded triumphantly around the campo, the puppets recovering their instruments and striking up a gay-spirited circus march quite unlike the pounding headachy noises they were making before. As they pass by the stage, the professor sees above it the psychedelically painted canvas he could not read before: GRAN TEATRO DEI BURATTINI. *"That's us!"* cries Pulcinella below his left buttock. *"Welcome, dear Pinocchio, to the Great Puppet Show Vegetal Punk Rock Band!"*

14.

GRAN TEATRO DEI BURATTINI

"*I want you stick to me, Pinocchio,*" Arlecchino rasps fiercely from beneath his stiff upper lip as he drags him off the back of the stage and down into the terrified crowds, "*like shit to a shovel!*"

"But my knees! I can't even—!"

"Don't argue, friend! This is *serious!*"

Just like a puppet. Doesn't understand the limits and hazards of human flesh. Il Dottore, as his fellow musicians now call him, *knows* it's serious. He can smell the bonfires. He can hear the screams. He knows what happened to the last Dottore. He's frightened, too. But he still can't move. Shifting his body is like moving a refrigerator or a heavy log: he has to tip it from side to side, rock it forward all in one piece, every inch costs him almost unbearable pain and effort. And at the same time he's so frail, the tiniest jolt sends him spinning off in another direction, making him feel like one of those airy little balls in a whirling lottery basket, a walking (speaking loosely) paradox. So, inevitably, they are separated, shit and shovel. The metaphor was all too apt. Shit always gets left behind. He can hear Arlecchino shouting for him through the awesome pack-up, but the shouts grow more and more distant. He tries to shout back, but he keeps wheezing and coughing instead. The smoke is getting in his eyes and tearing at his throat, aggravating the itching there. He is being stepped on, elbowed, crushed between frantic bodies, kneed and pushed, they can't see him down here. He longs for the relative safety of the rubbish bin. Though those too, he can see, are being tipped over and flattened by the panicky mob. He strikes out for the awning of a greengrocer's stall, hoping for a refuge there, but it disappears before he can reach it. "Striking out" is perhaps not quite the expression: most of the time his feet are not even touching the ground. But he manages to stay afloat in the human flood, one of his more conventional talents, even if he remains somewhat below the surface.

The last Dottore, he's been told, was taken apart stick by stick. The band's been outlawed, its members condemned, they're on the run, and the Dottore, too fat to run, got caught. The carabinieri were trying to get him to talk which was of course like inviting the hare to run, as Pulcinella put it, only they could not understand his garbled Latin, whoever could, so finally they had to torture him to *stop* him talking. Even as he was edifying his captors with his celebrated *at iam gravi* lecture about the wounded Queen and her raw sausages, they snapped the old philosophaster's limbs in two, split up the chunkier bits with hammer and chisel, then, with his own strings, tied all the pieces up in his big hat and shipped the lot off to Murano glassblowers for kindling. "But now you can be our new Dottore!" Flaminia exclaimed gleefully, meaning no irony at all, as they propped him up in front of the electronic keyboard, the newest member of the Gran Teatro dei Burattini Vegetal Punk Rock Band. "But I'm no musician!" he protested. "Neither are we!" they laughed. "Look! It's easy! Just hit this! Now this!" Arlecchino guided his hands and from the stiff poke of his fingers, frozen into gnarled little claws, vast sounds suddenly rocked the campo. "Now just keep repeating that!" The others picked up their instruments and gathered around him on the stage, improvising raucously upon his little phrase (which sounded suspiciously to him like "When You Wish Upon a Star"), electric guitars and theorbos, harmonicas, tambourines, flutes, lutes, and a set of amplified drums responding thunderingly to the touch of the virtuoso Burattini. *Pi-pi-pi!* they went. *Zum-zum-zum!* They made the whole square shake and tremble. It was fun, in a dizzying and anarchical sort of way, like the old days in Mangiafoco's mercurial puppet theater, and their friendship, however bruised he was by it, warmed his feeble heart.

The dizziness he suffered in their midst was not so much from the loud music or the smothering attention or even the fever which no doubt grips him still, but from all the head-butts he'd endured by which they'd first, ecstatically, recognized him. Indeed, down here in the desperate press and jostle of the fleeing multitudes, his head is still ringing from those blows, making it difficult for him to maintain any sense of direction, little good it would do him if he could. He sees the four public security police drag Corallina away, hears her screaming, but a moment later he cannot be sure whether she's in front of him or behind him. Arlecchino's fading shouts have seemed to spiral around him like a ball on a stretching string, almost as though the campo were expanding and he were being screwed deep into its tangled center. When Captain Spavento comes creeping by on all fours between the legs of the crowd, having just crept abjectly past in the opposite direction, the professor can no longer be sure, in his throbbing vertigo, that these are two separate events.

"Long live our brother Pinocchio!" they'd all cried on discovering him and the hugging and pinching and head-thumping had begun, everyone had a turn, he couldn't even speak it hurt so, he could only weep, and then they wept, too, but for joy, as they supposed he did, and kissed him some more and pinched him even harder as though to try to pluck him clean and banged heads again and crushed him with their wild loving hugs. And, in truth, for all the pain, he *was* happy, delirious even, it was as if, as they transported him out of the trash bag and onto their shoulders and paraded him through the snowswept square and up to the makeshift bandstand, he'd been suddenly and miraculously rescued, not merely from a lonely ignominious death, but from a whole lifetime of misguided exile and isolation, it was as if *this* was what he had come back for, this place, these friends, it was as if, as if a hundred years had never happened . . . !

"Remember the party that night? We danced till dawn!"

"Dancing wasn't the half of it! We all stripped and swapped parts and got our strings in a delicious tangle! Then Arlecchino stole Mangiafoco's swazzle and started playing it through his *bumhole!*"

"If it *was* his bumhole—might have been anybody's, things were pretty mixed *up* by then!"

"Listen, Pinocchio had just saved my can from the fire, the least I could do was *sing* through it!"

"As Arlecchino said at the time, he was thanking Pinocchio from the bottom of his heart and from the heart of his bottom!"

"I remember!"

"What a blast!"

"Then Rosaura challenged everybody to a pelvis-cracking contest with her polished cherry pudendum, and ended up splitting Colombina's mound and breaking Lelio's little thing off, not that he ever had any use for it!"

"She called it hardass cunny-conkers!"

"It never healed, I've still got a crack there!"

"It was a crazy night!"

"I was so happy . . . !"

"That party is a legend now!"

"But when was it? *I* don't remember it!"

"You weren't *there*, Flaminia. Must have been a century ago, maybe two."

"You were still just a gleam in old Mangiafoco's chisel!"

"And Rosaura," he asked then, craning his head about above the sea of faces, "where *is* Rosaura?"

"Ah, poor Rosaura, bless her wormy little knothole, has gone the way of all wood, I'm afraid, all except for her hardwood hotbox which Pierotto here inherited for a head when his old one got damp rot and fell apart!"

"It's made him a bit strange, but he's got a new *lazzo* with a chamber pot and a monocle you wouldn't believe!"

"But there are plenty of others here, you old rogue! Here, meet Corallina and Lisetta and Diamantina . . . !" They lowered him into the arms of these gay soubrettes with their bright-colored skirts and aprons tucked into leather leggings, their purple and magenta butch cuts, and safety-pin earrings through their wooden ears. *"Evviva Pinocchio!"* they laughed and they kissed him again and pinched and squeezed him and, just for fun, knocked heads some more.

"But why did you go away, Pinocchio? We were having so much fun! Why did you leave us when you said you loved us so?"

"Well, I—*ow!*—my father—"

"Loved us? *Loved* us?" roared Capitano Spavento del Vall'Inferno, rearing up then in sudden choler, his plumes quivering and waxed moustaches bristling. "He loved us as the wolf loves the sheep! As the whip loves the donkey! As the woodman loves the tree! No, no, let us say bread to the bread and bugger-my-ass to bugger-my-ass! This abominable imitation of humanity, this vile hodgepodge, this double-dealing French-leave-taking skin artist *deserted* us!"

"*Ahhh!*" gasped the three servant girls in unison and, tossing him in the air, shrank away as though from a bad odor. He would have crashed disastrously to the stage floor had not Arlecchino and Colombina deftly caught him, Colombina whispering behind what had once been his ear: "Is it true you left us because of a woman, dear Pinocchio? A painted woman with a mysterious past . . . ?"

"She wasn't exactly painted—!" he wheezed in dazed dismay.

"Ho ho! Beating about the bush, were you, you old gully-raker?" laughed Brighella, winking slyly. "Nothing like splitting whiskers for splitting friends!"

"It wasn't a woman, it was *fame* he was after," declared Pulcinella. "We weren't hot enough for the little showboat! He wanted to be the big pimple, not some second stringer out in the sticks! He wanted to be a *star!*"

"No, no: *money!* It was *money* made the donkey trot, it *always* is!" argued Pantalone, thrusting his pointed beard in the air like an accusing finger. "There was the passing of a purse, his palm was greased, I heard the insidious chink of gold! Money taken, friends forsaken—!"

"But—but it wasn't *any* of that, I just didn't *want* to be a—!"

"O blind counsels of the guilty! O vice, ever cowardly!" cried the Capitano, still in high dudgeon. "We took the little sapling in as our trusted friend and brother, but it was a viper we found at our bosoms, a copper-hearted two-timing turntail as treacherous as a deathwatch beetle!" He snapped his sword from its sheath and whirled it about menacingly, strutting up and down the cramped stage. "O evil, of evils most evil! There is no worse pestilence than a familiar foe! Such perfidy makes me snuff pepper, and when I'm aroused the seas duck under for cover, mountains shrink into the earth like iced ballocks, the sun is afraid to show its face, and even the mighty gods shit themselves in terror, so look out below! Down with your breaches of faith! Out with your double-jointed hybrid treachery! Avast! Avaunt! Oyez! Attento! The greatest achievement of a general is to smite the foe and chop the whoreson into little specks and slivers, so let me have at him! Don't hold me back! My heart detests him as the gates of hell!"

As Captain Spavento del Vall'Inferno, still brandishing his sword, whirled around and charged in his direction, the professor turned anxiously to the others for help, but they all seemed to be applauding the spectacle, or else grabbing up their musical instruments as though to use them for weapons themselves. Their painted faces and hard wooden smiles alarmed him, and he felt a sudden intense nostalgia for his old library carrel back at the university. "Wait! You don't understand—!" he gasped, but no one was listening. Arlecchino's and Colombina's grips tightened like shackles.

"Hasten with the sword," brayed the Capitano, bearing down upon him in full regalia and waving the others to follow, *"bring weapons, climb the walls; the enemy is at hand—IHAH!"*

Even as the old scholar ducked, Arlecchino heaved him up as though to ward the blow off himself. The effect, however, was to make everyone fall back, even the startled Captain, who dropped his sword and nearly fell off the stage, scrambling to pick it up again. *"Look at him!"* Arlecchino cried, holding him up by the scruff of his tattered coat and waggling him about. "Do you think he'd do this on *purpose?!"*

There was laughter and some rude whistling and murmurs of "It's true! what a calamity!" and "Povera bestia!" and when the Captain, recovering somewhat, started huffing and puffing again about collapsing the Hemispheres, shattering the Poles, sending heads rolling around the world like billiard balls, and, with his flaming sword inherited from Xerxes, Romulus, Caesar, and the Blind Doge, bringing on the final devastation, Lisetta took his sword away from him and swatted him on the behind with it until he cried. "Vergogna!" she scolded, as he crawled about on all fours, boohooing. "Keep your tongue, rotto in culo, and keep your friends, slander slanders itself! Chi pissa contro vento pisses on his own pants!"

"Remember that a wretched man, as a wise compatriot once said," continued Arlecchino solemnly, still dangling him on high like one of the cats of Venice, "is a holy thing, and vice versa, da cima a fondo, and to be without a friend is to be like a body without a soul, that is to say, a turd without a fragrance—nor is friendship to be bought at a fair, at least not at an honest price, except sometimes in a raffle, and even then, as they say, old friends are still the best bargain if they are not so old they are dead and beginning to smell. Pesce, oglio, e amico vecchio, we would all be wise to remember that famous old Venetian recipe, the secret of which is fresh basil, sturgeon eggs, a forgiving palate, and funghi porcini, when in season, as friendship always is of course if you have the liver for it. Yes, compagni, old wood, as they used to say in the old days, days so old they were never new, except on the Feast Day of poor little Saint Agnes, whose martyred maidenhead, preserved in a silver noggin, once rivaled the eyeballs of Santa Lucia as an object of veneration amongst our countrymen and made old days young again—old wood, they used to say, as I say now, burns brightest, old linens wash whitest, old friendships cling tightest, and old arses spread widest, so watch where you sit for it is a difficult thing to replace true friends who have been inadvertently flattened, may they rest in peace, or in pieces, as the case may be."

With this sobering reminder of mortality, the entire company of the Great Puppet Show Punk Rock Band, weeping and laughing all at the same time, crowded around him once more, kissing him and smacking heads and embracing him in their crunching hugs, even Captain Spavento, who swore eternal fealty to his brother Pinocchio, adding that if eternity were not enough, he would personally take Time by the throat and squeeze a whole new set of tenses out of the cowardly *stronzo*. They pressed him, peeking in his pants, for tales of his travels and transformations, and told him of their own troubles, the banning of the band by the Little Man gang, now running the city and cynically calling themselves "socialists," and the terrible persecution of their brothers and sisters that has followed. The Dottore, he learned, was not the only victim: the lovers Ortensia, Florindo, Lindoro, and Lavinia had been dismembered by the authorities and used for the making of grocers' crates, clothespins, and bird cages, though their heads were rumored to have been stolen by the mask-maker Mangiafoco, bastard descendant of the old fire-eating puppet master. The troupe's instruments had been smashed, their spare parts, props, and costumes confiscated. And poor Frittellino had been burned at the stake, the stake being his own master Tartaglia, or what was left of him: a few bent sticks, blue-rimmed spectacles, and a fading stutter. But Pulcinella did some backflips and headstands to show he was as spry as ever, Corallina tossed her skirts up to display her freshly varnished walnut behind, and Brighella reminded them all that "Hey, Father Goldoni was made to eat shit in this town, why should we expect truffles?"

By now, a fair-sized crowd had gathered at this end of the snowy campo, drawn by the novelty of vegepunk rock, university students mostly by the look of them (he gazed out as upon a lecture hall, suffering a momentary twinge of longing and bittersweet regret, or maybe it was only a heart attack, who knew what he'd lose next, but if she was out there, he couldn't see her), dressed in blue jeans and thick sweaters, heavy boots and seamen's caps, and growing impatient in the biting cold. *"We want the music! We want the music!"* they chanted, stamping their feet, and the puppets, conscious as always about how they were "coming down the strings," as they liked to put it, snatched up their instruments and began improvising an original number with the old professor himself, in his new role as deputy Dottore, at the keyboard. Though he seemed to recognize the melody he was pounding out, the words, barked in the Venetian dialect, were new to him, something about the world being half for sale, half to be pawned, and all to be laughed at, maybe they were making it up as they went along. The crowd seemed to love it, hooting and whistling and singing along: *"Lèzi, scrivi e tiente a mente, chi no sgrifa no ga gnente!"* they whooped, jumping up and down. *"Read, write, and never doubt it: If you don't steal it, you'll do without it!"* It was fun in a hypnotic and irresponsible sort of way, it was like drunkenness, like jumping, over and over, through a ring at the circus, and the old traveler, in spite of himself (for it was also somehow frightening, even his unwonted delight frightened him), found himself, eagerly, without thinking, wishing it could just go on like this: "Now that we're all together, let's stay together!" he cried, meaning it with all his heart, though they probably couldn't hear him, they were making a terrible racket —or, rather, *somebody* was: the Burattini, he saw now, had dropped their instruments and were staring grimly out upon the campo, he was hammering away all by himself, his hollow unaccompanied notes resoundingly challenged now by what seemed to be a great confluence of marching brass bands, arriving simultaneously from all directions like prancing caravans, beating out tattoos and blowing clamorous fanfares, joining in, as he mistakenly thought at the moment, in the fun.

"Vaffan—?!"

"Ahi! *la pula!*"

"The questurini!"

"It's a bust!"

"La madama!"

"And they've brought in the civil guards!"

"Those fist-fuckers!"

"And not only—!"

"Look over *there!*"

"The public security police! The carabinieri!"

"The highway cops!"

"And who's that greasy little dog's cock under the toyshop awning, the one with the whipsaw directing everything—?"

"L'Omino!"

"We're fucked—!"

"I hear motor boats!"

"The maritime patrol!"

"Look! Even the sanitation cops! The border guards!"

"Lido always gives us a warning! Where is he today?"

"The ecclesiastical police!"

"The vaporetto inspectors!"

"They've pulled out every prick in the province!"

"And they're all *armed!*"

In they paraded, hundreds and hundreds of them, long winding ribbons of vivid color, banded and braided, caped and cockaded, some in lance caps, others in shakos, tricornes, berets and busbies, their weapons gleaming, their shiny boots—notched, bossed, spurred, tufted, waxed, or gaitered—cracking snappily like ricocheting gunshots against the paving stones of the narrow passageways leading into the crowded campo. The Dottore-designate was still thumping away dutifully at the keyboard, grinning out half blindly on this resplendent spectacle, when Arlecchino grabbed his wrist.

"The show's over, my friend! We're hitting the road!"

"What—?! But I—!"

"It's too late!" Pantalone cried. "They've encircled the campo!"

"They've blocked all the exits!"

"What'll we *do—?!*"

"The pompieri! *They're building fires!*"

"Listen! Helicopters!"

"Tear gas!"

"Come on!" Arlecchino rasped, and suddenly, like the metaphorical

shoveled shit, he was out of his seat and flying into the turbulent crowds.

"*Help!!*"

"*Run!*"

"*ASSASSINI!*"

And now he has lost Arlecchino, he's alone in a mad crush of terrorized rock fans and puppets, trampling each other in their desperate search for an exit, it's worse than registration day back at the university. Helpless and confused and crippled with illness, the old professor is getting dragged along by the throngs, swept back and forth in waves as they flee from one police charge or another. There are bludgeonings, screams, the grind of buzz saws, howled insults, the exploding of tear gas canisters. Fires have been built, manned by the fire brigade, and, horribly, in one of them, he sees the pretty face of Flaminia melting. One moment he is jammed up against a flaking wall by a teeming mass, the next he finds himself sprawling, alone, as though he were suddenly the center from which all have fled, by the battered marble base of an ancient wellhead. Towering above him are two tall carabinieri, thin as nails, with cocked hats, drawn rifles, and flowing black capes, lined with blood red velvet.

"Is this one?"

"Hard to tell. Old bum, looks like."

"Let's throw him on, see if he burns."

"Oh, please!" he blubbers with what life he has left. "I'm *not* one of them! Can't you see? Sob! It's all a terrible mistake! I don't even know *how* to play a piano!"

"A likely story."

"A bad tool in any case. I say, throw him on the fire."

"*No! Please! Have mercy on an old man!*" he bawls as they reach down for him. "I'm *afraid* of fire—!"

"Sì, signori Cavalieri! Have *pity!*" someone cries nearby.

"Cavalieri—?! There are no cavalieri here, fool!"

"Signori *Commendatori*, then!" Through his tears the professor can see that it is Pulcinella in his loose white shift and sugarloaf hat. He seems to have popped out from under the iron lid of the well. "Have mercy on the old gentleman, Commendatori!"

"Commendatori—! Are you making fun of us, you turd?"

"Your Excellencies!" Pulcinella bows deeply, his rear in the air, his beaked nose at his toes. From this exaggeratedly abject position he winks soberly at the downed scholar and, while clucking like a chicken to mask his whisper, urges sotto voce: *"Run, Pinocchio! Run!"*

"Aha! I recognize you!" cries one of the carabinieri, grabbing the puppet by the scruff and hauling him to his feet. "You're one of those terrorist musicians!"

"Off to the fire with you, pricknose!"

"Wait—!" gasps the professor, rising, with difficulty, to his knees.

"Yes, wait!" echoes Pulcinella from under his raised beak. "My shoes!"

"What—?"

"The laces! I'll never burn with loose laces, gentlemen, I'll piss right through them and put the fire out!" he exclaims and, freeing his arms, stoops as though to tie them. The carabinieri reach down to collar him again, and he grabs an ankle of each to throw them down and run away: an old *lazzo* from the Commedia days. Only this time it doesn't work. Pulcinella grunts and strains, but he cannot raise either foot so much as a hair's breadth off the paving stones. "Made a frittata out of that one, I guess," he shrugs, as they lift him by his hump, his long arms dangling limply at his sides, "but that's how it goes in show business, Your Excellencies, no point in crying over spent milk, as they say, what's done has a head, so farewell, dear public! Your faithful servant Pulcinella is off to get his heart coddled and his buns toasted!"

"Stop! You can't do that—!" the old professor protests, but before he can even unlock his old knees and clamber to his feet, another policeman, dressed like a Cuirassier of the Guard in a steel helmet with brass ornaments and a black horsehair plume, a double-breasted blue tunic with silver buttons and red piping, the red cuffs and standing collar embroidered in silver wire, a sky blue sash with sky blue tassels hanging from the hip, silver epaulettes with silver bullion fringes, white breeches, and black jackboots, and carrying a rifle with a fixed bayonet, arrives and claims jurisdiction over the prisoner, asserting the divine right of kings.

"Kings? What kings? We have no kings, you fool!"

"The divine right of fools, then!" rejoins the Cuirassier and lays hold of Pulcinella to drag him away. "He who takes, has!" he laughs, a dry roguish laugh that can belong only to the band's lead guitar Brighella. "Possession, as the belly said to the nose, masters, is nine tenths of the law!"

"That still leaves *one* tenth!" the carabinieri reply, snatching at the slippered feet just disappearing into the roiling mob, whereupon a terrible tug-of-war begins with Pulcinella's body, Brighella at the head end, the carabinieri at the feet, Pulcinella whooping and yelping pathetically, sounding more like a chicken now than ever. Suddenly, the legs snap off at the groin, there's a frightful howl, the carabinieri tumble backwards into the crowd, tangled up in their capes, and the puppets vanish.

The professor knows he should do the same, but he is rooted to the spot. The crowds have shrunk back, he is suddenly all alone at the wellhead, center stage, the carabinieri, in a crimson rage, scrambling to their feet again, their sharp teeth bared, Pulcinella's sundered legs gripped in their fists like clubs—!

"*Pinocchio!* At *last!*"

"*Arlecchino*—! But you *shouldn't* have come *back!* They're *setting fire*—!"

"Tell me about it *later*, my friend! We have to split before these shits do the splitting for us! *Come on*—!"

15.

A GONDOLA RIDE

O nce, many years ago, in one of his less genteel embodiments, he had been sold for a few farthings to a bungling rustic who wanted to make a drum for the village band out of his hide. The lout tied a rope to a hind leg and a stone to his neck and kicked him into the water, then sat back with a pipe waiting for him to drown. Instead, a shoal of fish came along and ate him right out of his predicament. It was a strange sensation. Dragged down by the stone and donkey weight, he had sunk to the bottom, feeling all the while as though his body wanted to rise from within. Then, suddenly, there was this thrilling pain, a delicious nibbling away at his entire being, he has never felt anything quite like it before or since, not even what the starlets did with him in Hollywood came close, though he always had hopes, and his body, his new one, as though trying to express its exhilaration, popped like a seed from its old encrustations and floated exuberantly to the surface.

This time it is different. There is, as before, that same eery feeling of wanting to rise from inside even while the outer body, weighted down with coat and suit and flesh and shoes, steadily sinks, but this time there are no fish, nothing living at all so far as he can see, which isn't far, it's like trying to peer through cold bean soup down here in this quagmire of twigs and wattle upon which, improbably, an empire arose, nothing but curdled garbage, thin twists of opaque plastic, children's ruined copybooks and old sanitary napkins, lottery stubs, the occasional drowned cat, and otherwise just shapeless streamers of coagulated muck that wind around his limbs and grease his face as though to smear away that expression of joy and surprise painted there only a moment before by the unexpected sight of that which he has been, with such awesome consequences, seeking. Ah, with what fugitive, mad, passionate hopes did he go clattering ludicrously down that fatal underpass, his preposterous movements inspired by the demon whose peculiar pleasure it is to trample human reason and dignity underfoot, even when so finely nurtured and honed as his own, his giddy mind in abject travail, his senses so focused on the object of his quest that only now, deep in the fallen Queen's murky bowels and sinking fast, can he hear the cries he could not hear then.

That he has been able to complete this humiliating fall, out of the frying pan and into the pot, so to speak, is thanks only to Arlecchino, who came to his rescue back in the campo, popping theatrically out of the turbulent crowd, felt hat pulled down over his pinpoint eyes as though he were trying to hide inside it, just as the two carabinieri struggled to their feet and, wielding Pulcinella's broken-off legs like truncheons, turned, enraged, on the transfixed professor. "Hey, looking for you, old man," his brave friend laughed, "has been like trying to find a pearl in a hailstorm! Quick! Hop on my back! *A cavalluccio!*"

"*Hop—?!* I can't even—!"

Whereupon Arlecchino backed into him, reached down, and grabbed him behind the knees, and they were off, galloping clumsily over the icy stone flagging, the tall thin carabinieri in hot pursuit. "Hold it! Stop those two! They're dangerous criminals!"

He could feel bits and pieces flaking off as they jounced along, escape was costing him dearly, he knew, but Arlecchino was quick and cunning, leaping benches and wellheads, dodging in and out of the crowds, he had a thousand tricks, and it was working, they seemed to be losing their two pursuers, the pounding of their boots fading, their angry shouts gradually getting swallowed up in the larger uproar of the smoke-filled campo. He tried to tell Arlecchino as they galloped along how grateful he was and how much he loved him, and also about poor Corallina and Pulcinella and Flaminia and all the rest, but all he could do was wheeze and snort, his head bobbing loosely, his chest slapping Arlecchino's wooden back, popping the wind from his antique lungs. "Oh dehea-hea-hea-hear Har-Har-Harle—!"

And then, through his tears, like a miracle, he saw it: a flash of blue! *That* blue! "Stop! STO-HOP—!"

"What—what is it?" Arlecchino panted, staggering to a halt. The puppet's knees seemed to buckle and he set the professor down for a moment.

"I thought I saw—!"

"Whew, this used to be—*gasp!*—easier, old friend! I must be drying out!"

"Yes! *Down there!*" They were at the mouth of a dark passage through the middle of a building, the Sotoportego de l'Uva, he saw from the smudged sign above it, the Underpass of the Grape, and, at the far end of it, there she was, just drifting by as though in an angelic vision, her blond hair glistening with melted snowflakes, a fat pink bubble quivering between her puckered lips, and, jutting out from her unzipped plastic windbreaker, clad in soft blue angora and bouncing gently, those wondrous appendages which, for one magical moment that he desperately longed to reenact, had thawed him out this morning to the very tips of his being. *"Bluebell! Miss—! WAIT—!"*

"Pinocchio! Where are you going—?! Come *back!* We're not out of the woods yet, friend! We have to—*yow!!"*

"Hah! *Got* you, you impertinent little punk!"

"Pinocchio! Help me—!"

"Hey, look at the dummy's outfit! We've nailed the one the boss wanted!"

"You're screwed now, knobhead!"

"Ho ho! We're going to burn your wormy ass!"

"Pinocchio! Help!" Arlecchino was crying. *"Salvami dalla morte! I DON'T WANT TO DIE—!"*

But, lost in his mad trance, he was already halfway down the passageway, all this was far behind him, he was moving as he had not moved since he first staggered out of San Sebastiano, only now there was hope, real hope. This movement was not exactly running, nor even walking, it was more like some kind of goofy unhinged dance, the sort his drug-addled students used to dance a generation ago, his pelvis flying every which way and his arms and head moving more than his feet did. He caromed off the narrow walls, blackened with soot and wet moss, clattered into stacks of empty fruit crates, slapped through garbage, bounced off downpipes and stairwells, but he did make progress, slowly picking up forward momentum, his eyes fixed, no matter which direction the rest of him was momentarily aimed, on the opening at the far end, though she could no longer be seen there. *"Miss! Please! It's Professor Pinenut! That bath—! I've changed my mind—!"*

It turned out, however, there was no little street running alongside the canal at the other end of the underpass as one might have assumed, just watersteps leading down into the cold coffee-colored water below. Luckily, he saw this in time to start backpedaling, call it that. Unluckily, the steps were covered with ice and snow and there was an evil green slime below that, and so, for a moment, after an experience not unlike that, he supposed with a fleeting but bitter irony, of being pitched from a slick shovel, the venerable scholar and aesthete, former rock star, and erstwhile *cavalier servente* found himself hovering in midair, still backpedaling frantically, those partial misgivings he had felt since returning to this city now become a sore distress, a positive misery, his most cherished convictions vanished like the pavement beneath his feet, his dreams of truth, virtue, perfection, and a hot bath now just derisive memories. Alas, he thought, nothing blunts the edge of a noble, robust mind more quickly and more thoroughly than the sharp and bitter corrosion of knowledge. Then—*patatunfete!*—in he went.

And so, as though arriving at the final destination on that ticket purchased so impulsively back in America, he has come at the end to the beginning, to the very foundations of this mysterious enterprise and of his own as well: back to the slimy ooze and the ancient bits of wood, driven deep, holding the whole apparition up. "La strada è pericolosa," a creature once warned him, long ago on that fateful Night of the Assassins. "It is dangerous out on the road! Turn back!" Yet, though it has been brought home to him, now as then, that the failure to take such advice is, in the world's judgment, a capital offense (even as he struggles upward against his heavy clothing, his toes forebodingly touch mud), and though it may be true, as he has so often been told, that those who, in an excess of passion, rush into things without precaution rush into their own destruction, a sensible person never embarking on an enterprise (all the advice taken through the years is now passing before his drowning eyes as though it were his life) until he can see his way clear to the end of it, what is one to do, he asks petulantly, his wind giving out, his heart beating wildly in his chest, with failing eyesight? Stay at home? Faint heart and all that, remember! Better faint than defunto, fool! When will you ever learn? But I *have* learned, he rages, arguing thus with himself while trying to claw his way to the surface, which is not far above him, but the sludge is too thick and he is too weak: even as he kicks at the mire below him, his feet sink into it. I have done nothing *but* learn! It's not *enough* to learn—! He is still managing to hold his breath, he was always good at this, the girls in Hollywood used to throw him in the pool and see how long they could hold him under, they said it made them wet between their legs just counting the bubbles, and he let them, associating it with the excitement he had felt as a drowning donkey, but now it's over, he's not the youth he was then, his ancient chest is beginning to spasm involuntarily, he can't hold it any longer, *o babbo mio! o Fatina!*—and then, just when all seems lost, something hooks him under his collar and hauls him, snorting and choking and webbed in slime, halfway out of the water.

"Have a good bath, signore?" rumbles a gravelly old voice above him.

"Help! Help—!" he splutters, floundering about in thick icy water. From what he can see through the muck and tears, he appears to be dangling from the end of a pole held by a hulking figure wearing a straw gondolier's boater with the braid torn at the brim, tilted rakishly over a sinister red mask with hornlike brows. *"Save me!"*

"Hmm, I must think about that, signore. Why should I succor one who is running from the police? Save the hanged man and you'll be hanged by him, as they say—"

"I am *not* running—*splut! glub!*—from anybody! I am a decent law-abiding citizen! It's all a—*gasp!*—mistake!"

"So you say, signore! But why should one believe you?"

"But you *must!* I am the most truthful person in the world—!"

"Yes, yes, and you've got the nose of a titmouse, too! Ha ha!"

"But can't you *see?* I am an American—*glurp!*—professor! A professor *emeritus!* Everyone knows me! I am a—*blub!*—good man! *Un gran signore!*"

"Oh I can *see* the great man you are through the holes in your clothes, Eccellenza! Che spettacolo! Perhaps the little fish have been feeding on your 'poor festered amorettos'—?"

"Oh, shut up, you damned fool, and get me out of here!" he cries and—*thplup!*—finds himself under water again, this time unfortunately with his mouth open. *"Please—!"* he gurgles when next brought to the surface. *"I'll pay!"*

"Ebbene, at your service, padrone!" replies the devilish oarsman with a bow, lifting the professor out of the canal at last and, as though landing a crab, depositing his sodden catch on the black leather cushions of his gondola. "One must not be too hasty, you can never tell a tree by its bark, as I always say, or a pocket by its pants. So will it be the grand tour, signor professore, or famous murders, masterpieces, and executions, or perhaps the *Venezia esotica* of the poets and their param—?"

"No, no! I only want . . . I want . . ." What? He is dying. And soon. He knows that now. And what he wants, what he longs for, as he huddles there on the stiff black cushions, drenched through and trembling in the wintry wind, are his old down comforter, his snuggies, his hot water bottle. He wants a bed, a soft warm bed. "Did you see . . . go past . . . a young woman . . . ?"

"Ah! Una bambina—?"

"Yes—"

"Bella—?"

"Yes, yes!"

"Wearing a hat—!"

"No . . ."

"I mean, hair—"

"Yes . . ."

"Dark—"

"Ah—"

"But not too dark—?"

"Well . . ."

"You might almost say blond—"

"Yes!"

"Eh, how much money do you have, signore?"

"I-I don't know . . ." He tries to reach into his soggy pockets for the few notes that Alidoro and Melampetta stuffed there, but his hands are frozen into inflexible claws.

"Permesso!" the gondolier growls soothingly, and reaches in to help himself, pulling out a hairy handful of cheese, wet bread, a few soaked lire, and an ear. He cocks his head to peer at this collection through one of the eyeholes of his mask, the mask's expression of fiendish menace giving way at this angle to something more like red-faced bewilderment. "Is, eh, is this all there is?" he asks, sniffing the ear.

"It's all I have left," he whimpers through chattering teeth. The tears are starting. He isn't going to make it. "It's not my fault! I am not a poor man! I have been the—*sob!*—victim of a cruel deceit! I have lost everything! Please help me—!"

"Well, on a day like this, I suppose, somewhat is better than nothing," sighs the gondolier, tossing the ear and bread over his shoulder with a shrug, pocketing the lire, and popping the cheese behind the mask into his mouth with a slurp before setting off. "A little wood, as the saying goes, will heat a little oven."

As the gondola turns and noses its way up the canal, the oar splashing sluggishly in the snow-clotted water, the professor, slumped desolately in his wet rags and deprived even of the somewhat, describes through his tears, because, like the gondolier's proverbial bit of wood, it seems to warm him a little to do so, how those two ruthless thieves last night stole all his earthly possessions, leaving him alone and homeless in the bitter weather. "They threw me to the lions! Literally! It's true! *Sniff!* I was even chased by one! They took my clothes, my money, my papers, my medicines, my traveling garment steamer—"

"Ah, it is a terrible story, professore, my heart weeps for you!" commiserates the gondolier, reaching under his mask as though to wipe a tear, or perhaps to pick his teeth. "What a world we are condemned to live in, eh? Where can we gentle folk find a safe shelter? Well, but here we are! Step out, please!"

"What—? Already? But—!" They have bumped up against a small open campo, he sees, in front of a church whose bare façade today is striped with snow, giving it the appearance of a circus tent. They have not even left the area of the police operation. It is just across the canal, they have only circled around it, he can still hear the screams, the shouts, smell the smoke, people are fleeing this way, then turning around to watch the action on the other side. "But wait, this isn't—! You promised—!"

"Yes, yes, as requested, signore, thank you very much!"

"What do you mean, thank you very much—?! I gave you all my money! You haven't taken me anywhere yet! *This is robbery!*"

"Now, now, lower the comb," cautions the gondolier, glancing over his shoulder. "No sense drowning in a glass of water, as the saying goes, professore, so don't make an affair of state out of it!"

"But, see here, you—*Stop! What are you doing—?!*" The oar has caught him by the collar again, and once more he finds himself helplessly treading air, his coattails flapping soggily, over the murky brown waters of the snow-scummed canal. "*Help! Thief! He stole my money!*" he cries, appealing to the people in the square, even as he dangles from the gondolier's pole, but they only laugh and cheer, as though he were part of the daily entertainment.

"*Look at him!*" mocks the gondolier, waving a few soggy lire at the crowd. "*Il gran signore!*"

"Che bestiola!"

"He's too small! Throw him back!"

"*Put me down! This is an outrage!*"

"People who wear small shoes," the scoundrel declares portentiously, easing him down onto the snowy paving stones beside a little fat man, broader than he is tall, who seems, like everyone else, greatly amused by it all, "should not try to live on a large foot, dottore!"

"*Foot dottore!*" a blind beggar echoes, waving his white cane with the only hand he has.

"*You!*" he gasps, recognizing his old enemy at last. "You stole my baggage! You stole my computer, all my work! *You stole my life—!*"

"Ah well, that was long ago," rumbles the masked villain, dipping his head between his shoulders and leaning heavily on one foot. The fat man gives the rogue something, money probably, though the gesture is so fleetingly subtle as to be all but imperceptible. "Temporibus illis, and all that, dottore, if you please, let's pass the sponge over it, let's put a stone on it, as they say over on San Michele, let bygones be—"

"Bygones!" cries the beggar, and rattles his tin cup. "If you please!"

"*It's La Volpe! Don't let her get away!*" the old scholar wails, as the devilish creature pushes away with a tip of her tatty straw boater, slipping deftly up the waterway and out of sight. "*Help! Police!*" His voice is all that's left him, he cannot move, he cannot even point his finger. "*She's the one! She stole everything I had! Stop her!*"

But the police, not far away, have other things to do, and the gathered crowds seem merely amused, waiting to see what will happen next. What does happen is that the strange little fat man, his round rosy face split with a gleaming smile, turns to the water-logged professor, takes him tenderly in his arms, and squeezes him as though to wring him dry. "Pini, Pini, my love!" he gushes with a soft old voice full of loving kindness. "Safe at last!"

16.

THE LITTLE MAN

The low sky's sullen light is ebbing, as though swept up into the clouds of mothlike snow now blowing around the melancholy lilac-tinted lamps along the waterfront, by the time the rapidly sinking emeritus professor is lifted out of the rocking motor launch and onto his old friend's private dock on the Molo, the landing stage and promenade near the Piazzetta of San Marco. The ancient traveler is dimly aware, ravaged by illness and cruel abuse though he is, that he is making, at last, his proper entrance into this "fairy city of the heart," as Eugenio has just called it, quoting one or another of the city's agents, and it does not fail to occur to him, as his porters bear him ceremonially between the Piazzetta's two eccentric gallows posts as though through a turnstile, deep-throated bells ringing out their somber consent overhead, that had he somehow landed here last night, as so many who have preceded him to this city through the centuries have advised, the mortal disasters that have befallen him this past night and day might never have happened, a thought that, far from easing his despair, merely deepens it, reminding him once again of his deplorable ingrained resistance to all advice, no matter how noble and well meaning its source. He is that proverbial impetuous fool, who, rushing in, gets, over and over again, trod upon.

"Now, now," says Eugenio gently, sidling up and tucking his blankets more tightly about him, "stop carrying on so, my angel, take your courage in both hands, we'll be there soon."

"There" is Eugenio's palace, the Palazzo dei Balocchi, "my humble abode," as his old school chum called it, "my little capanna in the Piazza," which has been offered to the professor, not merely for the night, but for so long as he is able to remain, which, under the grave circumstances, may be, alas, the shorter span of time. He has been offered a suite of his own, centrally heated and "fitted out in full rule"

with built-in bar, medieval tapestries, a billiard table, marble bath-
room with its original frescos, sauna, Byzantine mosaic floors, and an
advanced electronic wraparound sound system, along with a staff of
servants, doctors, nurses, cooks, priests, pharmacists, tailors, secre-
taries, and cellarmasters at his disposal, and more: a curative herbal
risotto on arrival, silk pajamas, a new electric toothbrush, satin sheets,
and breakfast in bed, if he should last that long, even a personal hot
water bottle and all the credit he might need during this emergency.
"Indeed the whole city shall be laid at your feet, my exalted friend,"
Eugenio had exclaimed while still embracing him back there on the
little exposed campo where La Volpe had deposited him, "you'll be
sleeping between two pillars, as they say here, pillows, I mean, so
long as I have anything to do with it, trust me—to the laureate his
guerdon, the master his meed! Eh? So come along, contentment
awaits, dear boy, but hurry now, the night is cold and the way is
long! *Andiamo pure!*"

But, soaked to the core from his fatal dunking and fast icing up in
the bitter wind, he could no longer even speak, much less move, and
hurrying was like a forgotten dream. He could only lift his chin
creakily an inch or two and sneeze: "*Etci! Etci!*" Whereupon, with a
snap of Eugenio's fingers, two servants appeared with a kind of sedan
chair or litter, strapped him into it, bundled him up snugly in cashmere blankets, and hoisted him aboard the gleaming motor launch,
which had all the while been growling impatiently alongside them at
the foot of the bridge.

There was much, as the launch lurched away like a runner breaking
out of the starting block and went roaring, right through a red light,
down the narrow rio, darting in and out among the slower gondolas,
barges, and the honking express vaporetto, snow-thickened spray
flying from the bounding prow and water slapping stone and wood
along the sides, that was troubling the dying scholar, the smoke in
the air, for example, the remarks of that infernal Fox and then the
money that had passed hands, the very coincidence that had brought
Eugenio to just that little square beside the water at just such a moment on such a day and made his rescue possible, but all of this was
far at the back of his bruised and water-soaked head, and it disappeared altogether when Eugenio, declaring how sweet it was to go
simply *mad* over a lost friend found again, proceeded to recite, as

proof of his uninterrupted love and devotion to his old prepubescent pal, all of the grants, awards, fellowships, degrees (earned and honorary), prizes and publications, chairmanships, medals, titles, professional and honorary society memberships, special commissions, anthologizations, trusteeships, presidential citations, distinguished visiting professorships, biographies, eulogies, monuments, festschrifts, film credits, book and children's park dedications, and every single *Who's Who* entry of the professor's long and illustrious career, even mentioning the establishment, in his honor, upon the twenty-fifth anniversary of the first edition of *The Wretch*, of "The Annual 'Character Counts' Award" by Rotary International, and his more recent (politely refused) nomination as honorary president of the national "Nuke the Whales" campaign.

Whether it was this extraordinary exhibition of his boyhood companion's lifelong loyalty and admiration that set him off, or the sudden pungent awareness of the distance between that glorious past and his present misfortunes, the old wayfarer burst into tears and, taken generously into Eugenio's open arms, proceeded to unburden himself upon his dear friend's plump silk-shirted breast. Sobbing and wheezing, he has gasped out, as they've come spanking down the Grand Canal, engines wide open and sirens bleating, his terrible tale, in fragments only and in no particular order, getting blind monks confused with drunk lions, trash bags with turncoats, and grappa with graffiti, calamity tumbling upon calamity and all mixed up . . .

"And—*sob!*—he stole my computer!"

"The gondolier—?"

"Yes, but not—!"

"But, my dear boy, what were you doing jumping into the canal with a computer?"

"No, you don't—and the police! It was terrible! You saw—!"

"Now, now, boys will be boys, Pini . . ."

"But—*wah!*—my best friend! It was only music—!"

"We weren't afraid of a little music, ragazzo mio, we were worried about *you* in the hands of those Puppet Brigade terrorists! We were rescuing you from a possible kidnapping—!"

"Was that a *rescue*—? I was—*boohoo!*—in a trash bag—!"

"I know, I know, let it all pour out, my love . . ."

. . . And maybe not even entirely audible over the speedboat's wail and roar, but it hasn't mattered, Eugenio has seemed to understand and forgive everything, hugging him close, assuring him that his nightmare was over, truly over, he was with trusted and altogether human friends now ("And in Venice we value friendship dearer than life! I would be unworthy of the name of Venetian if I did not follow the example of my brave fellow citizens, who are the soul of honor!"), and consoling him with promises of the luxuries and unstinting cordiality that await him. "This is not only the world's most beautiful city, as has often been said, it is also, in case you have forgotten, amor mio, its most civilized and opulent host. Indeed, there is no other city quite like it! It is a kind of paradise, una città benedetta, set like a golden clasp, as someone has said, on the girdle of the earth, a boast, a marvel, and a show, magical, dazzling, perplexing, the playground of the western world, the revel of the earth—the Masque of Italy! Una vera cuccagna! Pleasure, Pini, is its other name! I *love* it, almost as much as I love you! So stop crying now, you silly creature, life here is like a perpetual holiday, and you are its guest of honor! Oh, I have such plans for you, my friend! What good times we shall have together!"

"But—for the love of God, Eugenio! *Sob!* I-I am *dying—!*"

"Then, sweet boy, we shall have obsequies the likes of which have not been seen here since the ninth century when those two mercantile body snatchers brought Saint Mark's stolen corpse back in a perfumed basket from Alexandria, an entrepreneurial coup the world has envied ever since! Ah, what a delicious funeral that must have been! Think of the crowds! The marketing possibilities! And they've never stopped coming! Those fragrant bones, planted in a mausoleum unequaled in splendor till our own age of the movie palace, seeded an empire! Indeed, the odor of sanctity bestowed upon these islands by the ever-ripe Evangelist, is, when the wind turns, with us still, a daily reminder of the debt we all owe to those two quick-fingered traveling salesmen, bless their shameless little hearts! And now, Pini, if it's your turn, I can promise you a send-off unmatched in modern times! I see a glass coffin, a single transparent bubble, hand blown around the dear departed by Murano craftsmen like a bottle around a model square-rigger! You will lie in state on silken cushions the color of biscuits and cream, trimmed with the finest Burano lace and stuffed with canary feathers, surrounded by candlelit displays of memora-

bilia, souvenirs, articulated miniature replicas, death's masks, and
other spin-offs, in the ballroom of one of the great Venetian palaces
—the Casa Stecchini perhaps, yes, why not? The House of the Little
Sticks—just over there, do you see it? On the left—!"

"I-I—*choke!*—can't see *anything*—!"

"I'm sure it can be arranged, and if not, we'll simply buy it for the
occasion, the media will love it! When word gets out, there will be
lines to view the body from here to Verona! It will take weeks! And
right in the middle of the off-season, too, what a golden opportunity!
We'll have screenings and readings, concerts, lotteries, public tributes
from your fellow laureates, art exhibits of your portraits from around
the world, fund-raising auctions and funny nose competitions, special
travel packages for little children, cruises for the elderly and the handicapped! Then, on some feast day, such as that of Saint Paul the
Simple, or Gabriel the Incarnating Archangel, or even, if the condition of the mortal remains permits such a delay, that of another Saint
Mark, he of Arethusa, who was stabbed to death, back in the perilous
days before felt tips, by the nasty little penpoints of his mischievous
students—!"

"Oh, please, Eugenio—!"

"No, wait, Pini, this is the best part! On that day, a flotilla of black
gondolas, the largest ever assembled in Venice and all of them heaped
with sage, narcissus, and laurel, along with bouquets of bleeding
hearts and woodbine, bachelor buttons and elderberry, dog roses,
fairy ferns, cat's paw and foxglove, and sprinkled with a touch of wild
oats, sea wrack, bitterroot, and rue, will bear your crystal casket up
the Grand Canal, the opposite way we've just come, under the Accademia Bridge back there, which will be closed off that day of course,
leased to all the world's major television networks, and on to the
vaporetto landing at the Ramo del Teatro. There, greeted by the
orchestra of the Fenice Opera House playing "Siegfried's Funeral
March" from our own dear Riccardino's *Götterdämmerung*, it will dis-
embark the entire cortege, composed of the greatest scholars, artists,
politicians, theologians, bankers, carpenters, movie stars, self-made
millionaires, and social reformers of the world, which will then make
its ceremonious way down the Streets of the Tree and the Lawyers
to the Rio Terra degli Assassini, chased thence up the Fuseri Canal
to the Calle dei Pignoli, the Street of the Pinenuts—henceforth, my

friend, in memoriam, *your* street! I *love* it! Meanwhile, in the Piazza San Marco—ah! a proposito, dear boy! *Here we are!"*

And so they have disembarked there on the stormy Molo, the ancient sojourner solicitously chaired in a traditional Venetian portantina, and made their way into the Piazza, Eugenio shouting: "Make way! Make way! *Largo per un gran signore!"*—though he cannot be sure, buried in blankets and blinded by the freezing wind, that there is actually anyone out in this wretched weather but themselves. He seems to hear voices and is dimly aware of passing under lamps and illumined façades, perhaps the Basilica itself, but his senses, he knows, can no longer be trusted, for he also seems to hear the murderous cries of squealing assassins, angels fluttering and making rude windy noises overhead, and a little whistling sound inside his skull as though something might be boring away in there, and the blur before his eyes is throbbing as though his pulse were beating on him from without. Even inside all his blankets, he is trembling violently, and his tears, shed on his dear friend's breast, have frozen on his face, threatening to split the exposed parts of his cheeks open. He feels light-headed and heavyhearted all at once, as though his bodily parts were trying to go in two different directions at the same time. It is not unlike the sensation he had while drowning in the canal, and he wonders, in his feverish confusion, if he might not still be down there, sinking into the slime, this rescue but a dying dream.

Or worse. Perhaps his whole rational human life has been nothing more than the dying dream of that poor drowned donkey, maybe he has only imagined that conveniently ravenous shoal of mullets and whiting, all the heroics thereafter and the transfiguration and the lonely century that has followed being just so much wishful thinking, certainly it all seems to have passed in the blinking of an eye, yes, maybe, all illusions aside, he is fated to be a drumhead after all, one more noseful and the mad dream over. He takes a deep snort: no , no such luck, just more frosty air, faintly Venetian-tinted, it has not yet, whatever *it* is, stopped going on . . .

"Ah, Pini, still with us! Good boy!" enthuses Eugenio at his side. "Coraggio, dear friend, we are almost there! But, ah! what a splendid night this is, a pity you're under the weather! It reminds me of the first night I came here all those years ago! It was snowing then, too, and dog-cold, but we were young and Carnival had begun, so what did it matter? No one to drag us in to baths and books, no one to make us keep our caps and scarves on, our pants either for that matter! Who could be happier, who could be more contented than we?"

The professor, too, is thinking, deep down inside his fever, where thinking is more like pure sensation, about happiness, and about all the pain and suffering that seems needed to make it possible. Everyone loves a circus, but to make the children laugh, his master whipped him mercilessly and struck him on his sensitive nose with the handle of the whip, so dizzying him with pain (yet now, when his thoughts are more like dreams, he knows—and this knowledge itself is like a blow on the nose—he was as happy as a dancing donkey as he has ever been since) that he lamed himself and so condemned himself to die. And as for that country fellow who tried to drown him, he was at heart a gentle sort who dreamt only of a new drum for the village band. No doubt some other donkey, even more ruthlessly treated, was eventually slaughtered for the purpose, maybe even someone he knew, because: who would want the village band to be without a drum?

"Oh, the lights then! the extravagant music and endless gambols! In the streets there was such laughter and shouting! such pandemonium! such maddening squeals! such a devilish uproar! It was like no other place in the world! It *is* like no other place in the world, Pini! *What fun it is still!*"

But should we, he asks himself, rising briefly out of the pit of his present distress, resisting the seductive lure of donkey thoughts, should we, aware of all the attendant suffering, deny ourselves then the pleasure of the circus, of the drum? Or should we, knowing that none escape the pain, not even we, seize at whatever cost (here he is seized by a fit of violent wheezing and coughing as though there were something caustic in the atmosphere, not unlike the foul air at faculty meetings) what fleeting pleasures, life's only miracles, come our way? In short, somewhere, far inside, something (what is it?) faintly troubles him . . .

"And *look*, Pini! Look how *beautiful!*" Eugenio exclaims, tenderly patting away the coughing fit. "See how the snow has been blown against the buildings! It's like ornamental frosting! Every cap capped, every tracery retraced, the decorative decorated! It's like fairyland! The Moors on the Clock Tower are wearing lambskin jackets tonight

and downy cocksocks on their lovely organs and all the lions are
draped in white woolly blankets! The snow is at once as soft and fat
as ricotta cheese, yet more delicate in its patterns than the finest
Burano lace! And now, do you see? in the last light of day, it is all
aglow, it is as though, at this moment, the city were somehow lit
from within! *Look*, Pini! *O che bel paese! Che bella vita!*"

Having been ever, or nearly ever, the very model of obedience, a
trait learned early and the hard way at the Fairy's knees, or, more
accurately, at (so to speak) her deathbed, or beds, the old scholar
cannot risk, in his own extremity, changing his stripes now (though
that is, he is all too dizzyingly aware, the very nature of his extremity), so he does his best to respond to the wishes of his old friend and
providential benefactor who clearly loves him so, poking his nose into
the wind and nodding gravely, even though to his fevered eye it is a
bit like gazing out upon a photographic negative, the ghastly pallor of
the snow-blown buildings more a threat than a delight. All the towers
and poles in the swirling snow appear to be leaning toward him as
though about to topple, lights flicker in the multitudinous windows
like chilling but unreadable messages, and the Basilica itself seems to
be staring down at him as though in horror with fierce little squinting
eyes above a cluster of dark gaping mouths, its familiar contours
dissolving mysteriously into the dimming confusion of the sky above.
All around him there is some kind of strange temporary scaffolding
going up like hastily whitewashed gibbets. Blood red banners,
stretched overhead, snap in the wind, a wind that tugs at the umbrellas of the few scattered early evening shoppers still abroad, stirs their
furs, and whips at the tails of their pleated duffle coats. Pigeons, dark
as rats, crawl through the trampled snow, no longer able to fly, their
feathers spread and tattered, chased by schoolboys who pelt them
with snowballs, aiming for their ducked gray heads.

"*No!*" he wheezes, struggling to rise up within his bonds. "Stop
. . . *stop* that—!"

"Ah, the mischievous little tykes," chuckles Eugenio. "Reminds
me of our own schooldays, Pini, when we used to trap the little beggars with breadcrumbs, tie their claws together, and pitch them off
the roof to watch them belly-flop below! What times we used to
have—!"

"*I never did!*" he croaks. "I *loved* pigeons! Don't *do* that, you young scamps! *Stop it, I say!*"

A boy near his litter looks up at him, grinning, his narrow eyes aglitter, his mittened fists full of snow. He drops the snow, reaches up, and pulls on the professor's nose. When it doesn't come off, he backs away, the grin fading. His eyes widen, his mouth gapes, then, shock giving way to horror, he runs off screaming.

"Ha ha! Well done, Pinocchio!" Eugenio laughs, as the boy, crying out for his mother, goes sprawling in the snow. "You haven't changed a bit!"

"Pinocchio—?" askes a feeble voice below. A dull gray eye blinks up at him from a crumpled mass half-buried in the snow. Eugenio has gone over to pick up the small boy and brush him off, giving him a number of kindly little pats and pinches. "Is that . . . Pinocchio?"

"What—? Who is it—?!" he gasps, peering into the dark blotch on the snow. "Can it be—?!"

"Did you . . . did you ever find your father . . . ?"

"Colombo! It *is* you! Yes, but that was long ago—!"

"I know, I know. At least the day before yesterday. I could still fly then . . ."

"But, dear Colombo—! How can it be you're still . . . ?"

"Alive? Don't exaggerate, my lad . . . As you see . . . But you're looking well . . ."

"Well—! I am *dying!*" he groans. "Just *look* at me!"

"Ah, I wish I could, friend, but that's gone, too, I'm afraid. Fortune's not satisfied, as they say, with a single calamity . . ."

"I know . . ."

"Can't see past my bill, or coo either, if you know what I mean, can't remember if I ever did, that's going, too, my memory, I mean, and . . . and . . . What was I saying . . . ?"

"That it was all going, your—"

"Going? No, no, I'm still . . . Ah, yes, your father! Well, at least I still have my memory! He was off in a boat somewhere . . . We stopped in a dovecote, do you remember, and feasted on bird-seed . . . !"

"I remember, green tares, I had cramps for a week after, nearly drowned—oh, but it was wonderful up there in the sky with you,

Colombo, galloping through the clouds! I've . . . I've often had dreams . . ."

"We flew all the way to Malamocco!"

"I thought . . . I thought it was farther . . ."

"It was far enough. What times those were! I can't believe I ever knew how . . ." The old pigeon, his dear strong friend of all those years ago, flutters a wing weakly, as though searching his memory with it. "What? Who's there . . . ?"

"It . . . it's me, Colombo . . ." Tears have started in the corners of his eyes again, melting the ones that had frozen there. He feels something deep down give way, popping and snapping like the banners in the wind overhead, releasing a rising turmoil of grief. He has soldiered on through so much, "carrying through" in the old way, "holding fast," and now, on the very threshold of deliverance from all his terrible trials, he fears he may not be able to keep his chin up any longer. Assuming he still has one. Eugenio has returned and seems to be poking at the bird curiously with his booted toe.

"Oh yes . . . Pinocchio. I heard you were in town. Someone . . . someone was looking for you . . ."

"For me? What—what was she wearing—?!"

"Ah, forgive me, dear boy!" exclaims Eugenio, snapping his fingers at the servants. "We must get you in out of this *abysmal* weather! Come along now!"

"Wearing? Nothing, so far as I could tell—"

"Nothing—?! But—*wait*—!" he cries as his porters pick him up again.

"No dawdling, carino mio, your risotto's already cooking, can't let it get cold!"

"Just an old fleabitten dog by the smell of him . . . But . . . who —who is that with you, Pinocchio my child? Is that—?"

"It's my old classmate Eugenio, Colombo! A true dear friend! He saved my—!"

"Ah, *bada*, Pinocchio—!" the pigeon gasps, trying to rise. "*Take care—!*"

"I've suffered so much, dear Colombo! If you only knew! And now—a real bed and doctors and—Eugenio knows everything I've ever—!"

The ancient pigeon gapes his gnarled beak as though to interrupt, but before he can manage so much as a peep, Eugenio, approaching the bird with a broad smile and full of loving kindness, steps on his head, crunching it into the stone pavement beneath the snow. The wings flop once and are still.

"What . . . what have you *done*—*?!*" the professor squeaks in alarm.

"The tedious old thing had some kind of cricket in his head, as we say—*qualche grillo per il capo*, ha ha!—and I, as it were, got rid of it for him!" chuckles Eugenio, wiping his shoe in the snow. He waddles back to the sedan chair and caressingly tucks the blankets around his old friend once more. "But, dear fellow, you're *trembling* so! It's like you're trying to shake yourself *out* of yourself—!"

"You—you've *killed* him—!"

"Now, now, let's not make an elephant out of a fly, precious boy! There are too many of these little shit-factories in Venice as it is! The commissions we get on the tourist seed stalls may be good business in the summer, but this time of year the little bandits are just a drain on the economy! So, here we go, it's off to the Palazzo dei—Pini, my love! are you there? Pini—? *Speak* to me!"

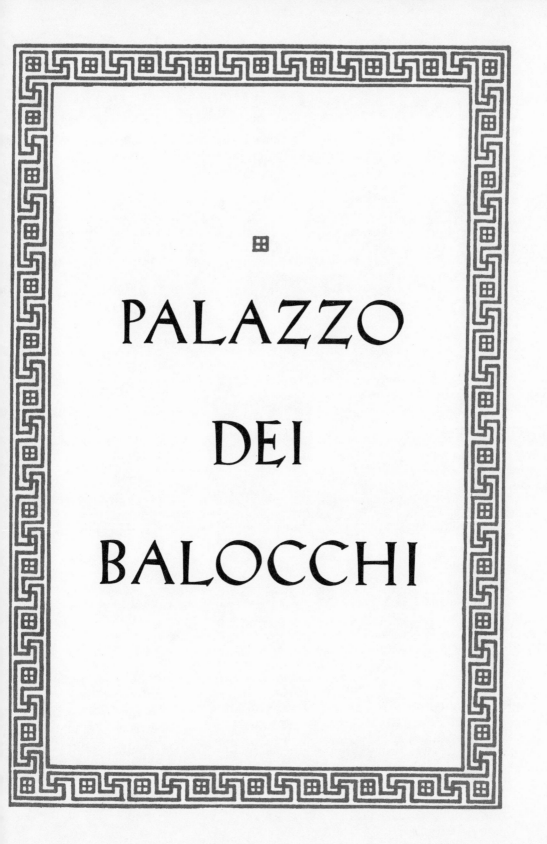

PALAZZO

DEI

BALOCCHI

17.

VIEW FROM THE
CLOCK TOWER

A cross the ruffled lead-colored waters of St. Mark's Basin, poised between crenellated Gothic fantasy and High Renaissance exuberance, Andrea Palladio's masterful church of San Giorgio Maggiore, with its sagging cheeks, carbuncular dome, and stiff cone-capped campanile at its rear (his grumbling companion has likened it to a belled cat with its tail in the air), sits gravely at anchor like an ordered thought within a confused sensuous dream, this damp dream called Venice, "the original wet dream," as his dear friend Eugenio likes to call it. The church's pale façade, caught obliquely in the winter sun's angular light and framed now between the two absurd columns of the Piazzetta like a carnival mask hung in a window, peers out past the growling, bobbing water traffic upon this shabby but bejeweled old tart of a city, the mystery of reason confronting the mystery of desire, and what it seems to be saying is: history, true, is at best a disappointment ("It is a fairy tale full of wind, master, you are right, an empty masquerade, a handful of dead flies . . ."), but it is also, in spite of itself, beautiful . . .

Not an easy idea for the old professor to accept, any more than that traditional Venetian notion of art as speech, as a discourse with time ("No, no," he is muttering now, his voice muffled by ruin and his thick woolen wraps, "that's not what I mean at all!"), a kind of ongoing dialogue between form and history, as Palladio, that Paduan Aristotelian, would have it. "Dialogue," after all, smacks of the theater and "history" of the storybook, and the professor, in his dedicated pursuit of ideal forms, has always rejected the theatrical, the narra-

tive, indeed *all* arts with concepts of time other than eternity. This
was, in his early days, his argument with Palladio, who drew echoes
of Venice's corrupt and mongrel history into his designs even as he
gently chastised the city with his intimations of a rational geometric
ideal, a compromise the professor himself, schooled in the categorical
imperatives of the Blue-Haired Fairy, was unable to make. Such an
accommodation to the moment was, he felt then, both patronizing
and delusory. Just as there were good boys and bad boys, there were,
the artistic image being the form given to thought, pure thoughts and
those contaminated by history. If art's endeavor, it being otherwise
useless, was to express man's ceaseless striving for perfection, then
history was what always went wrong.

"Yes, you have put your treacherous finger on the very sore, Excellency," snarls the old bewhiskered dark-visaged servant who, on
Eugenio's orders, has wheeled him out here onto the balcony of the
Torre dell'Orologio, muttering sourly at the time that he was "just
tying the donkey, as they say, where the master wants." The balcony
overlooks a Piazza San Marco decorously strewn this cold bright Sunday morning with the preparations for Carnival: raw yellow timbers,
metal frames and scaffolding, duckboards and bunting, all stacked
helter skelter below him amid the café tables laid out like chips in a
board game and the souvenir stands with their fluttering bouquets of
gondolier hats and the flocks of bundled-up tourists and feeding pigeons. It is a view of this glorious court, dizzying but thrilling, not
unlike the one he enjoyed a century ago, long before the Age of
Flight, when, clinging in joyous terror to the slippery pigeon feathers,
he flew on Colombo's back in search of his father. Ah, the excitement
of that flight! The freedom! He'd called Colombo his "little horse":
"Galoppa, galoppa, cavallino!" he'd cried.

"Gladly, master, but my instructions were to stay at my post while
drying you out in the sun."

"No, no, I didn't mean you! I was only recalling . . . a flight . . ."

"You wish to fly, master—?"

There is something wrong with this memory. Something out of his
recent ordeal that he does not wish to recall. Or, better said, that he
has simply forgotten, and probably a good thing, too, he needs to put
all that behind him like Eugenio says, his recovery may depend upon

it. Three café orchestras are playing all at once this morning, their whimsical cacophony interscored with the clangor of the city's multitudinous bells, the blast of recorded music, the whistling of hawkers and the honking of gulls and boats, the shouting and laughter in the square, the grinding of the clock mechanism beside him, all of it echoing and rebounding off the glittering waters of the lagoon like a single clamorous voice, which even he can hear in spite of having lost his ears, a voice which seems to insist upon the dominion of the present. Above him, the two huge bronze figures, known popularly as "Moors" because of their shiny black patina and their legendary genitalia, pivot stiffly and hammer out the morning hours, while, beneath them, under the symbolic Winged Lion of St. Mark with his stone paw on an open book and the copper Virgin and Child on their little terrace, the great revolving face of the zodiacal clock celebrates eternity with its serene turnings even as it intransigently mills away the passing moment, turning history into a kind of painting on the wall. "It is a devilish priest's game not worth the candle, a charade of charlatans, am I right?" hisses Marten the servant, keeping up his subversive *pissi-pissi* in his ear. "History! Hah! It is a veritable shit storm, master, *punto e basta!*"

"But, no, I was wrong then, you see . . ." For in time, tutored by Giorgione and by his beloved Bellini, he came to recognize that, if there were pure and impure thoughts, there were also simple and complex ones, and pure complex thought, which he was increasingly given to (he had taken on flesh, after all, he was no longer a mere stick figure), was obliged to embrace the impure world, else, blinkered, it found itself jumping, again and again, through the same narrow hoop.

"Uhm, excellent way to break a leg, padrone."

"Oh, I know, I know . . ."

"Or, heh heh, a neck . . ."

Moreover, as he himself had been a sort of walking parody of thought given form, assuming that what was in old Geppetto's pickled head was so noble a thing as to be called thought, he had been able to intuit (here, perhaps, the years in Hollywood helped) the hidden ironies in all ideal forms, and so began to perceive that thought's purity lay not so much in its forms as in its *pursuit* of those forms—whereupon: his "go with the grain" as a moral imperative, "character counts," his symbolic quest for the Azure Fleece, the concept of I-ness, "from wood to will," and all that. Already, in *Art and the Spirit*, erroneous as it might have been in its refusal to acknowledge the theatrical in Venetian art (what, he was obliged to admit, was the "emergence of archetypes from the watery atmosphere like Platonic ideas materializing in the fog of Becoming" but pure theater, after all, pure stage hokum?), he had begun, if not wholly to accept ("Ebbene, I too am interested in archetypes, condottiero . . ."), at least to understand and respect Palladio's position, and if he was once impatient, he was now more sympathetic, more prepared to make room for the human condition. Which was his condition, too . . . more or less . . .

". . . Provided the little stronzos are edible!" And Marten snatches, or seems to snatch, at a passing pigeon, throttle it, and stuff it into a bag at his side.

"Of course, it might just be my weakened eyesight . . ."

"Eh?"

Thus, from his lofty Clock Tower perch, coped and hooded in thick cashmere blankets with only his nose poking out, the old professor peers out upon this luminous spectacle and, face to face with Palladio's pale sober San Giorgio Maggiore across the sun-glazed bay, muses, his own pale and sober thoughts punctuated by the thick fluttering of pigeons and the rude interruptions ("Eh? Eh?") of Eugenio's impertinent servant, upon the folly of his youth and the debilities ("That fog, I mean . . .") of old age. Which, it would seem, contrary to his expectations of just a few nights ago, is not yet over. Like this crumbling old city, these famous "winged lion's marble piles" ("A damned nuisance, I can tell you, and no bloody cure for them either," he hears somebody grumble, might be Marten, he can't be sure) now scattered out before him in their antique devastation— pocked, ravaged, bombed, flooded, tourist-trampled, plague-ridden, pillaged, debauched, defaced, shaken by earthquake, sapped and polluted, yet somehow still stubbornly, comically afloat—he too, perversely, lingers on. Little more than, perhaps, but if by some misfortune he is not yet dead, as one of his doctors so wisely put it that night of Eugenio's rescue, then it's a sure sign he's still alive.

He had awakened, having apparently passed out in the Piazza, a Piazza he could not however at that moment recall (even now that bitter night with its monstrous snow-frosted shapes looming over him in the swirling wind like howling ghosts is little more than a half-remembered nightmare, in no way resembling the cheerful scene spread out before him now), in a soft warm bed piled high with down comforters, a hot water bottle at his feet, and three doctors at all his other parts, probing and prodding with various tools of their trade and debating the particulars of his imminent demise.

"It is my professional opinion," said one solemnly, flicking the old pilgrim's tender nose back and forth as though testing its reflexes, "that he is dying from top to bottom, or else from bottom to top, though one could conceivably hold the position that death was rapidly overtaking him, both inside and out."

"I quite disagree!" exclaimed a second, lifting a foot by a toe that snapped off like a dry twig. "You see? His condition is clearly as desparate at one end as at the other, even *if* the surface is as moribund as the core!"

"Gentlemen! Please!" protested Eugenio, who, for a confused moment, the dying scholar mistook for his old friend and benefactor Walt Disney with his apple red cheeks and pussycat voice and sweet soft ways, oily as whipped butter. "Is there no hope?"

"Well," sighed the first, pressing a stethoscope to the place where an ear used to be and rapping the professor's feverish brow speculatively, "if he is not dead by midnight, he may live until tomorrow."

"How can you say that?" cried the second, sticking a thermometer in his peehole, and glaring angrily at his watch. "He will certainly *not* live until tomorrow, if he is dead by midnight!"

"And have you nothing to say, sir?" Eugenio asked, turning to the third doctor.

"This face is not new to me!" that personage responded, pointing at the place where others might have a navel and he but a knothole. "I know him for a perfidious rogue and a shameless ideomaniac, buono a nulla, this faithless figlio di N.N., this good-for-nothing whoreson legno da catasta! Fortunately, all knots come to the comb, and to the lancet as well, this one no exception, so out with it, I say! Gentlemen, hand me my brace and bit!"

"Wait!" cried the first doctor suddenly, drawing back. "Could it be —not being otherwise, that is—the *plague?*"

"It *might* be," gasped the second, wiping his hands nervously on his trousers, "but then again, if it isn't, it's assuredly not!"

"Oh woe, *woe*, *WOE!*" exclaimed the third doctor, beating his chest and gazing upon the patient in horror. Certainly he could not have been a pretty sight, his hide foxed and tattered and falling away, bits and pieces of him missing altogether, his miserable water-soaked body wracked by fever and a rasping cough—as Eugenio remarked wryly, when first seeing his eyelids flutter: "Behold, gentlemen, there is the man who has been in Hell!" In truth, in his condition the plague might have been a mercy. "As one who has had it hammered into him by bitter experience," the third doctor continued, clubbing his own pate with a balled fist, "let me assure you that neither earth, nor air, nor water, nor flesh itself is a safe refuge for wicked little philo-sophasters under the lignilingual curse!"

"You mean . . . ?" Eugenio moaned, a pudgy hand clasped mourn-fully to his soft breast.

"Lamentably, sir, he is, as we say here," replied the first doctor, stepping forward, "truly between bed and cot! His hours are counted! He will soon be, morto e sepolto, making soil for the beans! That is to say—"

"On the contrary," interrupted the second, crowding in front of the first, "he is rather, sir, as the saying goes, more on the other than on this side! È bell'e spacciato! Dead and done for! Furthermore—"

"Ah!" screamed the third, bounding about the room and banging his head vehemently on the walls. "But what's the moral? *What's the MORAL?*"

"Exactly!" exclaimed the first.

"For once I agree with my esteemed colleague!" put in the second.

"Ohi, povero diavolo!" sobbed Eugenio, rubbing his eyes with his rolled fists. "He is my dearest sweetest friend! Surely there is some remedy—?!"

"Alas, I am afraid he is a tragic and more or less fatal victim of dermatological cytoclasis," sighed the first, stroking his beard, "for which no known cure has yet been found!"

"I am sorry to have to disagree once again with my distinguished colleague," argued the second, clutching his lapels firmly, "but the patient has clearly contracted a somewhat lethal dose of cytolysis of the epidermis, the cure for which remains, regrettably, a scientific mystery!"

"Idiots!" snapped the third, suddenly standing tall and composed beside the bed, staring severely down at—or into—the ancient traveler as though penetrating to the very core of his ignominy. "Can't you see? It is as plain as the face on his nose! This shameless ragazzaccio *is turning back to wood again!* Look at him! The little scoundrel is suffering from lignivorous invasions of all kinds, evil eruptions of xylostroma, probable sclerosis of the resin canals, peduncular collapse, weevil infestation, and galloping wet rot. He's starting to warp, too, disgustingly enough, and that offensive musty stench is unmistakable evidence that he's rotten to the very *pith!*"

"I resent your calling my colleague an idiot," complained the first doctor huffily.

"No, no," blustered the second, "it is *I* who resent your unwarranted abuse of *my* colleague!"

"But, gentlemen, gentlemen," pleaded Eugenio, "what can we *do?*"

"Very little," sighed the first doctor, and the second said: "Not much."

"The treatment is quite simple," responded the third doctor grimly. "The rot should be chopped out and burnt immediately, the remaining structures, if any, drilled and impregnated with fungicides and insecticides, using sprays or double-vacuum techniques to assure the deepest possible penetration, followed by total immersion of the subject in organic solvent–based preservatives for at least a week."

"Hmm, yes, I can see that," the first doctor conceded grudgingly, "but it's a stopgap measure at best."

"I am afraid my illustrious colleague is in error there," contended the second. "Such a treatment may be of temporary help, but only for a short time."

"Thereafter," concluded the third, "I recommend a restringing of all the joints, a thorough rubdown with fine sandpaper or steel wool, and finally repeated applications of linseed oil or else a few coats of yacht varnish!" Wherewith, he opened up his black bag and clapped it over his head, mashed his hat under his arm, and stalked blindly out, sending things rattling and crashing in the next room, his two colleagues following him in somber parade, quarreling about vocational dignity.

"This would be a most honorable profession," grumbled one, "if it were not for the wretched patients!"

"No, no, I must insist," objected the other, "it is precisely the patients who most dishonor this noble profession!"

During the days that have followed, as he slipped in and out of his feverish dreams, all too haunted by dark reminders of his recent folly, he has been lovingly cared for by Eugenio and his staff of servants and advisors and nurses in his private suite in the magnificent Palazzo dei Balocchi, which, as he came slowly to realize, looks out, here just below where he sits now, upon the Piazza itself. He has slept upon satin sheets, drunk his medicine from golden goblets, been fed Venetian liver and onions and bigoi in salsa and golden polenta and risi e bisi and other curative delicacies from a jewel-encrusted silver tea tray, said to have been part of the plunder from the sacking of Byzantium—along with the four bronze horses rearing up over the door of the Basilica of St. Mark just in front of him now—by the Blind Doge in the Fourth Crusade, and has attended to his daily needs, minimal as they now are, upon a fur-lined bedpan made of the finest azure blue Murano glass, hand-blown to his exact dimensions. Not only has he enjoyed the comfort of a hot water bottle, it is amazingly like the very one he had taken to bed with him each night since he first left for America, until it was lost to thieves that fateful night of his arrival here. Nothing perhaps has made him feel more at home.

"When you described it in your delirium, Pini," Eugenio told him, "it reminded me of one I had had as a child. It took a lot of hunting, but I finally found it!"

Ah, the great Eugenio! Very dear and very deep! Soon, after Sunday Mass, he will join him here on the Clock Tower solarium, and they will talk about the city and about the old times when they were schoolboys together and about the professor's illustrious career. Eugenio has promised to have him ported about the island to see once more before he dies all the masterpieces he most loves and has written about (his entire bibliography seems to be at his great admirer's command)—and may write about yet again, for Eugenio has also promised to replace in some manner his stolen computer, perhaps even with a similar model, a feat not beyond his resourceful friend's capacities. Already he has found for him some foot snuggies with the identical pattern of his old ones, a half bottle of his personal French Canadian brand of pine-scented mouthwash, and a pair of spectacles that fit him better than the ones he lost. So much Eugenio has done for him, dedicating to him from the moment of their fortuitous re-union all the treasures of his vast wealth and experience and attending to his every need, not least of all his daily oil treatments, applied personally by his own soothing plump hands, treatments which seem to have helped wonderfully, for if his condition is no less critical, the pain has lessened and the stiffness eased.

"Probably the belladonna," growls old Marten behind his ear, fuss-ing with the blankets.

"No, I wasn't even thinking about her," sighs the professor, though of course he was. He has been thinking of little else. As his life has ebbed, she has seemed to draw nearer, becoming once more the sub-text, as it were, of all his thoughts, rational or otherwise. Even these musings on Palladio and Venice, eternity and history, purity and its pursuit have really been little more, he knows, than coded medita-tions on that guiding spirit of all his years, at least the fruitful and noble ones. She was, after all, his first healer, just a child then like himself with her waxen face and strange blue hair and cold but nimble fingers. She dressed and undressed him like a doll, called him her little brother, poured bitter medicine down his throat and laughed to see his little faucet work. Sister, mother, ghost or goat, he loved her madly and, dying, he loves her still.

"Coast or float, Excellency? In the strange blue air? Still thinking about flying, eh? Ebbene! Detto fatto! Your least wish, padroncino: my urgent command! For as il direttore so graphically put it to me: 'Let his every twig, Marten my man, become a branch!' "

"What—?!" He realizes he has been pushed perilously close to the edge of the balcony and that his chair is beginning to tip forward. "What are you doing—?!"

"You pontificate very learnedly upon our exotic but delusive city, signor canino canarino, but perhaps you have missed some of the detail. I would like you to become more intimately acquainted with it! *Faccia a faccia*, as one might say!"

"Canino? Canarino—?! Stop! Don't you know who I am?"

"But of course, my devious little watchdog with the long nose, mister mock-Melampo, I know you well! For it has not been forgotten within our humble clan how, by your infamous theatrics, you did the shoes to our dear old nonno, betraying poor granddad and all his kinfolk to that ruthless henhouse tyrant, who not only had the entire brotherhood summarily executed, but had their earthly remains served up at the local inn disguised as stewed rabbit, a cruel and contemptible final indignity. '*Bù-bù-bù!*'—do you remember, my little barked barker? No wonder you are so fascinated by duplicity!"

"But wait—!"

"Wait? As my own elders, then so innocent, waited through that calamitous night? 'We stayed up till dawn for the old fellow and the great chicken festicciole he so loved to provide,' my grieving babbo used to say, tearfully recalling that tragic event which left him forever orphaned, 'but our beloved papà did not come home that night, or— *sob!*—any night thereafter!' It was a wrong bound to his finger, as is said, and so bound to mine in turn, and now at last it is time to give back bread for pie! You have sung like a canary, now let us see if you can fly like one as well . . . !"

"But it's not so simple as that—!" he protests, slipping forward in his seat ("Oh oh," rumbles a familiar voice nearby, "looks like another Palazzo dei Balocchi credit card's run out!"), as that enchanted square below, that fabulous open-air drawing room, that landing place that takes the breath away tips toward him now to take his own. Cocooned in cashmere, he cannot even move his arms, would it do him any good if he could. "What about the *chickens*—?!"

"Better strike the dinner hour, lads!"

"The chickens, master?"

"Yes, don't you see—?!" he cries, as above him the Moors suddenly hammer the great bronze bell and great flocks of pigeons lift off the Piazza below and rise with a vast fluttering communal roar like a black cloud of gathering mourners, beating their wings into the air, swirling before him down there like the great chain of being itself. "What *is* a good boy? What is *good?!* Can one love the eaten and the eaters too—?! Where is it all to *end*—?!"

"For you, Excellency, this curious philosophical enigma is, as they say, purely epidemic," snickers the servant wheezily, as this son of Italy, lost, found, lost again, slides out, untethered, into space, "for you are, heh heh, being sent on holiday! Bon voyage, master! Galoppa, galoppa, and watch out below! *Tim-BER*—!!"

18.

THE MIRACLE OF THE MIS-STRUCK HOUR

"If you think *this* is glorious, you should see it in the season of *acque alte*, Pini, when the sky blackens and the wind howls and the great foaming tides roll in," Eugenio rumbles wheezily in his ancient guest's earhole as they sit huddled together at his bedroom window in the palazzo, gazing out upon a more placid flooding, the celebrated lightness of the Piazza made doubly so this bright morning by its own crisp doubling in the square's limpid pool, this city of endless illusions seeming now to float in its symmetric fullness upon the reflected sky below. "Un tal pandemonio, as we used to say, un tal passeraio, un tal baccano indiavolato, you'd think, sitting here, you were in a ship on a boiling ocean! Waves crash against the columns and resound in the arcades below us, as if to loosen the palace from its very moorings and send us out to sea, the sunken street lamps standing then like rows of lilac-tinted channel markers out there showing us the way! Wastebins bob in the Piazza like buoys, inverted umbrellas tumble past like broken-winged birds, toothy predatory gondolas dart through the very porches of the Golden Basilica squatting helplessly in its stormy bath, and those red banners up there flap in the wind as though they might be wild wet sails, urging us upon our fatal course, as the entire trembling city seems suddenly intent on plunging downward to a watery doom!" Eugenio rakes up an emphysematous sigh from the depths of his sunken breast, no less ancient than the professor's, and, leaning back, exclaims: "Ah, Pini, Pini! This incomparable city, this most beautiful queen, this untainted virgin, as a celebrated whoremaster once said of her in his postcoital delirium, this paradise, this temple, this rich diadem and the most flourishing garland of Christendom—*I do love her so!"*

Although misfortune, most recently his being pitched from on high toward the stonier realities of this fantastic square, such mischief thwarted only by a spectacular rescue, which is already being referred to, he understands, at least here in the palazzo, as "the Miracle of the Mis-struck Hour," has conditioned the old scholar to see more of peril and duplicity in this mirrored doubling than any alleged paradisiacal beauty, he cannot entirely resist its shimmering appeal. Between his window and the Procuratie Nuove across the way, their stately arches now stretched in the reduplicating floodwaters to slender O's, the skeletal half-built Carnival platforms and the stacked scaffolding and ladders and barrier fences rise out of their own pooled reflections like the scuttled wrecks of ancient ships, disturbing the more timeless illusions, and they seem in their gentle mockery to be counseling him to accept his peculiar fate, which could be worse, after all, if not much, and let all the accumulated bitterness and suspicion of these past days, so alien in truth to his deepest nature, be dissolved once and for all into the pleasant watery vision before him.

His dear friend Eugenio, now gently oiling his creaking nape, has more openly urged this, extending to him all the amenities of his vast estates, and, in return, asking only that he surrender to the great love he offers him and to the pleasures which that love and his Palazzo dei Balocchi can provide. He has protested—"No, no, and no again!"— at each of Eugenio's many generous gifts, but in the end, having little choice, he has accepted them all, and often as not with tears in his eyes; that he should have come to this and that, in such adversity, he should find so great and true a friend! Moreover, the situation is only temporary. With Eugenio's help, he has written off to America for new credit cards and checkbooks, bank and royalty and retirement fund statements, and all his professional credentials, insisting that, even should he decide to remain a guest of the palazzo, he would wish to pay his own way, Eugenio smiling at that and observing that he always did suffer, even as a puppet, from an excess of woodenheaded pride. Meanwhile, at Eugenio's wise suggestion, he has signed his stolen cards over to the charitable institution of which his friend is presently director, Omino e figli, S.R.L., which will assume full responsibility for any misuse of them by the thieves, and which will have the power, under the labyrinthine Italian law, to prosecute them if apprehended. Eugenio has submitted all the requisite papers for a new passport and local visa, has bought him two new silk suits and a handsome woolen Tyrolean duffle coat with a felt borsalino to match, as well as a pair of green knee-high rubber boots to splash about in, has provided him with liniments, medicines, toiletries, and even a wonderful old-fashioned cotton sleeping cap, and has replaced the cracked waterlogged shoes he came here in with three new pairs, custom made from the softest hand-tooled Venetian leather, remarking as he threw out the old ones that they reminded him of those strange stiff shoes made out of tree bark that he used to wear to school.

"Devilish weapons, Pini my boy, especially for one with so free a kick as yours! Once—I *swear!*—I saw your leg whip clear around like a windmill, popping one boy on the chin on the way up, flattening another behind on the way down with a blow to the top of his head, and, still swinging on around, catching yet a third, trying to flee, right on his little culetto, delivering him such a stroke that it lifted the poor birichino five feet off the ground, as if he too were on strings!"

"But I was never on—!"

"No, it's *true*, my love! You can't deny it, I was *there!* How we feared—and coveted!—those bark-shod feet of yours! So *stylish*, too! And whatever happened to that *amazing* little breadcrumb cap you used to wear?"

"I don't remember. I think a dog ate it."

Sitting here today at his bedroom window, here in this ark of his own personal deluge, as he thinks of it, they have been reminiscing about those old school days together, about how they met and abused each other, and about all the wicked things they did, and with what consequences, and perhaps it is the seductive apparition of these reflected fantasies out in the flooded Piazza San Marco, or his old friend's soothing hands upon the back of his skull, or merely the miracle of his continuing survival, but the shame and disgust such recollections ordinarily arouse are today subversively commingled with nostalgia, disturbingly sweet. Eugenio has reminded him, for example, of the day he and the other boys cornered him in the school latrine and ripped off his wallpaper pants to see the little brass tap which Geppetto had plugged there between his wooden legs and which was, as Eugenio admitted, the envy of them all, despite their cruel taunts ("Your golden draincock, we called it!"), and what has come back to him most vividly from all that was not the humiliation he suffered but the comfortingly familiar pungency of those primitive open-air urinals and the warm sunlight that fell upon their innocent schoolboy curiosity. Just as Eugenio's account of that day at the beach when a math book thrown at him had missed and struck Eugenio instead, resulting in his arrest for murder (Eugenio had not been hurt at all, he confessed, he'd just been pretending, and when the two black-cloaked carabinieri had dragged Pinocchio away between them, Eugenio had sat up and thumbed his nose at them, laughing openly at his friend's distress: "That was very naughty of me, I know, dear Pini, but, eh, what can I say, io sono fatto così!"), has recalled for him not the terror of capture nor even the adventure of his famous escape—from the fire into the frying pan, as it turned out—but the delicious lure the sea had for him in those days and the way his disobedient truancy excited him and made his nose tingle.

"We were merely, after all, as one of our naughtiest boys here once said," murmurs Eugenio, his subtle caressing voice like that of a mewling cat rubbing at his ear, " 'cheerful creatures, whose most sinful deeds / Were but the overbeating of the heart . . .' "

"Nonsense! We were lazy unruly ragamuffins, seduced into brutishness by our own profligacy, wretched little asses bought and sold . . ."

"Well, as the Little Man himself used to say to me at the livestock auctions over there in the courtyard of the Convertite, whilst squeezing my bum affectionately: 'The world, Eugenio my precious little arsewipe, is half to be sold, half to be loaned out, and *all* to be laughed at!' "

"So it's true then, as I've heard," the old scholar sighs, "you too went to Toyland!"

"I never *left* it, dear boy!"

"Hrmff. I would have thought when you got hit by that math book, it might have knocked some sense into you."

"That it *did*, amor mio! That it *did!*" laughs Eugenio tenderly, pulling on the servants' bell rope. "I vowed never to get close enough to a book to get hit by one of the nasty things again! And you were, you must remember, then as now, our leader, our moral guide, our great exemplar of insubordination and mad adventure, whither thou went we could but follow! And so we did, dear Pini, each and every boy! And laughing all the way! You would have been proud of us!"

The old professor snorts ruefully at this perversion of what he has called in *The Wretch* and elsewhere his "long-eared mission" to "cast out, cast as, the outcast," an unhappy fate all great ideas and actions seem to suffer in this heedless world—but somewhere behind this rueful musing, in fact more or less at that spot just behind his ear which Eugenio's plump warm hand is oiling just now, or perhaps a bit lower, deeper, closer to the core, he is experiencing an acute longing for the strange exhilaration of that eery nighttime ride on the back of the weeping donkey with the bitten ears, his best friend Lampwick snoring like a bear in the cart behind him, the donkeys clopping down the dark road in their fancy white leather boots, the cart following mysteriously on its padded wheels like a sleigh on snow. They'd arrived at dawn, harness bells jingling and L'Omino blowing his coach horn like an exultant little bantam, at what, to a child's eyes, was paradise itself, so beautiful that it seemed rather celestial than of this world . . .

"Sports, cycling, acting, singing, reading, gymnastics—today we'd probably call it a kindergarten," chuckles Eugenio, giving another pull on the bell rope. "They even had us out there on the riva practicing soldiering! Ha ha! But how we loved it, eh? Gullible little gonzos that we were! Even our naughty graffiti was like an art class in finger painting, not so lasting a form perhaps as that of a Titian or a Tiepolo, but there's still a bit of it around, you know."

"I think I've seen some . . ."

"You asked us to a party, a kind of birthday party, you said, but when we turned up you weren't there! You'd gone prancing off, as I recall, with that dreadful boy Romeo—what did we call him—?"

"Lampwick. You remember him—?"

"Of *course* I do! Skinny and warped as that cue stick of his, very butch, with buttocks hard and red as a pair of billiard balls and a face like a knuckled fist, who could *forget* the vicious little mangiapane?! So, tell me, whatever happened to the dear boy?"

"He's . . . he's dead," gasps the old scholar, feeling afresh the loss and weeping now as he wept then. "He died as a . . . as a donkey. But—but why are you laughing—?! It was *terrible—!*"

"I'm—whoo! hee!—sorry, my love, I'm sure it was, I, ah, missed all that, you see. But you *must* tell me what it was like—I mean, all those parts just *engorging* like that, stretching and filling so suddenly all by themselves, it must have been quite *extraordinary!*"

"It hurt."

"Oh, yes, I know what you mean! Ha ha! I did try one once, a lovely little salt-and-pepper thing we'd once called Lucio. The pain was . . . *exquisite!* Hoo, dear! If they hadn't shot him, I'd have *died!* Now where *are* those wretched servants?" he complains, jerking impatiently on the bell rope. "I *do* miss dear old Marten, you know, it's been absolutely *impossible* around this place since you made me dismiss him, Pini!" He rises, wiping his hands on a velvet cloth. "It's well past time for your morning infusione and my corretto, dear boy, so you'll have to excuse me. It seems I must take care of it myself! But when I come back, I want to hear all about the donkey life!"

Ah well, the donkey life. Poor Lampwick summed it up in the last few words he spoke, lying there in the farmer's stinking straw, dying of hunger and overwork: "I am . . . not . . . who I am . . . Those shits . . . have stolen my life . . . !" Early in his career, in a monograph entitled "Reply to an Errant Friend on his Deathbed," modeled on the *Epistolae* of Cicero and Petrarch and later reprinted as an appendix to the fifth edition of *The Wretch*, he chided Lampwick for blaming thieves for his own easy charity. "No one can steal what is only yours to give. Spiritual penury with its attendant despair is a willed choice, dear Lampwick, like any other. If a man were to lose his watch to pickpockets and then recover it, would he ever put himself at their mercy again unless he willed to do so? As Saint Augustine reminds his disciple in Petrarch's *Secretum*, 'The deceived is never separate from the deceiver.' " Perhaps he'd shown too little respect for outright villainy, as some argued, or too little awareness of what those of a popular heresy of the day called "the conditioning power of social forces," but he saw these objections as little more than sophistical dodges, using the seemingly objective otherness of "history," a mere illusion of language, after all, to deny or undermine the individual will and its responsibilities, a package he came to call "I-ness," the uncompromising defense of which has brought him where he is today. Or was a week or so ago, anyway . . .

How differently their lives have turned out, his and Lampwick's! Of course it helped that he got sold to the circus instead of to some pig of a farmer to be starved and beaten and worked to death. Clearly, the Blue-Haired Fairy had been watching over him, even in his donkey days. That she had a box seat for his debut as the "Star of the Dance," for example, could not have been an accident. He was so startled to see her there, dressed in mourning garments and flashing her medallion with its portrait of a defunct puppet at him, that, jumping through the hoop, he fell and lamed himself, thus bringing on, as though spelled, his own execution, but maybe that too was a part of her pedagogy, his fall a mark of promised grace, her medallion not so much an omen as a vivid image for a little beast who'd not yet learned his letters to let him know that much in him still had to die before he could be hers again. Or so he learned to read those awesome trials in retrospect. His "Golden Ass" theory of redemption, as some have called it, and with reason, for there was much in Lucius Apuleius' youthful asininity, his buffetings and sorrows, and his eventual transformational rebirth (though he merely ate and was not eaten) into lifelong devotion to his protectress' sacred service, that paralleled the professor's own strange formation and contemplative career, and took him far from Lampwick.

Whom, however, for all his waywardness, he has never ceased to mourn, for a friend, as Cicero said, is like a second self ("True, true," murmurs Eugenio, at his side once more and holding the cup of hot medicinal tea at his guests's cracked lips, "and *old* friends, dear Pini —like old wood, old casks, old authors—are always best, especially when they are—ha ha!—all one and the same!"), and moreover, in Lampwick's case, as he explained in his great prose epic, *The Transformation of the Beast*, a *sacrificial* second self whose death prepared the way for his own salvation: Lampwick, dying, was lying, so to speak, on the last straw, put there in his emblematic extremity, he came to feel, by the Fairy herself. As the light went out in Lampwick's eyes, the light came on in his puppet head, and he became forever after the very model of entrepreneurial industry and scholarly ambition, winning thereby the Fairy's ultimate blessing. "Despise not this lowly ass," he wrote affectionately, many years later, "though he be in

appearance the most hateful beast in the universe, for, as William of
Occam observed long ago, God could have chosen to embody himself
in a donkey as well as in a man, and who is to say that he did not?"

"Ho ho! God in a donkey suit! I *love* it, Pini!" chortles Eugenio,
crossing himself hastily, then squeezing the old scholar's knee.
"Rather *changes* the holy manger scene, doesn't it, and makes one
wonder just *what* the Holy Family had been *up* to, eh? But to answer
your question, my boy, there's the testimony of our own precious
Saint Mark, for one," he adds, gesturing with a sweep of his hand at
the saint's great water-masked square before them.

"Who has no manger scene, honors the ass, and ends his evangel
with the terror of his witnesses," replies the professor, sipping at the
hot *infusione* held at his lips.

"Ah, is that so! Well, of course, I've never read it . . ."

The floodwaters in the Piazza are receding. A slate-gray line now
cuts like a smudge through the reflected arches of the Procuratie
Nuove, a kind of dry spine down the middle of the porous Piazza,
higher than the rest, and there the pigeons and tourists gather as
though on a crowded strip of beach, feeding each others' appetites, a
scene he gazes upon this morning with a certain affection, for only
yesterday those pigeons in their appetitive innocence saved his life.
Pinioned in blankets and tipped out like a seedpod into space by the
vindictive Marten, he could only, with that "horror of heart" said by
Ruskin to have been this city's original creative principle, gaze helplessly down upon the pale blank countenance of stony Death, rushing
upwards, when least expected, to kiss him cruelly face to face. Even
as he began to plummet, however, Death's face was all at once darkly
scrawled, as though moustachioed by a mischievous boy, as a massive
swarm of pigeons rose up, roaring round like a sudden black tornado,
alarmed, it seemed, by the striking of the great bronze bell above his
head: twice, though it was not yet noon. He'd heard the Moors' two
reverberant strokes as a personal knell, signaling, as did the Maleficio
of the Campanile in the old days, his imminent execution, not knowing what the pigeons knew: that it was in truth a dinner bell, the city
having traditionally fed its feathered mendicants, at public expense
and for generations beyond number, each day precisely at nine and
two, occasions that called for, in this ceremonial city, a ceremonial
ascent, orbit, and processional descent to table. He fell, light as a

cocooned moth, upon their arched backs and, bounced from one to another by their beating wings as though being blanketed, was lofted to within reach of the jaws of the stone Lion of Saint Mark on the clock tower—or perhaps the great creature, screened by the pigeons, left his pedestal and joined the flight, it was hard to say, certainly there was an awesome flopping about overhead, as though a helicopter might be hovering, and afterwards the old fellow, though poised as before with his paw on the book when next he looked, recognizing him now as the very beast that had pursued him through the snow his first night here in Venice, his nose flattened as though from hitting too many bell towers, did seem desperately winded, snorting and blowing like a beached walrus—and from the Lion's jaws, he was flung back into his wheelchair, or dropped there, much to his relief, having been, on top of his terror, nearly asphyxiated, just as Eugenio arrived, beaming sunnily, from Sunday Mass.

"Well, well!" he exclaimed with his jolly pink-cheeked smile, his slicked-back hair gleaming on his round head like a shiny plastic cap. "You're looking much better, my friend! So wide awake! The fresh air seems to have done you good!"

"I-I was thrown . . . out into the middle . . . the *middle* of it!" he squeaked clumsily, still dizzy from the vertigo of the fall, the pigeons' tossing, and the Lion's blindingly foul breath.

"In the middle? In the middle of *what*, dear boy?"

"I'm afraid, eh, the old fellow was actually asleep the whole time, direttore," growled Marten sotto voce. "He seemed to be having nightmares, so finally I woke him. You can see he's still confused—"

"No! There . . . I was out *there* . . ." he gasped, pointing, his arms bound, with his nose.

"What? You mean, in midair—?"

"He speaks metaphorically, padroncino," chuckled the servant with a conspiratorial wink, trying to bundle the blankets around his mouth. "As Checco Petrarca from up the street once said, some of us scrape parchments, write books, correct them, illuminate and bind them, adorn their surface; superior minds look higher and fly above these mean occupations . . ."

"Ah! Quite so! Well said, Marten!"

"No!" he cried, gagged on cashmere, tears stinging his eyes. "He —*choke!*—*threw* me out there—!"

"Ah! See how he trembles, master. He may have a dangerous fever—!"

"He-he tried to *kill* me!"

"Who tried to kill you, dear boy?"

"This-this-this-that—!"

"He lies, direttore."

"Lies? My friend Pinocchio?" Eugenio exclaimed, arching his tufted brows and peering closer with his little eyes. "There, my good man, I think you may have overstepped yourself."

"The . . . the Lion—!" he managed to gasp, "—saved me!"

"Just protecting the citizens below," the Lion rumbled grumpily from his pedestal, still puffing and wheezing. "We Venetians welcome strangers with open arms, but not at thirty-two feet per second per fucking second."

"Aha. So that explains the mischief of the bells . . ."

"Don't mind your drowning these wormy old dog-cocks out behind the Arsenale," the Lion went on, "no one gets hurt that way, but dumping the turds in my Piazza is going to get *some* fat little sporcaccione *stepped* on!"

"Now you see the trouble you've caused, Marten? The next time this happens, I am going to have to discipline you most severely—!"

"The *next* time—!" squawked the professor in disbelief, his blood rising, or his sap, whatever: "The next time I'll be *dead!*" Then, before he could stop himself, he blew up into a wild unseemly temper, screaming indignantly about "assassins and murderers" and "depraved prevaricators," castigating the entire city of Venice and all of its duplicitous and tyrannical history, accusing the grizzled old servant of everything from imposture, insurrection, and criminal neglect to pigeon poaching and senicide, even raging about Palladio and the cruelty of the climate and the Lion's halitosis, he'd never so lost control of himself since they'd tried to curb his franking privileges back at the university. It was shameful, really, a throwback to the ill-mannered tantrums of his days as a woodenhead, but effective. Though Eugenio was clearly reluctant to let his longtime servant go ("He doesn't steal *from* me, Pini, he steals *for* me—!"), two policemen finally appeared on the balcony and, at a snap of Eugenio's fingers, hauled Marten away between them. "All right, Pini, calm down, you've had your way," sighed Eugenio wearily when they were gone. "I hope you realize only a true friend would render such a great service! For you, of course, Old Sticks, it was a pleasure, but," he added, leaning toward him with a sly forgiving wink, "just don't eat rabbit in Venice for a while . . ."

Now, his grappa-laced espresso finished, his great friend and benefactor snores contentedly at his side. There are traces of rouge in his ancient cheeks and a dusting of powder around his eyes, a tender vanity. His thin slicked black hair catches light from the Piazza almost as a mirror might, hard and glittering. Out there, the dry spine in the middle has become a broad isthmus, once more populated by the familiar crowds of clicking and posing tourists, many of them already in Carnival masks and costumes. There are devils out there and royal couples, wild beasts and butterflies and ghostly spectres. The Caffè Quadri below him and Florian's across the way are setting out their tables again, and the orchestras are tuning up. At the edge of the receding waters and reflected in them, a camera, seemingly without an owner, stands on its tripod, the colorful film-advertising cloth thrown over it hanging silently in the bright still day, as if in its spindly solitude to speak to his condition or else perhaps to mock it. An illusion, of course. Nothing is being said. Not far away, a Harlequin approaches, hobbling on a cane, so fat his hairy behind sticks out from the rear of the costume, and accompanying him is a squat bent-backed Columbine with a moth-eaten tail who entertains the crowd by walking into stacked platforms and falling over café tables. Sooner or later, they will hit the camera and knock it down, he knows, and that, too, will have a certain meaning, and at the same time, none at all.

In that fractional moment, somewhere between the first stroke of the bell and the second, when, tossed from his chair, he hovered up there in the icy air as though afloat, the Piazza below appeared to him as an open book, a book he'd read a thousand times before, or perhaps a thousand books he'd read before compressed to one, its text dizzyingly complex yet awesomely simple, readable at a glance, yet somehow illegible, and it recalled to him his first terrifying encounter, when still a puppet, with his *abbiccì*, which (the Fairy said) promised him the world and more but gave him (under "N" of course, and this was the page he'd come to once again) *niente*. Nothing. And this, he thinks, slipping peacefully into a nap of his own, snug in his silk pajamas and monogrammed velvet robe, was the Miracle of the Mis-struck Hour: the pigeons rose and turned the page.

19.

AT L'OMINO'S TOMB

"It's . . . it's a long story," he replies hesitantly.

"What do you say?" Eugenio calls out over the start-up roar of the motor, as they lower him into the launch.

"He says it's quite *long!*" shouts Francatrippa.

"Aha! And I suppose, Pini, it gets *longer* the more it goes on . . ."

"I'd say it *stands* to get *harder* the more it goes on, direttore!" laughs Buffetto.

"No, no, the more it goes on, direttore," pipes up Truffaldino in his squeaky voice, hopping aboard, "the more it *grows* on you! The more the tension *rises* and the plot *thickens!*"

"Ha ha! Very good, my child!" laughs Eugenio, holding on to the wheel with one hand as they pull away from the island and out into the lagoon, reaching behind him for Truffaldino's backside with the other.

"But even when he *stretches* the *truth*, direttore," adds Truffaldino, backing down into the cabin and holding out his fist in a sailor's cap for Eugenio to pinch, "his moral is always *rigidly upstanding!*"

"He gives it to you *straight*, direttore!"

"*With a hard snout!*"

"*Right in your ear!*"

"But *tell* me, dear boy, please do," Eugenio has just pleaded, the immediate cause of all the raillery, "tell me the tale of your *nose*," the professor himself having just previously remarked in a rare moment of candor, touching upon that subject which has always remained, though unhideable, hidden: "It was as obvious, you could say, as the nose on your face. I was probably the last person in the world to figure it out, slow learner that I am—I mean, I was fifty-seven years old before I suddenly realized other people had nostrils!" Not true, though, that he's a slow learner. No, he's more like a fast learner and a fast forgetter . . .

It has been a day for candor, spent upon the moody emptiness of the wintry lagoon, touring Eugenio's varied enterprises, and lastly upon San Michele, the Island of the Dead, where Eugenio has taken him to visit the mausoleum of the Little Man and to lay fresh flowers there. "I've something special to show you, Pini," he'd said, and so he had, and there in that somber place, surrounded by vast gardens of graves and walls of stacked tombs like immense stone filing cabinets, there before an image that brought tears to his eyes, Eugenio has opened his heart to his old friend, telling him all about his long active life on these islands, his relationship with L'Omino, the Little Man, and his own boyhood experiences in Toyland. Which were different from his.

Before that, a day that began cheerfully enough, with Eugenio, in an ebullient mood quite out of keeping with the dour misty weather, or perhaps in resistance to it, offering to take him on a tour of his many civic projects, an offer inspired in part by his heated telephone negotiations before lunch with the government of Czechoslovakia, Eugenio seeking to recover the bones of Venetian native son Giacomo Casanova in time for reburial next week during the climax of Carnival, which was already well under way in the Piazza outside his windows. "If I don't get those bones for our Gran Gala, Eccellenza, siamo *fottuti!*" he'd shrieked wildly, slamming the phone down when he got disconnected, but then as quickly, spying the alarm on the professor's face, he'd broken into a warm ruddy smile and added: "Ah, but why make it a cause for war, eh? Where you cannot climb over, as the Little Man himself used to say, you must crawl under, there are other fish to skin, after all, other cats to fry—if we cannot retrieve that sinner's wormy remains, we might still have time, per esempio, to wrest dear Santa Lucia's eyes from the Sicilians to go with the rest of her we have here, steal them if we have to, pop them in place perhaps at the very moment of the midnight unmasking! Why not? Indeed, the world of scattered holy relics offers us an infinitude of opportunities! Even with what we already have here in Venice, we might be able to piece together a kind of saint of saints to preside over the festivities, and to the devil with that quasi-Bohemian minchione's disloyal and profligate bones! Eh? And, besides, in this dark solstitial season, are we not more than amply enriched by your own luminous presence, my friend?"

"A relic intact, you mean," he'd replied, adding gloomily: "More or less," and Eugenio had laughed his honeyed laugh and said: "You exaggerate, dear boy! To put *you* together again would be beyond even my considerable powers! Nor, were it possible, would I wish it so, for to tell the truth, dear Pini, I love you more each day, the less of you there is! But come now, let us escape these vaporous old stones and make our way out upon the open waters, and I will show you the empire that Toyland has built!"

But before they could even get started the palazzo was thrown into an uproar. Buffetto and Francatrippa, sent to the private hospital owned and operated by the Sons of L'Omino to bring back the personal effects of a deceased client, brought back the patient instead, very much alive, grinning dippily and still wired up to all his medical paraphernalia, which looked suspiciously like something made out of Lego blocks, colored balloons, a Meccano set, and birthday party straws. "No no, you fools, you went too *soon*, he wasn't *ready* yet!" Eugenio screamed, and in his rage he heaved an antique bejeweled chalice from Thessalonica at Buffetto, who ducked, the chalice striking the patient on the head instead, widening his witless smile and setting his ancient dilated eyes to spinning. "Must I do everything *myself?!*"

It was the sort of uproar all too frequent since the arrival at the Palazzo dei Balocchi of the new servants, hired to replace Marten and his brothers, summarily dismissed, if not worse (just yesterday Buffetto said to him: "Eh, professor, I saw my predecessor the other day!" "Marten? How—how was he—?" "Tasty . . ."), such that hardly a day has passed without Eugenio erupting with fresh fury and complaining about the loss of his beloved old valet and reminding the professor bitterly of his own instigating role in that unfortunate decision. Indeed, this morning's incident was not unlike that of a day or two ago, when an English lord, who had supposedly drowned after slipping off the walkway at the back of the Arsenal walls and whose tragic and untimely death had been duly lamented in the evening newspaper, found his way back to the palazzo in time for supper after wandering the city all day in senile confusion, expounding thunderously to all the gondoliers upon the greater glory of the British fleet and declaring that if this was NATO, he'd have none of it, little Truffaldino meanwhile returning draped in sewage and seaweed and bawling like a baby, having fallen in in the nobleman's stead, an event that would have elicited even more wrath than it did, had not Truffaldino with his sweet musical voice and soft winsome ways so swiftly become Eugenio's newest favorite.

The Palazzo dei Balocchi, the professor has come to understand, is operated by Eugenio on behalf of his charities as a sort of aristocratic retirement hotel, catering to banking magnates, oil barons, the nobility, former munitions makers and Third World presidents, gambling czars and diamond miners, all the successful diggers and owners and traders of the world, now purchasing for themselves in their final days a foretaste of paradise in paradisiacal Venice, he himself being housed in the royal apartments of this generous establishment, though as a friend of course, not a client. Not only are all the creature comforts provided, but much more besides, and always with Eugenio's characteristic touches of elegance and serendipitous anticipation of every need and appetite. Thus the professor, for example, while having little interest in the theaters and nightclubs, restaurants, regattas, shops, casinos, masked balls, and gondola serenades so sought after by the others, has discovered that sitting on the Grand Canal under the blue-and-white-striped awnings of the Gritti Palace terrace bar, across from the sweet golden serenity of the incomparable Ca' Dario, dressed in a clean silk suit and an ascot tie puffed up like a cloud at his throat, his feet dangling in their new shoes and his macabre condition otherwise hidden behind hat, scarves, and soft kid gloves, sipping a small glass of the official papal grappa made in the Picolit region while watching behind subtly tinted spectacles the water traffic go rumbling by, a book in his lap and pen and fresh paper before him, is precisely what he has wanted to do all his life and was in fact the very reason, though he may not have expressed it in just this way, for his decision to return here in the first place, something only Eugenio could have, tacitly and wonderfully, intuited and, without asking, acted upon. "Whatever you want, dear boy," Eugenio has insisted over and over, "I can arrange it. *Trust* me." And who, so blessed, not merely with comforts but with such fraternal understanding, would not?

But since Buffetto, Francatrippa, and Truffaldino joined the staff, things have not been the same. Sheets have been shorted and sugar salted, room and sauna assignments have been alarmingly confused, bringing on palazzo miniwars with international reverberations, purses and gondolas alike have sprung inopportune leaks, medicines are now jumbled together and dispensed at random from a golden punch bowl, with spectacular and sometimes explosive consequences, and Eugenio's best vintage Barolos, when uncorked, have been found to be mysteriously filled with canal water. The professor himself has discovered a live squid in his hot water bottle, chewing gum on the seat of his portantina, and dog hairs in his grappa, though these latter were left, Francatrippa insisted, by "some irascible old mutt who keeps coming by here looking for you, lucky she didn't raise her leg in it before the boss chased her off." Contessas hired to throw tour-group parties at their Venetian palazzi have been stood up, the guests appearing in rowdy Mestre discos instead, the roulette wheel at the Casino has stopped repeatedly on the same number for five nights running, forcing it to close its doors right in the middle of Carnival season, a group of randy old widowers from Bavaria, taken ostensibly to a house of pleasure, had their lederhosen down before they realized they were actually in the cloister of a convent, and only last night a group of American retirees from Nebraska disrupted a performance of *La forza del destino* at the Fenice, apparently encouraged to believe it was a public sing-along.

Still, though Eugenio fires the three of them every day, he hires them back every day as well, either from necessity, as he claims, or from some perverse attraction to the very perversity he pretends to deplore, or perhaps merely out of his dreamy-eyed infatuation for little Truffaldino, who today, when his companions were not only discharged but turned over to the police, arriving ominously as suddenly as summoned, fell to his knees at Eugenio's feet and, weeping copiously, begged forgiveness and pardon for his two friends, insisting that the fault was really his and that if the questurini must take someone away it should be him. "Ah, what talent!" exclaimed Eugenio, his heart softening, and he opened his arms affectionately. "You are a good brave boy! Come here, my little piscione, and give me a kiss!" Truffaldino leapt up, straddled Eugenio's globe of a belly, gave his master a magnificent wet smack on the end of his nose, then bounced away again before the kiss could be returned or in any way elaborated upon, wherewith Eugenio not only rehired them all but invited them along on this afternoon's excursion, explaining that he wished to instruct them in seamanship, speedboat handling, and the sailor life.

And so after lunch they had set off, the professor, still unable to get about on his own, ported to the motor launch in his sedan chair by the three servants, Eugenio waddling along beside them, expounding grandly on the glories of his city and pointing out the many prized possessions of Omino e figli, S.R.L., and its affiliates. Indeed every second building seemed to belong to one or another of Eugenio's enterprises, many of the banks and businesses as well, innumerable palazzi, even several churches and bridges and historical monuments, it being the enlightened policy of the city government, in which he and his friends, due to their deep sense of civic duty, are also active, Eugenio explained, to turn over to private enterprise the terrible responsibility of maintaining these landmarks in the face of the awesome challenges that Venice, for all her beauty, daily presented. He fell just short of laying claim to the Doges' Palace, but added with an intimate wink that, thanks to a recent windfall, negotiations were in fact under way to make his fondest dream come true, and that, if successful, the first thing he was going to do was add a penthouse for his own personal quarters and for his dear friend Pinocchio.

They roared away from the Molo, sending gondolas bobbing and flopping and vaporetti grinding into reverse and blowing their horns, out into the magnificent Bacino di San Marco, Buffetto at the wheel, swerving wildly at full throttle between the strapped posts which serve as channel markers and which looked to the professor like grieving old men consoling one another, but which Buffetto compared to ball players in a huddle, Francatrippa to stacked rifles, Truffaldino to clasped lovers, and Eugenio to *cazzi incatenati*, as he called them, chained cocks, each then shouting out his own interpretation of the black tips or hoods of the posts and the little white gulls perched on each of them as though by assignment from the Tourist Office. They flew next up the Giudecca canal, slapping against the water churned up by other craft escaping their path, the encircling faces of the Palladian churches glowering at them in gape-mouthed disapproval, but Eugenio responding with squeals of unabashed joy—"Ah, this thrice-renowned and illustrious city! This precious jewel, this voluptuous old Queen, this magical fairyland! Love of my life and forger of my soul! I wish only to clasp it to my bosom! Una vera bellezza! Ah! *Ah!* Mother of God, I think I am *coming!* Faster, my boy, *faster!*" —while Truffaldino entertained them all with astonishing acrobatics on the cabin roof, even as they tipped and swerved and bounced through the busy canal. "Ah, life, *life!*" Eugenio cried, hugging his belly as though he had just named it. "It's so much *fun!*"

With like and in truth infectious delight, his round appley face flushed and black eyes twinkling, he pointed out to the professor his many projects for the lagoon, beginning with his desire to tear down the Giudecca and rebuild the entire island in the old aristocratic style of rich villas and exotic pleasure gardens that had characterized it in the time when Michelangelo stayed there, perhaps converting the old Stücky mill at the far end into a private academy or university to be named after the professor himself ("No, no, do not object! You deserve no less, my friend!"), and certainly reclaiming the famous Convent of the Converted Ones, now a women's prison, and restoring it as it was at the turn of the century when the Little Man used it as a marketplace for auctioning off his donkeys. "Our friends at Disney are definitely interested!" he exclaimed secretively above the roar of the speeding boat, clapping his little fat hands.

Whipping around by the Lido, Francatrippa now gleefully at the speedboat's controls, Eugenio pointed out the projected location of the new lagoon entrance tidegates, told him of his plans to seek commercial sponsorship of the gondolieri and sell advertising space on their shirts and straw hats, and described for him how, by digging between Malamocco and Marghera a channel deep enough for sixty-thousand-ton tankers, they could create what he called the Third Industrial Zone, making the Veneto region the rival of Osaka, Manchester, and New Jersey, though he admitted that, having done much the same thing twice before, even though the project would be immensely profitable, worth more perhaps than all their other investments put together, his heart really wasn't in it. "Besides, it would only increase the size of the working class, un fottio di cazzi as it is, God knows, a veritable plague, my dear, which is ruining the democratic process and turning the world into a fucking dungheap—no, no, I ask very little of this world, being at heart a modest man, only let me live the rest of my days, the few that remain, among the superrich! That's who this noblest of cities, sole refuge of humanity, peace, justice, and liberty, is truly for and they are the only ones who will save it! But just the same, my love," he added, leaning close and wrapping an arm around his old friend to wheeze into his earhole: "if you're looking for a hot real estate tip, you could do worse than to buy in to Malamocco!"

"I used to think it was the end of the world . . ."

They were now barreling through the triumphal arch of the Great Gateway, past the statue of a lioness, strangely elongated like stretched taffy, and into the main canal of the Arsenal Vecchio, and, as they went ripping past the huge brick barns and rusting drums and the thick bunkers skulking like cement elephants, spray flying from the prow, Eugenio explained to him how he hoped to convert this great Renaissance workshop, once civilization's most famous shipyard and now little more than a rotting hulk, into a vast eighty-acre marina for the world's most luxurious private yachts: "It has a bigger basin than Monaco, Pini! Think of it! It will create a whole new generation of seagoing pleasure craft! Venice will again rule the waves! It will take money, of course, but not only are we rich in public funds right now, we also have the whole world's hearts in our pockets and our hands in theirs, and, so long as our Socialist Party stays in office, I can promise you, we shall not lose sight of this noble goal!"

As they came plowing out through the low arch cut into the crenellated wall at the back end, Francatrippa and Buffetto now fighting like schoolboys over the wheel, Truffaldino at the same time hugging it head downward and arse high and, feet kicking, demanding his own turn, the launch reeling drunkenly through the lagoon and slicing a straying gondola clean in two ("He'll *drown!*" the professor cried in alarm, craning around to watch, but Eugenio only laughed and said: "Nonsense, my boy! You forget how shallow the lagoon is—he can *walk* home!"), the cemetery island of San Michele with its trim brick walls and cypress canopy suddenly loomed into view, and Eugenio, taking over the boat's controls so as to avoid hitting it, leaned over toward the professor and, Truffaldino having barely escaped getting bit on the bottom before scrambling away, stage-whispered above the motor's diminishing roar: "I have something to show you over here, Pini . . . something special . . ."

They moored next to the vaporetto landing stage and, after stopping to buy flowers just inside the cemetery walls, Eugenio led them in a little procession down the long cypress-lined gravel paths to the far end of the raftlike island where the route became increasingly mazy as though in imitation of the neighboring island these dead once called home. Along the way, women, carefully tending graves as though they were pieces of heirloom furniture, washing them, brushing them, shining up the photographs, changing the flowers and the water in the pots, paused to greet Eugenio as he passed, a regular visitor here, it would seem, and taken as one of their own. The professor could not help remarking how dry-eyed they all were, by contrast to his own wild unrestrained grief at the tomb of the Blue-Haired Fairy. In fact, he felt it again now, churning up inside afresh, that old graveyard fever, punctual as saliva.

"They are making their husband's beds," Eugenio murmured, his voice hidden behind the labored rumble of heavy earth-moving equipment digging somewhere nearby, "the beds they had in truth been making for them all their lives. They are happy now, this is their true vocation. When I am feeling morbid, Pini, I sometimes wish I had one of the dear things . . ."

The twisting path, leading them down narrow labyrinthine passageways between stone condominiums of the dead, stacked five deep and sometimes two or three to a niche, opened out suddenly upon a splendid little campo, lined with cypresses and rosebushes and dominated by an immense yet graceful semicircular mausoleum built like a kind of marble stage with a raised platform, ceremonial central stairs, shielded wings protected by poised angels, and a recessed proscenium arch supported by fluted Corinthian columns like a ring of folded curtains. In the middle of the stage was the tomb of the Little Man, an ornately decorated marble sarcophagus, laden with fresh flowers piled up sumptuously around a perpetually burning oil lamp in the center. Above the sarcophagus hung a crucified Jesus with the familiar sloping hips, smooth feminine limbs, and soft pierced abdomen, his face turned heavenward in agony, or perhaps in ecstasy, while around him plump naked cherubs played in melancholic abandon. The legend on L'Omino's tomb was that famous line of his which every little boy along his route had heard sooner or later, and one which even now caused the professor's heart to sink: "Are you coming with us or staying behind?" *"Vieni con noi, o rimani?"*

"Io rimango," he thought to himself, recalling his futile resistance, as futile now as it was then: here still, but not for long. He was not getting well. He was feeling less pain, no doubt thanks to Eugenio's pharmaceuticals, and he was able, if carried, to get about a bit, but if anything his disease was worsening. The bits that had fallen off were gone for good, awash somewhere in the waterways of Venice, and more vanished every day, teeth and toes in particular, and the patches of flesh that kept flaking away, fouling his sheets with dusty excrescences sometimes as large as dried mushrooms. And what was left of him, once waterlogged, was twisting and splitting now as it dried out, he could hardly move without startling those about him, himself included (this is not *me*, he continued to feel deep in his heart, or whatever was down there, there in that dark place inside where all the weeping started, this *can't* be me!), with awesome splintering and cracking sounds, his elegant new clothing worn not merely to conceal the surface rot, but to muffle the terrible din of the disintegration within. He would shed the rest of his flesh altogether and be done with it, but it sticks tenaciously and bloodily to his frame like a kind of stubborn reprimand, his attempts to scrape it off causing him excruciating pain. Far from transcending flesh, he was dying into it. Into the tatters of it. Only, as he shrank toward oblivion, his love for her and a certain bitter dignity remained . . .

"I *loathe* small deaths," Eugenio was saying. "Death is our great master, but must be met with the grandeur it deserves!" The old professor, emerging from his revery, realized that Eugenio had been describing for him the magnificence of the Little Man's final rites, beginning with a great requiem Mass in the colossal church of Santi Giovanni e Paolo in the company of twenty-five dead doges and the skin of Marcantonio Bragadin, who was flayed alive by the Turks at Famagusta (perhaps Eugenio had told him this in response to his own complaints, or else, speaking his thoughts aloud, he had complained of his own slower flaying upon hearing of that of the hero of Famagusta, whose skin at least was whole enough to be saved as a relic and not shaken out each day with the changing of the beds), followed by a solemn funeral procession around to the Fondamenta Nuova with all the bells of Venice tolling (as, from over the lagoon, they were hollowly, as though in wistful remembrance, tolling at that moment), the hearse drawn by sixty-nine leather-booted donkeys who were later driven into the sea and drowned. There, the Little Man's coffin was removed to a gold and black funeral gondola, heaped with orchids and roses and palm branches, and, followed by other gondolas carrying the statues of the angels now mounted on the tomb and all the thousands of L'Omino's admirers and lovers, brought across the Laguna Morta to this island, the church here draped that day in black and silver and bearing, freshly engraved on the cloister gateway under Saint Michael and the dragon, where it could be seen still, another of L'Omino's immortal lines: "While the world sleeps, I sleep never."

"I-I never realized," the old scholar stammered, filling the momentary silence, "he was so-so-so . . ."

"Loved? Oh yes, but it's not what I brought you here to show you," Eugenio replied with a sly vulnerable smile. "Lift him over here," he instructed the servants and, crossing himself as he passed the tomb and genuflecting gently, he led them to the naked angel, stage right, poised balletically on one foot as though in imitation of the beautiful angel in blue on the Pala d'Oro. "Look, Pini. Do you recognize him?"

Not exactly an angel after all, he noted, for it had a little inch-long uncircumcised penis and two tiny testicles like polished glass marbles which Eugenio now fingered affectionately. "I-I'm not sure . . . The, uh, face . . ."

"Yes, you have guessed it," Eugenio groaned, leaning his head almost shyly against the angel's pale thigh. "It is I, as I was, when L'Omino first loved me." He ran his finger in little loops through the artfully scrolled pubic hair, traced the contours of the childish abdomen, poked the tip of his finger into the deep navel. Yes, that's right, the creature also had a navel. "Now . . . now it sticks out like . . . like a little clitoris," Eugenio confessed, touching his own round tummy. He tried lamely to laugh through the tears that were now streaming down his cheeks. It's true, the professor thought, squinting up at the marble face with its pursed bow-shaped lips, its long-lashed eyes and flowing locks, it *did* quite resemble the Eugenio he once had known, and in particular—perhaps in part it was the ghastly pallor of the stone, or maybe the halo, tipped back like a cockily worn school cap, the wings attached to the shoulders like bulky bookbags—that Eugenio who lay sprawled on the beach that dreadful day, seemingly dead or dying after being struck down by the math book; but at the same time this was a *different* Eugenio, a more mature one to be sure, a more intense and self-assured one than the boy he had known, but also (he was gazing up at the eyes now, eyes not unlike those he had seen in certain paintings as the light of the Renaissance dimmed) one clearly in touch with the nuances and deceptions of power and exchange, one who had already come to know pleasures and the pitfalls of pleasure and who had ceased to search for something that could not be found, one privy—like an angel, one might say—to the world's bleakest secrets . . . and embracing them . . .

The living Eugenio, the short butterball one with the fat crinkly face and slicked-back hair, was running one thick bejeweled hand up a taut thigh, hugging it to him, while caressing the marble buttocks, their luster attesting to the frequency of such devotions, with the other. "Ah, che culo!" he exclaimed throatily, covering it suddenly with passionate kisses and wetting it with his freely flowing tears. "How I wish now, Pini," he blubbered, "I could fuck myself as I— *choke*—was then!" He bawled there for a moment, cheek to cheek, his arms around the statue's hips, and then, when he could, he gasped: "You see, dear friend, that sweet bottom won L'Omino's heart, and —*sob!*—changed my life forever! It made me, fundamentally, in a word, what I am today! Che culo, we say: what luck, eh! And it gave good value. He beat it, bit it, slapped and tickled it, slept on it, sat on it, used it as a canvas, a pincushion, a footstool, a musical instrument, ate his supper off it, whispered his most intimate secrets to it and, as you might say, wrote his will on it. By the time its glory had begun to sag, L'Omino was dead and it was I who was choosing favorites . . ."

Then Eugenio wiped his eyes and blew his nose and, still embracing the statue affectionately, told the professor about his own life at the Land of Toys, which was not at all like the one he and Lampwick had known, nor could they even have imagined it. "It all began," Eugenio sighed, "that first night when the Little Man lifted me up onto his lap and let me hold the reins as we bounced down the road to Toyland. The other boys all envied me, but in truth, I soon felt shackled by those unfamiliar straps tugging insistently at my hands. Such a strange dark journey, Pini, the little donkeys clopping along in front of us in their white leather boots, the only things you could see by that night's eery light, and making odd snuffling and whim-

pering noises, while the Little Man shushed them with ominous lul-
labies sung through clenched teeth and cracked them with the whip
which whished terrifyingly past my ear from time to time. I tried not
to cry, but I couldn't help it. I was trembling all over like a leaf in a
temporale. The Little Man, in his fashion, consoled me. By dawn, I
was no longer a virgin . . ." Eugenio sighed tremulously and stroked
the statue's buttocks tenderly as one might to soothe a tearful child,
then went on to tell him how, when they arrived and all the other
boys ran off to play, he was carried under L'Omino's arm like a pig
from market, arse forward, school knickers still in a twist around his
ankles and blood trickling down his thighs, to the Little Man's private
rooms, then in a modest corner at Venice's eastern tip near where the
soccer field now stands, itself a commemorative gift to the city from
Omino e figli, S.R.L. Here, L'Omino kept a little stable of his favorites whom he treated like donkeys but left, at least most of the time,
in the shape of boys, the games they played being the sort one might
associate with a stable. "Well, tutti i gusti sono gusti, as the Little
Man himself used to say, his own being mostly of the Tyrolean
sort . . ."

Eugenio gave each cheek a misty-eyed farewell kiss, pocketed the
rosary which he'd been fingering with his free hand, then, on the way
back to the motor launch, took the professor on a quiet meditative
tour of the cemetery island, describing for him as he waddled along,
the old scholar ported at his side by the three servants, his long and
happy life in Toyland, which he still held to be the most beautiful
place in the world, a land of dreams, *un paese benedetto*, the very goal
of human civilization, and he the preserver of its sacred flame, becoming over time L'Omino's dearest beloved, subjecting the adorable man
in his declining years to his least whim and fancy, including his
signature on the documents that created Omini e figli, S.R.L.

"I was a good little boy, Pini, loving and obedient, and everything
came true for me, just as the Little Man promised!"

The professor, somewhat befogged and guilt-ridden, as was his
wont in the midst of tombstones, did not know what to answer to all
of this, and finally, as they were making their way back to the landing
stage, twilight by now dimming the sky and darkening the hovering
cypresses, what he said was: "I-I have never known the careless freedom of youth . . ."

"Ah, poor Pini!" smiled Eugenio, taking over the controls as they reboarded the motor launch. "And now with your little thingie gone . . ."

"Well, it's—it's not exactly gone . . ."

"No? But when I was oiling you, I saw nothing there but a—"

"I mean 'it' wasn't . . . *it* . . ."

Whereupon, the others urging him on as the launch, growling softly, slides out into the wet dreamy lagoon, the ancient wayfarer commences to tell them, with all the candor that the day has inspired, the tale of the world's only Nobel Prize–winning nose . . .

20

THE ORIGINAL WET DREAM

"So it's all true, then," murmurs Eugenio in the echoey darkness, "all those old jokes . . . ?"

"Yes, all the pornographic films and comic books, the sex
magazine cartoons, the party songs and burlesque routines, just pages
really out of a depressing case history. The boy who had to wear on
his face what other people hid in their pants. Watch it misbehave.
Watch it get punished. I always felt insulted by the names you called
me in school, not recognizing at the time that it was not much worse
than calling me 'Faceface' or 'Footfoot.' And people laughed at it, but
they were afraid of it, too. It took a lot of abuse. What was old
Geppetto's assault on it that day he made me, after all, but . . . ?"

"My thoughts exactly, dear boy! An attempt to emasculate his own
son! But that you should remember it all so vividly is most extraordinary!" Eugenio and the servants have become just faceless shadows
hovering over him, faintly silhouetted against the distant glow of the
city. The boat motor is off, the lights as well, and they bob silently
now on the lap of the black lagoon, the cool night mist having gathered round them with a motherly embrace, as though to soothe away
the anxieties aroused by their visit this afternoon to the island of the
dead. "For the rest of us, our beginnings remain forever a strange
unfathomable mystery. A bit terrifying in fact . . ."

"Actually, I forgot most of this when I became a boy. Only lately
has it been coming back to me . . ." Not all of it, there are vague
scary bits for him, too, mysteries he too cannot penetrate. But he
does have a clear and precise memory of his babbo's clumsy affection-

ate strokes as he carved and fluted his wooden hair and whittled out eyes for him to see by, eyes he rolled mischievously at the old fellow just to make him jump and reach for his grappa, and he can almost feel still the impatient hewing and hacking up and down his body as Geppetto roughed out the rest of him: a mouth with its own mocking tongue, thumbed but fingerless hands with which to pincer away the old boy's yellow moth-eaten mop of a wig, feet for kicking him in the nose, and then a nose of his own, fashioned from scraps chopped out between his new legs and wedged into a hole gouged in the middle of his face, a nose that started to grow as soon as it was plugged in, a trick he had no control over and which frightened him nearly as much as it did the old man, who erupted into a kind of blind squeaky rage, accusing the thing of insolence and deviltry and slashing at it wildly with his rude tools, sending splinters flying about the room, bits and pieces of him lost forever, alas, he could use them now to patch up his losses. And still the perverse thing kept shooting out in front of his startled eyes, irrepressible as that infamous beanstalk, stretching and quivering, the tip of it sore where his father whacked madly away at it, but somehow itchy and tingling with fresh raw excitement at the same time, insisting upon its prefigured but ludicrous length even as Geppetto went on lopping it off. Even as he wept, loudly disclaiming it, he could feel himself coming to identify with it in some odd way, as though it were somehow, in its unruly defiance, expressing his own deepest and truest nature, as though it were, in a word, taking a stand in his behalf, or rather, taking a stand that would become his own, he in the end, until the Blue-Haired Fairy taught him how to master it, the captive appendage of the obstreperous nose.

But though he can remember all that as though it had just happened, can indeed remember his entire birth right down to the beveling and pegging of his articulated joints, the drilling of his bottomhole, chased decorously with a chamfer bit, and the planing of his belly which made him whoop and giggle, there are also things he cannot recall, and which cause him deep disquiet when he tries to think about them. His earlier life on the woodpile, for example: When did it begin and where did he come from? Was he always just an impudent log, a sentient chip from a dead block, nature's freak, a useless piece of yattering driftwood, as his father called him when he washed up inside the fish's belly, or did he have, so to speak, a family tree out in the world someplace, its amputated limbs a lost brotherhood? And then, when Maestro Ciliegia found him there on the stack of firewood, how did he, without eyes, see, and, without a mouth, how speak? Still enclosed in his thick bark, how did he, when presented to Geppetto, shake himself free of Maestro Ciliegia and strike Geppetto on the shin, setting off the free-for-all that so delighted him? *How did he know "delight?"* And if, as a log, he had no ears, no legs, how distinguish what was "between" them? Or, put another way, all those pieces chiseled away, the slivers and shavings and even the sawdust: were they nothing more than the dead crust of the hidden self within, discovered by Geppetto, mere packing material, as it were, or were they lost fragments of a being once whole, monadic scraps of his original wooden integrity, now tragically scattered?

"Such as those splinters that he hacked away from your nose like a great harvest of foreskins, you mean?" Buffetto asks softly.

"Yes—"

"Were they dead as clipped fingernails, you mean," adds Francatrippa, marveling, "or did they think? Did they feel?"

"Did they talk back?"

"Were they naughty?"

"Yes, and, if so, do they, are they, somewhere, still . . . ?"

"Woo! Spooky!" whispers little Truffaldino from the prow, perched out there beyond Eugenio's reach. "It makes you wonder if anything is really what it seems to be!"

"Nonsense, my little marinaio," replies Eugenio, sitting anchored in his dark shadow behind the wheel. "Everything is *exactly* what it seems to be. That's the sadness of it. Now, come and sit here on my knee, my child, and let us explore reality together while we still share in it!"

"I am afraid if I did, master, I would lose my share to you! I would be in only half of my reality, you would be in the other half!"

"Macché! Pleasure is never diminishing, ragazzo mio. It would not halve your reality, but double it!"

"But I can barely clothe and feed the reality I have now. What am I to do with twice as much?"

"Then I will double your income, sweet boy, with each doubling of your reality!"

"Ah, very good, direttore! And if I increased my reality, by, say, fifty percent?"

"Why, how would you do that?"

"Like this, master!" Truffaldino puts his feet on the deck of the launch, or seems to, and walks over to Eugenio, even while remaining sitting on the prow. He puts his hands under his chin and lifts his silhouetted head to arm's length—then the arms themselves seem to periscope upwards in the darkness, raising the head another foot or so in the night air.

"Che roba! And can you do that with *all* your parts, you wicked boy?"

"Only in the darkness, master," sighs Truffaldino, shrinking back into himself, leaving Eugenio snatching at air. "That's, as you say, the sadness of it . . ."

A moment of wistful silence descends then, through which, as though from some other time more than another place, come, across the dark waters from the other side of the island, the distant hollow reverberations of revelry: amplified voices, waves of laughter like sullen heartbeats, whistles rising into the night and muffled shouting, the beat but not the melody of music—the sounds of Carnival. The peace of his suite in the Palazzo dei Balocchi is not what it once was, but he dare not complain, for the recent restoration of the Venetian Carnival is virtually the invention, or reinvention, of Eugenio, yet another of his host's acts of homage to his legendary mentor, for whom Carnival existed twelve months of the year. Besides, the professor expects to move any day now into quieter quarters of his own, as soon as his new credit cards, checkbooks, and personal documents, requested for him by Eugenio, reach him through the anarchical Venetian postal service, though the bag of mail they saw floating in the Giudecca canal today made manifest the hazards.

The old scholar leans his head back and gazes up at the night sky. The hovering mist seems to be breaking up, letting a few stars shine through, scattered here and there in abject loneliness like chips struck from the moon. Star light, star bright, he thinks. But what is he to wish for? To be free from his disease? A death wish. To be free from his fear of death? A kind of madness, the dubious blessing of senility, a greater terror. Perhaps just to *know*. But he already knows so much and what good has it done him? No, no, he knows all too well what he desires, she has been on his mind all afternoon, she whose graven tombs once marked his passage like milestones. He wishes—it is quite simple—he wishes only to be held again. Taking them to the heretics' corner of the cemetery island this afternoon to show them where he hoped to enshrine the bones of Casanova, Eugenio led them all through a section devoted, it seemed, to those who had died young: children climbed stairs to heaven, youthful lovers sprawled erotically on marble deathbeds, babies reached for the arms of Jesus. And there, in the dim light, half buried amid the grander monuments, he saw, or thought for one heart-stopping moment that he saw, that selfsame little slab of marble which once announced the Blue-Haired Fairy's death of a broken heart: *"Qui giace una bambina,"* he read, even from his bobbing portantina, "Here lies a child," and the words *abbandonata* and *fratellino* jumped out at him as though the stone itself were crying out. *"Stop!"* he gasped, and begged that he be taken closer. No, not her, he saw through teary eyes, some other little sister gone, and *abbandonato*, the brother, not the girl, deserted, but that was how he felt, too, and, no doubt startling Eugenio and the servants, he sobbed out his grief there on that stone, not for the dead child but for the little brother left behind, who was himself, exiled forever from the consolation of her hugs and kisses, her sweet embrace. *O Fata mia!*

"Look, direttore! Do you see—?"

"Sshh! Come here, my child! Quickly!"

He made some foolish remark then, to cover his greater foolishness ("But why should you be interested in a little thing like me, master, when you have a Nobel Prize–winner on full display?"), about life's cruel brevity, the stony permanence of death, and Eugenio, laughingly reminding him of the old wisdom, which he credited to Dante Alighieri, that "He who comes from tinche tanche, goes in the end to gninche gnanche," guided them all back to the gloomiest, remotest, most desolate corner of the island where bad boys, he said, were buried and where all the tombs were sinking and collapsing, the headstones broken, the busts and crosses cracked and fallen, the pieces scattered about like garbage floating in the canals. It was a strange, wild, darkly canopied place with spiky plants and stunted trees and thick beds of moldering leaves among the broken stones and rampant weeds through which fiendish little black and emerald lizards skittered while pale butterflies hovered in the coiling mists above like flakes of dead flesh. *"I ta morti!"* Francatrippa exclaimed, and Buffetto concurred, "Un merdaio, compagno, a veritable shithole," Truffaldino pointing silently to a sign at the entrance that read: DEAD END. Eugenio ordered them to set the sedan-chair down and to jump up and down as hard as they could. As they did so, whooping and grunting cheerfully, the entire area began to wobble in little waves that spread slowly out to the four walled edges. Tombs tipped and toppled, cracked apart, dumped their dead flowers, cast off ornament, and sank another inch or two, as the ground rippled under them like a shaken carpet. With a soft sucking noise, two or three of the graves disappeared altogether. Overhead, cypresses leaned and fell against one another like grieving or drunken friends, and the walls coughed out loose bricks that plopped softly to the earth as though falling into thick pudding. He could feel the tremors beneath his chair, which seemed as it shook to be tipping and sinking just like the tombstones, and the fright he felt was not unlike that he'd suffered as a puppet whenever the Fairy, in despair at his misbehavior, would go pale and cold and fall down with her eyes rolled back, showing only their whites, remaining like that until he hugged and kissed her and wet her all over with his tears, her limp lifeless body slowly vibrating beneath his sobs just as the earth was doing now, a kind of loose ripple that seemed to spread from the middle out and come bouncing back, building slowly until at last her body would be shaking him as much as he was shaking it and she started to come alive again, groaning and sobbing, or maybe laughing, it didn't matter, and hugging and kissing him as feverishly as he her . . .

"*Che sborro!* What a *cannon!*"

"If we had a sail, we could use it for a mast!"

"Maybe we should put a light on it to warn low-flying aircraft!"

"Standing at attention like that, I can see why it got the Nobel for keeping the peace!"

"Though it won the Nobel Peace Prize," the professor sighs, gazing up at the bright star his nose is fingering and silently making his futile but heartfelt wish ("No request is too extreme," as that old hymn goes), "it itself has had no peace. It was cited at the time 'for standing for the truth in the age of the Great Lie.' This was on the eve of World War Two, the film had just appeared and was being viewed as a realpolitik fable, with Geppetto as a kind of Swiss neutral, Stromboli as a bearded Mussolini, Foulfellow and Barker the Coachman as fifth columnists, Monstro the Whale as the German U-boat menace, the Miss America–like Blue Fairy representing the wished-for Yankee intervention with their magical know-how, and my mystical nose as a mark of the divine, visible proof that we, not they, were the designated good guys. Like many a victim of the political repression of that time, it had been imprisoned, tortured, humiliated, reviled, and in countless other ways persecuted, and so stood as well for courage and integrity in the face of tyranny, even while exhibiting a peaceful, rather than warlike, stance. In the film it is shown sprouting a branch in which birds nested, and this was interpreted as being an olive branch. Of course all that changed when war came . . .” That was when the jokes began. The world was more aggressive then. Military units wore his nose into battle and fighter pilots painted it on their fusilages: “Always Hard.” It appeared on condom packets sold in PXs and USO canteens. Still, he didn’t figure it out. Or rather, he knew full well, had known since he’d become a boy, if not before, but kept forgetting, *that* truth elusive as a dream. The expanded version of his Nobel acceptance speech, *Astringent Truth*, which became a classic of moral philosophy, never mentioned it, and even in his more autobiographical writings such as *The Wretch, Sacred Sins*, and *The Transformation of the Beast*, works which won him his second Nobel, this was a truth, naked as it may have been in the world, which remained largely under wraps. With all the dignity of his great career he carried his nose through the world as though it were only a nose, he alone beguiled by his own pretenses. It might have been otherwise. There were students who wanted, who might have . . . but whenever they got too close his nose would start to smart and shrivel as if the Blue-Haired Fairy’s woodpeckers were at it again, a painful humiliation far worse than any imaginable pleasure, at least any that he in his innocence could imagine, and so he distanced himself from them behind his professorial demeanor. Anyway, they were never his best students . . .

“Ah, poor Pini! And still a virgin, then!”

“Well, not quite . . .” He lowers his head, his nose inscribing its usual ignominious arc through the liquid night air, and stares out at the lagoon, pitch black except for the glittering gold coins cast on its surface by the yellow lamps of the channel markers and illusorily deep as an ocean. He lets his gaze drift out upon it, losing focus in its seeming immensity, floating deep, deep into the void, acknowledging his lifelong yearning to hide himself from life's profuse terrors and confusions upon the bosom of the simple, the vast, and surrendering for a moment to his ancient appetite, as perverse as the day Geppetto chopped out his rough-hewn little torso, for the absolute anarchy of the eternal emptiness, that incommunicable but ineradicable truth of his pagan heart, which the Blue-Haired Fairy so abhorred. In effect, civilizing him, she taught him, if not his intractable nose, how to lie . . . "There was the night I . . . I became a boy . . ."

"Aha . . . !"

He'd been wearing himself out, doing the sort of donkey work he'd been spared in his donkey days, harnessed to the primitive water-wheel that had killed his old friend Lampwick, just to earn a glass of milk each day for his grappa-crazed babbo, now on his last legs. The times were hard. Since their escape from the monster fish, they'd been holing out in an abandoned straw cottage that was insect-ridden and stank of goats, sleeping on beds of rank straw, dressed in rags and half starving. The farmer he worked for was a tyrant, but no worse than his old man, who hated him still for dragging him out of Attila's innards, the best home he'd ever had. At the time, he'd felt that he was saving him, but now he didn't know for what. The old loony, now calling himself San 'Petto, raved all day and often as not all night, spat out the milk he brought him from his backbreaking labor, peed spitefully on their straw mattresses, left his other evacuations around the cottage wherever he felt like. Saint's relics, the old boy called them. So as to have something to trade at the market, he'd taken up basket weaving and, whenever he was away at market or off pushing at that murderous waterwheel, his father would throw his handiwork down the well or set it on fire or chop it up and try to make grappa out of it. He'd knocked together a little cart to use on his trips to the market, and Geppetto had torn up three of his best baskets, braided a whip out of the raffia, and bullied him into pushing him around in the thing. That was all right, at least it kept him quiet, if only while he was in it, and the whip didn't hurt, the old brute was too far gone to do more than wave it about like a blind man's cane. It was the meanness of it that hurt. The Disney film had captured something of Geppetto's stupidity maybe, but not his malice. On one of his trips to market, he had picked up an old coverless primer with half its pages missing, the very one perhaps he had sold for a ticket to Mangiafoco's puppet theater, and had begun to teach himself to read and write, and in this book, under "M for Madonna," was a picture that, though he did not know it at the time, was eventually to change his life: a reproduction of Giovanni Bellini's "Madonna of the Small Trees." He could not keep his eyes off it, returning to it time and again. Maybe he identified with the stunted trees. Whatever, it utterly absorbed him. "M" was the letter he learned best in the alphabet, and it was still his favorite. It was no accident that the title of his final opus, only five letters long, was to have had three of them in it. This primer was the treasure of his life and his sole consolation. Until Geppetto mustachioed the Madonna of the Small Trees and drew a penis in her mouth, then drank up all his fruit-juice ink and smoked the shredded pages, "M" the first to go.

"Poverino!"

"It was awful. I couldn't help but feel sorry for myself. I cried all the time. The Fairy was out of my life forever, I was stuck with this mad old man, I'd watched my best friend die a miserable death that seemed to foretell my own, I was working fourteen-hour days and getting nowhere and I felt like all my joints were coming apart from the physical strain, I was cold and hungry most of the time, and I was utterly alone. My old enemies the Fox and the Cat were somewhere in the neighborhood, down on their luck, Il Gattino who'd once feigned blindness as a beggar now blind in fact, La Volpe crippled and her tail gone, both of them desperately needy but also probably dangerous. I'd chased them off but knew they might return at any moment to steal what little we had, the scraps of food, the baskets, the few coins I'd managed to put aside from my market dealings. So one day, deciding I'd better spend those coins while I still had them, I took them to market to buy myself some new clothes. As I walked down the road, I imagined myself making a fresh start. You know me, always the irrational optimist, fields of miracles, money trees, *zin, zin, zin,* and all that. Why not, I thought. I knew at least half the letters in the alphabet by then and figured I could fake the rest and so perhaps move up into the professional classes. But . . ."

"Ah yes. With you, dear friend, there's always a *but* . . ."

"On the way I met La Lumaca, the Blue-Haired Fairy's sluggish maid, the one who once took twelve hours to bring me plaster of Paris bread and alabaster apricots when I was sick from hunger."

"Ha ha! And she told you the Fairy was dying, no doubt, and was temporarily short of funds . . . !"

"That's right. She said she didn't even have enough to buy a crust of bread. I gave her all I had."

"Ah, poor Old Sticks!"

"It was nothing to me. I was overwhelmed by hope and despair at the same time. I ran back home and started making more baskets. I doubled my production in a single evening even though I was crying so hard I could hardly see, the tears streaming down my nose like a rainspout. I was going to save her life with baskets. I'd work till dawn, and then till dawn again, and for as many dawns as it would take. But I was too exhausted. About midnight I fell asleep. And I had a strange dream . . ."

He was back in the Fairy's little snow white house in the dark forest. He didn't remember how he got there, but there was something before about pushing his sodden father, or perhaps the carcass of his dead friend Lampwick, in the little wooden cart he had made. Whoever it was was very heavy and the going was slow. Far far ahead in the dark night he could see the old Snail, lit up like a porcelain-shaded nightlamp, and crying: "Hurry! Hurry! You'll be late!" But pushing against the cart was like pushing the terrible waterwheel. La Lumaca disappeared and the night came down on him like a coal sack. But then, without transition, it was he who was being carted, just like the first time, into the Fairy's cottage. She was little like she was when he first met her with her waxy face and spooky eyes and strange blue hair, and they were playing doctors again, or something like it, though this time he was completely dead. She laid him on her bed and took all his clothes off. Then she removed his feet, took his knees apart, unhooked his legs where they were pegged into his body, popped his faucet out like pulling a cork. She did the same thing with his arms and head and all the rest, took him apart joint by joint. Though it should have been scary, it was in fact very relaxing. When she unplugged his nose he felt like he could really breathe for the first time in his life, even though he was dead. She put all the parts together in a pile and played with them for a while like wooden blocks, making little houses with them and knocking them down. It didn't hurt and he felt freed from responsibility, though it made him dizzy when she rolled his head around. When any of the pieces got dirty, she licked them and rubbed them clean on her dress, which was more like a winding sheet. They seemed to need a lot of cleaning, so she took off her clothes and rubbed them all over her body, which was smooth and slippery like a bar of soap, kissing them and licking them and caressing them at the same time. It felt wonderful, especially when she pushed the pieces down between her legs, where her softest parts were. She was on her back now, fondling and stroking all his segments, and though he couldn't see very well anymore, he could feel how each part of him got pushed up into the warm wet place between her thighs and scrubbed around in there and then came out again, hot and soaking, his torso too, though he didn't know how she managed it, little flat-tummied thing that she was. When his head went in, he caught just a glimpse of the crimson slash amid the waxy pallor like rose petals buried in ice cream, and he was afraid she might have hurt herself, she was moaning and yowling now and pitching about as though in horrible pain, but she slapped him playfully and growled at him to "Close your eyes, you little scoundrel!" in a voice that didn't sound like a little girl at all, and pushed him on in where everything was soft and creamy and utterly delicious, he didn't want to come out again, he just wanted to push deeper and deeper and stay there forever. But while he was in there—his head at least, he could still feel the rest of him in a wet scatter outside—he seemed to hear her speaking to him: "Bravo Pinocchio!" she said. "Because of your good heart and other parts I forgive you everything!"

"Wonderful! And so you woke up a real boy!"

"Not yet. When my head came out I found myself lying on her bed where she was reassembling me. I was still drenched from head to foot. What is all this wetness, I wondered? Why, it must be sweat, human sweat! I'd never sweated before, and I realized now that something truly grand was happening. When she put my hands back on, she lifted them up and pressed them to her nipples. I could feel her breasts puff up like spongy little balloons to fill them up, and she blew me a sly kiss and winked. I felt whole and happy, but vaguely frightened. Amost whole. There was one part still missing, forgotten until now."

"Ah! I see it! Your nose!"

"I was rather hoping it had gotten lost. I'd always hated it, it had caused me nothing but trouble and humiliation, and it seemed I might be free of it at last. I'd not lost the sensation of it, however. Wherever it was, it was encased in a plump fragrant warmth. As it turned out she was sitting on it. She plucked it out from beneath her and held it up between us, as though it might be a wicked secret we shared. Her azure hair was snarled and wild, her eyes strangely glazed, her lips twisted into a grin that bared her teeth, and, somehow aware that I was dreaming, I began to fear this might turn into a nightmare. She licked it all over, then blew on it teasingly. I watched it grow in her hands, felt it growing at the same time, felt her tongue on it, her lips, her breath, even though she was sitting far away from me at the foot of the bed. It was a very peculiar sensation. Perhaps this sort of thing happens in everybody's dreams, but for me it began to feel like something utterly new in the world, not unlike a sudden visitation of angels. As she put it in her mouth, wallowing it about with her tongue and sucking it deeper and deeper down her throat, I began to suffer a terrible tension around the hole gouged in the middle of my face, and my eyes and teeth felt like they were about to leap from their sockets. It was frightening, I was literally petrified, but I couldn't stop it, nor did I want to. When a little acorn appeared at the end of it and she nipped it off with her teeth, I nearly screamed with something compounded of both terror and delight, and then she put it up in that place where all the other parts had been. It was too much. I couldn't hold back anymore. 'Grow wise,' she said, 'and be happy.' I sneezed. I woke . . . I was covered in flesh . . ."

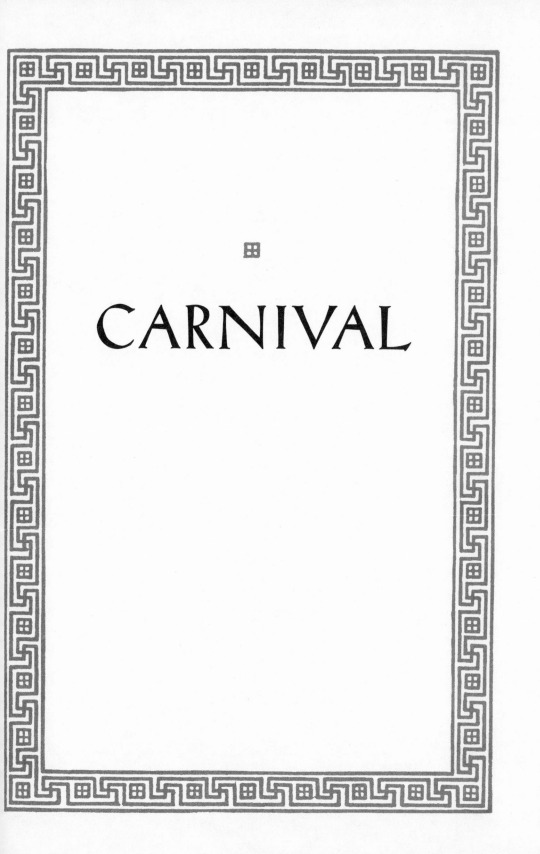

CARNIVAL

21.

PLATO'S PRANK

"Gee, Professor Pinenut," Bluebell exclaims, snapping her gum in his tender earhole, "that's a real masterpiece, hunh?" It is not. It is one of the most idiotic paintings he has ever seen. He cannot stop looking up at it, though. Chagrin would be his middle name, he thinks bitterly, if he had more than one in the first place. "I mean, when you look up at the ceiling and see a stark naked old man as ugly as that who's supposed to be, you know, 'The Universe,' it makes you realize what a *mess* we're in, right? Standing up there on that croc as though to say that's all it is, you know, just a big crock, see you later, alligator, whoo! That's really *deep*, man! I can see why you dig it!"

"He is *not* the Universe, that happens to be the River Nile he is standing on, and in any case that is *not* why I—"

"No? Hey, wait, don't *tell* me it's that cute tootsie with her big jugs spilling out like the Milky Way that's—*crack! pop!*—got your old eye, teach! Jiminy! I feel like I'm back in your classroom again, down mammary lane in the Beak's lecher hall, arse pimples, dix pix, cunny funnies, and all that!" That vulgar creature up there does indeed have his weary eye, but by the decree of—first, crack, then pop—Fate, as it were, not by election. Fate and Plato. That his beloved mentor should have helped to do this to him makes him feel doubly betrayed. "Whoa, speaking of your old clit classics," Bluebell whispers, her red windbreaker rustling as she leans down to press her warm cheek next to his, "I just *realized!* From where *you're* standing, you can see right up the little sweetie's ballooning sky blue skirts, can't you?! Wow, the art of introspective, just like you taught us! Dimples and all!" She gives him a conspiratorial squeeze. "Never know what you'll see if you just keep looking, right?"

"The details in this instance are insignificant, Miss," he snaps in his old tutorial manner, his irritability provoked not by her, for in truth he has been longing all the while, though he had forgotten this, to see her again, but by his present predicament, disconcertingly pathognomonic, preferring an aesthetic explanation for it, however contrived, to the humiliation of the mechanical one. Or, more precisely, the wooden one. "What matters is the, ahem, overall composition." Which doesn't matter at all. What matters in a cheap hamfisted pastiche as bad as this one is who commissioned it and why that cretin and the painter weren't both gibbeted in the Piazzetta or hung out to dry in a cage at the top of the Campanile. But, given his seemingly intense scrutiny of the wretched thing (what is worse, he can feel his incorrigible nose acting up again, even as he speaks), what he says is: "That and its position, both in, eh, historico-cultural time and in physical politico-geographical, as you might say, space."

"Oh yeah, I get it! You don't have to point! Like, right beside it there's that painting of 'Modesty,' right? And so that whole bare-assed scene of the Universe or whatever it is up there becomes like an assault on—*splupp! crack!*—decency itself, a case of aggravating rape by a dirty old man, you might call it! I *love* it! And then in this one up here—gee, I'm sounding just like you, Professor Pinenut! I *told* you you taught me everything I know!—in this one we got this gorgeous hunk in the red bikini holding up the earth, or else maybe the mother just came down and—*squit! fpooff!*—bopped the sucker in the neck, and right over there we got Fortune—am I warm?—with her naked buns spread like fat on lean on a round dead stone, same size as the world on the hunk's back, as though to say that that's—*spopp!*—what this whole ball o' wax is gonna come to, right? Diddly-squat and let's hope her rectum's clean!"

As far as this blue Monday is concerned, it has been pretty much diddly-squat from the beginning. There were masked Carnival revelers whooping it up outside his windows all night until the early hours, and then, after an hour or two of vague stifling nightmares about interminable tenure committee meetings back at the university, which he couldn't escape because the chairman, an old crab, had his claw clamped on his elbow, warning him to "void evil companions," he awoke to the shrill squealing of schoolchildren in St. Mark's trying to hold up armloads of feeding pigeons, a "Ladies' Marching Band" made up of bearded and mustachioed men dressed in pinafores and blowing trumpets and tubas, and the hammering together of the viewing stands for the Mardi Gras Gran Gala on the other side of the Piazza. He had a pounding headache, his backside felt as if it had been coarsely sandpapered all night, and there was a fresh weevil infestation in his right elbow, telltale sawdust in the soiled sheets. On his return from the cemetery island of San Michele, he had resolved to press on immediately with his life's work—if he hoped to recover his discipline and integrity, it was now or never—and his worsened condition this morning made that resolution all the more urgent.

Of course he had to gauge his remaining strength. Though never afraid of the difficult, willing to confront challenges few other men of letters would even contemplate, he had never undertaken the impossible, knowing that was just another form of cowardice. His great *Mamma* opus was irretrievably lost, he knew that, and he also knew he could never reconstruct it, much less rewrite it, an effort as useless as trying to make an omelette out of a hatched chicken, but he believed he could capture something of its intent in a concentrated monograph, and such a project he might well have the time and energy to complete. In effect, he would write that final chapter that had brought him here in the first place, summarizing the salient points of the lost book and incorporating his recent Venetian experiences as paradigmatic fables of a sort, much as Saints Augustine and Petrarch used their own more vulnerable moments to provide dramatic contrast to their eventual unwavering commitment to higher principles, a commitment he intended, rejecting folly now once and for all (as though he had not done so many times before, but never with such a prospect of looming finality), to emulate. As his body weakened, he felt his spirit strengthening, as if being purified by the very impurity of his physical decay: home at last in the figurative lap of virtue, so to speak, all of a piece or not. This would be his theme, together perhaps with Wagner's dream of "dying in beauty," a dream which that musical impresario eventually realized upon this very island, though probably, as always, sooner than he'd hoped. With that in mind, then, he thought he might conclude the essay with the image of that tombstone on San Michele, the one he thought for a moment was hers, an artifact hard as an idea but pulsating with transcendent emotion, and ultimately something other (more abstract, in effect, more indefinite) than it appeared to be, an image that would thus reveal much that was at the very core of his personal aesthetic, he who, dying in beauty, had always lived in it as well, though more in the abstract than in the particular.

What was here unfolding, he felt, or rather was already in full bloom, was what one might call, as another who died here once did, the "miracle of regained detachment," that ingenuous but contemplative state of mind from which all true creativity flows. This detachment was difficult to sustain, however, with that rude din just outside his windows, it was worse than those head-butts the puppets had given him, so he decided to escape the palazzo altogether and, in preparation for that spiritual task which, like a kind of artist's holy purgation, awaited him, to embark upon his long-planned pilgrimage to the works of Giovanni Bellini, poetic painter of Madonnas, whose many masterpieces anchored the city in that high serenity for which it was named and kept it from floating off through Ricci's and Tiepolo's silly ceilings. And where better to start than in the Accademia with the painting that had changed his life, "The Madonna of the Small Trees"?

But Eugenio, in a pink-faced dither, would have none of it. "Out of the question, dear boy! I need everyone *here!* My costume has to be *completely* remade, the bodice just *won't* do! Then there are the masked balls, the decorations, and I haven't even *started* on my introduction speech for the Gran Gala! *Tomorrow night!* Martedì Grasso! Can't you *see?*" The palazzo staff was indeed in great turmoil, the servants scuttling about feverishly, racing hither and thither on Eugenio's screamed orders, out one door and in another, crashing into each other on thresholds and tumbling down stairs, though it was not certain anyone was actually doing anything. "And now Count Agnello Ziani-Ziani Orseolo is on his way here with the deeds to the Palazzo Ducale! I *told* you I had something extravagant boiling, Pini! The Count is the direct descendant of nine doges, but he's at the green, as the saying goes, and we've got the gold! Think of it! The central building in the world! This is a chance that comes only once every Pope's death! But we have to grasp luck by the hair and the bull by the horns, my boy, a botta calda, while the drum's pounding—!"

"But you *promised!* You said I could have anything I *wanted!*"

"But, Pini, all the way to the Accademia—?! Be reasonable! I have *five* Madonnas right here in the palazzo. One of them might even *be* by Burloni!"

"Bellini."

"Bollini, Ballone, I simply can't *do* it, my dear! The Count is due here any moment! *History* is being made! Buffetto! Quickly! Take the professor to the Gritti and buy him a Picolit grappa!"

"I don't *want* to go to the Gritti!"

"Ahi, what a plague you are, Old Sticks! You always *were* such a restless thing, I did think you'd learned better!"

"It's *not* restlessness, it's my *life's work!* My Venetian monograph! I insist—!"

"Believe me, the worst thing you could possibly *do*, amor mio, is write another book about Venice!"

"But it's not about—!"

"Wait! How about the Biblioteca Marciana? Eh? Just the other day you were complaining that it was easier for you to visit a distant island than the Marciana across the way!"

"But there aren't any Bellinis—!"

"*Tomorrow* the sodding Bellinis! Today Petrarca! Cicero and Pliny! Marco Polo's will and Fra Mauro's map! The Grimani Breviary! The Bessarion Codexes! A million precious volumes, Pini, if we haven't sold them! Not to mention the 'Wisdom' of Tiziano hanging up there someplace, and the immortal 'Philosophers' Gallery' in the Great Gilded Hall! How can you *resist?*"

"Well . . . but—"

"Francatrippa! Buffetto! Hurry! Transport the professor across to the Sansovino Library *immediately!* This is important! Can't you see the dear man is *waiting?* His life's work *depends* upon it! And come back at once! Count Ziani-Ziani is on his way! *The future of Venice awaits us!*"

"Back in a crack, direttore!"

"In a pig's whisper, direttore!"

"In quattro e quat—!"

"Non fare il coglione, you impertinent blowhards! Get your feet *out* of here, or it's off with your *heads!* And I don't mean the ones with *ears* on them!"

And so they'd not even gone for his litter chair, they'd just swept him up by his armpits and gone clambering madly out of the palazzo as though escaping a burning building, bustling him, feet dangling, down the back stairs into the alleyway behind with its stale kitchen odors, clinking of dishes, and BLOWING GLASS FACTORY ENTRANCE sign, then through a tiny sottoportico past camera, clothing, and junk shops into the Piazza itself, startling the patrons of the Laverna as the three of them collided with the marble tables and sent the yellow café chairs tumbling; then, his feet fluttering behind him like a wind-whipped flag, they went racing pell-mell across the open end of the Carnivalized Piazza, under the rearing bronze horses and past the towering Campanile, colossal father figure of all bell towers, now sounding from on high its throaty five-mouthed alarums, putting white-masked tourists to flight as they charged down upon them and churning up clouds of terrified pigeons, barreling finally at full gallop through a doorway flanked by a pair of caryatids, massive and glossy as body builders on steroids, and bearing the legend: BIBLIOTECA NA-ZIONALE MARCIANA: LIBRERIA VECCHIA; without pause, he was hauled on up the marble stairs, now under workers' scaffolding, the vaulted ceilings and precious gilded grotesqueries hidden behind tented sheet-ing, and deposited hastily in the barren Great Hall, stripped of its display cases and undergoing restoration, no book in sight, not a person either, and there, without so much as a brief farewell, aban-doned, his protest—"Wait! Stop! Damn you, take me back!"—un-heard.

Stand there he could, but little more than, his knees shaky but holding, just, there in that cold empty hall, surrounded by a kind of cartoon gallery (he recognized Tintoretto's facile ink-stained hand) of ancient philosophers mocking him with their robust good health and their evident immunity to folly. Not a one with a wooden head. He felt cruelly judged. Was one of them his master Petrarch? No doubt. Perhaps that one in the golden robe, teetering on a loose pile of books, piercing him through with his dark sagacious gaze. Petrarch had be-queathed to Venice his entire library, the most splendid private col-lection of its time, launching the idea of this building in which to house it, and then had taken the whole lot back again. The professor had flown here from America with the poet's *Epistolae seniles* under his arm, and it might now be said their roles had been reversed, he now (it was the dank sad smell of the place perhaps that suggested this) in the great man's armpit. Francesco Petrarca, alias Petrarch, Petracchi, Petracco, Petraccolo, and Petrocchio: like himself the most celebrated scholar of his age, one who also blended art and theology, promoted the classic vision, opposed folly and deceit, and became an exemplar in his lifetime for all humanity, the old professor not excluded. He had stopped short of producing bastard children, but had otherwise emulated in all ways the noble life of his fellow Platonist and Tuscan, even in ways unpremeditated, for Petrarch had also, upon becoming a boy (this is said to have happened when he saw Dante in Pisa at the age of eight), lived a pious and studious youth, suffered a Hollywood-like period of dissipation on foreign soil (Petrarch's faucet worked better, there were consequences), then found his true vocation through an idealized love, abjuring lust and devoting himself thereafter to a lifetime of scholarship, writing, and tenured self-denial. They both had wandered the world in pursuit of truth and beauty, and had both ended up finally here in Venice, though Petrarch had lived long enough to die elsewhere, something the old professor doubts will be granted him. They both struggled their lives long against Aristotelians (Sophists they scorned outright), Petrarch finally driven from this city on that score, no wonder he took his books back. And they both were, it could be said, composers of tombstones . . .

On either side of the doorway through which he had been ported in such haste, posted there in their voluptuous robes like candidates for honorary degrees or guests at a royal feast (Veronese again, to be sure, that sybaritic host) and coldly examining him now in his doddering ignominy, stood the warring figures from his own and Petrarch's intellectual history, Aristotle and Plato. Plato's gaze, though full of disappointment and sorrow, was essentially benign, like that of a forgiving lover, but Aristotle, dressed as a Moorish prince, appeared to be glaring fiercely at him, giving him the big eye, as they say here, as though enraged at the bad press the professor had given him all these years. He had made Aristotle—and standing there on his trembling pins, feeling the chill of hostility in the air, needing all the friends he could find, he nevertheless did not regret this, and so, bravely, with what eye remained, returned the glare—the emblematic target of his lifelong dispute with those who substituted mere problem solving and art-for-art's-sake banalities for the pursuit of idealized beauty, and thus of truth and goodness as well. Aristotle and his vast camp following had unlinked art from its true transcendent mission, reducing it to just another isolated discipline, one among many, the worst of heresies, he deserved no quarter even had he any, in his extremity, to give.

Perhaps a cloud went by, or else it was a trick of his old eyes, but Aristotle seemed to wince as though at a bad odor and turn away, dismissing him with a contemptuous shrug, while Plato's austere expression, contrarily, appeared to soften, a faint appreciative smile curling the great sage's lips. His aged disciple, confused but moved (though move in fact he could not), dipped his nose in modest homage to the master, whereupon Plato, his rosy robes rustling gently, lifted one hand, puckered his fat lips, and, with a coy wink, blew him a kiss. The professor started, Plato's eyes rolled up to stare in alarm at the ceiling, he jerked his own head back and—*crack! pop!*—there it stuck, his rot-decayed neck locked, his nose pointing up at Il Padovanino's barbarous allegorical roundel, while around him the venerable philosophers wheezed and giggled like mischievous schoolboys. Which is when Bluebell came in and said: "Hey, Professor Pinenut! What a surprise! Whatcha lookin' at?"

There was a time once, he was still a young man in his early sixties, when he decided that writing about the decline of art in the Western world was not enough, he had to become a painter himself and establish the new classical norms by example. Futurism, expressionism, cubism, surrealism, abstraction, op art and pop art and all the rest: just forms of iconicized naughtiness, when you got down to it, and he felt it was up to him to recover art's ancient integrity, its sense of duty, its inherent grandeur. No more self-mocking irony, no more moral shilly-shallying, but true devotion: this was his cause, so he bought himself a box of paints and pencils and turned up at life-drawing class. It was not something he could accomplish overnight, he knew that, his eyes were open, but no one understood the history of art better than he did and he had been pretty good at basket making, so he figured it was just a matter of time, a year or two perhaps, he could be patient. He took to wearing berets, smocks, and neckerchiefs, and let the four or five hairs on his upper lip grow.

As it happened, the model for the art class was a student in his Art Principles 101 (was it *this* student? he couldn't be sure, but he thought not, remembering the girl as shy and delicate with body hair the color of burnt sienna dulled with a touch of Sicilian umber, which he had to go out and buy separately since it wasn't in his paint box), and about three weeks into the semester she came to see him late one afternoon during office hours. This was before the time of tights and miniskirts, it was more a ponytail-and-bobbysocks time when skirts were full and long and often pleated, and so, as she came in and sat down in his office, her flexing hips and legs were more like the subtle implications of hips and legs enveloped as they were in the soft contours of her flowing skirt, and, he thought as she gathered the folds around her, expressing a thigh here, hiding a knee there, much more provocative than when seen in the flesh, which he tended to look on primarily as a technical problem. That choice of roughly five parts of burnt sienna to one of Sicilian umber to capture the soft dark luster of her body hair, for example, was dictated in part by reality and his close examination of it, and thus captured something of the absolute for which he was always searching, but it was also tempered by the inconstant flesh tones of her circumambient thighs and abdomen, which seemed sometimes pale, almost bluish, and at other times tenderly flushed, almost aglow, and so threatened him with that relativity he so abhorred: if not even private hair color was constant, what then was Truth? An important question, perhaps none more so, yet one that seemed strangely irrelevant in his office that afternoon as he caught a teasing but imprecise glimpse of pale shadowy thigh when she crossed her legs and said: "That's just it, Professor Pinenut: it's— it's your nose!"

"What—?" He realized then it had been growing and had become engorged and feverish at the tip, and, as always on such occasions, he ducked his head and buried the unruly thing in a handkerchief. "Sorry, Miss, just a bit of a—!"

"I always get the feeling, you know, in the studio, that you're *painting* with your nose, and it gives me a very eery feeling, not so much in the art class itself where it seems almost natural, even when it bumps the canvas and gets paint on the end of it or when it's down between my knees when you're mixing colors, but in your lecture class when you're all dressed up in your nice wool suits and standing up there on the platform in front of everybody like the president or something and pointing it straight at some art slide you're showing, and, well, it's suddenly so—so *naked!*" She blushed and pushed her trembling hands between her knees, tightening the skirt around her hips. "It—it almost scares me, and I get this funny feeling between my legs like, well, like *God's* there, you know, *doing* something, and I can't even hear what you're saying anymore and everything else just disappears and all I can see is your nose and I can hardly breathe and I'm wet and trembling all over and probably the other kids around me are laughing but I don't even know they're *there*, there's just nothing in the world except your nose, pointing at *me* suddenly, like it is now, and this weird overwhelming feeling, even now I can almost —*oh!*—almost not stop it!—and what I'm wondering, Professor Pinenut, what's—*gasp!*—got me scared is, well—*ah!*—am I the Madonna?"

That was when he shaved his upper lip and gave up painting. And that was when he stopped blaming individual painters for the tragic decline of art. He now knew they couldn't help it. It was just how things were.

Which is more or less what he is thinking now when Bluebell, who is still cuddled up close with her arm around him, whispers in his earhole: "You know, Professor Pinenut, sometimes I think I don't even *like* paintings, even great ones like that one up there on the ceiling. They just seem so dead or phony or something, like those photos they put up outside movie theaters to advertise the films they're showing and which aren't anything *like* the films at all. But just watching you *look* at a painting like you are now—I don't know, maybe it's your nose or something, how *intense* it gets, how *excited*, like it's really *on* to something—whatever, I just get this tremendous feeling that, even though I'll never understand it, something *great* is happening, and it's enough for someone like me just to be close enough to pick up the vibrations. If I'm too dumb or insensitive to feel what you feel, you know, at least I can feel you feeling it!"

He knows he should tell her the real reason he is staring at this stupid painting, just as he should have told that teary-eyed student in his office that day that she was not the Madonna and stopped her from licking his nose all over, but he hates, now as then, to break the spell. Bluebell has moved behind him and, taller than he, now stands looking down, their heads pointed in opposite directions, into his eyes, her blond hair falling in curtaining wisps, her soft breasts, unzipped from the windbreaker, resting snugly on his shoulders like a kind of furry foam rubber warming pad. It is wonderfully relaxing. He can feel the back of his neck unpopping, unsnapping, almost like magic. He squints up past her smiling eyes and wonders if he sees what he sees. "The—the roots of your hair—" he whispers hoarsely, as she blows a quivering pink bubble toward his forehead and at the last second sucks it back between her bright white teeth: "—are they —are they *blue*—?"

"Oh yeah," she laughs lightly, giving her head a little shake to tickle his face with its strands, her breasts bobbling gently around his ear-holes. "Just a silly college stunt. A bunch of us girls thought it'd be neat to dye our hair some weird punk color, and I did mine in this funky blue to, like, you know, go with my sweater. Pretty dumb, hunh? Thank goodness, it's finally growing out—only the roots are left."

"Ah . . ." The stiffness in his neck seems to have melted away. He finds he can lower his chin at last and his headache has utterly evaporated, though his face feels flushed and pinched in a not unpleasant way. He wonders if, in some mysterious way, he has found the illusive closing image for his monograph . . .

"Speaking of my sweater, prof," she adds, holding something strung on a gold chain in front of his nose, "you left this *inside* it last time." It is his ear, now blackened and shriveled up like a smoked oyster. He can feel his headache coming back. "I thought it was maybe kind of a present, you know, like a fraternity pin or something, so I've been—*snap! ffpoop!*—wearing it, but if you need it for anything . . . ?"

"No—!" he squeaks.

"Gosh, thanks a million, Professor Pinenut," she whispers and gives him from behind a tender little hug. "I'll always wear it next to my heart, just where I found it! Right here—see?"

He turns his head, following the dangled ear, and, encouraged by her pointing finger, presses his earhole into the warm blue hollow where its dessicated outer shell is snuggled. As he listens to the accelerating thump within, nodding in concert with it, his nose stroking lightly the fleecy breast, he tells himself with an outburst of rapture that what he sees there before his crossed eyes is beauty's very essence: form as divine thought, the single and pure perfection which resides in the mind, of which an image and likeness, rare and holy and soft as a powder puff, is here raised up for adoration. He wishes to explain this to her, discreetly of course, never once forgetting that she is the student, he her teacher and moral exemplar, wishes to tell her that beauty, my dear Bluebell, beauty alone is both lovely and visible at once, and indeed touchable as well, it is all that we can know of the spiritual by way of the senses and is the discriminating person's route to it, if approached with the appropriate fear and reverence and without getting overexcited, if you can help it, just a matter, the route that is, of following your nose, so to speak—but before he can even get started on this little essay the servants Buffetto, Francatrippa, and Truffaldino come storming in with his portantina, shouting: "Come quickly, master! We have something to show you!"

"No, no!" he cries in alarm, as they snatch him up and strap him in. "I want to stay *here!*"

"There's nothing to see here, professore, it's closed for renovations, as you can see for yourself! Come now, we've got to run! There's a new Bellini at the Accademia!"

"But I don't *care* about—!"

"It's the Madonna of the Organs, dottore! Il Conte Agnello Ziani-Ziani Orseolo has brought it! A masterpiece! You have to see it to believe it!"

"A new acquisition!"

"A gift to the city!"

"He's the heir of eleven doges!"

"Twelve!"

"And he's brought the deed to the family palace!"

"We have to escort the Count back to the Piazza for his official reception! Hurry! There's not a moment to lose!"

"No! *Stop!*" he protests, tears coming to his eyes. "You can't do this! *My—my life's work—!*" But they have already bundled him out of there, not even time to glance back, and now they go clattering down the marble stairs and out onto the busy Piazzetta, past the diapered Ducal Palace and the stiffened digits of the patron saints' twin monoliths, racing at full tilt toward the motor launch.

22.

THE PROCESSION IN
HONOR OF
COUNT AGNELLO ZIANI-ZIANI
ORSEOLO
AND
THE MADONNA OF THE ORGANS
(NEW ACQUISITION)

"Ah! casa mia, casa mia!" exclaims il Conte Agnello Ziani-Ziani Orseolo, his old head thrown back, pointed gray beard thrust high in the wintry wind, his eyes closed, his immense dripping phallus bobbing with the tremulous ecstasy of his wide-armed embrace of this city he calls his *dulce domum* and *summum bonum, il suo paese, bell'e buono*, first cause and final hope: "My fulcrum! My feedbag! My fetish! My fenny fount and fungous funiculus! Floating fleshpot of my fancy! My foolscap, fizgig, flophouse, and fantod! My foreskin! My fistulae!" Thus, to the cheers of his strange audience there on the Campo della Carità, the Count glorifies the alleged city of his birth, exhausting the alphabet in his exaltation, or at least all the F's, prompting Melampetta to bark out finally from beside the professor's portantina: *"Ma, fammi il favore! Va' a farti fottere, faccia da culo!"*

Which, far from arousing the ire of the Count or the crowd, only draws more cheers ("Viva! Viva! Go fuck yourself, buttface!" they chant lustily, led by Francatrippa, who conducts them with a candy-striped phallus of his own, Buffetto and Truffaldino bounding gaily about the campo doing handsprings and cartwheels: *"Va' a farti fottere! Va' a farti fottere!"*) and incites the old graybeard to even loftier flights of grandiloquence: "Ah, Venezia! Mother of all my pleasure and profit!" he cries, striding about manfully, gripping his phallus with both hands to keep it from slapping the pavement as he goes, the onlookers ducking and scattering to make room for the monstrous engine. "Father to my glorious misdeeds! Uncle of my wild oats, sown and unsown, mother-in-law of my exile, and second cousin of my throbbing green-isled imagination! Great aunt by marriage of my melancholic flatulence! Grand nephew of my noble erections and half-sister to my sweet ruin! Venezia! *Veni etiam!* Your errant prodigal has indeed come again! And again! Clasp me close to your bosom as a scrotum clasps its restless testes, let me wander no more! Those of us who have changed our homes and pleasant thresholds, and sought a country spreading its legs beneath another sun, as a great Roman publicist was wont to say, ought to have our heads examined, if we can find them, stuffed up our irrespective rectums as they waywardly are. No, no, propria domus omnium optima, or oppressa, or obstupida, and/or words to that effect, home is where the hard is, he who lies everywhere, gets laid nowhere, eheu, eheu, sic passim!"

This oration draws more applause and cheers (*"Bravo! Viva la faccia!"* they shout: *"Ipse dixit! Viva il Magnifico!"*) which the Count acknowledges by leaning back and raising his glitteringly decorated organ on high like a bejeweled flagpole, others in the assembly at the Accademia landing stage responding in kind as their constitutions permit, the monumental Madonna of the Organs for her part reaching into the scarlet folds of her glistening vagina with both hands and pulling out her ovaries which she proceeds to flick on their fallopian strings at the Count's shaft like little pink yo-yos. Her face, true, the professor has to admit, does, except for the hollow eyes and the fringe of ink-black beard peeking out from under her chin, resemble that of Giovanni Bellini's "Madonna of the Small Trees," but the rest of her is more like an oversized walking anatomy lesson, an elaboration of sorts upon the traditional Madonna of the Bleeding Heart, in that not just her heart (which is bright green) is outside her body, but *all* her glands and organs are dangling from her generous flesh like Christmas ornaments: her spleen, kidneys, liver, brains, bladder, stomach, larynx, pancreas, and all the rest, her lungs worn like water wings, her mammaries like shoulder pads, her intestines looping from her rear like a long spongy tail or a vacuum sweeper hose.

Il Conte Agnello Ziani-Ziani Orseolo's first act, upon the arrival of the emissaries from the Palazzo dei Balocchi, the exchange of greetings, the display of the deed, the windblown dissemination of the billion lire, and the Count's knighting, as it might be called, of the professor, was to present the Madonna as a gift to the city *("Urbi et orbi!"* he'd cried, making the sign of the cross over her in the Byzantine fashion with his ithyphallic appendage, the genuflecting citizenry in the Campo della Carità replying with a communal breaking of wind and a whooping ovation), observing that, as he pointed to her exuberant crimson-petaled gash: "Heroes have trod this spot! Poets have slept here and signed their ineffable names! Merchants have here lost all their earthly goods, philosophers their minds! Only a few intrepid explorers, venturing into its labyrinthine depths, have returned to tell the tale in their epistles and travel guides of the fatal gift of beauty, the very sight of which sets us afire with pain and longing and sends us plunging, lance hoisted, blind to dangers, into the awesome abyss! Ah, but roses, roses all the way, good friends and figsuckers, so loving and so lovely, nature herself shivers with ecstasy at the sight of this toothsome apparition! She walks the waters like a thing of life! Beauteous even where beauties most abound, she is the answer to our bedtime prayer that womankind have but one rosy mouth, to kiss them all at once from North to South!" Which is what they all did, lined up to lap, more to the south than to the north, at the Madonna's fluorescent lips, which some said exuded a dewy liquor not unlike zabaglione laced with rum and holy water and went eagerly back for seconds, the professor in his dark temper demurring, furious still at having been dragged away from his former student (he felt that some grave academic principle had been ruthlessly violated, but his threats and protests had gone unheeded) and subjected once more to the cruel abuse of the elements and the callous masses.

On their way here, as they came spanking up the blustery Grand Canal in the roaring motor launch, Truffaldino, Buffetto, and Francatrippa had driven him finally into a sullen silence with their breathless overlapping accounts of the triumphant arrival in Venice of the

famous Count, descendant of at least thirteen doges ("No, no, *fifteen!*"
cried Francatrippa vehemently: "*Fifteen* doges! And three *popes!*"), the
splendor of his entourage, the undeniable authenticity of his deed to
the Palazzo Ducale, attested to by 579 recognized doctors of law,
living and dead, for which he had already received from Omino e
figli, S.R.L., a preliminary down payment of a billion lire, and his
gift to the city of the newly uncovered Bellini masterpiece, "The
Madonna of the Organs," which they called "a living miracle." "Well,
yes, it's *sort* of in the style of the 'Madonna of the Small Trees,'
master, only more like a 'Madonna of the Stunted Kidneys,' as you
might say!"

What they meant by this became clear when they rumbled up
under the green steel frame and dark heavy timbers of the Accademia
bridge to the vaporetto landing stage of the great museum and were
met there by his onetime boatyard hostess Melampetta, serving as
official watchdog in the absence of Alidoro, and now yapping out
something between a joyful welcome and an angry scolding; a motley
assemblage of hundreds of citizens, local or otherwise, many of them
bearing or wearing gaudy organs of their own, together with a number of wild animals, demons, extraterrestrials, monsters, and plague
victims, all cheering the new arrivals with grunts and roars and exposure of their backsides; a squadron of regally dressed attendants to
the Count, standing at attention, their genitals where their faces
should be and their faces between their legs, and each with a barrel
of wine on a little cart in tow; the Count himself in the crimson cap,
vest, and tight breeches of his ancestral dogeship, his flowing black
gown lined in crimson satin and trimmed with sable, his yellow gloves
and golden mules in the Turkish style, and his colossal erection
emerging from the gaping money pouch hanging between his thighs;
and finally, towering above them all, "The Madonna of the Organs"
with all her insides on her outside, including her disproportionately
small kidneys, sticking out at either side of her ample waist like shriveled tree-shaped little handles.

"Here he is!" Buffetto exclaimed, as Truffaldino and Francatrippa
unloaded him from the boat and onto the landing, elements of the
bearded Ladies' Marching Band beating out a drumroll as they disembarked. "L'Omino's dearest and oldest pal! Old Sticks himself! Un
gran cultore! Winner of the No-Balls Prize and, as you see, a worthy

challenge to any present! Make way! Make way! *Largo per il Gran Nasone!"*

He was paraded in his litter chair, with much pomp and swagger, past the ticket booth and up a kind of aisle beside a small garden, the scraggly bushes crowding up there like groundlings, a bank of outdoor phones standing in the front like spectators in the orchestra seats, to be deposited eventually, seething still with rage, mocking cheers and applause ringing in his defoliated tympanic cavities, in the middle of the broad campo under a massive yellow brick wall with tall dark windows, flat as a backdrop, a wall he recognized from the postcard pictures of Canaletto, prince of the *vedutisti*, to be that of the defrocked church become Venice's celebrated Temple of Art. His temple, too, alas, and there, in its scowling shadow, looked down upon, as it were, by those very masters to whom his own long life had been devoted, he was obliged to exchange his new felt borsalino for the tall conical sugar-loaf hat of someone called Il Zoppo, a red-tipped prophylactic device was slipped on over the end of his nose and unrolled to his cheeks, around his neck they hung a sign reading "ECCE NASUS," and then Count Ziani-Ziani tapped him on each shoulder with his huge phallus and declared him an Immortal Member in Firm Standing in the Great Privy Council of the Illustrious and Lubricious Republic of Venice.

Throughout all this—and the subsequent exchange of greetings, toasts, and tributes, which included a brief memorial to the original Little Man in the form of a chorus of *"Viva i balocchi!"* and *"Abbasso l'aritmetica!"* followed by the unscrolling of the ancient parchment deed to the Palazzo Ducale, doodled on, it was said, by Doge Sebastiano Ziani himself, decorated with architectural fancies, and colorful as a circus poster, then the scattering into the wind of the billion lire, which the Count somehow managed to discharge explosively out the end of his upraised phallus, much to the squealing and scrambling delight of the vast crowd, and finally the presentation to the city of the "Madonna of the Organs," an unveiling that was more like the opening of a pop-up book—the venerable scholar sat hunched in his portantina, dunce-capped head ducked, beating with impotent fury at the chair arms with his little balled fists, and grinding his teeth so hard that most of the ones that remained fell out in his lap. What most galled him was his awareness of how much his own wooden-headed resistance to well-meant advice, that ancient bane, was responsible for his present distress. It was as though he were inhabited by some kind of demonic antibodies to common prudence and sanity! Oh, he had blundererd in public before, exposed himself, played the fool, but now it was as though he were making a career of it!

"There, there, don't pull the snout so, dear friend," growls Melampetta at his side. "True, it's about as pretty as a blackhead, this cazzo di niente we call life—'un bel pasticcio,' were the Abbé de Montfaucon de Villars' immortal words for it, I believe, as he lay dying in the road in a bed of horse dumplings, asking only that they pass the parmesano—but as Horace Il Poetastro once counseled the constipated Augustus Caesar whilst feeling his way hopefully in the dark, 'Nil desperandum, padrone, there's a plug here somewhere!' So cheer up! Not all sorrow comes to bring damage! Besides, I have a surprise for you!" When he first arrived, Melampetta had, less generously, greeted him with a bitter howl of invective and reproach, quoting everyone from Alexander of Abonuteichus to the Zenos of Citium, Elea, and the Zattere on the subjects of ingratitude, bad manners, false friends, the corruptions of power ("Was it not our own Zan Petrarca who denounced in these very streets those who 'swallow a gazeta and shit it in silver—?' "), sins of omission, faithless love, broken promises, and blind folly, and not forgetting in her citations Zosimos of Panopolis, whose mystical vision of a world alchemically bonded by interlaced dogs and puppets, here betrayed, led the sagacious old gnostic to rewrite the incommunicable axiom to include "arf!" and "cucù!" and to remark on his deathbed that the only dangers to universal happiness were a warm nose and a cold arse. But her desperately wagging tail revealed her true feelings and she soon took pity on his dire condition, even acknowledging his justification in abandoning the doghouse and taking refuge in the Palazzo dei Balocchi: "It's an old prole's dream, after all, to live the life of Michelaccio among the filthy rich, vicious unprincipled pricks though they be. But just the same, comrade, you might've stopped by the yard from time to time to scratch my ears and let me give you a lick or two . . ." Now she reaches beneath her tail with her teeth and strips a watch off her hind leg, holds it up to him: it is his own, the one he threw through a window the night he came here. "Alidoro managed to wrest it away from those pirates down at the Questura, but when he got back where he'd left you, you weren't there."

"Something . . . came up. Another . . . another engagement . . ."

"The bright lights, break a leg, a star is burned, and all that, you mean, yes, yes, Lido found your crazy tracks, heard the commotion, but by the time he reached your venue the show was over. Nothing but greasepaint smears and ashes. They'd rung down the curtain and then burned that, too. Nobody left onstage but a few of his pals from the pula, toasting their garlic sausages and warming themselves like sanctimonious Parsees around the embers of their fiendish bone-fires, as they are properly called, according to Saint Elmo of the Smoldering Ecstatics, or else it was Saint Anthony the Great in his bone-on fever. The mangy old mutt was heartbroken, of course, until he picked up your scent in an underpass and saw your ear floating in the canal at the end of it. He didn't know if you'd been thrown in or fell but—"

"I *fell*—!" Yes, he had almost forgotten: the wild ride, the mad chase, the icy green slime underfoot—

"Without thinking, something the fart-brained testardo always did find harder to do than fly backwards, he jumped in to try to save you—"

"Alidoro—?! But he can't—*he can't swim*—!"

"From all the available evidence, amico mio," growls Melampetta, scratching her ear with her hind foot, "that would seem to be a reasonable deduction. The driveling old eyesore, at no loss to the general aesthetics of this open sewer, has not been seen since."

"Oh no . . . !" Though Alidoro later rescued him from fire, sealing the ancient bond between them, they had met, so to speak, in water, the powerful young police dog having leapt into the sea to chase him, only remembering after it was too late that he did not know how to swim. It was the first time he had ever had the authorities at his mercy, and he reveled in it. He taunted the drowning mastiff, toyed with him, exacted promises, swam teasing circles around him. Finally, convinced the miserable beast was too bloated from all the salt water he had swallowed to pursue him any further, but still wary of the fanged jaws, he took hold of the thick tail he still had in those days and dragged the half-dead creature back to the lido. Alidoro could not even stand up, but lay helplessly on his side, draining from all his orifices like a punctured balloon, blubbering out his gratitude. Pretending to be administering artificial respiration, he jumped up and down on the prostrate body, just for fun, and kicked the turgid belly-bag like a football, then jumped back into the water, daring the police dog to follow. Only later, on the lip of the Green Fisherman's frying pan, did he come to understand that he had made a friend for life, a real friend, perhaps the truest one he ever had.

"Now, now, no need for tears. There are those who would say the poor dim brute should have been put down years ago. He was a good comrade but something of a backslider in his old age and stupid as warm water, alla fin fine he may have done us all a favor."

"But—*sob!*—why didn't you *tell* me—?!"

Melampetta tips her head and gazes up at him quizzically, but before she can reply, the Count, who has been lamenting in the high style on behalf of the dripping kidneys and swollen bladder of the Madonna, not to mention his own leaking instrument, the removal from this campo of a municipal urinal ("Here, where a great public facility once stood, and where many great public figures thus stood as well . . ."), now announces his intention to conduct them all, en route to their official civic reception in the Piazza San Marco, on a sacred pilgrimage in memory of what he calls the original fourteen "pisciatoi della Via Crucis," commencing with a communal pee of homage and protest from the Accademia bridge.

And so the old scholar, weighed down now with grief, is hoisted once again by the palazzo servants and, led by il Conte Agnello Ziani-Ziani Orseolo and the Madonna of the Organs (New Acquisition), with the rest of the zany assemblage trailing behind, the Count's personal attendants with their bodily parts *a soqquadro*, as they say here, bringing up the rear with their cartloads of free-flowing wine, he is ported ceremonially up the massive wooden staircase, past a priest and a blind nun posted there at the foot like sentinels of conscience, nodding lugubriously as though tolling the knell of the passing sinners, and, at the bridge's crest, is tipped foward, portantina and all, so that just his nose with its translucent red-tipped rubber sheath droops over the railing.

Alongside him, up and down the bridge, the rest of the Count's cortege bring out organs of every size, color, and description and dangle them over the side, those without baring their behinds or else their breasts, or something resembling all of these, and, upon the Count's appeal to his "friends, roamers, and dribbling cunnymen, as Marcus Aurelius was said to have declared on the eve of the Battle of Thermopylae, lend me your tears and other bodily excretions, for our noble causeway depends upon it," let fly a veritable downpour upon the Grand Canal below, sending motorboats swerving and gondolas pushing desperately for shore, those on the decks of vaporetti ducking inside for cover, or else replying with similar, if only token, gestures of their own. The old professor, gripping his newly recovered watch with trembling fingers, seems to see through his bitter tears the sodden body of his old friend Alidoro floating by on the dark ruffled waters below, though it is probably only the usual plastic sack of garbage, of which the canal is always full. "I-I'm sorry!" he weeps, his chest riven. "I loved you so!"

The tall spindly hunchbacked character next to him with whom he had been forced to exchange hats, the one known as Il Zoppo, opens up the flies of his baggy white pantaloons, and a face leans out of them, spews a mouthful of wine over the railing, then turns to him and says, in chorus with another deeper voice above: "No need to be sorry! We love you, *too*, dear Pinocchio!"

Though charred and disfigured, it is a face he recognizes: the once-beautiful Lisetta of the Gran Teatro dei Burattini! There is still a trace of magenta in her hair and a safety pin in her wooden ear! But then—?! He cranes his old head up stiffly, peering through the tears and biting wind: "*Pulcinella!* Is it—is it *you—?!*"

"As you see, my friend," replies Pulcinella, tipping the professor's hat from on high, and from inside the pantaloons Lisetta says: "Yes, Pinocchio my dear, it is we!"

"But I thought—! I was afraid—!" And suddenly it all comes rushing back to him as though the evacuations cascading down from the bridge were releasing a torrent of dammed-up memory: his rescue from the wastebin, the kisses and pinches and dizzying head-butts, his brief career at the electronic keyboard (but how had he forgotten all of this? He must have nothing but woody pulp up there . . . !), and then the police parading in, the brutal charges, the bludgeonings and screams, the mad crush of the terrorized mobs, the frantic bodies kneeing him, pushing him, the smoke tearing at his eyes and throat, the two tall thin carabinieri bearing down on him, swinging brave Pulcinella's torn-off legs like nightsticks—"I saw—! Oh Pulcinella! *What they did to you—!*"

"Ebbene, compare, don't cry, it could have been worse. Others lost the lot. I've always walked as well on my hands as on my feet anyway —I was out of there in less than it takes to say it! Poor Lisetta here was not so lucky! They threw her on the fire!"

"Mangiafoco turned up and pulled me out in the nick of time! Burned my face black as a pewit's, I lost both arms, and my tits aren't what they used to be, but the bottom bits are all still good as new!"

"I'd lost my legs and Lisetta her arms, so Mangiafoco put the two of us together by nailing me to her shoulders."

"Nailing—?!"

"The joints and hinges were all gone, nothing left to pin new limbs to, it was the best he could manage."

"It's all right."

"It's kind of fun!"

"Of course, back flips aren't so easy any more."

"What I miss most is not being able to clap."

"But we do a double act now."

"We've worked up some new *lazzi*, Pinocchio, you wouldn't believe!"

"The old Siamese twin gags, you know! With a new angle, as you might say!"

"With a bit of a twist!"

"Not everyone's got a woman's head in his crotch!"

"Not everyone's got an asshole behind her ears!"

"But . . . but the others—?" he asks uneasily. "Brighella? Colombina—?"

"Ah . . . well . . ."

"You know . . ."

"Where there's smoke . . ."

"It was a real horror show, friend . . ."

"Mass pupicide . . ."

"Poor Arlecchino . . . they used a hacksaw on him . . ."

"They drilled him full of holes . . ."

"They soaked him before throwing him on the fire . . ."

"You know, to make him burn longer . . ."

"His screams would have broken my heart, if I had one," sighs Lisetta from inside Pulcinella's pants, as Pulcinella reaches in to wipe the tears from her eyes. "Fortunately I've always been a bit wormy in that part . . ."

"At least you did what you could for him, dear Pinocchio!"

"Well . . ."

"At least you didn't turn your back on your dearest friend!"

To his horror, just as he is about to reply, in all honesty of course, as is his wont, if not indeed his onus, he suddenly sees the same flash of blue that he saw then: she is sitting out all alone on the bow of a battered old No. 1 waterbus lumbering up below on its way to the Accademia landing stage, seemingly oblivious to the excreta showering down upon her, gazing up through it as though in stunned disbelief at the professor, crowned ludicrously in Pulcinella's peaked *coppolone*, his nose hanging limply over the railing, still in its silky sheath, like that stupid character in the World War II graffiti. His heart plummets. "Forgive me!" he whispers in his pain and confusion as she slips past. His mortification is complete. "My . . . my love—!" And then she is under the bridge and out of sight, and he is, though numbed by shock and utter despair, under way again, the procession setting forth once more, Count Ziani-Ziani having just pulled up his crimson breeches and declared: "As the great Zan Bellini, painter of the famous 'Incontinent Fortune,' shown relieving herself blissfully from the side of a gondola with a granite blue globe in her fragrant lap, used to say, *'Forbirse el cul col sasso tondo, xe la piu bela cossa de sto mondo!'* The loveliest thing in this world that's known is to wipe your ass with a round stone! And now, fellow citizens, it is time, as they say, to jump, having blessed it, the ditch! The city babbos await us! So soak your beak and let it leak, our solemn round proceeds!"

23.

THE LAST CHAPTER

In a cramped busy campo like many others they have visited on their pilgrimage to the Fourteen Urinals of the Cross, the procession of Count Agnello Ziani-Ziani Orseolo and the Madonna of the Organs (New Acquisition) is interrupted suddenly in the middle of one of the Madonna's bizarre purification rituals by the clamorous headlong arrival of the Winged Lion of Saint Mark, flapping in either to join or to assault the party, but, already well in his cups, seriously misjudging his approach, catching his forepaws on the tent top of a makeshift costume stall and somersaulting heavily into a marble wellhead, roaring out an alarming stream of drunken obscenities all the way. A human butterfly, pirouetting decorously on the convex lid of the wellhead, is sent flying when the yowling Lion slams into it, stone crashing upon stone, while from within the collapsed stall come cries of "Rape!" and "Earthquake!" and "Help! Murder! It's the Red Brigade!"

"Che cazzo—?" bellows the Lion in his querulous stupor. *"By the Virgin's verminous and fulsome cunt, I'll kill the turd who did that! Oh, I am fucked! Get me something to drink, you cretinous pricks! I am dying!"*

The three servants hastily set the old scholar down in a quiet corner of the little campo, warning him not to run away or get into mischief or talk to strangers, and rush off to attend to the raging Lion, who seems prepared to eat the poor crumpled butterfly if he can just get on his feet again and if he hasn't lost all his teeth in the calamitous fall, Count Agnello Ziani-Ziani Orseolo ordering that an entire barrel of wine be poured down the old fellow's throat as a kind of holy libation in recognition of the once-glorious empire and designating him Honorary Chaircreature and Despot of their entourage for their triumphal march into the Piazza San Marco.

Left alone, the professor, crushed by sorrow and chagrin, buries his veiled nose in his lap, the condom's red tip hanging forlornly from the end like a bloody drip, and fretfully twists his silvery watch as if he were telling his beads, gripping the skittish thing with both hands in the old way, before he had fingers, thinking bitterly: what a paltry bauble time is! He's had more than his share of it, and what good has it done him? He can't even see the face of it. All he can see is the shock and disappointment on Bluebell's innocent upturned face as she passed below him back at the Accademia bridge, a famous phrase from his early writings returning now to haunt him: "The bridge between It-ness," he wrote in *The Wretch*, elucidating a concept first introduced in *Art and the Spirit*, "and I-ness is *character*, whether staunch or frail, artfully made or haplessly jerry-built, and that which flows below is not Time, but *the ceaseless current of implacable Judgment!*"

As Buffetto and Truffaldino ported him down the broad wooden steps of the brdge, it recalled for him an earlier descent from another bridge, that night he first arrived here, full then of hope and joy and something like intellectual rapture, the city, silenced by snow, awakening in him an almost mythic sense, as it felt at the moment, of being a witness to eternity. He had plunged into the alluring labyrinth of the magical city that night on his damaged but still functional knees as a lover might enter the body of his beloved (speaking poetically of course), experiencing that rare creative communion between the spirit and the body that prophesied a happy conclusion to his final work-in-progress and thus to his long exemplary life as well. And now all that noble joy had come to this. That reckless eager plunge into the masked city had been his undoing. As they looped back toward the Piazza San Marco, whence this newest misadventure today began, he felt caught up in loops within loops, his fraudulent life a mad skein of recurrent self-deceptions, and he wished only, the tears streaming down the craquelure of his cheeks, to make it safely back to his room in the Palazzo dei Balocchi and to hide his terrible face there forevermore.

Around him, meanwhile, the Count and his followers celebrated with wine and song and wild abandon. Drums beat out a processional march as they wound their way from the site of one vanished urinal to another through the dreary Venetian labyrinth, the Count squirting his monstrous phallus on them all from time to time as though dispensing holy water, the Madonna waddling about seductively with her exaggerated Trecento dehanchement, wagging her intestines, her organs jouncing and bobbing like bangles, teasing passersby to give her parts a little squeeze. Feet went by with eyes and noses on the soles, an immense penis passed with semen dripping from a white mask at the tip, there were copulating rodents and horn-blowing bottoms and birdlike creatures with phallic beaks and pretty young novices with devils' faces winking from their bare behinds. But to the tormented professor, hunched over in his litter chair, they were all mere mourners at a wake, their revelry a dirge, their bawdy songs a last lament. Cast down in final defeat, he could only stare darkly at the recovered watch in his trembling hands, sinking ever deeper into that pit of inconsolable grief, regret, and bitter self-reproach into which he had fallen, or, as it were, been pushed. Most of the flesh had fallen away from the backs of his hands, and he noticed now how the grain stood out like reticulated tracery, the softer parts of the wood eaten away. It was as though its encasement of flesh had fed upon it like lichen. He tried to pick off a scabby piece of skin, but the pain, as ever, was harrowing, as if it were determined to hold fast, to carry through, even if he were not.

This power of flesh to go its own way became the subject (perhaps he had been talking aloud again, quite likely) of several of the Madonna's ceremonial performances as they went along the route of late lamented pissoirs. She would light the seminally blessed votive candles with her apple green heart, which worked like a kind of miniature blowtorch, empty her bladder on the site of the displaced *pisciatoio*, and with her spleen lead a communal prayer for making public urinals and ridotti out of all the city's banks and churches: *"Più cessi meno chiese!"* they would chant. Then, after Count Ziani-Ziani had recited from what he called the Ancient and Holy Testament of Latrine Grafitti, she—or, more precisely, her organs—would sermonize briefly on various topics such as individual organ and glandular rights, cruelty by civic neglect of the tragicomically fused genito-urinary twins, or the body politics of visceral autonomy versus a united organic front, the various glands and organs sometimes getting into heated debates and even duels with one another, all trying to shout at once, the liver blackening with rage, the stomach turning sour, the bowels complaining rudely, the heart winning most arguments finally with its lethal blowtorch, the Madonna's body becoming a kind of strange traveling puppet booth, the organs her fractious tattermen. Finally, the larynx or the adenoids or the vagina would bring all the spitting and screaming and squirting of this anatomical psychomachia to an end by singing the *Benedictus*, the anus at the end of its long undulatory tube providing the resonant antiphon, and then the Madonna would deliver a few dozen marzipan Jesuses from her womb and pass them out to the children.

Here in this campo, after the opening rituals, she and her organs, having paused to reflect upon martyrdom, had taken up as a case in point the professor's nose, on rubber-masked display above his "ECCE NASUS" sign, debating the question: which was the true martyr, his nose or the rest of him? Not surprisingly, the more exposed parts opted for the abused and repressed ("Hamstrung," was the way the hamstrings put it) nose, the glands and internal organs arguing contrarily on behalf of the inner humiliation and suffering brought to the whole by the offending part, which the fulminating colon called an intolerable pain in the butt and the uterus said wasn't worth a dried fig and, for its sins, as much of omission as commission, probably ought to get the chop. "I've had it up to my hair with the stuck-up thing!"

"That's right," agreed the adrenal glands, "let the snotty nuisance stew in its own juices!"

"I see what you mean," observed the eyeballs on their little strings. "At first glance, the little blowhard does appear to be something of a fist in the eye and more than a bit uppity, but it is our view that only the branch can be said to be martyred when the tree, for its own good, is pruned!"

"Right, I can swallow that," piped up the esophagus, and the shrunken kidneys, siding with the eyeballs, added: "Moreover, if the fault is in the handle, as the saying goes, so then is the anima: dismemberment hallows the honker!"

"I speak," said the heart, flaring up briefly, "from the heart when I say that your argument, my dear kidneys, doesn't hold water. The holy martyrs were canonized for their good hearts, not good hooters!"

Thus, inevitably, the debate, which grew increasingly tempestuous ("You're getting up my nose, you cardiocentric four-flusher!" screamed the sinuses, and the ovaries started throwing eggs again), evolved into a raucous theological dispute about the true location of the soul, each organ staking its claim as sole container of the elusive stuff, the lungs bellowing that insufflation had been the true sign of life since God first puffed up Adam, the brain retorting heatedly that the soul was inseparable from the logos and that to think otherwise was unimaginable idiocy, the mammary glands doing a bit of breast-beating of their own, and the rectum airing its "gut feeling" that, since everything else in the world got stuffed up it, the soul must, willy-nilly, be there as well. "Macchè! I haven't the stomach for this," rumbled the stomach acidly, burned by the heart and vainly seeking relief from the spreading crossfire, which came finally from on high with the head-over-heels arrival of the Winged Lion, explosively interrupting the performance.

Throughout all this, the professor had been watched at some distance by the mournful old priest he had noticed back at the foot of the Accademia bridge, standing now across the little campo, together with his companion, the blind nun, under a circus poster for tomorrow night's Gran Gala. Perhaps they were waiting for him to resolve the dispute of the organs with one of his famous Augustinian disquisitions on the "changeless light within," an image he had once found useful in trying to recapture the peculiar essence of his prenatal (so to speak) life on the woodpile. No, I am sorry, my friends. No resolutions. The light's gone out. He has never been afraid of course to speak of the "soul" or "spirit" ("I-ness" was in effect a word for this), though he has often wondered why men born to real mothers did, and indeed it could be said that his entire *Mamma* project had been really little more than a homiletic account of his idiosyncratic search for the magic formula by which to elevate his soul from vegetative to human form, as though body, far from being a corrupting adversary, were in itself a kind of ultimate fulfillment. Soul itself, in the particular.

Now, left alone by the Lion's crash landing to savor, hunched over his scabs (has he found at last, he wonders, picking at them, his closing image?), the manifest ironies of his life's quest, he is approached deferentially by the limping priest and his ancient companion, stumbling along on a cane. "Scusi, signor professore!" rumbles the holy father softly in his gravelly old voice, bowing slightly and tipping his black hat, and the nun, nodding circumspectly, whispers as though in awe: "Professore!" "We are profusely honored, il nostro caro Dottore Pignole," the old cleric continues with another little bow, "to have your sublimated presence among us! We hold your nugaciously pleonastic writings here in grand esteem, alla prima, and consider them to be, as the saying goes, of the most beautiful water!"

"Yes," whispers the nun, her old head bobbing, "your water is very beautiful!"

"They have, as we Veneti say," the priest is quick to add, "*la zampata del leone*, the paw of the lion, that is to say, the indisputable footprint of genius and caducity. We few, to whom such things still have provenance, from the bottoms of our unworthy souls, if indeed they have bottoms, exalted sir, and who would know better than you, thank you!"

"You are welcome," replies the antiquated nun, then wheezes deeply as though suffering a sudden pain in her lower ribs.

"I-I am not who or what you think I am, father," the old professor confesses abjectly.

"You are not Professor Pinenut—?" asks the priest, peering closer. The nun, in seeming confusion, turns to hobble away, but the priest snatches her by her habit and draws her back.

"Yes—no, I only meant—"

"Ah. You speak metaphorically, of course, true to your majestic and incogitant stylus. We are all, souls masked by bodies, other than what we seem to be, and yet what we seem to be, in the soulless barter of the bodied world, we also are, and so, though *not* Professor Pinenut, you *are* he nonetheless! I trust then you will not deny us a trifling favor, good sir: to wit—"

"Good, sir," says the nun. "Do it."

"—To wit, to sign one of your noble and predacious tomes for our parish library, hoping that is not too magnanimous an imposture for such a gran signore—?"

"No, of course not, but I'm afraid I don't—"

"Have an opus at hand? Do not concern yourself, maestro, for we have traduced a little volume of our own. *Psst!* The *book*, you little turk's head!" The nun, he sees now, has a book clamped under one arm, but the arm seems disabled. Reaching for the book with her other arm, she drops the cane. Stooping for the cane, she drops the book. She feels around blindly for the book, but the priest steps crunchingly down upon her black-gloved hand and, sighing deeply, picks up the book himself, hands it to the professor with an uncapped pen.

"Your—your colleague, she's—"

"Yes, blind in all her two eyes, excellency, from too much devotion to the noble battologies of your ambagious texts. Now, if you would be so kind . . ."

Wearily, he opens the book to the flyleaf. He has signed millions of these things in his lifetime. The gesture is automatic. The book, however, is not an edition he recognizes. After signing it, he turns to the title page. For a moment he cannot comprehend what he is seeing. The letters stand there on the page like a row of rigid pine trees or the teeth of a saw. "Where—*where did you get this—?!*" he gasps, as the priest takes the book back and loses it in the voluminous folds of his cassock, the nun still whimpering under his planted foot.

"Why, in the little bookstore by the Rialto bridge, dottore. Everyone is reading it. It is a worldwide success!"

"But—but that's *impossible—!*"

"Ah, you are too modest, signor professore. I insure you it has been festooned by the most fulsome praise and garlanded with the ambrosia of excessive honor!" grimaces the priest, holding back a wheezing cough. The nun, too, on her feet once more, is shaking so hard with inner convulsions, she has to lean against the priest not to fall down again. "Perhaps you would like to peruse some of the recent reviews from *La Repubblica* or the *Corriere della Sera?*"

He takes with trembling fingers the clippings the priest hands him. "*Mamma*, the final opus magnum of the Nobel Prize–winning art critic and historian Dr. Pinenut," he reads through his blurring vision, a shudder shaking him violently from head to foot, "has been universally declared, upon its posthumous publication this week by the Aldine Press, in cooperation with the executors of the author's estate, to be, if not his greatest masterpiece, certainly his most revealing work. Although the unusual scrambling techniques of the early sections make them exceedingly obtuse, the patient reader will eventually find his reward in the clarity and simplicity of the final chapter, 'Money Made from Stolen Fruit,' with its extraordinary sentimental eulogies to his early mentors La Volpe and Il Gatto, from whom he admits most of his ideas were taken. 'They made me what I am today,' the great scholar confesses, providing fresh and startling new insights into the true sources of his peculiar, though now perhaps questionable, genius . . ."

"*Mascherine!*" the professor hisses between clenched jaws. He feels he is about to explode. Even this they have stolen! His work! His reputation! His very life! "*Assassini!*"

"Are you all right, master?" asks Truffaldino softly, leaning close. "You don't look so well . . . !"

The priest and nun are long since gone, of course. As is, once more, he notes, his watch. "Take me home," he whispers hoarsely, his whole body trembling. It is all over. Like his beloved San Petrarca before him, he is tired in body and soul, tired of everything, tired of affairs, tired of himself . . . "I have lived long enough. I am ready to die."

But then, just when ("Why not," he can hear Truffaldino saying with a shrug, "we're going that way anyway . . .") all hope vanishes, something occurs that reminds him forcibly of his old babbo's favorite saying. "One never knows, carogna mia," he would say, tipping his dirty yellow wig slyly down over one eye and sucking wickedly at his grappa jug, "what might happen next in this curious world . . ."

24.

LA BELLA BAMBINA

I t is to be believed, as Father Tertullian once said, leaping from paganism to the Apocalypse in a single bound, because it is absurd. It is certain because it is impossible: Tonight he is to have her at last! In his case, too, the miracle has owed something to the Apocalypse, though he can hardly be said to have leapt, and the Apocalypse in his tale of redemptive grace was a Carnival ride on the Riva degli Schiavoni: no mere mystical vision, that is, but an extraordinary and dizzying reality. Even now, he seems to lose his balance whenever he thinks of it, an experience he has never felt when contemplating something relatively so frivolous as the end of the world —and *that* magical ride was as nothing compared to what is yet to come before this day is over! "At last, tomorrow," Eugenio promised him yesterday, after making the arrangements, "your biggest wish will come true!" His mind cannot even quite take it in, though the rest of him is certainly more than ready, his whole body trembling in anticipation of that which, for his staggered imagination, remains ultimately unimaginable. As Bluebell put it on the Apocalypse yesterday, begging him to hug her close: "Wow! I'm so excited, teach, I feel like I'm about to wet my doggone pants!"

"Easy, master! You'll tip us over!"

"We'll be there soon enough!"

Yes, they are rocking dangerously, standing huddled there together in the frail gondola in the middle of the Grand Canal, both shores now lost to view in the damp cold fog of this wintry Mardi Gras morning, lost to *his* view anyway, but it doesn't frighten him, nothing frightens him since his wild ride on the Apocalypse, he feels reckless and manly and heroic, invulnerable even, and he responds to their silly fears with devil-may-care laughter, which unfortunately comes out more like deranged cackling, no doubt making him sound to the servants porting him completely *pazzo*, as they'd say—as indeed, in love, he is. Stark staring.

"Brr! What a cold stinking soup this is!"

"It's like the old Queen let one and it froze!"

"If this cacca gets any thicker we'll have to shovel our way across!"

For the professor, the dense fog which rolled in last night is full not of threat but of tender promise, an obliging curtain dropping upon the past, dissolving its regrettable angularities, so harsh and obstinate, in the sensuous dreamlike potential of the present. It is as though the city were masking itself in buoyant anticipation of secret revels of its own, hiding its shabbiness and decay behind a seductively mysterious disguise which is not so much a deception as an amorous courtesy. "The important thing about Carnival," he wrote recently in a note intended as part of his monograph-then-in-progress, "is not the masking, but the unmasking, the revelation, the repentance, the re-establishment of sanity," but, as always in all the days before yesterday, he was wrong. The important thing *is* the masking. What is sanity itself, after all, but terror's sweet foggy disguise? And love the mask that shields us from the abyss, art its compassionate accomplice?

These poignant thoughts come to him unbidden, full-formed already in a language, though chaste, clearly steeped in Eros's ennobling power (only now could he write that monograph which now he knows he will never write), swirling through his quickened mind as easily as do the coiling twists of fog here upon the still gray surface of the Grand Canal. This fog has caused the suspension this morning of all motorized water traffic and so forced upon them this slow labyrinthine journey to the mask shop by foot and now traghetto, a journey whose purpose is, in effect, to initiate a healing, providing him the means, designed by Eugenio, by which to rejoin, after the misguided century, his life's lost theater. He will put a new face on and, in love's name, learn to lie again, free at last from the tyranny of his blue-haired preceptress with her "civilizing" mania, her cruel tombstone lessons. The long oar splashes softly behind him as the black-snouted bark carves its perilous way across the silent waters, drawing a line erased as soon as drawn, thus celebrating, not the line, dull as death itself, but the motion that has made it. The others stand in a cluster in the rocking gondola like passengers on a crowded bus, holding him up between them, chattering nervously and peering intently through the purling mists for a glimpse of a landing, as though afraid that what they cannot see might not exist. Though impatience grips the old scholar, fear does not, and, least of all, the fear of *movement*, once such a bugbear that even melody's traveling line offended him and his gardens all were paved so as not to have to witness growth. No more. Movement, after all, was his very *raison d'être*, he was made for it. "To dance and fence and turn somersaults in the air," as his father advertised. His concept of I-ness, as he tried to explain yesterday to his former student, aboard the whirling Apocalypse, was never more valid: he could not, without doing violence to himself, be other than what, at the core, he was. "And only here, dear Bluebell, right now, where I am, am I truly what I truly am!"

Or words, in his cross-eyed, thick-tongued, mouth-stuffed delirium, to that effect . . .

"*Ecco!*" cries Francatrippa as the gondola strikes its dock, unseen till hit, and slides, bumping and scraping, into its berth. "We're here!"

"Where else," asks Buffetto impatiently, stepping onto the bobbing dock and reaching back to help with the portantina, "*could* we be?"

"Well, if I were here and you were there," replies Francatrippa, as the two of them lift him out, "and vice versa, then we'd be, both, both here *and* there, would we not?"

"And if I were here and you were there," pipes up Truffaldino, following them ashore, "and he were neither here nor there, then we'd all be both here and there and neither either, too!"

"Hrmff! And yet here is where we'd each still be for all that," insisted Buffetto. "Isn't that so, professor? But now come along, if you are to find the romance and adventure that you seek, we must find the guise for it. Am I right? Tonight's the night!"

Yes, so he believes, though twenty-four hours ago he would not have thought it possible. Nothing seemed possible then. His desire to go on living, guttering out, had dimmed to nothing more than the simple wish to be able to die in his bed at the palazzo beside his hot water bottle, and even that wish was more like the memory of a wish than the thing itself. Moreover, as he thought about that hot water bottle, there, surrounded by Count Agnello Ziani-Ziani Orseolo's raucous court with their drunken taunts and fountaining organs, dunce cap on his lowered head and condom on his nose, bereft, grieving, his manuscript pirated and his watch stolen for the second time, the realization slowly invaded his consciousness like a last lethal wounding that it *was* his hot water bottle, the snuggies, too, also his, the bent spectacles, the half-empty bottle of pine-scented mouthwash, and certain very grievous patterns began to emerge, not least the lifelong pattern of self-deception: he had known all along that was his own hot water bottle, there could not be two of them.

The procession had reached the Bocca di San Marco. Through the columns and beyond the temporary stands and stages built for Carnival, a vast assembly of the island's smart set and power elect could be seen congregated together in full regalia under the Clock Tower, prepared to receive the venerable Count Ziani-Ziani, now poised arm in arm with the Madonna of the Organs, his free hand tucked in his vest of crimson velvet à la the builder of this final wing of Venice's so-called "open-air drawing room," his chin high and pointy gray beard fluttering in the gusty wind, his immense phallus held aloft with the help of little Truffaldino. On a cart being pulled along beside him, the Winged Lion snored drunkenly, a sign around his neck reading "THE GOOD SOVEREIGN." Il Zoppo, as Pulcinella and Lisetta were—or was—now called, stepped forward from the crowd and raised a horn to Lisetta's lips, prepared to lead the multitudes into the Piazza, and just at that moment he heard it again, as though in fulfillment of some grim brassy oracle: "Oh my *Ga-ahd!* Lookit *this!* What a lotta crazy *lolly*-pops! Ding-*dong*, man! It's like a—*ffpupp! squit!*— little girl's dream come *true!*"

The professor sank even deeper into his litter chair, wishing there were a hole in it he could fall right through. The American strutted, hips swaying, through the spellbound crowd in her fringed white boots and wet blue jeans, tweaking organs and peeking into empty eyeholes and slapping the smirking faces on bared behinds, cracking gum between her dazzling white teeth and blowing fleshy pink bubbles, hooting and wisecracking ("Hooboy, I *love* those little faces down there, fellas! Is that what you call—*ssffPOPP!*—'masked balls'—?!") and circling inevitably around to the cringing scholar in his portantina. "Hey, *wow*, prof! *This* is a surprise! What are *you* doing here—?!"

"I—*kaff!*—it's not what—! A-a monograph I'm working on . . . !"

he stammered helplessly down between his knees, and felt his shameless nose bounce and waggle goofily in its latex wrapper.

"Jeepers, teach, that freaky rig is *beautiful!*" she exclaimed, clapping
her gaudily ringed and bangled hands together. "I hadn't *seen* you as
such a fun-loving *guy!*"

And then she did something quite extraordinary. She peeled the
condom away, pulled it on over her wet blond curls like a shower
cap, and, leaning over, her red windbreaker rustling between them
like a whispered secret, gave his nose a tender lingering kiss, tonguing
it at the tip and pinching it gently between her soft lips before letting
it go. He felt for an alarming but exquisite moment that he might be
going blind. "Yum!" she sighed, her breath warm on his ravaged
cheek, then added: "But gee whillikers, prof, look how you're shivering! You must be freezing to *death!*" Cold was what he did not feel.
But he could not argue. He could not speak. He could not even close
his gaping jaw, but could only stare in stunned amazement as she
tossed her windbreaker over his knees, stripped off the azure blue
angora sweater, and, while blowing a huge rosy bubble, the only
thing his bedazzled eyes could see, tucked the sweater around his
chest and shoulders. Then she pulled the windbreaker on again, leaving it unzipped, and grabbed Francatrippa's grand candy-striped
phallus away from him: "Hey, gimme that, man! Whoopee! I always
did want one of these doodads!" She gave it a squeeze and a jet of
milk spurted out the end of it, making those nearby duck and shriek.
"Yipes! Whaddaya know! It even *works!* C'mon, gang! *Let's go!*"

And so, with condom-capped Bluebell in the vanguard, carrying
her particolored phallus over her head like the troop ensign and
switching her behind provocatively, they all paraded triumphantly
on into the great open light of the Piazza, unloosing in those delicate
symmeteries a mad cacophony of shouts and squeals, honkings and
blarings and other rude noises: Count Agnello Ziani-Ziani Orseolo il
Magnifico behind Bluebell with his long nose in the air, his much
longer organ on little Truffaldino's shoulders, and his flouncing Madonna on his arm; the slumbering Lion on the wine cart alongside
him, wearing his crumpled sign like a belled cat; the bearded Ladies'
Marching Band, led by Il Zoppo blowing a trumpet out the flies of
his/her white pantaloons; the old professor, sugarloaf-capped and

shawled in blue and ported by Buffetto and Francatrippa in his litter chair, his astounded gaze locked helplessly on their bewitching bare-breasted standard-bearer; the Count's royal attendants with their inverted anatomies, dragging along the now much lighter barrels of wine; and finally the multitudinous throngs of zany and improbable creatures who had joined the procession along the way, Melampetta yipping and barking at the periphery, first on one side, then the other, like a sheepdog rounding up the drunken strays. At the far end of the square, the awaiting dignitaries arose en masse, either in homage to the visiting Count or else aghast at the apparition descending upon them through the Mouth of the Piazza, while overhead the terrified pigeons, displaced by the clamorous invasion, let their frantic droppings fall upon the Piazza like confetti.

They emerge now from a narrow passageway so tight they have been scraping the walls into a campo too broad and thick with fog to make out its shape or exits. "Which way *now?*" asks Truffaldino tremulously as the other two set the professor down. "I'm *afraid* — *!*"

"Don't be stupid! That way, of course!" reply Francatrippa and Buffetto more or less in chorus, one pointing to the left, the other to the right. Glancing at each other, they quickly switch directions, pointing at each other, then switch back again, and Truffaldino bawls: *"Help!* We're *lost!*"

Just then the heavy silence is broken by a scratchy two-way radio announcing something about a thief in a junk store, and a moment later two carabinieri materialize out of the fog, clattering past at full trot, their black capes fluttering behind them, rifles gripped at the ready in their white-gloved hands. *"Wait!"* the three servants cry out as one: *"Mangiafoco's — ?!"*

"This way!" shouts one of the policemen as both are swallowed up once more in the swirling fog, the smacking of their boots on stone fading slowly away to a distant ticking sound like an animal's claws on glass, and then everything is submerged once more in a dense muggy silence.

"Ebbene," sighs Buffetto as he and Francatrippa pick up his litter chair again. "We'll never get there by standing still! Andiamo subito!"

Subito is not exactly the word. They pick their way across the campo like ants, the pavement emerging in front of their wary toes as it vanishes behind their heels, a sharp contrast to yesterday's roisterous Carnivalesque crossing of the Piazza San Marco. If Eugenio was incensed by the irreverent congregation that approached him, he did not show it. He greeted the Count Ziani-Ziani with a deep bow and prepared eulogies, departing from his script only briefly to remark upon the nobleman's prodigious scepter, referring to it as "The Great Disseminator of Empire" and "The Magnificent Lion-Planter," citing it (at this reference to lions, the "Good Sovereign" awoke suddenly with a startled stupid look, bawled out *"Che cazzo—?!"*, then, blood-shot eyes crossing, dropped his shabby old head back in his paws and nodded off once more) as demonstrable proof of the Count's lineage and pointing out to the wide-eyed city fathers gathered around him that: "You see before you the true cause of that envy that stirred our sister states in times gone by to so malign our great Republic and bring about through deceit, intrigue, and spiteful tongues her eventual and untimely ruin! The Turks, for all their famed endowments, came up short in *their* rash challenge to it, and similar fates befell the impudent Franks and Goths, who simply overreached themselves! In a later age, Napoleon in his impotent rage raped and pillaged our most beautiful Queen, swallowing up everything on the island he could lay his lascivious hands upon, but this, her true glory, he could not, for all his voracity, engorge, though a fateful glimpse of it is said to have embittered his dreams to the end of his tormented life!" He then suggested that, while the city officials were examining the deed, according to the law, the Count might like to join him privately *in camera caritatis* to sample some grappa distilled in the time of his ancestors and toast the success of their transactions.

The Count, introduced as the direct descendant of four popes, at least three of them male, six cardinals, and nineteen doges, replied that he was indeed honored to have his pockets picked by such a distinguished assembly of impenitent thieves and whoresons, true heirs of the pustulous glories of the Serenissima, but that, while gladly surrendering the deed for their exanimation, he would have to decline the Director's kind invitation to visit his privy chambers, not because he suspected treachery or doubted his host's integrity— "You'd *better* doubt it, that rotto in culo is as bent as a *forcola!*" barked Melampetta from the edge of the multitudes, and Eugenio turned to the Inspector General of the Questura at his side and, smiling unc-tuously through clenched teeth, growled: "Somebody go muzzle that damned bitch!"—but because, in his present state of arousal stimulated by his return to his debauched and beloved homeland, he might do damage to its Renaissance splendors and would in any event find it painful to negotiate the stairwells. About this time, the Lion rose up once more and roared out a string of sour melancholic oaths, threatening, for the greater glory of Venice, to bite the heads off every infidel present, starting with the Archbishop—"*Soul to God, body to the crypt, asshole to the devil for his tobacco dip!*" he bellowed—but the Madonna calmed him down by feeding him some of her organs, and soon enough the decrepit creature was sonorously back asleep again.

For the professor, bundled up in the blue angora sweater with its warm milky odors, deliciously stupefying, all of this was happening as a sort of remote theatrical backdrop to the only event left for him on center stage and the focus of all his entranced attention. As his former student pranced about, so full of life, spraying dignitaries and revelers alike from her gaily striped machine, or clamping it between her thighs and riding it like a bronco, or challenging other phalli to duels, she occasionally afforded him glimpses of smooth creamy flesh and bouncing breasts with generous nipples that excited him as no masterpiece had ever done. Her worn blue jeans were molded around her abundant thighs and hips like a second skin, freely exhibiting to the delight of his captive eye every thrilling line and posture of her piquant body, which he, with an outburst of what would have been, before the Blue-Haired Fairy stole it from him, rapture, told himself was ideal beauty's very image and all he would ever know of the divine, forget all previous pretensions of his long misdirected life. He was utterly disarmed, overpowered, intoxicated with fugitive, mad, unreasoning hopes and visions of a monstrous sweetness: in short, oh joy, he was, alas, too late, in love.

Seeing him stare at her with such pained tenderness, Bluebell gave the giant phallus back to Francatrippa and, zipping up her windbreaker against the cold, came over to her old mentor's portantina. "Politicians are just so darn *boring!*" she complained, cracking her pink gum. She stripped off the condom and shook her blond curls out. "C'mon, teach! Whaddaya say we get the heck outa here and go have some *fun!*" He could not in his smitten state find breath to speak, much less words to use were even breath available, but, deftly reading his wistful devastated gaze, she unbuckled him from his litter chair— "What're they doing, prof, holding you *prisoner—?*"—and lifted him up into her arms. "Holy moley, you're light as a parakeet feather! Look at you, poor thing! You're nothing but skin and bones! Or . . . whatever." She gave him a little hug and whispered in his earhole: "Let's sneak down to the waterfront and have a ride! C'mon! These goofballs'll never miss you!"

And so it was that he found himself on the Apocalypse. There were other choices out on the cold windswept riva: bumper cars and whips and fun houses, pirate ships and merry-go-rounds, looping airplanes, spinning teacups, but for Bluebell, who had tried them all, only the Apocalypse still gave her a thrill. "Present company excluded of course!" she added with a tinkling gum-snapping laugh. In all his life as a human being, he had never been in or on any of these things, and he had disdained those who had, but now the very prospect brought tears of joy and excitement to his eyes, as he huddled, shivering, against Bluebell's soft slippery windbreaker, clasped like a child in her strong young arms. Music was playing separately from each of the attractions, a chaotic dissonance, diabolically loud, but the riva was empty, they were all alone, their Carnival fling like a secret tryst behind closed doors.

What followed was the most exciting ride of his life. Not even his flight on Colombo's back could match it. At first it wasn't fun at all, it was sheer terror. So whipped about was he by the sudden violent wheeling and swooping and plunging that he worried he might start coming apart. Flakes of dried flesh were flying from him like dead moths from a shaken carpet and his insides were in such turmoil he was afraid he'd end up like the Madonna of the Organs. Bluebell, seeing his plight, quickly opened up her red windbreaker and tucked him inside. "*Yow-eee!*" she howled as they dipped and whirled, her golden locks flying and her bright white teeth sparkling in laughter. "*Hot* dog! I *love* it!" For a moment he suffered a terror of another sort. Not since Hollywood had he been this close to a woman's fleshy parts, and never when they were jouncing and bobbling so crazily as this. He grabbed on as best he could but it was like trying to hug a runaway exercise machine. Her naked breasts literally flew up and whopped him on the nose, and her knees were sometimes as high as his head. *"Whee-ee-ee!"* she squealed and wrapped her arms and legs around him and squeezed him tight.

Then, as the mad ride continued, he began to find an anchor in that very motion. The earth was flying about them everywhere and they were being severely shaken still, but it was as though they were becoming one with the very forces that, so powerfully and so primordially, shook them. This: *this* is truth, he realized, with such a jolt of recognition, he knocked his head on her chin and set off another giddy burst of whooping and squealing: "You made me swallow my *gum!*" she yelled, and then suddenly they were upside down again and hanging on to each other for dear life. All these years, he thought as they plummeted, then shot upwards again, instead of riding with it, he had been trying to stop it in artificial freeze-frames, made light-headed by anything that twitched, but now, suddenly, he began to feel most centered, most contented, when most ferociously flung about. "I feel *alive,*" he gasped, as, headlong, they looped and dived and spun, "truly *alive,* for the—*ahi!!*—first time since the day I-I . . . grew up!" It helped of course to be held by and holding Bluebell and to be pillowed in her lovely bobbing breasts, whose nipples, he saw now, and this was just another amazing revelation among many, were exactly like the rosettes of Ca' Dario across from the Gritti Hotel where he used to take his grappas, but it was more than the breasts, more than the hugging and squeezing and bouncing against one another, and the glorious fragrances that wound him round, it was a true mystical communion with the Other, the most ecstatic and visionary moment in his life. And, well, even if it *was* just the hugging and the breasts, et cetera, one thing he knew without *any* qualifications: whatever it was, he didn't want it ever to stop . . .

They are lost again. Truffaldino, whimpering, wants to go back to the palazzo, but Buffetto reminds him that, as they are lost, they don't know where that is either. They have just crept over another bridge, having almost missed it on the other side and fallen in, and now they find themselves in another open space in fog too thick even to see each other if they lean away. They set the portantina down and, holding on to each other, feel about them in the fog. The whole purpose of this hazardous journey is to procure a certain mask for the professor, who, though he plays no part in the servants' deliberations, is determined to carry on, *per amore o per forza*, as the saying goes. The plan is Eugenio's. "Leave it to me, Pini," he'd said with a sly knowing smile. "Yes, yes, tomorrow night, I can see it all! *Trust* me!" And so here, wherever it is, they are, preparatory to his night of nights, whatever the deceptions, whatever the costs.

On the Apocalypse yesterday, as he grew accustomed to the violent motion, he tried to speak to Bluebell about his affection for her, indirectly of course, joking abstractly about the laughable folly of old men and referring to certain scandals that had happened at his university over the years between professors and students, never to him needless to say, though who, ever, dear Bluebell, is wholly immune, and telling her about a movie star he once knew, quite famous, who kissed him once—for the cameras, of course—in a very special place, finding it difficult as he spoke to keep Bluebell's wildly bouncing breasts out of his mouth. This seemed to make her giggle, so he let it happen more and more until, his more reasoned approach abandoned, he was lapping at them and gumming them and scrubbing his nose on them quite shamelessly. She laughed at his clumsy gaiety, gasping as the Apocalypse whipped them about that she always thought of him as such a stuffy old bird, and he tried to correct this impression by bragging about running away from home all the time and about his bad-boy past in the Land of Toys. "We wuh' weawwy—*shplurpp! glop!—wicked!*" he squawked around his mouthful of convulsive breast. He offered to take her places in the motor launch, to Torcello or Chioggia, for example, wherever, it didn't matter, he was just hanging on, hanging on to *everything*, making desperate plans for the future, and she asked if they couldn't go out on an American Express "Venetian Night" package tour instead. "We'll go dancing! And to the Casino! No museums, no churches, just fun! We'll take gondolas! With singing gondoliers! It'll be *wild!*"

And then suddenly the ride ended and she carried him back to the Piazza and, the official ceremonies over and his portantina gone, deposited him in the palazzo doorway in the Sotoportego del Capello, took her sweater back, rang the bell, gave him a little kiss on the top of his head, popped a bubble, and said: "Well, in case we don't see each other again, Professor Pinenut, have a happy Carnival!"

He was shattered. He felt like he felt whenever the Fairy died. He turned, once he knew who he was, to Eugenio.

Police whistles blow not far away and there are shouts and the sounds of scuffling. "Per carità, gentlemen! What are you doing—?! A poor holy man! *Ow!* In nomine excelsis and de profundis gloria, have you no shame?" cries a gravelly old voice from out of the fog. "What ficcanaso has sent you here? Eh? What bad tongue in partibus infidelium has misled you? *Ih! Ih! Ih!* Mercy, gentlemen! A frustulum of indulgence, if you please! A bit of nunc dimittis and ite, missa est! I am no thief! Upon my faith! See, here is my money! Take it if you wish! I have made vows of poverty! Look at my hair shirt! Per amor del cielo, let me go and I will forgive you! See, it's only an old tail, not worth the novena of spades, as they say! Who would want to steal such a thing! *Uf!* Be reasonable, gentlemen!" There are heavy booted footsteps and the sound of something or someone being dragged, but the sounds seem to come from every direction at once. And, as suddenly as they began, they cease.

"Signori carabinieri . . . ?" Truffaldino calls out hopefully into the murky silence. There is no reply. The little servant starts to cry.

"What—? Who is that malcontented guttersnipe out there?" comes a waspish voice from out of the coiling yellow fog. "Unbutton yourself, you blubbering turd!"

"It's us!" wails Truffaldino. "Help! We are lost!"

"Lost! Hah! We should all be so lucky!"

"I'd give an arm and a leg to be lost!"

"Easy for you to say, dearie!"

"Please! We've walked all the way from Saint Mark's—!"

"Oho! The little pap-sucker walks! He talks! He's a bloody miracle!"

"He's probably even got one of those lumpish things between his head and his feet—what do you call them?"

"Let it all leak out, piss-brains, we're on burning coals . . ."

They take a step toward the voices and faces materialize around them in the fog. The old scholar recognizes them—the pink-cheeked sun, the angel with the cherry-red lips, the camel, the skull, the freckled face with red hood and yellow braids—"Hey! It's the maskmaker's!" cries Truffaldino. "We've found it!"

"It's found us, more like," mutters Buffetto, then falls silent as the towering figure of Mangiafoco with his fiery eyes and his rampant black beard like flung ink crowds into the doorway, filling it, his head half lost in the swirling mists high above. *"Ma che cazzo fai—?"* he roars, making the masks rattle on the wall. Peering down through the fog with his glowering eyes, he spies the old professor. "Eh! What's this—?!" He bends down to look more closely. A big toothy smile cracks his plaster-stained lips. "Oho! So *this* is our great Casanova, enh? Ebbene! Enter, signori! I have just the faccia for the little ciuco!"

The masks titter furtively as they enter, making the collective sound of mice scurrying through the walls. The old scholar is fully aware that he is the object of some ridicule. He doesn't care. There is not time left in his life to care. This American student will be his, whether the foolish milk-fed gum-popping creature knows it or not. Nothing will stand in his way. Not his long unyielding life with its heroic devotion to truth and art and virtue. Not his terrible fear of confusion and humiliation. Not all the "civilizing" precepts and ruthless pieties of his despotic blue-haired catechist. Nothing. "Nothing!" he tells the walls of brightly colored faces, all the red ones, white ones, green, black, leathery brown, and Venetian gold ones, the flesh pink ones and those of dreadful azure blue: *turchino.* Cassiodorus called this blue the "Venetian color." It was the color of the darkness which came over the sun at the time of the desolation of the Gothic kingdom. The color of his own desolated life. No longer. Eugenio has promised. *"Tonight!"* he declares, twisting round defiantly in his portantina.

And then he sees her. Just behind him in the middle of the room. Tipped back in a barber's chair in a winding sheet with only her blue jean cuffs and fringed white boots sticking out, hands crossed, face waxen, eyes rolled back, lips slack and parted. Dead. Dead—?! He feels faint. His vision blurs. He cannot breathe. There is something so dreadful about this sight that his mind will not take it in, but continues, stubbornly, even angrily (what has she *done—?!*), to contemplate a future now utterly erased: She will come to him. (She cannot.) He will have her. (There is nothing to have.) She will love him forever. (Forever is over.)

25.

COOKED IN LOVE

The august professor emeritus, embedded in molded pizza dough, has an uneasy premonition, as they back him into a bread oven with only his head sticking out ("Don't worry, Pini, you won't melt!" Eugenio assures him, beaming ruddily from beaded ear to beaded ear: "Just like baked Alaska! You won't feel a thing!"), that this night is not going to turn out exactly as he had so ardently hoped. He had asked for a proper philological costume, a mysterious and somber *bauta* perhaps with ruffle and tricorn and wig and cape—he had practiced taking short steps about his room in the palazzo, more or less erect, imagining the cape fluttering majestically yet secretively around him as he staggered along—but, as Eugenio explained when they opened up the box from the maskmaker's and, to his wailing dismay, found instead the donkey mask inside: "Now, now, a bauta mask would not even fit correctly over your . . . you know, your *thing*—and besides, there will be *thousands* of capes and bautas out there tonight, dear boy! How will she find you if you are not somehow different from the rest?"

"Find me? I thought we were to be alone—!"

"Well, er, of course! But not at first . . ."

"You mean it's some sort of masked ball?"

"Precisely! A masked ball! Is it not Martedì Grasso? What did you think? So now stop being such a little fusspot, Pignolo my darling! I promise you, it's going to be *beautiful!* A night you will remember for the rest of your life! *Trust* me!"

And so they have brought him to the kitchen, stripped him of his fine clothing, his silk suit and monogrammed hand-tailored shirt and his satin underthings, and wrapped him in layers and layers of heavy pizza dough, stuffing in prawns and olives and onions and pepperoni and wild mushrooms and tuna and golden pimientos and eggplant, with a whole garlic salami wedged up between the thighs, a stiffened mane made of wild asparagus beribboned with prosciutto curls, and with anchovies and artichoke hearts and extra cheese on the hind portions—"Best bits for last!" Eugenio enthuses, patting the enriched rump, his plump cheeks flushed with excitement and an overly tight corset (he doesn't look at all like the person the professor mistook him for yesterday, he must have been reeling still from that mind-churning ride)—and now, six cooks all helping at once, they ease him on backwards on a little trolley into the bread oven.

Eugenio is mistaken about not feeling a thing. The intense heat actually soothes his inner wooden parts, penetrating like muscle balm to the damp rot lodged deep there, but the burning dough expands around his outer fleshly remains with all the blistering ferocity of a red-hot iron maiden, piercing him through with the most agonizing pain and squeezing the breath right out of him, making him gasp and scream and beg for mercy. Even as he bawls to be let out—"*Ih! Ah! Please!*"—his breath seizing up in his chest and his cries emerging like raw heaving croaks ("Let him cry," Eugenio urges the startled kitchen staff with a tender chuckle, "the little ass can laugh when he gets laid!"), he has a sudden total recall of the dream he had while burning his feet off on his father's brazier all those years ago, a simple dream about *leaping*. At first it was only common everyday real-life leaping, over hedgerows and thorn bushes and muddy ditches—he'd only been a puppet for a little while, his legs were new to him, but already, barely able, with Geppetto's help, even to walk, he had gone bounding off, full of short-lived joy, leaping as high as he could, but running straight into, as though ordained, the nose-grabbing fist of the constabulary (such troublesome impetuousness, already on the move even as a shapeless lump of wood, where had it come from?)—but gradually, while his feet, as remote from him in his sleep as if they belonged to someone else, blackened and turned to ashes on the brazier, he felt himself in the dream growing lighter and lighter, he could suddenly leap over carts and houses and could even leave the world behind altogether, and as he rose above all the rooted trees and planted houses far below, he was overwhelmed by an intense sense of freedom, of being truly *alive*, his nose out of the reach of all earthly constraints and rising even higher than the rest of him rose. But then, as he soared higher and higher, he had a thought. A very simple thought, one of his first: that his freedom only made sense, only truly *was* freedom, if he could get back down there whenever he wanted to. With that, he began to fall. Feet first at the beginning, then head, finally just tumbling wildly, nose over heels and out of control. It was terrifying. He was screaming like he is screaming now. He fell with the awesome clatter of a sack of wood thrown from the top of a house, scaring even himself. When he awoke, his feet were gone. He thought they'd been eaten and blamed the cat.

"Stop carrying on so, Pini! You *are* out!"

So he is. But he is still burning up. Inside and out, baked to a turn. "Innamorato cotto," as the faces on the maskmaker's wall mocked, tittering and hooting (he didn't care) when his little American student left him all agape and askew on the shop floor, chewing gum stuck to the side of his earhole, their ridicule now becoming prophecy: an old fool literally cooked in love. His darling Bluebell, too, had prophesied: "cute as a blister," she'd called him on their Carnival ride. He is crying so hard he cannot even get his breath. His surface is bubbling and the salami between his legs has shriveled and is dripping hot grease.

"Ahi, what a nuisance you are, carino mio!" shouts Eugenio over his desperate howling. "*Chetati!* You are drying me *up!*" He sniffs appetitively at the professor's sizzling hindquarters, reaches in with a bejeweled finger, plucks a meatball stringy with melted cheese. "Roll the tedious beast into the meat locker and cool him off!" he commands irritably, popping the hot meatball in his mouth with a loud smack. "Ow! Yum! See what you get for doing someone a *favor!*"

He has asked for it, it is true. He'd had a terrible shock after his ride on the Apocalypse yesterday when Bluebell had abandoned him so abruptly, dropping him in the palazzo doorway like an old unwanted toy, and an even worse one when the door opened: for there, towering above him like an avenging angel, her arms folded majestically over her bosom and her face half in shadow, was she whom he'd thought dead these hundred years, returned as it were from the grave, or graves, his sister, mother, bedtime hair-raiser, drillmaster, and erstwhile benefactress: "O Fata mia! *Forgive me!*" he'd cried, utterly stupefied and undone (where *was* he?), and he had tumbled to his knees there to hug hers, sobbing out his confession together with an account of his many and ghastly trials, and not excluding his most recent truancy and all his sinful thoughts while buried in his beautiful ex-student's rosette-nippled breasts, shameless recreant that he incorrigibly was, but regretting this even as he did so: perhaps . . . perhaps, even with her strangely fat knees, she could help—?

"Ah, while you are down there, dear boy, would you care to suck my lecca-lecca?"

"*Eugenio—?!*"

"But of course! I don't know who you *thought* I was, sweetheart, but I am *supposed* to be the Queen of the Night!"

"I-I've been through so much I can hardly—!" His bewilderment was such that he could not even see, he felt numb and dry-mouthed, as though his senses were falling away with the rest of his bodily parts, maybe that wild ride had done more damage to the lignified mush in his brainpan than he'd thought. Only one thing was clear in all this dreadful blur. "Eugenio! Listen to me! Dear old friend! I-I know now what I want! You said I could have anything—!"

"Oh, I know. The American bambina, no? I thought you'd never ask, you wicked boy! But it goes without saying! I already have a plan!"

"You do—?"

"Tomorrow night! I promise you! She is yours!"

And so this, this is the plan. He can feel the crust, like fate itself, hardening around him. Still, he clings, speaking loosely, his blistered arms spread beneath him, locked in stiffened pizza dough here in the meat cooler, to his one hope—absurd, abject, perverse, yet at the same time spiritual, and even, for he is after all who he is, venerable —because: what else is there left to believe in if not love? Yes, love is the word of the day, *his* word, his only one. Her mask shop confession rings still in his inner ear, the only sort he has left, like celestial music. She is, the sublimate of his otherwise vaporized concept of perfect beauty, all he can see. If she is expecting an ass tonight, he will, with all his smitten heart, be one.

When he saw her this morning, stretched out in her winding sheet in the barber's chair, her eyes rolled back and her blue lips slackly parted, he was not able to breathe. He had gaped his mouth, but no air entered. He felt like he was strangling. His gnarled fingers tore at the straps of the portantina. Feverish chills shook him, and guilt, dismay: Had his own demented desires done this—?! Oh no! "I-I'm *sorry!*" he had gasped. He fell out onto the floor of the mask shop, bruising the patches of flesh that remained, crawled toward her. When he reached her boot, he kissed it passionately, wetting it with his tears, his nose pressed into her blue jean cuffs, then pulled himself up to hug her knees. "Oh, Bluebell!" he sobbed, abandoning all his greater learning for that simple and terrible formula, the abject confession of a stricken heart: "I-I *love* you! Don't die!" Gripping her belt buckle, he hauled himself up onto her lifeless body, blind to the danger of being caught in so mad an attitude, crawling over her sunken belly, her flattened breasts, pausing to weep there, his face buried in what, until a moment before, were his greatest joy on earth, shapers of his very destiny; then, using them as wobbly handles, he dragged himself on up to her precious face, ghastly in its ashen pallor, and kissed tenderly her cold lips, still faintly bubble gum–perfumed. Her lips moved beneath his lips. They stretched into a smile. *A miracle!* She opened her eyes, sighed, gave him a little smack on his behind, and said: "Now, now, teach! Be nice!"

He tried to speak. He could not. He felt cruelly deceived and impossibly jubilant at the same time. *She lived still!*

"C'mon, don't take it so hard, prof, just having a little fun! I saw you coming, I thought you'd get a kick out of it! You gotta admit it's a great costume, right? But down you go now, I've turned over a new leaf, no more spreading it around, I'm saving it for the man of my dreams!" She lifted him by his armpits and set him down dismissively in his litter chair again, as though clearing her lap of a minor nuisance. "I learned about him from a little fat man who has, well, you know, *befriended* me. He told my fortune, like, and said I'm gonna meet my true love tonight! In the most scrumptious drawing room in Venice! In a mask! It's all worked out! That's why I got this crazy costume! Jeepers, isn't it *romantic?!* Tonight! Who do you think he is—?"

"Ah . . . !" What could he say? He felt a terrible weight upon him. He had never lied before. Not like this. But if he told her the truth, she wouldn't come. He would never see her again. He gazed upon this lovely apparition, now wriggling out of her grave clothes like a beautiful thought, softly bodied forth in denim and angora, his eyes delighted afresh by each familiar curve and hollow as it emerged, quiveringly alive, and he knew, drunk with mad desire, grateful merely that, this night at least, she lived, he lived, that (his nose alone would have told him this) he was lost. "He . . . alas . . ." he wheezed, desperately trying not to tell her what he could not but tell her, "it is only . . . !"

"Honest, you know what, prof?" she whispered then. She leaned down to press her warm cheek next to his, so dizzying him with fragrant memories of their fairy-tale ride on the Apocalypse he had to close his eyes, and, shyly, almost breathlessly, she added: *"I hope it's you . . . !"* When he opened his eyes again, feeling her cheek still pressed hotly on his own, he'd fallen out of his portantina and she was gone.

He has been, all day, since that confession, and until the costuming began, in a state of constant dreamlike euphoria, a state unlike any he has ever known, even as a puppet. "My, how perky you are!" Eugenio had laughed when they returned from the mask shop, by vaporetto this time, the fog beginning, much slower than his spirits, to lift, and in reply he had crawled out of his litter chair and performed a feeble little bowlegged jig, bowing afterwards to the general applause. Ah, the theater, the theater! he'd thought, blowing kisses to them all. Why have I turned my back on it all my life? It is time made real, it is movement, it is passion, it *is* life! All the rest, the dead paintings, the statuary, the tiresome books, all those pompous "images of eternity": just so much bullpoop, as his dearly beloved so eloquently put it. Perhaps, in spite of himself, he *had* taught her everything she knows! Eugenio, surrounded by a flock of clucking tailors and seamstresses making emergency repairs in his costume, the seams of which had largely given way under an excess of flattering tucks and "modelings," had smiled benignly at all of this and, fluttering his long false lashes, wheezed: "Dear boy, love is *good* for you!"

Oh yes! Oh yes! His heart is full, as they liked to say in Hollywood. (He *adored* Hollywood, why did he ever leave it?) All day he has been embracing everyone who came within range, the busy servants, the doddering and incontinent clientele of the palazzo, the police officers who came with the news of La Volpe's arrest, the seamstresses with their mouths full of pins, the Omino e figli, S.R.L. lawyers, laden with briefs and deeds, and the contessa offering to give up her claim to the Rialto bridge in exchange for an efficiency apart-

ment in the new Palazzo Ducale, the maids stripping his bed down
and emptying out his closets and drawers, building contractors with
plans for converting the Bridge of Sighs into a love nest, even the
electricians stringing up lights outside his windows and hanging the
new red banners—he has so much love in him he has felt he must
share it or die! Madness! But eagerly he embraced that, too! Let it
come!

And he has forgiven everybody! His mean old babbo, all the tor-
mentors of his youth and age, the bad painters and jealous reviewers,
the Fairy, the upstart department chairman who tried to take away
his second office and limit his franking privileges, the student who
wrote THE BONG'S LONG, ART'S SNOT—SENECTA on the blackboard,
even the old Fox, his ancient nemesis, apprehended at last today and
jailed, held on the charges from the professor's own denunciation.
Which he now regrets. She had apparently been trying to use the
money from the piracy of his *Mamma* manuscript to buy back her old
tail, now not much more than a ratty piece of frayed rope and no
longer useful even as a fly swatter, her mistake being, as the police
explained it, that for the first time in her life she was attempting to
purchase something instead of simply stealing it, and, unaccustomed
to legal barter as she was, she had gotten into a violent argument with
the dealer complaining that the price was too *low* for so precious an
object, the dealer finally calling the police, fearing he had a lunatic on
his hands. The professor tried to persuade Eugenio to intercede for
her, but to no avail: "Let the old reprobate stay there overnight,"
Eugenio snapped reedily, scarcely able to breathe in his tightly laced
corset. "We'll all be richer for it!"

But then, when the sad news came that poor blind Gattino, without his companion, had walked off the wrong side of a vaporetto in
the fog ("When the tipo hollered out the stop, Il Gatto repeated it
loudly and stepped off the other side! He never came up, master, all
they found was his white cane . . ."), he made another urgent appeal
for La Volpe's release, fearing for her when she got the news, begging
Eugenio to help him drop the charges, but his friend threw up his
hands in despair, crying: "Madonna! We've worked so hard to *catch*
the infamous whore! How can you ask for such a thing after all she
has *done* to you—?!"

"I forgive everybody! I forgive even you, Eugenio!"

"How nice, dear boy, I forgive you, too—but this is completely bizarre! And look at the hour! I can't do anything now!"

"But—!"

"*Tomorrow*, Pini! *Maybe!* For now, I tell you, we haven't a minute to lose!"

He had to accept that, his own costume was not even begun, and already the bands were playing in the Piazza and the darkening square was filling up with masked revelers, exciting him with a sense of romance and adventure not felt since he first heard the *pi-pi-pi* and *zum-zum-zum* of Mangiafoco's magical marionette theater in the last century. He had sold his primer then for a ticket and he would sell it again now, together with all his degrees and books and honors, only to have Bluebell's cheek next to his once more.

His excitement was evidently contagious, the entire Palazzo dei Balocchi has seemed abuzz with it all day, the staff, the clientele, the visitors, and its Director, too, alias the Queen of the Night, giddy as a schoolchild about his big party this evening (he has been dropping hints he may have acquired Casanova's bones for his great Mardi Gras Gran Gala tonight after all, for he is also laying plans for elaborate Ash Wednesday obsequies on the morrow, inviting, it would seem, the whole world to them, as though reluctant to let the glorious season come to an end) and priding himself on being the new owner and resident-soon-to-be of the Doges' Palace. He has already ordered up new stationery. When the professor expressed his doubts about the authenticity of Count Agnello Ziani-Ziani Orseolo's deed, Eugenio replied that "a country which has happily accepted the legitimacy of fantasy titles purchased by mail order from a remote German king, my love, can as easily accept the legitimacy of *this* entertaining document!" Various charges have been brought against the Count by the city meanwhile, including "the illicit erection of a public display intended to violate the true Christian meaning of Carnival" and "contributing irresponsibly to an increased risk of *acque alte*," and Buffetto, Francatrippa, and Truffaldino have been sent out this afternoon to supervise his arrest by the authorities, Eugenio assuring them that, if by some unfortunate circumstance the Count should be martyred in the course of his pursuit, an appropriate plaque would be mounted on a wall of the Ducal Palace, commemorating his historical visit here and specifically honoring all emissaries of the occasion.

By the time they roll the old scholar out of the meat locker, his new hide, as it might be called, has cooled as firm as a body cast, though he is stinging all over as if his cauterized flesh might have become suffused somehow with the baked pizza dough. His head hangs limply from its weary neck like a turtle's dangling from its shell, and his breaths are coming in short dry patches as though they might be his last. "Ah, *that's* better!" gushes Eugenio, lifting his former school-chum's drooping chin up and wiping his tears with a scented handkerchief. It is dark outside, bands are playing, and the crowd noises have mounted: there are shouts and screams coming in through the windows, and bursts of wild laughter and, underneath it all, the intense rumble of anticipation, as in a stadium before a big match. "It is almost time now for your great adventure, you old rogue! She is already out there waiting for you!"

"Out—? Out where?"

"In the city, dear boy, where else? That fabulous house of pleasure, that opulent place for perfect licentiousness, that lubricious refuge of love with its illusion of the incredible, its wondrous aura of fairyland—!"

"But you said a salon—!"

"But of *course*, Old Sticks! Have I ever said otherwise? And look at you! Beautiful! I am in love with you myself! Ah, but one last thing to make you perfect!"

Eugenio, whistling a happy little tune, bores a hole in his rear with an apple corer and works in a jauntily upright tail made of long crisp cannoni, filled with sweet ricotta. Then, following the Director's instructions, the kitchen staff move him from the trolley onto one of the wine carts from yesterday's procession, perhaps the one the old Lion slept on, it smells like it, securing him to it by way of ropes around the neck and butt of the creature in whom he now resides. Earlier today, the old professor was convinced he was ready for this. Now he is not so sure. Only Bluebell's whispered wish sustains him. But if this is how she expects to find him, what is it she expects to do? He tries to conjure up stimulating memories of his ride on the Apocalypse, his snuggle with her in the mask shop, but it is as though, in his present position, his memory has plummeted into his sinuses somehow, closed to recall, merely making his head heavier on his tired neck. Carnival, perhaps, is not meant for everyone . . .

They lower the professor, imbedded in his donkey-shaped pizza loaf, to street level in the freight elevator, joined by two bleary-eyed old ladies who squat in a corner to pee, and at the bottom they roll him out into the Sotoportego del Capello, the dimly lit alleyway behind the palazzo. Through the narrow underpass there, he can see the bright lights and the massed crowds of the decorated Piazza San Marco, but back here it is damp and silent, like the darkened wings of a musty theater. He has supposed they would be heading down an obscure calle or corte somewhere: isn't that where assignations are always held? Eugenio, however, bubbling with excitement, seems prepared to march them all out upon the raucous Piazza. This is not good news. Does he mean to inaugurate the Bridge of Sighs tonight? The two ancient ladies, a Russian princess and the heiress to a rubber fortune, clients of the palazzo, have exited the elevator with them and wandered confusedly off into the night, somewhat shackled by their drawers, and now two soft splashes are heard at the far end of the Sotoportego del Capello where the gondolas dock at night. Eugenio sends instructions out into the square to commence the fanfare and then carefully fits the donkey mask over his old friend's face, attaching fresh white camellias behind the upright ears. "And now, my dear little mammifero," he says, peering in at him through the eyeholes with a look full of loving kindness, his voice like honey oozing from the comb, "the rest depends on you!"

Before they can set off, however, they are interrupted by the clamorous arrival of Buffetto, Francatrippa, and Truffaldino, staggering down the alleyway, wailing and groaning, their clothes torn and bloodstained, their arms and heads bandaged, Buffetto and Francatrippa on crutches, little Truffaldino crawling toward them on all fours. "Ahi, direttore! What a terrible fight! We are dead!"

26.

THE STAR OF
THE DANCE

He knows everything now. What's happened to him. What
happens next. Forget secret assignations. Forget dreams
come true. Remember instead the words of Melampetta as
attributed by her yesterday to luckless Pierre Abelard in his presumed exegetical marginalia upon Saint Bernard of the Cisternian
beekeepers, "known in the underworld," as she (or perhaps he) put
it, as "Doctor Mellifluus": "Honey in the mouth, amico mio, sting in
the culo!" "But he has been so good to me!" he'd protested, and she'd
growled back: "If I know the Little Man, compagno, you've been
good to yourself!" That's right, he thinks now, staring out upon the
demonically Carnivalized Piazza through the eyeholes of his donkey
mask with increasing apprehension and terror, there's probably nothing wrong with the mails either. His retirement funds may well have
just bought the Doges' Palace. His old classmate's "recent windfall"
was a pinenut. He has probably lost everything but the clothes on his
back. So to speak.

Overhead, meanwhile, wisps of fog, like ghostly fish, twist and
curl around crimson banners announcing the celebrated native son's
Gran Gala top-of-the-bill performance tonight as the "Star of the
Dance," and the stage toward which Buffetto and Francatrippa are
rolling him is tented in strings of colored lights and decorated, even
to a golden hoop, like the center ring of a circus. Eugenio as the
Queen of the Night goes before them, switching his behind provocatively and calling out in his reedy falsetto: *"Permesso! Permesso! Largo
per il Ciuchino Pinocchio! La Stella della Danza!"* On his back, Truffal-

dino, or whoever he or she is, does handstands and backflips, as the well-stung wayfarer, dismally at one with his freshly baked outer image, is paraded on his creaking carriage, to the hoots and cheers of the riotous multitudes, across the great square, which, notorious metaphors aside, is something less than the "sumptuous drawing room" his perfidious friend had led him to expect, though he is all too aware that his expectations have always been led less by the likes of Eugenio than by his own mad unrestrainable fancy, and that he deserves whatever he gets, insofar as getting and deserving have anything to do with each other, not much. Wretches are born, not made. Don't count on character. The grain goes with you, I-ness is an illness.

Thus, with each fateful turning of the cartwheels, the venerable scholar's most abiding convictions fall away as lightly as those flakes of pizza crust, a truer tougher mask, kicked loose now by Truffaldino's acrobatics on his donkey back. It doesn't hurt. Neither the acrobatics nor the collapse of his precious ontology. He recalls (even as, on all fours, he is hauled through the bright lights and pressing mob) that solitary moment in his darkening office back at the university in America, when, left all alone on campus in the backside of the festive season (yes, he was feeling sorry for himself, a sure spur to folly) and despairing of a happy conclusion to his current, perhaps definitive work, he had been struck by the vision which propelled him here. He had been staring out of his office window, meditating upon his singular relationship to the Blue-Haired Fairy, as intuitively clear to him at that moment as had been the Trinity or the hypostatic union to Saint Thomas Aquinas, but also as resistant to formulation within language, a resistance which had thwarted his hopes of closing his epic tribute to his beloved preceptress with his latest chapter, just completed, "And The Wood Was Made Flesh and Dwelt among Us." He would have to try again. One more chapter. And the image that came to him then, as his thoughts floated back to that revelatory moment here on this island all those years ago when abjectly he dropped as though felled to hug, in joy and in sweet repentance, the Fairy's knees, no longer bony and childlike as when he'd played with them last, but now full-fleshed and maternally solid, was one not of absence and desolation (this was what he saw out his office window) but of generosity and abundance and throbbingly intense beauty. He seemed to be looking between her virtuous knees as between the two famous columns on the Piazzetta (perhaps two dead trees in the yard, topped and amputated, had helped bring this image to mind), gazing in wonder upon that succulent composition of plump Christian splendor and lacy Oriental fantasy which, from a different angle and diabolically transformed, confronts him now, and he felt suddenly as if he were peering, his gaze drawn toward the dark labyrinth of the Merceria twisting its way into the distance beyond the radiant Basilica, into his very source. Yes, yes, the truth must be *seen*, he reminded himself then, the good *felt* (his hands, he saw, were pressed against the office windowpane, he was licking the glass). And so it was that, only hours later, as though compelled, with Petrarch's cautionary *Epistolae seniles* under his arm to curb his almost childish excitement (and what had happened to that book? he must have left it on the plane . . .) and his *Mamma*, seeking resolution, in his hastily packed bags, he had found himself on his way here, visions of climax dancing in his old wooden head like Bellini cherubs.

No cherubs out here tonight, alas. Climax is happening without them. Everything but, however: he is encircled by a crazed menagerie of the impossible, massed up hundreds deep. The racket is deafening. There are bands playing, whistles blowing, flashguns popping, fireworks crackling, and the costumed revelers, the most terrifying of them wearing Pinocchio masks of their own, are dancing about drunkenly and shouting out his name: "Evviva Pinocchio!" "It's him! È proprio lui!" "This is gonna be fun!" As he rolls through the bedlam of the square, lit up bright as day, he scans the crowds in vain for a friendly face, even the hint of a friend behind a face. Not even the Count or the Madonna, perhaps dead or chased off after all. Ah, this, *this*, my poor dear Fox, is the devil's very flour, he laments as paper streamers and confetti flutter overhead like tossed seasoning, and I am in it . . .

"Yes, you are truly buggered, my tender friend, becco e bastonato, and worse to come," Buffetto, who is perhaps not Buffetto after all, murmurs in his donkey ear. "But, as we say here, 'Zoga el coraggio a l'ultimo tagio!' Play your nerve at the final serve! At the last hand, old man, take a stand!"

He had hoped for a moment, back in the darkness behind the Palazzo dei Balocchi, that Buffetto, Francatrippa, and Truffaldino might be coming to his rescue, or at least to whisk him off, as planned, to his assignation with little Bluebell, but this was not to be. "Ohi, direttore, what a terrible fight, we are dead!" they had cried, staggering up the alleyway on crutches, all bruised and bandaged, Truffaldino crawling along on all fours, and Eugenio, slapping his palm impatiently with a folded fan, had snapped fiercely: "If not, you soon will be, you worthless louts, unless you come with the news I want to hear! The hour is late! Quickly! *What has happened to the Count!*"

"We apprehended him, master!"

"We seized him!"

"We surrounded him!"

"Good!"

"But he escaped!"

"Escaped—?! I warn you—!"

"*Tried* to escape, direttore! We pursued him!"

"Ah!"

"But he got away!"

"What—?!"

"But we caught him again! By the very throat! What a battle!"

"You can't imagine, direttore! That retinue! We were up against witches and wiverns and hundred-armed fiends from outer space!"

"Gryphons and ghouls!"

"Hellhounds and harpies, master!"

"Yes, yes, and so—?"

"Enh, what could we do against such an army?"

"They were merciless!"

"They drove us back!"

"They *what*—?!"

"Then we drove *them* back!"

"Aha!"

"Into the sea!"

"The sea?"

"Well, into the canal!"

"Very good! And—?"

"They had gondolas waiting!"

"They were swept away before you could blink an eye!"

"But surely, mere gondolas, you must have been able—"

"*Motorized* gondolas, direttore! One minute they were all drowning, the next they were roaring away!"

"Into the fog!"

"You couldn't see them—!"

"*You let the Count get away, you imbeciles—?!*"

"No!"

"No! We, uh . . ."

"We . . . ?"

"We chased him in the motor launch!"

"That's it!"

"Aha! Then finally you —"

"They sank it with their submachine guns!"

"They sank the motor launch—?!"

"We fired back and sank the gondolas!"

"It was frightful, direttore! There were bodies everywhere!"

"The canals were full of them! You could walk right across without getting your feet wet!"

"The gondolas couldn't move even if we didn't sink them!"

"What do you mean? Did you sink them or didn't you?"

"Well, the fog . . ."

"All those bodies . . ."

"It was confusing . . ."

"If you *didn't*, you fools, *it's Marten's fate for you!*"

"We did!"

"*Pum! Pof!*"

"Blew them right out of the water!"

"The canals were running with blood, direttore!"

"And guts! Blood and guts, direttore!"

"It was a fight to the death!"

"It was hand-to-hand!"

"And foot-to-foot!"

"I was killed at least eleven times, master!"

"But the Count, the *Count*, you damnable wretches—?!"

"Who?"

"Don't 'who' me! I'll have your *heads—!*"

"Ah, the Count! He's dead."

"The Count's dead? You're sure—?"

"He must be! Everybody was dead!"

"But you didn't see him—?"

"What did he look like?"

"Short fellow with a bald head and a wrinkled—?"

"Enough! *Enough!*" Eugenio screamed, his mascaraed eyes flashing in fury. "You'd better take confession tonight, you insolent vermin, *your afterlife begins tomorrow!*" And he turned sharply on his high heels to stamp out into the noisy and luminous Piazza San Marco, crying: "Now follow me, you little shits! And bring that wretched thing there on the wagon with you!"

The three servants, anxious to please, threw away their crutches and, with Buffetto pulling, Francatrippa pushing, and Truffaldino helping at the side, they rolled the little wine cart into the tiny underpass leading to the Piazza. In the momentary darkness there, before the light and roar beyond, Truffaldino hopped nimbly up onto the professor's donkey back, then leaned down to whisper into his pointed ear: "La Volpe is dead, dottore!"

"What—?! *Dead—?!*"

"Hanged herself. With her own tail. Isn't that funny? When they told her about Il Gatto. And your charges against her."

"Ah . . ."

"She left a note for you. In her pocket. Shall I read it?" The old scholar could not reply. He knew the nausea overwhelming him was human nausea, associated with his human flesh, what was left of it. " 'To my dear friend Pinocchio,' it says. 'Do not judge your old traveling companions too harshly. Remember that it is more shameful to distrust friends than be deceived by them.' " He hated the tears running down his cheeks, the lump crowding his less than wooden throat. He wanted no more of it, he wanted it all gone, wanted to be free of this appalling human sickness once and for all. Why did he ever want to be a boy? Why did he let them do this to him? Who talked him into it? Running away with Lampwick, though they didn't run far enough, was probably the wisest thing he ever did. Even being a donkey, a real one, was better than this. " 'As proof of my love for you,' she writes, 'I would like to return your watch, but, worse luck, Gattino was wearing it when he made his final blunder.

All I have left is my old tail, which is yours, dear friend, as soon as I am no longer using it.' Signed, 'Yours in the bran, La Volpe.' "

He was bawling by now, his heaving sobs catching in his imbreaded throat. He knew what it sounded like. He knew what he was.

"Poor Pinocchio, I am really sorry for you," whispered Truffaldino in a voice suddenly familiar to him. "Be brave, dear friend. Whatever happens . . ."

"Colombina . . . ?" But his voice was drowned out by the tumultuous uproar that greeted them as they emerged from the underpass and, under a blazing explosion of floodlights, filed out here into the eerily transformed Piazza: "Pinocchio! It's Pinocchio! Here he comes!" they screamed, and scream still, raising their voices above the din. "È Pinocchio davvero!" "Hooray!" "It's the Star of the Dance!"

As they rumble along now in the gaudy tumult, headed for the circus ring, they pass two tall caped carabinieri, mustachioed and thin as sticks, perhaps the same ones who chased him during the puppet band bust, now helping to keep the crowds back for his grand entry. Between them, on a leash, is a dog, masked by a steel muzzle: it is Melampetta, a friend at last! He aches to reach out to her, but he cannot move inside his bready cast. On seeing him, or perhaps, more correctly, on smelling him behind the pizza, the old watchdog throws her muzzled head back and lets out a pathetic wordless howl, for which she receives a whistling slash of a horse crop from one of her trainers. "Stop! Don't—!" the professor gasps, but of course he cannot be heard in the demented cacophony of the square, nor would they listen to him if he could be. Melampetta's miserable howl continues, as do the dialectical whip strokes, fading into the general pandemonium that fills in around him as they lift him off the cart and onto the stage. He is passed ceremonially through the great golden hoop, stretched with tissue crisp as old silk—pfUFff!—and, to a crescendo of applause and wild howling cheers, is deposited finally on a little round platform, rotating slowly in the center of the ring.

"Rispettabile ed irrispettoso pubblico!" cries the Director, stepping to the microphone and raising his pale plump arms, glitteringly bangled. "Welcome! Welcome, my dear fiends! All of you beastly boys and ghastly ghouls! Welcome to the Pizza San Marco!" The sudden roar is deafening and disturbingly appetitive. The professor cannot turn his head, can only stare straight ahead at the strange masked faces slowly circling past as he rotates on the little platform. "Ah, what a moment, my noble and nubile congregation! Here we are in Venezia, the most magical city in the world! And it is Carnevale, Martedì Grasso, the most magical night of the year! Magic squared in the magic square! *What cannot happen?*" The din of the Piazza seems not to diminish when Eugenio speaks but to mount from phrase to phrase like the heavy steps of an approaching monster. "And oh! oh! what a banquet we have for you tonight! A subtle delight, like our voluptuous metropolis itself, for *all* the tender senses! For at this time I, the Queen of the Night, debauched trollop that I am, have the inestimable honor and license, as well as the infinite pleasure, naughty and otherwise, to present to you for your admiration and delectation, the feature attraction of our Gran Gala: our own Marco the Pole come home to us like so much drifting flotsam stumping back to his deepest roots!" Around him the deadpan masks blankly circle, belying the savage frenzy boiling up behind them. The three servants seem to have disappeared. He is alone on stage with the mellifluent Eugenio, who, with a sleight-of-hand flourish, has turned his fan into a little scarlet whip which he cracks now above his donkey rump to the rhythm of his exhortation: "A mere sprout of native undergrowth when he left here, a green little sap pegged for the pen, he penned his way, as he grew alder, to become the world's most distinguished woodenknob, spunkily taking on all the knotty problems of the wormy world, branching out into his-tree, sophis-tree and rudiment-tree ribal-tree, a hack of all trades, and now, au currant, a seasoned sage laureled, lacquered, and lionized!" *Snap! crack!* goes the whip with each phrase, as Eugenio goads his delirious audience on, many of them now pressing toward the stage, leaping and bobbing and throwing themselves about like fiendish ecstatics. "So here he is, this most poplar fella and perennial favorite, for whom two's company and tree's a crowd, this legno da catasta who became a man of many letters, nine to be exact, the evergreen fantoccino who is nobody's dummy, with a cherry before and a cork behind, shy o'veneer but with balsa walnut and a peach of an ash, the puncheon from Puncheon Judy, our very own boneless bosky-boy, yew all know him of gorse: the one and only, the world-renowned, the great, that inimitable old chestnut, nose and all, *Pinocchio!*"

A moment ago, crossing the square, the old professor, much honored for a fleshly condition he now abhorred, that condition's alleged wisdom not excluded, had the impression, trusting that fleshly wisdom as he knew he should not and thinking, as usual, about himself, about his present fate and how he got here, all on his own, in the old way, bad company, drifting attention and all that, that he knew everything now. He was, once again—oh, how he weeps!—mistaken. For, with the platform's slow turning amid the mounting lunacy of the Piazza, he has seen his love again, somber amidst the maddened merrymakers, dressed in mourning and wearing his ear like a memorial medallion on a long gold chain around her neck, only the whites of her eyes showing and her head slowly spinning on her shoulders as though in derisive parody of his revolving platform. Around and around it goes, seven times, then stops and goes the other way. And so, though her curls are still mostly blond, he knows her now, a new and bitter knowing that makes all other knowing the merest trifle. He feels his heart shrink to the size of the deathwatch beetle gnawing at it. He waits for the platform to bring him around again that he might, though it be his last breath and unheard in the thunderous furor, cry out his loathing of her, that all the world might know her for what she truly is: *assassina!*

"You all know his story, he's held nothing back, his life as they say is an oaken book, he's logged it all! You know how he came to this island all those years ago, brought here then by donkey cart, soon to become a donkey himself, headed for the circus life as the Star of the Dance, trained to play dead, jump through a hoop, and dance the polka on his hind feet! You know how he lamed himself, was sold to a peasant for his hide, and thrown into the sea to drown, but was rescued by a school of fish that nibbled away his donkey flesh, revealing the puppet still within like the stick in a lollypop! Well, we had hoped to have the radiculose little peckerwood here in his glorious person tonight—in the bark, as it were—but, by juniper, wooden you know it, as you can see, *the little sucker has done it again!*"

Whoops and howls muffle the hour being struck hollowly up on the illuminated Clock Tower, a nebulous blur in the high rolling fog, as the platform slowly wheels him round again toward the Blue-Haired Fairy, she who, whipping him with guilt and the pain of loss, has broken his spirit and bound him lifelong to a crazy dream, this cruel enchantment of human flesh. In effect, liberated from wood, he was imprisoned in metaphor. Even his shabby career has been a sham, for, all these years, he has really only had an audience of one. Millions have read him, only because they too were all puppets like himself, hapless creations of the insidious Blue-Haired Fairy. But, though on his last legs, all four of them, trapped in pizza dough and confronting, he knows full well, an imminent horror, he will at last repudiate her. He will, though crushed by chagrin and sorrow, be free! He will do, dying, what he—*but what's this—?!* Too late! She is gone! Vanished. And her being gone is worse than all the things she has done to him, a final devastating punishment. She has lured him to his terrible fate, then mockingly abandoned him. His heart, still there after all, withered raisin though it be, is agonizingly wrenched, his eyes fill with tears, his mind with a blackness deep as the midwinter night beyond the fog . . .

"But alas, my hale, hellish, and hearty friends, there are no little fish here tonight, it is we who must eat the little ass out of his sorry plight! We must be of good mouth and do the little shoe, as they say, we must lick the poxy platter clean! Don't be shy! Dig in! You know the saying: If you touch wood, it's sure to come good! So come now, my ostrich-bellied butchers, and put your fangs into it! A capriccio! He's as good as bread, as they always said, da cima a fondo! Ammiratelo! And judge for yourself! Al passo! Al trotto! Al galoppo, you crapulous maniacs! *Let the feast begin!*"

The guest of honor, unable even to flinch in his cumbersome infrumentation, can only gape in wide-eyed terror at the mayhem that erupts at the edge of the stage and gradually closes in upon him, as the revelers, many with painted faces or their masks flung aside, their eyes aglow with a bestial appetite, their sharp teeth bared, battle each other for first bite. There is only one pizza pie. There are thousands of snapping and laughing and frothing mouths. Eugenio stands rooted in the crazy melee, a bit alarmed by the anarchy he has unloosed, but giggling so hysterically he seems about to pop his corset stays, his colorful wig bouncing gaily on his sleek round head. The professor catches only the briefest glimpse of all this—and then he is upside down, there are hands grabbing at his legs, trying to tear them from his body, he is dragged one way, then another, is tossed and thrown, he sees someone eating his papier-mâché mask, another with her mouth full of half-chewed camellias, others rabidly biting each other, and then he is lost in the sea of rending teeth. It is not like the time with the little fish. This time there is no sensation of his body wanting to rise from within. No delicious nibbling, no thrilling tingle, no ecstasy of release. And the fish at least knew when to stop . . .

27.

THE FATAL
MATH BOOK

"In the old days, I never even knew little piss-pockets like this existed in the city, but probably they were here all along, dark and filthy as an old whore's cunt, the swampy cold creeping up through the cracked flagstones like death sticking a finger up your asshole, and so quiet you can hear a pigeon shit," rumbles his companion, stretching his stony wings briefly and fluttering them to shake the damp out. The rattle they make bounces off the crumbling brick wall facing them and then slowly dies away through the black labyrinth of canals in a fading echo that sounds like dry cackling laughter. "But now I know better. I know now this is the real Venice, has been all along, ever since that first desperate wanker, pissing himself with fright, nested here like a marsh bird a couple of millennia ago—no, fuck all the famous pomp and grandeur, the bloody glorious empire and all the tedious shit that went with it and made such strutting ninnies of us all, all that was just for show, a kind of mask the old Queen put on to hide her cankers and pox pits, her true face was back here all the time, just like the devil's true face is on his arse. And you know what, my little cazzo buffo? It's fucking beautiful. I love it!"

The old Lion takes a long meditative suck from the grappa bottle and hands it to what remains of the senescent professor, now huddled, shivering, in the great beast's gritty fossilized mane, and naked as Saint Mark himself at the arrest of Jesus, nothing left but a few bloody tatters of flesh and flakes of pizza dough still clinging to his wooden frame. The grappa is cheap raw stuff, but, vile as it is— "Good for clearing the passages," the Lion growled, pressing it on him, "burns the moss out of your throat and kills off the vermin that crawl in . . ."—he soaks it up, fuel against the bitter nighttime chill, deadener of the ache in his heart. What's to happen next, he does not know. That he is still here at all is a miracle in itself, short-lived as its effects are apt to be. And, except for his "new feet," as he has always called them, the ones Geppetto made for him when the original ones got burned off and now nothing more than raggedy gnawed-off stubs, he is still amazingly "all of a piece," as his old friend Captain Spavento del Vall'Inferno put it, helping to smuggle him out of harm's way, Colombina responding: "True enough, compagno, but a piece of *what?*" But then, no sooner rescued and he was in trouble again, terrible trouble, and now they are on the run, having escaped here to this secluded little corner after flying hastily out of the uproar of the Piazza just before the police arrived to arrest him. It was Brighella's idea: "Get him as far as the Teatro Malibran! We'll take it from there!" So here they crouch, the decrepit puppet and the venerable marble Lion, outlaw and monument, pressed together in the wet shadows and dense eery silence under the unadorned pediment at the back entrance of a derelict theater with a plaque on its wall commemorating another wayfarer of mixed fortunes who allegedly once lived here, the two of them sharing a half-liter flask of his winged redeemer's fiendish spirits and waiting for he knows not what.

The end probably, there being no imaginable future. Though, if the end, at least not the one he had seemed fated, only a short while ago, to suffer, there in the Piazza San Marco in that collective maw of omnivorous mouths and gnashing teeth—getting swallowed by Attila was, relatively, a civilized experience. Trapped in his donkey suit and pinned to the cold slick paving stones by all the crazed revelers who fell upon him and upon each other and by his own crushing despair, he could do nothing but surrender to the horror of raw human appetite, helpless as the day he ended up on the Green Fisherman's plate. By the time his friends from the theater intervened, he had lost all hope, had even forgotten what hope in such a world might be. Most of the pizza pie had by then been eaten away or ripped off and passed around and now the delirious celebrants were trying to do the same with what no doubt looked to them like yet another costume: nothing could be that grotesque and live. They munched at his wooden limbs, tore off scraps of flesh with their teeth, bit his face and hands, chewed his feet up altogether, their prey meanwhile, though in mortal agony, sinking deeper and deeper into himself, as though to distance himself from the dish of the day he had become, his gaze locked on the top of the Campanile, glimpsed flutteringly beyond the bobbing heads of banqueters as though in slow-cranked film frames, half lost in the fog, which swirled about up there like teasing wisps of bluish hair, and seeming (or perhaps he wished it so with the last wish left him) to lean toward them, ready to come crashing punitively down upon their mad ruthless feast.

Then, suddenly, there was a tremendous explosion, and when the smoke had cleared, Buffetto was standing over him on one side gripping an immense blunderbuss and, on the other, Il Zoppo with a huge hole in the crotch where Lisetta's head should have been, masked and painted faces peering through the hole in stunned alarm from the other side. Il Zoppo, eyes crossing, toppled over like a felled tree, scattering startled merrymakers, and, before they could recover, Francatrippa came leaping over the fallen body, wielding a scimitar with both hands. "Stand fast, you craven turd, and measure swords! I'm a man of blood and, not to strain courtesy, you've stroked me up the wrong way with your gutless buggery! Prepare now to pitch and pay and pray your paternosters, you perfidious poltroon! *En garde!*" Buffetto raised his blunderbuss to fire again, and Francatrippa, crying out, "Death to all tyrants! Liberty for the people!" and "Viva Inter!", slashed Buffetto's hand off at the wrist.

There were shouts and screams and outbreaks of panic at the fringes of the mob, boos from Juventus fans in the masses beyond. Buffetto, undaunted, drew a saber of his own with his remaining hand and, remarking that "those who try to shit turds bigger than their assholes end up with tears in their eyes," commenced a furious blade-clashing duel with Francatrippa over the remains, as it were, of the communal repast, their dangerous leaps and strokes, though agile and successful in driving the crowds back, threatening to do more damage than all the mad ravening revelers had done. In one such parry and thrust, though the erstwhile Star of the Dance felt nothing in his benumbed desolation, Francatrippa seemed to trip over what was left of him and fell, dropping his scimitar. "Haha! Time to let the gas out, you pompous fartbag!" laughed Buffetto, jabbing his saber at Francatrippa's breast, but before he could drive it home, little

Truffaldino came swooping in from overhead, clinging to a rope of some kind, and, reaching out as he passed by, cut off Buffetto's nose with a rapier. By the time he had swung away and back again, both Buffetto and Francatrippa were waiting for him: *slick! slack!* went Truffaldino's ears in twin strokes, and then, *zzzip!* the head, both blades crossing each other as they sliced through the neck, the headless body, now fountaining blood like popped champagne, still hanging on the rope and swinging like a gruesome pendulum.

By now there was general panic spreading throughout the Piazza, and when Count Agnello Ziani-Ziani Orseolo, his gigantic member clad in gleaming armor, stepped into the fray, shouting *"Terrorists! Terrorists! It's the Puppet Brigade! Stand back or we'll all be killed!"*, the stampede was on. The Madonna added to the pandemonium by flinging about her organs, which exploded in great magical puffs of colored smoke wherever they fell, and in the confusion which followed, the moribund dancing donkey emeritus found himself being strapped secretively to the underside of the Count's phallus by Buffetto and Francatrippa, the Pulcinella half of Il Zoppo holding the thing up at the head, Lisetta whispering in his ear through the blasted hole in the white linen pantaloons: "Time to cut and run, dear friend!" And before they could even say it, they were out of there, a disappearing act so deft even Eugenio had wanted to know later how they had done it.

"It used to be bigger, this place, you know," rumbles the old Lion, passing him the grappa flask and lapping his stony jowls melancholically with his rough tongue. The coarse wet grating sound is echoed faintly by the inky waters of the Rio di San Lio lapping at the stone steps below them. "There was a time you couldn't fly from one fucking end of it to the other. I mean, literally. I wasn't sure I could say what its limits were then, any more than I could tell you how long God's devious pox-ridden cock was. Of course, I was just a cub then, I wanted to hump everything in sight and was eager for action, I took a lot of detours—Dalmatia, Crete, Byzantium, Cyprus, Crimea, and Galilee—I'd head out after breakfast, wouldn't get back for three years. So I admit I wasn't all that good a judge of distances. But, look: that guy Polo whose house used to be here somewhere? The restless coglione dragged his ass all the way to fucking Mongolia, other side of the world somewhere, came back and wrote a book about it, *Il Milion*, they called him, because of how the cunt stretched the truth, or else for all the money he made. But ask him if he'd seen all of Venice, he'd tell you straight to your face: Impossible. No one has or can. The distances are unimaginable. That's true, that's how it used to be, mate. I shit you not . . ."

The naked wayfarer, hovering disconsolately in the beast's abrasive mane, takes a deep pull on the grappa bottle, pincering it between both hands, having lost a few fingers back there in St. Mark's, and, trying not to cough or wheeze, hands it back, recalling the grandeur and seeming infinitude of the stage upon which, when young, he too had strutted, a spatial concept which he has often defended as being "an intimation of Being, ultimately dimensionless, and *therefore* real." Rising up out of the demented frenzy of the Piazza astraddle the Lion's slippery back, polished slick by the centuries, and clinging desperately to the mane with his mutilated fists, he had seen in one vertiginous glimpse how small it all was, how illusory the fantasy of "Being." "Un cazzo di niente," as the old warrior piloting him would say. "A lotta bullpoop": someone else. And yet, he knew, too, that in thousands of hidden corners of thousands of hidden artworks in all the hidden churches and museums in all the hidden alleyways throughout that disintegrating but multilaminous island down there, there were whole discreet worlds to be found like DNA clusters or nested microchips, belying their material limits. Ah well, the "real." He is coming to the end of a long life devoted intransigently to a pursuit of it, and, truth to tell, he still doesn't know what it is. All he knows is that, whatever it is, he is in it. And soon won't be . . .

"Some years later," his companion goes on, swigging from the flask, "I went away for a while. I was pretty old by this time, and suffering from mange and anemia and buboes and crotch rot and delirium tremens and all kinds of depressing shit, I couldn't even get it up anymore, I was just a useless fucked-up old boozer, sick at heart, jerking off limply at the world's keyhole. Napoleon came here then, just walked in and kicked my miserable hemorrhoidal butt around like he owned it, and nobody gave a moldering fig, not even me. Then he took me off to Paris for a while. And, though I hate to admit it, I had a pretty good time . . ." The old Lion tips back the bottle, finishes it off, tosses it into the black waters of the canal, belches resonantly. "When I got back, this place looked different somehow, shriveled up, tackier, fucking pathetic really. It was never ever the same after that." He lifts one paw and scratches himself ruefully between his hind legs, making a sound like bricks rubbing and clattering against one another, a sound that rebounds thinly from the wall across the softly plashing water, dimly lit by the single dull yellow bulb above. Drifting down the canals toward them now with the wisps of cold fog as though carried on them come, faintly, the distant sounds of Carnival: music, laughter, whistles, horns, shouts, drumbeats, sirens. Then they fade away again. He stares at the little arched bridge a few meters up the canal from them as though to see the sounds lingering there, but there is only a bleak dark silence. Did his puppet friends get away, he wonders. Or . . . ? He is afraid to consider the alternatives. "And now, shit, I'm nothing but an emasculated flea-bitten old clown, I know that. A fucking joke, too old to merit another telling. Hrmff. Still got my figure though. Eh? *Wurrp!* Damn right! Not worth the dingleberries on a stray cat's ass, but I'm still something to look at!"

When they got back to the Palazzo, the three servants having unstrapped him from the Count's giant penis and carried him gingerly up to his apartments, they found a glass coffin in the hallway outside his rooms, the rooms themselves stripped of his personal possessions, and a wizened Third World monarch, still wearing his crown, sleeping in his bed. They poked and prodded the ancient potentate but he seemed to be brain dead, so Buffetto and Francatrippa, peeling off their human masks to reveal themselves as his old Gran Teatro dei Burattini colleagues Brighella and Capitano Spavento del Vall'Inferno, dragged the royal person out onto the floor, while Colombina, whose head had popped up to replace Truffaldino's severed one, prepared now to remake the bed. "Yes, it's me, dear Pinocchio!" she laughed when she saw him staring up at her. "One of my most successful roles ever, though it hasn't been easy! I had a hard time keeping the Director from grabbing at something that wasn't there!" And she lowered her breeches to show him her hard hairless pubis, slightly cracked, knocking on it—*bok! bok!*—with her wooden fist. "Come in!" Brighella shouted ("In emergencies, I had to use everything from clothespins to broom handles!" Colombina was laughing), and the Captain muttered ominously: *"Cazzo! Il tristo nominato e visto!"*

"What are you *doing*, you idiots?!" screamed Eugenio, storming in in his disheveled Queen of the Night costume, no doubt red-faced under all the smeared paint. "Why is His Royal Puissant Majesty lying on the floor in his nightshirt? Are you *mad?!* I come back to powder my nose and freshen my lipstick and what do I *find—?!*"

"Easy, easy, direttore," urged Brighella, hastily pulling on his noseless Buffetto mask. "There was someone in the professor's bed—"

"Of *course* there was someone in his bed, you cretinous scoundrel! He doesn't *live* here anymore!"

"No? But then—?"

"Traitor!" the abused pilgrim squawked feebly from where he lay. *"Monster—!"*

"What? Ah, so *there* you are, Pini! How on earth did you get here, dear boy? I couldn't believe my eyes! There you were, in the middle of the crowded Piazza, quite the center of attention, and then suddenly a puff of smoke and: *vanished!* Into thin air! I thought they must have eaten you up! How ever did you manage that?"

"Murderer! See . . . what you have *done* . . . to me—!"

"What's that? Speak up, Pini," Eugenio complained, turning to primp in a gold-framed mirror, "I can't hear a word you say! As for your room here, if that's what you're mumbling about, I regret to say, your credit has run out, dear old chum, and I must ask you to leave. No hard feelings—"

"Run out—? Credit—?"

"Yes, credit—did you think it was Cuccagna around here? In the real world, things cost *money*, my dear, as a Nobel Prize–winner you should at least know *that* much!

"But all my savings—!"

"Your bank accounts are as empty as a Venetian well, your credit cards are used up, your properties sold or seized, your royalties bequeathed to, eh, charity, there's simply nothing left."

"My retirement funds . . . ?"

"Tsk tsk. I am afraid they're gone, too, Pini. You've been a very expensive guest!"

"You took even my—?!"

"Everything, carino mio. I am nothing if not thorough, as the Little Man himself would have told you long ago." Applying fresh ruby red lipstick, Eugenio puckered his lips in the mirror and winked coyly at himself. "And, please, I didn't *take* those little baubles, you forgetful old thing, you *gave* them to me. Still," he added, adjusting his wig, then turning away from the mirror and snapping his purse shut, "for old time's sake, if you stop fussing, I will let you stay on one more night. *I'm* certainly not coming home tonight, I'm having the most *delicious* time, so you or this grand imperial nabob here may use my rooms for the time being, whichever one of you promises to be continent."

"But—but what about *tomorrow?*"

"Tomorrow is a lifetime away, amor mio. We will take off our shoes, as we say here, when we come to the water! Those of us who still have them, that is. Now, now, don't put on such a face! I *do* love you, you know. And just to prove it, I have a little present for you! You there without the nose! Go to the library immediately and bring me what you find there on the Cinquecento papal secretary! Snap to it, you unsightly rogue!"

Almost before he had left, Brighella/Buffetto was back, cradling an all-too-familiar portable computer. "That's *mine!*" the old scholar croaked as the puppet-servant set it on his old writing table by the window. "You've—you've had it all the time!"

"Have I? Well, how should I know?" snapped Eugenio petulantly, turning away from the window where he had been throwing kisses and hallooing in his teasing falsetto to someone down in the Piazza below. "I buy and sell things all the time, that's what I *do*. I can't keep up with all the details! Now, really, I *must* get back to my party. We only live once, you know! Be a good fellow and don't disturb the other guests! And get something on, dear boy, you look a fright!"

"Wait! The—my student—how did—?"

"Ah, sorry about that, Old Sticks. I'm afraid she stood you up."

"No! I mean, what did she—did you—?" But Eugenio, with a flamboyant swish of his brocade skirts and jangling his jewelry like little beggars' bells, was gone, squealing: *"Here I come, you naughty boys, ready or not!"*

So he would not know. Perhaps he did not want to know. Knowledge, he has written somewhere, leads to the abyss. Knowledge *is* the abyss. How proud he had been to take that notorious path and, beating his breast for all to see, to walk the perilous rim, failing to perceive the true abyss opening up behind him with every footstep he took! One look back, and—!

And, well, here he was.

On his writing table sat the most recent instrument of his own daily acts of self-deception and -destruction. The very sight of it filled him suddenly with an indescribable loathing, a hatred of what Eugenio had done to him, of what he had done to himself, and of his long wretched life so wrongfully spent. Feeble as he was, he lurched to his feet, desiring to reach the thing, and it was then that he discovered his feet were gone. The clatter he made on the marble floor alarmed the puppets.

"Ahi! Be careful, dear Pinocchio! You're splintering!"

"There's not much holding you together!"

"It's the climate, you know! You must—!"

"Take me . . . over there!" he gasped.

"What? To your table?"

"You wish to write, dear friend?"

"You should be in bed!"

"Now! Please! While I'm still able . . ."

Reluctantly, Colombina rolled his leather swivel chair over to the table and Brighella and Captain Spavento set him in it, propping him up tenderly with goose-down pillows as they'd always done. "Great artists must always work when inspiration strikes them, I suppose," Colombina said dubiously, pulling a blanket off the bed to tuck around his shoulders. It took every last ounce of strength left him, but, summoning up all his rage to assist him in the final thrust (it didn't help that the infernal chair was on casters), he managed to push the computer out the open window, feeling as he did so the weight of a century lift from his frail weather-beaten shoulders.

"Free at last!" he rasped bitterly.

There was a sickening *k-thuck!* sound and then screams and shouts rose up from the square below. Oh no. He had forgotten about the Carnival crowds. He gripped, gripped by dread, the sill and, wishing not to see what he feared he must see, pulled himself forward to peek over, the three puppets squeezing around him to gape over his shoulder. At first he thought he had struck a woman. There at the mouth of the little underpass beneath his window, she lay lifeless, limbs outflung, wearing the fallen computer like a large square cartoon head. But then he recognized the tender butterball knees splayed out beneath the tossed brocaded skirts, the plump bejeweled hands. Blood pooled out richly around the computer, as though the Piazza were flooding from below. This time there was no mistake, Eugenio was as dead as he could be.

"Che colpo di scena!" whooped Brighella. "And what a *shot!*" The other two were already down the stairs, running to join in the festivities erupting around the body. Il Zoppo was down there, attempting celebrative back flips that were more like lanky pratfalls, and also the Madonna of the Organs and Count Agnello Ziani-Ziani Orseolo and all his bizarre retinue, the Count tipping back his mask and laughing the fierce strident laugh of the Venetian Lion-Planter, Pantalone the Magnificent. His monumental phallus was slit open by Colombina and Captain Spavento, just arriving, and out popped Pierotto, Lelio, and Diamantina, while other Burattini emerged from the costumed entourage, leaping and dancing wildly. "Viva Pinocchio!" they shouted. "He has saved our lives!"

Their presumptive hero, however, was not celebrating. He was weeping grievously, head drooped over the sill as though on the block. "Oh Eugenio, Eugenio!" he sobbed. "What have I done? Get up, Eugenio! This is *not* why I came here! Damn you! You mustn't die!"

The Madonna of the Organs took off her mask and wig, and the figure inside, the huge bearded maskmaker Mangiafoco, tipped his hairy head to one side and, peering up at the palazzo window, his eyes blazing as though with an inner fire, asked: "Who is that little woodenpate filling the air with sighs and watering the ground with his tears? Eh?" They might well be the last tears he would ever shed, already he could feel the tear sacs drying up, perhaps he should save them, he thought, things might get worse, but he could not stop them from flowing, it was like a wound that could not be stanched. "Yes, Pinocchio! Why?" the puppets cried. "After all he has done to you?"

"I-I don't know! I c-can't help it!" he bawled, feeling ashamed of his answer, his tears, his uncertainties, and of his very shame all at once. It was as bad as when he found himself in old Giangio's stable, crying like a mooncalf over a dying donkey. "He was a schoolmate of mine! And—and now he is *dead!*"

"Ah well," laughed Mangiafoco toothily, spreading wide his arms costumed in the pale likeness of flesh, "but that, signorino, is the very nature of our comedy here—!"

"*Wait!*" Pantalone cried out, beaked nose high as though testing the air, gray beard bristling. "*Listen!*"

Sirens wailed distantly. Beyond the Molo blue lights flashed. "It's the carabinieri! They're on the way!" "La madama!" "What do we do now?!" "We must rescue Pinocchio!" "He saved our lives, it's the least we can do!" "But how? They'll be here before we can even get him out of the palazzo!" "They're already at the Ponte della Paglia!" "They're coming down from Santa Maria Formosa!" "We're surrounded!" "They're at the Bocca! All is lost!" "Ahi! Ahi! Poor Pinocchio!" "Who will save him now—?!"

Whereupon began that heavy overhead flopping now no less familiar to him than the smell of the lagoon, as the Winged Lion of Saint Mark, for the second time, flew down to save his life, if his present condition could be so generously labeled. And this time, tossed out the window by Brighella onto the great beast's glossy back instead of into its jaws, without the torment of the creature's lethally fetid breath. Which, nevertheless, nestled here now on the Fondamenta del Teatro in the old fellow's pebbly mane, he has to admit he finds somehow less odious than before. Of course, the grappa probably helps.

"Helps—?"

"Your halitosis."

"My drinking grappa does?"

"No, *my* drinking it."

"Well, hrmff," grumps the old fellow, a bit miffed but with that sour, melancholic dignity that marks his character, "for centuries the citizens here fucked one another over by stuffing my mouth full of anonymous accusations. A shitty diet like that, what can you expect?"

The ghostly bulb overhead, casting no more light than a glowworm, barely illuminates the munched bricks in the wall right beside it, much less the little elbowed platform down here whereon, like cornered fugitives, they huddle, the dark wet walls and mazy canals beyond lost in an impenetrable darkness, yet he has the distinct impression that something large and secretive is moving now under the nearby bridge. The old Lion notices it, too. "Che cazzo—?!" he rumbles, flexing his clattery wings and beginning, slowly, boozily, to rise. The large dark shapes, darker than the darkness behind them, sway and bob furtively, moving slowly this way with the soft treacherous sound of rustling leaves. Then, like a dead man's hand reaching from its coffin, the silvery beak of a gondola emerges from beneath the bridge, followed by a second, and then a third. The occupants still are hidden in the shadows of the arched bridge, but, unless his ancient eyes deceive him, the ashen figure standing at the prow of the lead gondola, sightless and bloodied, broader than he is tall, one hand at his breast, or breasts, the other pointing accusingly straight at him, is Eugenio.

28.

THE FIELD OF
MIRACLES

"Porca Madonna!" whispers someone at his side, as, drawn up together, they stare in awe at the ghostly little campo, eerily lit by the single blue bulb hanging in the mists above. "Am I dreaming?"

In the middle of the softly undulating campo, where a wellhead might otherwise be, stands a strange tree, no larger than a leggy Tokai Friulano grapevine, leafed with crumpled thousand-lire notes and plastic credit cards and bearing clusters of silvery coins that glitter like lapis lazuli in the spectral blue light, though the sound they make is not so much the *zin-zin-zin* of his childhood fantasy as the *kunk-kunk-kunk* of old postwar leaden coins, the credit cards and dog-eared banknotes, ruffled by the cold damp breeze, adding a listless continuo of *futter-futter-ffpussh* to the blurry plunking.

The gondolas are already perilously overladen with treasures looted from the Palazzo dei Balocchi, but the lure of the mysterious money tree is irresistible, and soon the ancient anthropoid emeritus is alone once more, as his companions scramble up the broad watersteps to gather in cautious amaze around the luminous spectacle. He peers up through the blue mist at the sign engraved on the crumbling brick wall above him and sees: CAMPO DEI MIRACOLI. So here he is again. The Field of Miracles. It looks a bit different from the time he last saw it, returned then to search in vain for the gold pieces he had, with an innocence that shames him still, buried here. It has been paved over for one thing, though it is still as washboardy as a harrowed field. And it seemed larger and wilder to his childish eyes, he doesn't remember the pretty fog-masked Renaissance houses crowding in across the square from him or even the little church here by the watersteps with its façade of precious inlaid porphyry and marble, iridescent as mother-of-pearl, but then, what did he care about such things then, artless little gonzo that he was? In the lunette above the closed paneled doors of the church, a pensive stone Virgin gazes down at her naked baby, who seems to be pointing, amused, or perhaps alarmed and about to cry, at the even more naked figure hunched, trembling, in the gondola below, singling him out for reproach in much the same way that Eugenio, to his terror, seemed to be doing a few moments ago.

When he'd first seen the ashen bloodstained ex-Director of Omini e figli, S.R.L., floating toward him out of the mists, his pointing finger raised in angry denunciation, he'd hardly known what to think. He'd seen Eugenio dead, he had no doubt of that, this ghastly hollow-eyed apparition approaching him now could not be alive—and yet . . . Stripped of everything else, he feared his sanity might be going, too. And whatever else it meant, he was sure, as he shrank back into the rough mane of his growling companion there on the little gloomily lit fondamenta, that his own retribution was at hand.

The outstretched arm bent stiffly at the elbow as the grim figure approached, and slowly the pointing finger rose to point directly overhead. *"The devil teaches how to make the pot,"* intoned a hollow voice that seemed to come from the bottom of a well, Eugenio's painted scarlet lips moving slightly like a clumsy ventriloquist's, his face expressionless except for a tear glistening on one cheek, *"but not, dear boy, the cover!"* The empty eyes began to glow and rays of light emerged, beamed directly on the accused. *"Murder will OUT!"* The hand pressed to the costumed bosom swung out abruptly and the padded bodice slipped to the waist, then, as though by itself, popped back up again, the hand overhead dropping quickly to clamp it in place, the other hand flopping loosely for a moment, then rising steadily once more, elbow bent, until it covered the tearful face, extinguishing the beams of light. *"No evil more terrible,"* bemoaned the echoey voice from behind the hand, *"than to give an old friend such a bloody headache! It's a technological scandal! What good is a friend with an empty attic, not one turd of a brain in his bean?"* As though to demonstrate the consequences of this condition (snorting sourly, the Lion of Saint

Mark dropped his blunt snout back into his paws, and the escaped fugitive, too, felt the danger, if not the horror, pass), Eugenio's arms opened wide, the bodice plopped down and rose again, the hands waggled on their wrists, then the elbows angled upwards, the hands flopping loosely like laundry on a line, while the eyeless head rocked from side to side until it shook its wig off. One of Eugenio's thick white legs rose rigidly to one side, pushing against the brocaded skirt, and fell, then the other did the same. Then both legs rose straight up out of the gondola until the feet, still in their Queen-of-the-Night high-heeled shoes, were higher than the lurid head, hands falling limply between the fat thighs. *"Più in alto che se va,"* sang the voice, or voices, which now might have been coming from any part of the body, the flabby arms spreading apart like an opening curtain, *"più el cul se mostra!"* This reprise of the familiar Gran Teatro dei Burattini Vegetal Punk Rock Band ballad was followed by clackety wooden applause from the other gondolas and the cadaver's sudden collapse, its animators Pierotto, Brighella, and Diamantina peering out from behind it to take their bows.

"Meat!" grumped Brighella in disgust, as he and Pierotto, Pierotto first plucking the crystal tear off Eugenio's face and putting it back on his own cheek, heaved the corpse into the canal. "It's got no *style!*" Then he sprang in one great leap from the gondola to the fondamenta, followed by all the other members of the troupe, the laden gondolas left bobbing on their own, spilling into the canal loose Trecento artworks, silver goblets and golden candelabra, and there he led them all in a strutting, high-spirited, double-jointed celebration of woodenness. They scaled the wall of the theater, then fell from the roof on their backs, wept lugubriously in unison, broke into wild knee-slapping laughter, fanned at each other with wooden or imaginary swords, danced, somersaulted, bounced rigidly as though on hidden springs, pirouetted, walked on their hands and kicked their wooden heels together, flew through the air from kicks they gave one another, swaggered about stiff-legged and flat-footed, spouting Latin nonsense, then turned into potbellied hunchbacks one and all, competing with one another in a wind-breaking contest. Throughout all of this, Il Zoppo, somewhat handicapped, put on his/her own show, a kind of choral version of the other puppets' acts, weeping and laughing at the same time, farting in Latin, walking on Pulcinella's hands while strutting on Lisetta's feet, and falling down even as she/he was getting up. Finally the two of them formed a kind of arched bridge from fondamenta to near gondola over which the others hopped, skipped, tumbled, pranced, or leapt.

When they were all back in their gondolas, they turned to smile and wave up at him. "Come along, Pinocchio!" they cried. Captain Spavento maneuvered his gondola over to the watersteps so he could get in. "This house is played out! We're on our way to Rome!"

"Paris!"

"London!"

"Hollywood!"

"Look at all the loot we've got!"

"We're rich! We sacked the palazzo!"

"What parties we will have!"

"Anyway, we have no choice," said Brighella. "The carabinieri are right behind us."

"And are they *mad!*"

"Pantalone's wearing the Madonna's gash and stalling them with his stolen cazzo act!"

"They can't seem to find the corpus delicti either!"

"Ha ha!"

"But why didn't you laugh at our show, Pinocchio?" Lelio wanted to know. "We did that famous 'Dead Meat Lazzo' just for you!"

"It's one of the oldest routines in show business!"

"It's a real bitch, too!"

"Hardest puppet act there is!"

"Especially in a gondola!"

"He weighed a ton!"

"And the mask was too old and stiff. Maybe we should have left all that mucky stuff inside and used the whole head on a stick or something."

"No, no, it was great! Those flashlight eyes were fantastic!"

"I saw the lips move!"

"So why didn't you think it was funny, Pinocchio?"

"Maybe he's seen it too many times."

"Maybe he's not really one of us. Maybe he's still—"

"Of *course* he's one of us!" Colombina argued hotly. "He killed the Little Man, didn't he? He saved our lives! And he did it with style!

He added to the repertoire! He invented a whole new lazzo! And look at him! Of course, he can't last long, the rot's too deep, the pith's gone, and even his knotholes have knotholes, but one of us? What else *could* the poor little splinter be? Oh, I know, Lelio, I heard you complaining about the fungal spores and woodworm and other infestations, that they might be contagious and all that, but since when do we abandon a brother in his extremity just to save our own bark? *That's* not show business! *That's* not being one of us!"

"Bravo!" exclaimed Lisetta from inside Il Zoppo's flies. "Clap for me, you cretin!" she called up to Pulcinella, who, clapping, said: "But he still doesn't want to come with us. He's just sitting there."

"Because he hasn't got any *feet*, peathead! Have you forgotten what it was like? Somebody give him a hand!"

"Hurry! They'll be here any minute!"

So he was lifted aboard one of the gondolas, the Winged Lion of Saint Mark turning down their offer to join them, accepting instead a handblown bottle full of centuries-old grappa from the pillaging of the Palazzo dei Balocchi as a farewell gift, and after many hugs and "Ciao!'s" they set off, the Lion flapping westward to misdirect their pursuers, the puppets heading east for open waters, dreaming aloud about the grand adventures that awaited them. Hardly had they begun, however, when, sliding out from under a low arched bridge, they came upon this little campo bathed in blue light with the money tree in the middle.

It means nothing to him. He has no illusions, no hopes, no plans. All eaten away. He's going nowhere, he knows, even though he cannot stay. Does he hear sirens? Perhaps. It doesn't matter. He slumps, shivering, in his tapestry-upholstered gondola chair, watching his shipmates encircle, wide-eyed and breathlessly, the strange tree, drawn to the idea of wealth rather than to the thing itself. After all, their gondolas are already full to overflowing with fabulous cargo from the sacked palazzo, now tumbling piece by piece from the rocking barks into the sludge of the canal to become part of what holds this whole preposterous caprice up, they hardly need expired credit cards and coins worth less than the metal in them. Fairy gold . . .

Ah! The thought alarms him, waking him from the stupor into which, like this lagoon city, he had been irretrievably sinking. Is it possible? "My friends!" he croaks weakly. "Come back!"

But Lelio has already reached for a fat cluster of coins. There is a blinding flash as the unfortunate puppet goes up in flames, the tree disappears, and in its place, aglow in the pale blue light, stands a small tombstone with an inscription carved on it. Even before poor Lelio's ashes have settled, the puppets are back in the bobbing gondolas and grabbing madly at their oars, having lost half their plunder in the frantic reboarding.

"Wait!" whispers the former scholar, unable, even in such extremity, to break old habits. "Brighella—?"

"No way, old friend! Did you see that?! We have to get our lumbar regions *out* of here!"

"Please . . ." If there is something to be read, he cannot but, fearful of missing a message, *the* message, read it. "That may be for me . . ."

Violent arguments break out among the frightened puppets and there is talk of abandoning him there with Lelio's ashes, but finally, Captain Spavento threatening to slice up anyone who disagrees into cheeseboards and drink coasters, his oldest friends prevail and he gets his way: they use his gondola chair as a makeshift portantina and, slapping sullenly back up the half-submerged watersteps, carry him in it to the center of the small campo. Afraid to stay alone back in the gondolas, the entire company joins them there, gathering in a tight little cluster behind him, staying close to the church as though for protection, muttering about the need to keep moving before the madama catches up with them and complaining about the sudden deadly chill in the air.

He leans forward and squints his eyes, but either the light is too dim or else too radiant. He can see the letters but he cannot make them out. "Come on, come on, old vice! Get *on* with it!" complains Diamantina, glancing apprehensively over her shoulder, then, with a demonstratively impatient grunt, she stoops down and, peering close, reads it out for him: " 'I shall forgive you this once more,' it says, 'but woe betide you if ever again you are . . . you are . . .' There's moss or dirt or some kind of shit growing there, I can't read it. It *looks* like 'nauseous,' 'if ever again you are nauseous,' but . . ." She reaches forward to rub away the dirt.

"No!" he squawks. "It says 'naughty!' *Don't touch it—!*"

Too late. There is another flash as Diamantina flares up and, along with the tombstone, vanishes, leaving only a sooty smudge on the cracked flagstone. At the same moment, the church doors behind them open slowly as though by themselves and a thick creamy light, faintly rose-hued, flows out into the campo, accompanied by a strange ethereal music which might be harp music played on an organ, or else organ music played on a flute and theorbo. Or more likely none of these things, instrumentation having nothing to do with it. He sits alone in the light and music, of course; the puppets are all back in the gondolas once more, frantically preparing to push off from the steps and head with all haste for the high seas.

"Stop! We forgot old Pinocchio!"

"We *can't* stop, Colombina! The curtain is *down* on this horror show!"

"But—!"

"Leave him! Think of him like a dropped cue! A line that got stepped on! Tough, but that's showbiz!"

"It was his fault anyway! Come on! Let's blow this mud-hole!"

The beautiful inlaid marble walls now glow like alabaster lit from within and, above him, colored lights flicker and dance teasingly from window to window. The center of the lustrous façade is creased at the navel by a dark shadowy cross, and he sees now that the dazzling entranceway below it is bearded in a spiky blue moss, the Virgin's glistening white head peeking out overhead as though to inquire who might have put their foot in the door. He knows where he is. He has been here before. It is the little white house. The same one he saw between the Fairy's legs all those years ago.

"But we can't just leave him there, not Pinocchio," he hears Colombina protesting, and, in spite of a lot of short-tempered growling, there eventually seems to be general agreement about that, though less a consensus about who would go pick him up and bring him back. Finally, by offering up her share of the booty, she is able to persuade five others to come with her, the six of them creeping up on tiptoes, doubled over like chicken thieves, peeping up uneasily from under their lowered hat brims at the transformed church.

"These fucking miracle marts give me the creeps!"

"Eat me, drink me—they're like a fast food chain for vampires and cannibals!"

"Last time I played one of these houses, they called me Perverse Doctrine. Must've been centuries ago. Worst beating I ever got!"

"You'll get worse if you don't move your stumps! Grab the old board up and let's go!"

"No, no! Not that way!" he begs as they pull on his chair. "I want to go in there! I *must* go in there!"

"Now, now, dear Pinocchio," counsels Colombina, leaning close to his earhole, then speaking as to a deaf person, "as your best friend, let me give you some advice. It is very late, the night is dark, and we're up to our mildewed bungholes in death and danger as it is! We've already lost poor Lelio and Diamantina tonight. And the law's right behind us! Things are bad enough, as the saying goes, so don't blow on the fire!"

"Yes, you are my best friend, Colombina," he replies with his dry cracked voice. "I have almost no one left but you. If you don't help me, I-I don't know what I'll do!"

"But, Pinocchio, my love, this is crazy! Do you remember what our dear late lamented Arlecchino used to say? 'What do you gain by hanging yourself?' he used to say. 'Does that put any flesh on your bones? It does not, it makes you thinner!' Now, for goodness' sake, or at least for your own, and for mine, too, if you love me, be sensible! Come with us while there is still time!"

"Please! Just take me inside. I can't get there by myself. Then you can go."

"Go? But aren't you coming with us?"

"I-I don't know."

"Ahi, my dear Pinocchio, you are impossible!" she cries.

"Perhaps we could just toss the old cazzo inside on the count of three and make a run for it—?" Pierotto suggests.

"Or maybe we could nail a couple of those fancy crosses we stole to what's left of his knees and he could toddle on in on his own," says another.

"Bad luck," mutters Brighella. "We've your nut for a hammer, but we're fresh out of nails."

"No, if we're going to do it, let's at least show some style, let's go clean—like they say in the trade: if you slip in the shit, make a dance out of it!" Colombina insists, and, with an exasperated sigh, the six of them lift his gondola chair in unison like grim-faced pallbearers, sharing out not the weight, little of that that there is, but the dread. The other Burattini, being old troupers after all and superstitious about splitting up an act, reluctantly pile out of the gondolas yet again and join them, huddling closely, for their collective entrance.

"Mamma mia! Is this dumb, or what?"

"We must all be out of our waterlogged gourds!"

"Look at those crazy lights playing around up there! It's like some kind of Grand Opening!"

"Yeah, well, just so what gets opened isn't me!"

"This church, is it . . . is it used for last rites?" he asks faintly.

"No, never. Lust rites, more like. It's a wedding chapel."

"The brides are off-loaded from those steps out there."

"The only things that get buried here, old chum, are little birds in ripe figs."

"Ah . . ."

"But never so deep they can't be made to rise and sing again."

"And again."

"This is the only shaman shed in town where the Second Coming is not sufficient cause for celebration."

"Let's just hope we don't lose any more than the brides lose!"

"What did you say?"

"What?"

As they reach the blue-wreathed doorway, the liquid glow from within seems to grow more intense, troubling their sight and hearing alike ("Loose enema, then: what—?"), the music, which is more like a fragrant lullaby than a hymn or a wedding march, now reaching them less through their ears than through their noses as a rich harmonious brew of incense, gentle arpeggios, hot peperonata, and Venetian lagoon.

"Listen! The bells!"

"It's nearly midnight!"

"And tomorrow—!"

"I can't hear them, but I can feel them kicking!"

"Tell me when we're in Paris!" whimpers Lisetta, only her nose sticking out, and Pierotto complains: "What's that? I can't hear a thing! I've still got poor Diamantina's ashes up my nose!"

"Now, come in here, and tell me how it happened that you fell into the hands of assassins!" intones a grave windy voice that seems to come from another world, and is not so much heard as felt like a cold finger down the spine. The gondola chair is dropped on the flagstones there

in front of the open door with an answering bang and the trembling puppets fall clatteringly together like a sackful of shingles.

"Who was that—?!"

"Assassins? What assassins—?"

"I'm suddenly losing interest," Captain Spavento wheezes solemnly, turning shakily on his heel, and the top half of Il Zoppo gasps: "Whoa, old pegs! Any further and I'm getting off!"

"Button your pants, Pulcinella! Don't let me look!"

"You close this farcetta on your own, Colombina! I'm butting out of here!"

"Me too! I'm so scared I think I just split myself!"

"This is not in my contract!"

"No, don't go!" he cries. "Please! Capitano! Brighella—!"

"But they are right, dear Pinocchio!" agrees Colombina. "This is not our pitch! It's clear we've all been cast here for tomorrow's Ash Wednesday magic makeup kit! We must go—quickly!—and you must go with us!"

"But—!"

"No more 'buts'! 'Buts' have caused you nothing but trouble all your life! Come now! The show must go on, old trouper!"

"But that's just it!" he gasps feebly. "Look at me, Colombina! Dear Brighella! Capitano! Can't you see?! My part is over! I've got no feet, no ears, no teeth, my fingers are dropping off and everything else is warped and cracked and falling apart—I can't move without fracturing and splintering, my cords and ligaments have rotted out, and my insides are nothing but wet sawdust! There's nothing alive and well in there except the things feeding on me! And Lelio was right, though I love you, I'm not one of you! Flesh has made a pestilential freak out of me! Even I don't know who or what I am any more! There's only one thing left for me now. But I-I can't do it without you!"

His desperate plea has silenced them. Brighella has returned. Pierotto looks over his shoulder from the foot of the watersteps, the tear on his cheek gleaming like a sapphire in the blue light there.

"You've touched me to the very core, dear Pinocchio," Colombina sighs. She gives him a tender little hug, and the miserable sound of wet twigs snapping makes her groan and hug him again, whatever the damages. "What is it you want us to do, my brother?"

"I want, how can I say . . . ? I want you to help me make . . . a good exit."

"Ah . . . !" The puppets turn as one toward the blazing blue-whiskered doorway of Santa Maria dei Miracoli. This is something they all understand. A proper exit needs timing, boldness, clarity, purpose, but, before anything else, one must command the stage. What they feel, standing here in the misty wings, is worse than stage fright to be sure, but it is no longer mere woodenheaded panic. They are professionals, after all. Those who have fled to the boats now return, and though there is still some surly grumbling to be heard at the fringes, the general mood as they pick up his tapestried gondola chair once more and step pluckily on through the resplendent portal (the Virgin, under a punctuated cross lit up now like a pinball bumper, seems to spit on them as they pass beneath her, or perhaps she is squirting her breasts at them, or little Jesus, lost in the dark tangled foliage, might even be peeing on them all, it is hard in the confusion of their senses wrought by the musical light, or luminous music, to be sure) is more like that of getting stuck with a lean part in a bad show in front of a cold house: grim but steady, and prepared to see it through.

MAMMA

29.

EXIT

They crowd in under the overhanging ridge of the Nuns' Choir at the back of the little Santuario di Santa Maria dei Miracoli, gazing in awe, their senses still somewhat bedazzled, at the fabulous scene before them, which reminds the much-traveled old wayfarer of nothing so much as his visit to Attila's innards. The sheer marble walls, pale as old bone and glistening dewily, seem to be pulsating with the strange pumping music, as do the softly clashing gold-framed Pennacchis, arched above them like the plated back of a prehistoric beast. As, cautiously, the puppets port him down the aisle between the ribbed pews, they are assailed by the delicate aromas of frankincense, ambrosia, and myrrh, along with something headier, reminiscent of the sweet decay of wens and bogs, which may be the odor of the throbbing music. In all the church, except for the celestial gallery of portraits in the gently billowing vault above, there is only one painting, a Quattrocento Madonna and Child, mounted on the high altar standing atop broad marble steps crisp as vertebrae and surrounded by balustraded galleries and filigreed marble carvings delicate as living tissue. Two hanging Byzantine lamps swing at either side of the altar like blood red pendulums under an expanding and contracting cupola, and the crimsoned painting itself seems to glow from within as though the Virgin, robed in midnight blue and holding the haloed child like a ventriloquist's dummy, were standing in the midst of a blazing fire. *"Gentlemen, I should like you to tell me,"* the painted Madonna calls out to them in that whispery otherworldly voice they have heard before, *"I should like you to tell me, gentlemen, if this unfortunate puppet is dead or alive!"*

The Burattini pull up short, wooden mouths gaping from ear to ear, their knees knocking in the sudden silence like a whole marching

band's drumsticks being rapped together. "Who-who said that—?!"
they gasp severally.

"O Fatina mia, why are you dead? Why you, so good, instead of
me, so wicked?" squeaks the long-nosed deadpan creature the Madonna is holding, its right hand rising and falling mechanically. Her
hands deftly but in full view work the marionette from underneath,
pulling the wires down there, and her lips move perceptibly as the
wooden-faced baby's lower jaw claps up and down: "If you truly love
me, dear Fairy, if you love your little brother, come back to life!
Aren't you sorry to see me here alone and abandoned by everyone?
Who would save me if I were caught by assassins? What can I do,
alone in a world like this?" Then, though the little figure continues
its singsong recitation of the famous "Puppet's Lament," the text in
this century of tragedies, operas, and countless requiems throughout
the world, the Madonna's cheeks puff out, her lips pucker up, and
between them a shiny pink bubble emerges, slowly fillng with air
until it is as big as the talking infant's mouth, its head, its halo. "Who
will give me something to eat? Where will I sleep at night? Who will
make me a new jacket?" continues the whining voice, the hinged jaw
clopping up and down like slapsticks, even as the bubble expands
until only the Virgin's right eye peeks slyly over the top of it. "Oh, it
would be a hundred times better if I died too! Yes, I want to die! *Ih!
Ih! Ih—!*"

The crescendoing sobs are interrupted by a sudden bang as the
bubble explodes like a firecracker, splattering the faces of the Madonna and Child, and indeed some of the painting's fiery background
as well, with pink bubble gum. A breathless quivering hush seems to
grip the little wedding chapel. Even the music has stopped. The
Virgin, blinking through the impasto of gum as though through
thrown pie, pushes her hand deep into her son's body, then pokes out
the eyes from within, waggling two long rosy fingers at her awestruck
audience like insect feelers. Her own mouth gapes, webbed by moist
streaks of gum, and the damp windy voice wails: *"Birba d'un burattino!
Are you not afraid to die?"*

"That does it! I'm off!" cries Capitano Spavento del Vall'Inferno,
letting go his side of the gondola chair and wheeling round. "You can
only carry friendship so far!"

"No! Stop!" the old pilgrim gasps, twisting around in the dropped chair, heedless of the wrenching and splitting within, but the mercurial Captain, sword drawn and striding as though into battle, is not to be held back. He charges full tilt at the doorway, now overgrown with blue brambles, slashing at the wiry thicket with his sword, and —*FFRISST!*—there is a sudden brief blaze in the shape of Captain Spavento, gone before seen. His ashes hang like a shadowy afterimage for a moment, then settle silently to the floor.

Everything is changed. The curtain of blue bramble has vanished. The door is closed. The smooth bare walls, encrusted with precious marble the color of fresh air on a dull day, are merely walls now, holding in the solemn silence. The fifty Pennacchi portraits gaze down from above like the sober voyeurs they have always been, the altar lamps have stopped swinging, and the ancient painting displayed there is once more flat and lifeless, the Christ child's stare a bit askew perhaps with two dark holes where the fingers poked through, but otherwise, except for a streak or two of sticky pink, a work abused only by the passing centuries. Slender white tapers have been lit in front of it and throughout the chapel, and there is everywhere a great profusion of fresh-cut flowers, in all the pews and on the walls and statues and columns, in the pulpits and windows, and heaped up on the high altar like whipped cream and spilling into the choir galleries and through the ornamental balustrades and down the stairs and center aisle to where, clustered around the ancient figure in the gondola chair, the puppets press together in benumbed terror, their collective gaze riveted upon the strange person in the snowy white shift, her azure hair flowing down her back like a bridal train, sitting now, her back to them, on one of the two carved and upholstered stools before the altar. The other stool is empty.

"Su da bravi, Burattini!" comes a voice from the front of the chapel, a voice he knows all too well, soft as canary down and sweet as panna cotta. It is the voice that changed his life, and its seductive power is undiminished. He feels his resolve crumbling like hot *favette dei morti*, the *favette* she always baked for him when he came home from school or mischief, saying tenderly as she popped them in his mouth: "You see how I love you, ragazzo mio? But if you want to stay with me, you must always obey me, and do as you are told!" With pleasure, mammina mia! Oh, with pleasure! Che bello! Che bello! "Do you see that poor half-dead puppet there?" the voice continues now. "Take him up gently, bring him to me, and sit him on this cushion here beside me. Do you understand?"

"*No!*" he rasps, shaking off the terrorized puppets when, as though spellbound, knees rattling and eyes popping, they reach for him. It takes all his courage not to surrender to her immediately, such is the lure of her great power to one so powerless as he, and so desperately lonely, but he knows that, having lost everything else, the withholding of that surrender is the only expedient left him if he is to attain the end, or ends, he seeks. Or indeed any end at all, beyond abjection's shoddy but, alas, appealing joy . . .

"What are you muttering between your teeth?" asks the voice up at the high altar. "What is the matter now?"

"So you lied to me again," he wheezes, speaking up as best he can. "You are not dead, after all."

A deep echoey sigh flutters through the little church, making the flower petals tremble and the candles gutter briefly, and setting the stupefied puppets' knees to clicking like wind through a cane brake. "It seems not," admits the voice, so wistfully affectionate he almost cannot bear to prolong his separation from her.

"All these years of mourning my precious mamma's early and tragic death! 'Poor Fairy! The victim of a thousand misfortunes and too poor to buy a crust of bread!' Do you remember your little joke? I have carried the harrowing sadness of it with me all my life! All that I have done or have not done has been confused and tempered by it. Even now, my final years have been devoted to its bewildering mysteries, it is why I am here, why I have suffered so—and it has all been just a farce! Ah, Fatina mia! Why have you done this thing to me?!"

"Because idleness is a dreadful disease, my boy, of which one should be cured immediately in childhood: if not, one never—!"

"Oh, yes, yes, I've heard all that before! You always were the *good* little fairy, weren't you? Society's little helper! Civilization's drill sergeant! But I was free! I was happy! And you, with your terrifying heartbreaking parade of tombstones and canon, put strings on me where there were none. You cheated me! All my life," he squawks, lifting up the twisted splinters of his arms and rattling them at the blue-haired figure on the bridal stool, "*I have been nothing but a puppet!*"

Slowly, though she keeps her back to them still, her head begins to rotate on her shoulders, and the waxen face of the little Bella Bambina of old appears with her strangely rigid smile and rolled-up eyes, bringing a startled gasp from his friends, pressed tight about him. "I love you," the Bambina stage-whispers, piercing him to the quick with her terrible intimacy. "Stay with me! You shall be my little brother, and I will be your darling sister!"

The sight of the Bambina, the dearest playmate he ever had, gruesome as her games could sometimes be, makes his arms drop and would bring tears to his eyes if they had not all been spent, like everything else. How good she was, or seemed to be! How tender, even if she did leave him hanging all night in the oak tree, swinging in the wind like a bell clapper, her loving care! And does she not offer him what he now most wants: just to play again? "I have thought about your little white house, Fatuccia mia," he croaks at last, summoning up all his strength to resist her, "and how much pleasure you promised me in it. Yet when I tried to return to it, you took it away and put a tombstone in its stead! I went crazy with grief for a while, but I learned my lesson well."

"So my medicine really did do you good?"

"I can truthfully say, though I have been diligent, obedient, truthful, and circumspect, I have not had a wholly happy day since. I might somehow have found my way back to one little white house or another, but I was always too afraid. Pleasure was death and dissolution. That's what you taught me. Fun was fatal. No. I will not play with you."

"My child, you will be sorry," sighs the Bambina as her grinning head recommences its slow grim turning. "You are very ill . . ." When the next revolution begins, the head is joined by the upper torso, swiveling at the waist, and this time it is Bluebell. "Hey, wow, teach, you don't look so hot!" she laughs, snapping her gum in her bright white teeth. She reaches up with both hands to pull away the lacy shift and out pop her spectacular young breasts like fat rabbits from a hat, bringing fresh gasps of amazement from the puppets surrounding him. Those breasts, last seen on the Apocalypse, are dizzying alive, the scintillating rosettelike nipples, lightly gilded, throbbing as though with excited little heartbeats of their own. "You need some *nourishment*, Professor Pinenut! So, why don't you scoot your cute little boopie-doops up here and grasp, as you like to say, my 'civilizing principles?' "

This glorious sight, for which, so recently, he was ready to throw away honor, dignity, life itself, steals his breath away, what little there is left for theft, and he feels riven (literally: he can hear the stifled creaking and snapping deep inside) with an unendurable yearning, not to fondle them—what would he fondle them *with?*—but simply to rest his dying head there, to hide himself, as someone has said, on the breast of the simple, the vast, the ineffable . . . "I see," he rattles drily, hanging on to his chair arms with both gnarled fists, "you are still wearing my ear."

"You better believe it, Daddy-o! It's my good luck charm!" She reaches up to finger the shriveled black brooch, making her breasts wobble teasingly. "So, hey, what'll it take to trade you for the rest, prof?"

"Certainly, you deceitful ogress, more than those puffed-up things you are flaunting so, a mask like any other. Put them away! The dead ear suits you better!"

She looks crestfallen, deflated, the rosette nipples withering to something more like smallpox vaccination scars, and he almost regrets his own deceit, hoping his nose is not giving him away. "You're right, teach," she says finally, perking up a bit, "I could use a good dressing-down! I've been really rotten, I admit it! A dirty dog! C'mon! You can treat me as rough as you please! I *deserve* it!" She hesitates, gazing at him hopefully ("That's a pretty good offer!" one of the puppets whispers in his ear, and another asks: "Do you think we could all have a go?"), but when he makes no move, she turns away sorrowfully and begins to rotate once more.

When she pivots around again, it is with her whole body, though the stool at the top of the steps remains in place. He is not quite sure how she does this because his gaze is fixed on the creature appearing before him. This he has not been prepared for. It is his mamma, to be sure, she could be no other, but she has changed. At first he thinks she must simply have aged, he hasn't seen her since the last century, but then he catches a glimpse of the Bambina's wicked smile, Blue-bell's milk-fed complexion and fluorescent eye shadow, and hints, too, of a Hollywood starlet he once knew, maybe more than one, a colleague at university, several students, his interviewer on a television talk show, the doctor who removed the peculiar growth on his nose a year ago and prescribed a long voyage, an admiring museum curator who confessed to a platonic affection, his traveling companion in the limousine to the Nobel awards in Stockholm, even (the stray blue hairs on her chin perhaps, the ridge of her forehead) the blue-haired goat he passed on his way into Attila's gut. These features, or suggestions of features, seem to exist not simultaneously but sequentially (now it is the Bambina's waxen complexion he sees, Bluebell's gum-smacking cherry-lipped grin), in a kind of moving montage, flickering across her face like unstable film projections. It is like being under water in a Hollywood pool with naked starlets swimming by and his eyes full of chlorine. Or like trying to put a half-forgotten face together with a half-remembered name.

"Deceitful ogress—?! How can you say all these horrible things about me, my child?" she asks with a forlorn sigh, and it is as though she has reached in, penetrating easily his fragile defenses, and pulled the little lever that floods his chest with guilt and regret, just as she always did in the old days. "That I cheated you or was unkind to you or abandoned you or misused my power or misled you or indeed did anything all your life long but love you with all my heart? 'Assassina,' you called me tonight in front of everybody! How could you do that, you wicked boy? Civilization's lackey! An avatar of Death! The Great Destroyer! Really! And, 'a son pregnant with his own mother,' what an idea!" She seems almost to be crying, but he cannot be sure, her eyes do not stay in one place long enough. Those fleeting traces of the familiar are now blurred by the strange. Claws on her fingertips. An iron tooth. Smoke curling out her nose, which seems to change shape with every breath. He has seen a scar grow, cross her brow, and rip vividly down her cheek and throat, then as quickly fade and vanish. A moment ago, her ears, peeking out from under hair twisting like thin blue snakes, seemed to be pointed, but now they look like his mamma's once more, the ones he snuggled against when she let him nuzzle his nose in her azure tresses, then—and now again—silky and soft as a passing cloud. "I am just a poor lonely fairy who fell in love with a stupid puppet's good heart and wanted to, well, make him beautiful. And happy." An eye slips out of a socket, she pushes it back. Or perhaps the socket moves to cup the errant eye. His fascination is such that he begins to worry: is this yet another seduction? "You are right about one thing, however. I *have* always wanted to be a *good* fairy. I was never one to suck navels or sour the cow's milk. I loved humans and wanted them to love me, even if they were pretty silly and didn't last long. I wanted to live among them in their nice little towns and villages, I never cared for the bog life, but somehow, even when I was being good, I was always scaring them. Maybe I had a way of doing things too suddenly, or maybe it was the holes in my armpits, I don't know, but they were always very nervous around me. I tried my best for a few hundred years, but I never managed to fit in. It was a kind of racism, as you'd call it now, I suppose, and probably I had grounds for complaint, but we fairies, as you know, are not much given to such tactics. We merely poison the wells, smash a few eggs and babies, and infest the beds with rectum snakes. My own response was to try to die. Dying seemed to carry a lot of weight with humans, I thought it might help. But it wasn't in my repertoire, really. I gave it all I had, but I just couldn't get the hang of it. Which disheartened me all the more. And then, just when my spirits were lowest, you came along . . ."

"I see it now," he says, not too appropriately, inasmuch as his tired old eyes, struggling in vain to fix the Fairy's face, which, if anything, is growing increasingly fluid and monstrous, have lost all focus and seem to be swimming in his head. "If dying carries weight with humans, so, if not more so, does mothering. If you couldn't win them over one way, you'd try another. I was just another trick to play, your surrogate, your convenient dummy, your marketable change-ling."

"There! You're being cruel again! What have I done to deserve such an ungrateful son? When you came back here to our island looking for me now, I was so happy. I thought we could be together again. In the old way, like we used to be before you got changed and went off into the world. But you have disappointed me, my boy, slipping back into all your old habits, falling in with unwholesome companions, breaking promises, acting on impulse, running away, getting in trouble with the police, refusing advice—and now, to have degenerated into the theatrical arts—I ask myself, what was it all *for?*" As she scolds him, the floating ambiguities fade and she resolves into his mamma once more, firm, exasperated but loving, intimidating, beautiful . . . "And just look at you now! Flesh would no longer even stick to such a shameless ruin! Couldn't you at least keep your warm wraps on? How many times did I tell you—?"

"It wouldn't have made any difference. Sooner or later, I would have ended up like this anyway. You didn't do a very good job . . ."

"I know, and that is why I have forgiven you." She sighs, settles back, casting a last quick loving glance at him before her features again melt into a pool of possible features, an inconstancy that now spreads to the rest of her body, causing all the edges to waver and blur. It is as though the *idea* of her is too big for her canvas. "The trouble is, though I always tried to be a good fairy, I wasn't quite good enough. In the end, proud as I was of the proper little man I'd made, I found I loved the naughty puppet more than I should have and was afraid of losing him, or at least his good heart, and couldn't quite let him go. So I left just the tiniest seed inside. A bit of the sneeze, as you might say, that got held back. I didn't think it would do any harm. And this way, I felt, we had a kind of bond between us . . ."

"We were both monsters, you mean." She smiles, or seems to, her mouth spreading to her ears, dispersing her teeth like fence stakes, her eyes at the same time receding deep beneath her brows and flaring up as her head flattens to her shoulders, the rest of her turning shaggy and ballooning out in all directions, but only for a moment, just long enough to give him a glimpse of something beyond mere rhetorical flourish and make him catch his breath. "Ahimè! Fata mia! How can I resist you?"

She seems to blush at that, though the colors are ambiguous and none of them pink, and a light comes to her eyes, or her eyes to the light, and she spreads her knees a little, causing the banks of flowers on the steps and in the aisle between them to rise and fall softly as though mice were running through them. He too feels a vague stirring somewhere, nothing prurient, more like . . . more like getting shifted on the woodpile . . . "Come, my child!" she croons in a voice so resonant with desire it sets the organ pipes to humming. "Burattini! Bring him to me!"

His puppet friends stagger out of their weak-kneed crouch around him to take a fearful grip on his gondola chair, but, though dizzy with the intensity of his own peculiar desires, he stays them with a restraining gesture. "Dear Fairy, I am yours," he says in his thin scratchy voice. "But first I have three small requests, which I am sure you will grant me."

"Ah!" She draws back, her colors changing (frustration perhaps, rage, he can't be sure), and the flowers close and shrink flat as a woven carpet between them. The light in the chapel may also have just dimmed, though it may be he who is losing the light. "What's wrong with humans? Why is there always this haggling—?"

"The first is that you let my friends leave here unharmed. I don't want anything more to happen to them."

"Oh, is *that* all," she sighs, and Bluebell's healthy complexion returns, the Bambina's rigid smile. "Yes, of course they can go, peace and prosperity to them, but, well, don't be mad, but . . ."

"But—?"

"I was afraid they'd take you away. So I sank the gondolas."

"Ah . . ." He turns to his companions. Pierotto sniffs. Colombina shrugs. "Megio no aver bezzi / che el cul in diese pezzi," mutters Brighella, apparently quoting a Gran Teatro dei Burattini routine, for the others pick it up like a murmured antiphon: "Better broke than your arse / broken up in ten parts!"

"Thank you, my friends. The second request, dear Fairy, is a little more difficult, but I believe you can do it. When I was turned into a boy, something happened which, though at the time I thought little of it, has troubled me increasingly all my life. I have written about it, but not well. Too much guilt maybe. When I woke up a boy, the straw cottage had been transformed into a beautiful house, I had brand-new clothes and a purse full of gold pieces, my dying babbo was suddenly healthy as a fish and back at his lathe, and—"

"Well, that is because when children who—"

"No, no, that's not the part I mean. What bothered me was that the wooden puppet I once was was still there, outside of me, the old Pinocchio, I saw him, collapsed against a chair in my father's workshop with his legs doubled up under him and the rest unstrung and dangling."

"Oh yes . . ."

"I want you to let that puppet live again. Do that, and my friends here will bring me to you."

"But what are you saying, my son? You have lived a long and illustrious life, an impeccable example to all humanity. Your bibliography is one of the ten longest in the world, and few men in history have been more honored. A university has been named after you—"

"It's not a university, it's a junior high school—"

"But don't you see? If that stupid puppet lives on, all that will have been in vain! Your own beautiful life, the one I *gave* you, will have been meaningless!"

"That's right. It's what I want."

"You won't know anything about it, you know. It's not like—"

"I know. It doesn't matter." The Fairy slumps back darkly onto the stool. Stools, rather, she is sitting on both of them now. She doesn't look anything at all like his mamma at this moment. More like Attila actually. He hadn't realized she would take it so personally. "I love you, mamma. But he, as you might say, stands between us . . ."

Reluctantly, composing herself, she nods, her shifting features gathered up once more into something like maternal melancholy: "It's not a very nice thing for a good fairy to be doing," she says with a sigh that sends the flowers at her feet cascading down the steps, "but it's done."

"Thank you, mamma!" he whispers, showing her a bit of a smile, which bring on another loss of outline and rush of color, then he turns to the puppets encircling him: "You may take me up to her now."

But they seem rooted to the flower-strewn floor, a little petrified copse in the field of petals. Only the rattling of their knees gives them away. "Are you kidding?" one of them whimpers. "After what happened to Captain Spavento?"

"That's just putting the straw next to the fire!"

"Already my head feels capped with phosphorus!"

"All that's over. Don't be afraid. You won't be harmed."

"Can you put that in writing?"

"Why can't that thing with the fright wig come down here? Hasn't it got any legs under that drapery?"

"Compagno, don't ask!"

"Friends, please! You promised—!"

"I just dried up! Can't remember a thing!"

"I seem to recall another engagement—"

"No, brothers and sisters, Pinocchio is right. It's his drop scene and we're the support, the feed, don't you see? We can't stick now! Not when he needs us most! We can't spoil his curtain!"

"I don't know, Colombina. I'd tear myself to pieces for the little fantoccio, you know that. On the other hand . . ."

"We could sing a song," he suggests. "What was that one you taught me? Da-da-da-da-da-da-DUM—?"

" 'Lèzi, scrivi,' you mean?"

"How does it go—?"

Someone hums a bit of it, Brighella raps out a beat with his hands on the back of a pew, others make instrumental noises through their noses or pick up on the words, and soon the troupe is in full throat and marching together down the flower-carpeted aisle toward the altar, his gondola chair raised on high. He joins in, celebrating all the naughty truths of the world, sung to the tune of his Hollywood theme song, his final performance with the Gran Teatro dei Burattini Vegetal Punk Rock Band. They port him up the fourteen steps to the altar and at the top lift him out onto one of the two stools there, the Fairy having discreetly withdrawn for the moment to a side gallery, and then, with hugs and kisses and tearful break-a-leg jokes, they leave him.

Even as, descending to the pit, they slip from view, he finds himself, home again, on the Blue-Haired Fairy's pillowy lap. Tenderly, clucking and sighing and, it may be, weeping, she goes over him from head to shredded shins, testing the hinges, brushing away the vermin and pizza crumbs, kissing the sore spots. "Poverino!" She raises and lowers his limbs, listens to his heart, picks him up and turns him over, pokes and knocks at what she finds there, gasping with pity when her finger pushes into the soft bits. She does a little makeshift repair work to the crumbling mortise and tenon joints between head and shoulder, then, laying him on his back again, dresses his wounded stumps with wet motherly kisses and twists of her azure hair. "You forgot your third wish," she remarks teasingly as she binds him.

"No," he whispers. "You know it, mamma!"

The luminous flush returns to her cheeks and throat and he feels a damp dense warmth engulf him for a moment. Her eyes lose focus, though whether in ecstasy or in grief he cannot say, and her blue hair, alive once more, spreads out like a veil above him, then flutters down, the tingly strands flowing over his body like water, curling round all his parts, penetrating the innumerable gaps and fissures, swathing him wholly in their writhing embrace for a moment of what seems to him the very quintessence, although abstract, of passion, as if he were being gripped by a delicious idea. Then, as quickly, her hair slithers away again, releasing him to her subtler ministrations, her kisses, nibbles, soft caresses. "You've been well plucked, my son," she murmurs. "There's not enough left here for a sandwich and a cigar box. You're not even worth burning. I'm afraid there's nothing left to do but send you to the pulping mills to help ease the world paper shortage." She leans down, little more than a loving shadow to him now, to kiss his eyes closed, whispering down the long receding tunnel of his earhole: "We'll make a book out of you!"

"Ah!" he replies with his vanishing voice, grateful for the line she has, in her wisdom, thrown him. "But a talking book, mamma! *A talking book . . . !*"

Though his eyes are closed, his senses withdrawn, for one vivid moment he sees himself at a distance in the Fairy's arms. He has not moved from those arms, has indeed fallen deeper than ever inside himself, yet the view seems to be from the back of the church, near the door, looking down a long polished nose at an altar bedecked with flowers and flooded with soft light, the rest of the little chapel now in darkness. What he sees up there is a decrepit misshapen little creature, neither man nor puppet, entangled in blue hair and lying in an unhinged sprawl in the embrace of a monstrous being, tented obscurely in her own wild tresses, but revealing, as she picks and nibbles at the ridiculous figure in her lap (it feels, remotely, very good . . .), glimpses of tusk and claw and fiery eye. She is grotesque. Hideous. Beautiful. She leans toward the little man's head now as though to suck at the orifices there (yes, he can feel it go, feel it all emptying out), and then the eyes at the doorway turn away from the light and he is finally and for all that infinite span of time still left him, infinite because he will never know its limits, be they but a hair's breadth away (the thought escapes him, even as he thinks it), in the dark. Somewhere, out on the surface, distant now as his forgotten life, fingers dance like children at play and soft lips kiss the ancient hurts away. And . . . is she doing something with his nose? Ah . . . ! Yes . . . ! Good . . .

R O B E R T   C O O V E R is an Iowan who now lives in Rhode Island and Europe. Among his awards are the William Faulkner Award, the Brandeis Citation for Fiction, an American Academy of Arts and Letters award, the REA Award for the Short Story, and fellowships from the Rockefeller Foundation, the Guggenheim Foundation, and the National Endowment for the Arts. He is a member of the faculty at Brown University.